To John,

Hope you enjoy Gold Watch. I'm confident that you will.

C. Raymond Taylor

GOLD WATCH

GOLD WATCH

.

A NOVEL BY

C. RAYMOND TAYLOR

ISBN
978-1-312-49883-9

Printed in the U.S.A.

C. Raymond Taylor

To my triune God and my family. Both of whom I love dearly, and both of whom have saved me from myself. The former on several occasions, which He knows so well.

Acknowledgements

I would like to thank the following people for their invaluable assistance, without which "Gold Watch" would continue to be a fervent unrealized hope instead of a reality.

First and foremost, I'd like to thank George Roush, whose technical expertise, marketing concepts, and patience were key in the creation of the final product. Also many thanks to his friend Tom Whittle for getting George and myself together. Kudos to Carla Erbe for her professional editing of the novel. Karen Wellman deserves a double round of applause not only for the sterling artwork which is the front cover of Gold Watch, but also for her faith that something would actually result from our efforts.

I greatly appreciate the formatting assistance provided by my son Matt, and daughter Britt – hats off to you both again! To my friends Dave Garner and Larry Stenger I offer my profound thanks for your suggestions and for being in my corner during the latter stages of the decision-making process. Not to be remiss, my appreciation goes out to Kristin Clifford and Johanna Dickson at Media Connect for their patience and assistance.

Lastly, but certainly not least, I'd like to thank the dozens of you who read copies of the manuscript and for your kind and honest evaluations which truly kept me believing in the dream. I thank you one and all!

Author,

C. Raymond Taylor

CHAPTER 1

A recurring belief of the human condition holds that when faced with imminent death, a person's life flashes before their eyes. David Spangler, at this moment, could attest to the truth in that belief, as he continued to be mesmerized by the kaleidoscope of images marching across the silver screen of his inner eyelids. A parade of people, places, events, dreams, and material possessions came into his mind's eye to be witnessed and cherished one last time.

This succession of visual images proceeded at an orderly pace from left to right across his imagination as his life unfolded in front of him. The rate of David's flashback was less frenetic than that normally associated with those about to die, because he had the "luxury" of extra time in which to contemplate his certain demise. This was due to the fact that at this moment, David was freefalling from an altitude of 9750 feet above sea level at terminal velocity toward a small group of oak and elm trees in Ohio without benefit of a parachute. This would ultimately end in David's untimely death. That portion of David's cerebellum, which somehow controls the timing of such functions, was now dictating the speed at which he reviewed his past.

Almost immediately upon being unceremoniously dumped from the plane while unconscious, David had been revived by the extreme cold and the rush of howling wind. Together these elemental forces served as a slap in the face enabling him to recover sufficiently to take stock of his hopeless predicament. While passing through clouds around the 11,000 foot mark David had ultimately accepted the sheer reality of his impending doom. At that point his subconscious took over, putting David's consciousness on autopilot as it commenced to begin the fast forwarding of David Clayton Spangler's life from beginning to end.

Once again David found himself reliving his childhood, playing with his sister Nadine and his brother Terry. Pleasurable memories of vacations, amusement parks, neighborhood sporting contests, and past infatuations were recalled. These were interspersed with remembrances of chores, homework, boredom, and embarrassing moments that had also replayed themselves. Elementary school, junior high, high school, and college all came and went.

Long forgotten episodes came flooding back into David's psyche, startling in their luminosity and clarity. Color became very important to his memory banks as the portrait of a brilliant rainbow, following a warm soft summer rain revealed itself. This was succeeded by a zoological visit, the highlight of which was a tumultuous peacock spreading its multicolored plumage in Oriental fan fashion for all to admire the magnificent palette. Fourth of July fireworks exploding against the top of his cranium showered David's senses with scintillating vividness. Visions of reds and purples were interspersed with greens and whites dynamically projecting spectral spider legs that extinguished themselves against the black background of a long ago summer sky. Jagged shafts of lightning from a 1992 thunderstorm pierced David's core, as it seemed his very soul was attempting to wring every last drop of excitement from the sponge of his life's experiences.

As the relive button of his life slowed from "fast forward" to "play", David lingered upon the image of his father, dead these many years. He was able to admire once again the laughing eyes and jovial countenance that were his father's trademarks. God how he missed him! An impression of his beloved mother softly began to replace the paternal visage before him. Her beauty caused the life recorder to hit the cerebral pause button as he greedily drank in every detail of her gracefully aging face. Tears came to his eyes as he realized that he would never see her again. This can't be. THIS CAN'T BE! IT ISN'T FAIR! Hadn't they had just celebrated the first anniversary of her remission from cancer? Hadn't things begun to improve financially in that he'd just received a good raise at the hospital where he worked as a male nurse? Hadn't he just formed a lucrative partnership with that tall mystery man who...

David's eyes flew open wide as his conscious self beat back his subconscious in a last gasp effort to make some sense of the fact that he was now freefalling the last 7000 feet of his existence. With almost superhuman willpower David fought back the waves of hysteria and anxiety that threatened to overwhelm his being. He focused every shred of thought power and concentration on spending his last few seconds of life determining how and why he was about to die this way.

David forcefully closed his eyes again, in part so as not to see the green canopy below rushing upwards to meet him, but also to help him focus on his dilemma. A throbbing ache in the back of his head offered a significant clue as to the "how" portion of his impending doom. Reaching behind his head, David felt an egg sized lump and his hand was streaked with his own blood when he brought it back in front of his eye slits for inspection. Once again squeezing his eyelids shut and gritting his teeth for added determination, David was able to visualize himself back in the cockpit of the small plane. The last thing he could remember was being asked by his mysterious new partner to reach under his seat for a small pack of some kind. Bending forward to accomplish that task was in fact, the absolute last remembrance prior to his having discovered himself falling. From that point it was not difficult to surmise that he must have been hit over the head by a blunt object, perhaps a blackjack, or the butt of a gun. Reconstructing the cockpit size and factoring in the obvious strength he had assumed from the 6' 5" athletically built pilot, he figured it would have been no problem at all for him to undo David's seat belt, force open the passenger door and push him out of the plane. Satisfied that he had solved that part of this grim mental exercise, Spangler turned his attention to the more daunting question as to the reason behind the soon-to-be murder.

Initially David thought it would be child's play as he reached behind to feel for the wallet that he was certain was no longer there. To his surprise he could feel the familiar square-shaped bulge in his rear pocket. Since it made no sense for a crook to have gone through the trouble of replacing his wallet, apparently theft was not the motive. At least David could be somewhat reassured that when his body was found he would not be a nameless corpse. David resumed his contemplative efforts as he zoomed past a startled eagle that had been drawing lazy circles in the sky, 5900 feet over the Ohio countryside.

His mind wandered back three months ago to a February day when he'd been performing his duties at St. Josephs Charity Hospital in Cleveland. While pushing his gurney of soiled linens, bedpans, and other sundry items, David noticed that he was being watched. A tall dark stranger in a black leather coat was paying attention to his every move. The stranger nonchalantly looked away, but not before David's brain registered his thick black mustache and piercing blue eyes. A fleeting image of the old Marlboro man entered David's thoughts before he dismissed the encounter as being totally devoid of meaning while he continued down the wide brightly lit hallway to dispose of his gurney's contents.

Three hours later, at the end of his shift, David pushed through the heavy metal door that opened to the fifth floor of the hospital parking lot. Raising his collar as protection against the cold, he plunged into the concrete abyss in search of his nine year old Chevy Malibu. As he inserted the key into the door lock, he sensed a car slowly approaching and heard the whirring sound of a window being electronically lowered. Turning the key and detecting the reassuring click of the unlock mechanism engaging, David was about to pull the frigid door handle towards himself when he heard his name being called in an insistent but non threatening manner. Turning slightly to see who was hailing him by name, David was taken aback when he discovered that it was the same leather jacketed individual he had noticed in the hallway many hours ago. He was seated behind the wheel of a black Mercedes E-series sedan.

"May I help you?" asked David as he slowly began to pull open the door to allow himself a little more margin of error in case this encounter should suddenly turn unfriendly.

"On the contrary my good man, it is I who can help you David Clayton Spangler."

Curious that this stranger should know his name, and yet apprehensive as to why he would have an interest in him, David warily remained by the now half opened car door.

"What could you possibly have that might hold the slightest bit of interest for me?" David queried."

No sooner had the last word left his mouth whereupon an envelope emerged from the Mercedes window and unerringly flew the short distance between the vehicles landing precisely at David's feet. Cautiously David Spangler picked up the manila envelope and lightly brushed a thin dusting of powdery snow off of it before bending back the metal clasps to observe the envelope's contents. Reaching inside, David pulled out a smaller white envelope which had the flap inserted over the material inside. Pulling the flap up revealed a thick wad of crisp currency. David counted out $2000 in $100 and $50 bills.

Just as he finished counting, the mustachioed stranger with the piercing blue eyes and jet black hair stated "There's double that amount available to you on a regular basis if you play your cards right my friend."

Shaking the hypnotic effect that the money had temporarily inflicted on him, David started to put the bills back in their envelope.

"I'm sorry Mr. Who-ever-you-are, but I don't get involved in drugs, guns, or contraband."

"Nothing of the sort is involved I assure you Mr. Spangler. In fact if you would be so kind as to follow me to the Mark Charles restaurant where I have a table reserved, I will show you that truly altruistic motives are involved."

With those words the window of the black Mercedes quietly ascended and the vehicle majestically began the slow descent to exit the hospital garage. David pondered his next move. Though a semi conservative man by nature he, like the majority of humanity, had more bills than money at the end of most months. In addition, he was trying to help his mother with unpaid hospital bills she had incurred during her recent bout with cancer. Patting the envelope in his hand several times, David decided that there was no harm in talking. This was especially easy to rationalize when the meeting was to take place in a public place such as the luxurious Mark Charles restaurant. Perhaps he also might indeed be helping people, if Mr. Black Mercedes was being truthful.

David's mind spiraled back to that fateful decision he had made to join his newfound benefactor for dinner that evening. He reflected on the restaurant's opulent surroundings and valet parking. He once again marveled at the plush velvet carpet and rich mahogany décor of Mark Charles as the restaurant's haughty maitre d' had escorted him to the table where his host awaited him. His salivary glands involuntarily moistened as he recalled dining on the exquisite feast that was billed on the menu feature page as "A dinner to dill for!" The main entrée was a large fillet of grilled Alaskan Steel River salmon glazed with a carmelized apple preserve, butter-wine mixture and sprinkled with dill, and paprika. The salmon was passed with a savory white sauce, which was enhanced with just the right combination of fresh dill weed, white wine, white pepper, and a dash of paprika. The side dishes of glazed coriander/dill carrots and mashed new red potatoes prepared with dill, garlic, butter, cream, parsley, and chives, were the perfect compliments to the salmon. They, along with a slice of cheesecake and an after dinner snifter of Courvoisier, helped set the mood for agreeable conversation.

Introducing himself as Trevor Graham, the mystery man opened the discourse by apologizing for having startled David in the parking garage. Sensing correctly that David was not interested in small talk, Mr. Graham jumped right into the reasons he had approached him.

"Mr. Spangler, I represent an organization outside of this country that is involved in discovering cures for many diseases. This organization's main goal is the eradication of pain and suffering through the elimination of as many diseases as they can possibly accomplish. As I'm sure you are aware, there is a great deal of gratitude, platitudes and fame which accompanies the successful conclusion of eliminating a scourge of humanity as can be witnessed by the household names of doctors Salk, Sabin, and Mme. Curie. Also as I'm sure you are aware, there is a great deal of money to be made by a company that holds the patents of disease curing products. In order to develop cures, an incredible amount of testing must be done. This requires an ongoing supply of bacterial and viral specimens. That is precisely the area that my client hopes you can be of some assistance to them. An orderly or nurse at a hospital is ideally positioned to have access to various infected articles such as used tissues, bodily function samples, washcloths, disease laden linens, hospital gowns, etc. that can be useful for my clients' purposes. You of course would be handsomely rewarded for your efforts as you have already seen. Your thoughts on that which I have just presented would be of interest to me at this time Mr. Spangler."

With only a slight bit of hesitation David began "Mr. Graham, you bring to me a very intriguing proposition, which I admit holds a certain degree of interest. However, a few thoughts come to mind. What you have offered seems overly generous for what you are proposing. I guess the questions why me, why here, and why so much, need to be answered to my satisfaction before we proceed any further."

"All excellent questions indeed my good man, which in part helps to answer the first question which was I believe, why you? You see, my associates and I have been observing you for some time now, and we have been impressed by your professionalism, your dedication, and your intelligence. Furthermore, we have noticed that the hospital staff gives you free rein in your duties because they appear to trust you and respect your ability to do your job. This affords you a certain degree of anonymity, which would help you in furthering my client's interests. This would allow you to remove articles from the rooms of ill patients without question. You of course would be coached as to which diseases interest my client the most, and how to furnish useable samples for testing purposes. Naturally we would prefer to maintain a low profile in order to keep the competition from learning which diseases are being focused on at any particular time. You would be sworn to secrecy and periodically monitored to insure that your discretion was above reproach.

This brings us to the second question, which was, why here? That is in part due to the aforementioned low profile aspect of our work. Cleveland, Ohio, while being world renowned in heart care and enjoying a large number of quality medical facilities, does not come under the same intensive scrutiny as many other areas of the country when it comes to disease control. This provides us with more freedom in our efforts. Another reason for having selected this area pertains to quality. Initially locations in other countries were thought desirable for our purposes. We soon discovered that due to poor handling, poor medical training, and lack of professionalism in general, our samples were usually tainted and our supply was unreliable at best.

In response to your third question, why so much? I would like to remind you that we will be asking you to obtain samples of terribly debilitating and deadly diseases. This type of work, even for a dedicated and trained professional like you, is not without risk. Payment will be based upon a number of criteria such as obtaining good quality samples, obtaining samples of those diseases most desired by my client, maintaining your anonymity, and keeping discreet about our partnership. Are there any questions?" The slow movement of David's head from side to side sealed the deal, and David's new life began.

A blur of training details came back to him concerning methods of maintaining disease potency during transfers, drop locations, cover-up alibi's, and myriad other concerns. These details tended to give the appearance of an espionage operation. Above all, David remembered the money. The envelopes of cash in unmarked bills passed to him at prearranged secluded meeting places, and never less than $3000. In fact he once hit the jackpot with a payoff of $6,000 for a sample of Legionnaires disease that he had been instructed to secure if possible. Suddenly the thought that there must have been something extraordinarily important about that particular sample to have made it worth so much to his benefactors occurred to David. Why was that one so important? Could it possibly have anything to do with his current situation?

The last thought that David Clayton Spangler was to have in this life was that of an outrageously huge black question mark. The question mark changed instantly to a brilliant white color as David's chest impacted the top of a stately elm tree. Momentum from the fall forced his body inexorably down onto a thick limb, impaling his torso in the process. Rivulets of crimson ran down the question mark turning the symbol blood red as his fatally pierced body came to a complete stop, 73 feet above the Ohio soil. The now red question mark was obliterated by sharp static type lines, which were abruptly replaced by a deep pitch black that bespoke of finality! The all-encompassing blackness gave way to a tiny pinprick of far off light. The light began to march forward, gaining a foothold on the Stygian darkness. Black turned to charcoal, which evolved to slate, which became light gray, which gave way to cream, as a hollow ever expanding shaft of luminescence rapidly approached David's inner self. An overwhelming feeling of peace and contentment, coupled with a sense of homecoming began to surround the spirit of David. A new sensation of immense joy and total love welcomed his soul, as a new journey began for him.

The Cessna 414A Chancellor touched down on the runway of a small airport in southern Ohio. Isaac (Ike) Steele a.k.a. Trevor Graham, a.k.a. twenty other aliases carefully guided the small plane to a controlled stop. He parked in front of a tiny building that served as the operation center/terminal/snack bar/car rental/and maintenance office. Ike climbed out of the cockpit and methodically removed his black leather gloves. He walked unhurriedly toward a plain looking mid size sedan carrying a black leather Gucci briefcase in his left hand. As he settled into the driver's seat of the sedan, Ike opened the briefcase and took out a small cell phone. While adjusting the shoulder harness, Ike quickly punched in the telephone number that he knew only too well.

A curt "Yes" after one ring indicated the call had gone through.

"The drop has been accomplished," spoke Ike.

"Excellent, compensation will be handled in the usual manner."

"That will be satisfactory."

Ike switched off the phone and put on his designer sunglasses for the 3-1/2 hour drive back to Cleveland. He made a mental note to add the details of his latest victim to his journal. Ike allowed himself a brief smile as he envisioned the hundreds who would soon die due to his efforts these past few months. "Damn I'm good!" he said to the steering wheel as the hilly countryside flew past.

CHAPTER 2

"Bill Feller, how the hell are ya?" bellowed Don Macklin across the crowded ballroom floor.

"Pretty friggin' fine now that Pharmacor's finally booting your lazy butt out to pasture," quipped Feller.

"You know, that's what I always liked about you Feller," replied Macklin.

"What's that," Feller asked.

"Nothing," roared Macklin nearly spilling his Crown Royal on the rocks as he doubled over with laughter. "What's it been, ten years now since I saw you, ya old bag of crap"!

"Not quite ten but close to it you good for nothing peddler," responded Feller.

The two men embraced in an awkward but enthusiastic bear hug as they met in the middle of the dance floor. "When I heard they were throwing this big ass retirement party for the outgoing sales manager, some guy named Macklin, I figured I ought to come and check it out. I couldn't believe it could possibly have any connection with that skinny big-mouthed Macklin guy that I was in pharmaceutical sales training with 35 years ago. Boy, Pharmacor must've really been hard up to stoop to putting someone of your dubious talents on as National Sales manager!"

"Well that just might've been true, but we haven't had much trouble kicking your two-bit company's butt around the block a few times since you left us," countered Macklin.

A few more good-natured barbs followed, accompanied by liberal slugs of whisky as the two former friends reunited.

"If the truth were to be known, I have to admit that we lost a good one when you went over to Windsor Labs" said Macklin. "What are you there now, head janitor of the night shift?"

"Try Chief Financial Officer," replied Feller.

"Whooeee! I didn't even think you'd be able to spell C.F.O., let alone be one. And of a Fortune 500 company no less! Well I guess desperate times call for desperate measures. Hey Bill it's really good to see you again old friend, but as the quote/unquote guest of honor, I suppose I'd better get back to mingling. Out of curiosity, from which one of my many enemies here at Pharmacor did you wrangle an invitation to this elegant affair?" queried Macklin.

"Would you believe that new prick of a C.E.O. of yours Jonas Trina sent me a personal invite. He wrote that he'd found out that you and I were old buddies and that even though we weren't on the same side of the fence anymore, he thought you'd enjoy having me attend this festive occasion. Who knows, maybe that arrogant S.O.B. has a soft spot after all, although I still find it hard to believe that he'd do something nice without having an ulterior motive," Bill said.

As they were about to part company Bill asked, "Hey Mack, why is it that there doesn't seem to be any of the current crop of Pharmacor flunkies here this evening? No offense, but almost everyone here is our age or older. The only people that I remember seeing here not qualified for Medicare yet were those two "hotties" that presented you with that ceremonial gold watch tonight. Don't you people have anyone working at your place under 65?"

"That same thought occurred to me earlier, but then I remembered that Pharmacor is having their National Sales Meeting down in the Keys this week, so all of my company friends who are still employed are down there. Typical of that inconsiderate jerk Trina to not consider the timing when setting up this send-off, but since the company's footing the bill for tonight, I guess I shouldn't bitch too much. I suppose us old fogies had better just pop in our false teeth, kick up our heels, down a few pints, and make the most of it! Nice seeing you again Bill. We'll talk later," yelled Macklin as he was whirled away to dance by a Reubenesque septegenarian.

Hours later as the end of the evening approached, a bleary eyed Don Macklin slurred his final goodbyes to a handful of guests as they loitered near the main entrance of the ballroom, not wanting the party to end. A significant amount of noise and commotion made it somewhat difficult to communicate as the band packed up their equipment. A small army of maintenance people busied themselves folding up tables and chairs. Amidst this cacophony of sound and frenetic movement, a lone uniformed security guard stood watch to ensure that all was as it should be. Lost in this flurry of activity were the unhurried movements of a tall white shirted bartender in the far corner of the room. The size of the expected crowd had dictated that a portable bar be set up in two corners of the room to facilitate efficient drink service for the guests.

While the other bartenders were busy counting their tips, the tall bartender at the far edge of the room was already in the process of wheeling his collection of silvery cylinders away from his station and towards the front entrance. As he passed the security guard they exchanged pleasantries and he continued on his way. Ike Steele's blue eyes twinkled and his teeth sparkled as he smiled his way out the door and headed towards his van with the cylinders in tow. The rear hatch of the van popped open in response to the command he had issued from his keychain.

"Hey buddy hold up there a minute," a voice called out to him.

Wheeling around Ike saw the security guard trotting towards him with something dark in his enclosed hand. Ike put his right hand inside his vest pocket intent on taking out his .38 snub-nose pistol concealed there for emergency purposes. His fingers involuntarily closed on the handle as the approaching guard drew ominously closer. A split second before Ike finalized his decision, the guard spoke.

"You dropped this at the door," he offered as he casually underhanded a black bowtie in Ike's direction.

Neatly releasing his grip on the gun, Ike removed his hand from his pocket and nonchalantly caught the article with a deft movement. "Thanks," he said to the retreating guard who had already turned to resume his post.

"Don't mention it," the guard shot back over his shoulder. "I always enjoy helping good people," he yelled as he re-entered the building.

Ike put the van in reverse, and as he backed out of his parking space he couldn't help but contemplate the irony of what had just occurred. He had just committed one of the most heinous crimes in U.S. history, and the one person in authority who had the possibility of fouling up his plans had praised him for being a good person. Wasn't life funny! Ike put the car in gear and headed for the highway. After driving for over an hour he determined that he was far enough away from the scene of the crime to dispose of the evidence. Pulling off the highway, Ike drove five miles down a lightly traveled country road until he crossed over a small bridge. Parking the van on the shoulder of the road, he opened the rear hatch of the van and took out the silver canisters.

Ike donned a pair of surgical gloves and put on a respiratory mask. Reaching under the back seat he removed a long pair of barbecue tongs. Unscrewing the tops of the silver cylinders, he turned each one over in turn and emptied the remaining liquid from each on the ground. Out of each cylinder dropped a large sponge. Taking a container of acid from the van Ike gathered up the sponges with the tongs and hiked down an embankment to the water's edge. Placing the sponges on a large flat rock in the water Ike poured the acid onto them. Immediately the acid began to dissolve the spongy material leaving only a small amount of fibrous residue in its wake. Ike turned the large rock over to hide any acidic evidence, and proceeded back to the van. The cylinders were disposed of in an industrial dumpster which was scheduled for collection the following day. Now all that was left was to sit back and watch the news for the results of the past evening's efforts.

Three days after the retirement party, Bill Feller awoke at his mansion in Rochester Michigan at his usual 5:15 A.M. wake up time to begin his morning routine. This morning though he didn't seem to have his normal energy. In addition to being rather lethargic, he also had a bit of a headache and his muscles felt achy. Fighting off the urge to call in sick, Bill padded down the hallway to the bathroom with the thought that surely a nice warm shower would make him feel better. While the shower temporarily made his muscles feel less achy, he noticed that he was having a little bit of difficulty breathing. Dismissing his symptoms as the onset of a cold or perhaps the flu, Bill drank a large glass of orange juice, took 2 aspirins, and went into work.

As the day progressed, Bill's condition deteriorated. The muscle aches returned with a vengeance and were accompanied by an ever worsening fever and increased breathing difficulties. By early afternoon Bill Feller could take no more and left work early. Refusing to take any of the offers to be driven home or to a doctor's office, Bill painstakingly made his way to his Lexus sedan and managed the 15 miles from the office to his estate. Leaving word with the housekeeper that he was not to be disturbed so that he could rest uninterrupted, Bill donned his designer pajamas and gingerly made his way to bed. He rested fitfully, with sleep being impossible due to the onset of a dry raspy cough that had joined the host of other symptoms. Marshalling all of his determination, Bill pulled himself upright in bed. By making slow movements and taking rapid shallow breaths through his feverish parched lips, he was able to stumble his way to the master bathroom. Rummaging through the medicine cabinet he found some sleeping pills, knocking numerous bottles out of the cabinet in the process. With trembling hands he shook 3 sleeping pills out of the bottle and somehow managed with both hands to get them into his mouth. With great effort he was able to turn on the tap and fill a glass with cold water that he greedily sloshed into his mouth spilling half of it on the marble floor.

Closing the cabinet door he was confronted with his face in the mirror. That reflection scared him as few other things had done in his life. Staring back at him was the vision of a dying man! The eyes were bleary and more bloodshot than he imagined humanly possible! His blotchy complexion had taken on a grayish hue due to lack of oxygen, which was the result of the dry raspy cough. Not only was he perspiring profusely, but he was also experiencing significant pain and discomfort due to the severe muscle aches which were accompanying his affliction. He looked away, unable to take anymore of the sight in the mirror. As he turned his head to depart the bathroom his body was racked with a violent coughing jag that produced a large amount of sputum, which he managed, with great difficulty, to deposit into a tissue. Bill tripped over the threshold of the bathroom doorway and found himself crawling back towards his bed, unable to muster the strength to get to his feet. Sweat was pouring off his body, and he was incapable of filling his lungs with any air at all. If only I can make it back to my bed and fall asleep everything will be all right Bill deliriously told himself. If only I can make it back to... If only I can... If only...

Bill Feller's wife discovered his body when she came home from a bridge party. The first E.M.S. unit to arrive on the scene recommended that the house and all of its occupants be quarantined. Whatever had killed Bill Feller had done its job quickly and efficiently, and if it proved to be highly contagious then containment was critical in limiting its spread. The Detroit medical community quarantined the residence, and a specially trained field unit was dispatched for analysis and determination. After 16 hours of intense effort on behalf of the unit, the cause of death had been established. A particularly nasty strain of legionella pneumophila had been the culprit. This bacterium causes Legionnaires disease, so named after an outbreak killed a number of people attending an American Legion convention in 1976 at a Philadelphia hotel. In that case the disease had spread through the ventilation system of the hotel. For the next two weeks Detroit area hospitals were on a special alert to keep a keen watch for other suspected cases of Legionnaires disease. Fortunately, the Feller case would prove to be the only case in the entire state of Michigan.

Not so fortunate was Michigan's Buckeye state neighbor to the southeast. Ohio, particularly Northeast Ohio, had been hard hit. Over 250 cases had been reported in an 8-day period, with most of the cases having occurred within a 50-mile radius of Cleveland. Scores were dead and almost 100 others were either listed as critical or in intensive care. Through investigating the whereabouts of the victims and establishing commonalities in their collective travels, it did not take long to discover at what event the contamination took place. A retirement party at a hotel in Cleveland was certainly where the victims had come into contact with legionella pneumophila. How the contagion had spread so rapidly to so many would never be discovered for certain. Pennsylvania reported 18 cases and 7 deaths, with New York and Indiana each contributing an additional 5 deaths to the grim tally. The final toll in what the media insensitively dubbed "The Fatal Farewell Party" was 307 reported cases with 123 confirmed deaths. Don Macklin was listed among the fatalities.

On a gleaming white sand beach in Cerromar, Puerto Rico, a lovely dark skinned native vixen playfully slid to a stop in the sand. She came to rest inches away from a tall middle-aged man with jet-black hair, dark moustache, and vivid blue eyes, lazing face up on a beach towel. The fingers on his hands were intertwined behind his head for support.

"Here ees your precious New York Times Trevor honey," she remarked teasingly as her brilliant white teeth flashed in the sunlight. Her bright eyes twinkled, still enraptured with the memory of last night's furious lovemaking, as she plopped down on the beach next to her current par amour. "Darleeng look at thees. Eet says here that 123 people have been killed by some Legionnaires disease theeng back in your country.

"Pity, but I guess we've all gotta go sometime," replied Trevor. He rolled over and delivered a sharp smack on the young lady's shapely bottom. "Now be a good little girl. Throw me the sports page and then go get us a couple of margaritas," he casually ordered as he turned on his towel to admire the fetching figure of a passing nubile Latin lovely.

"You men are all peegs," she sighed as she got up to fetch the margaritas.

As she did so, Ike Steele donned his designer sunglasses to shield his eyes from the hot tropical sun and returned to scoping out the territory.

Back in the United States over 100 funerals were held to honor those who had died from the outbreak of Legionnaires disease. At each funeral, the largest floral arrangement was that sent by the Pharmacor Co. C.E.O. Jonas Trina. Each arrangement contained a beautifully scripted letter of condolence on elegant Pharmacor company stationery. Each letter bore the signature of Jonas Trina. The letters were personalized for each victim's family, which touched the hearts of both attendees, and Pharmacor employees who learned of this extraordinary gesture on behalf of the corporation. This made them a little bit prouder to work for such a caring company and elevated Mr. Trina in many of their eyes.

At home in his sprawling estate situated in the exclusive Hunting Valley community east of Cleveland, Jonas Trina punched in his secret code on the keypad outside of his plush private office in the bottom level of his opulent mansion. The locking mechanism of the heavy door issued an audible click. Although the entrance system weighed hundreds of pounds, having been copied on the manner of medieval doors and hewn out of solid oak, it opened easily pivoting on its solid brass hinges. Jonas closed the door and proceeded across the 60x80 foot room towards the far wall. This office was Jonas' sanctuary and it reflected his style, taste, and dramatic flair for living in excess and flaunting his station in life.

Regardless of where you looked in this incredible room, you could not help but be struck by the sheer grandeur of its appointments. The floor was exquisite Italian marble, punctuated by four huge support beams of solid granite. As Jonas crossed the threshold, his footfalls reverberated off the mahogany paneling. Turning to the right upon entering the room, Jonas proceeded straight to the wet bar and pulled open a pair of mahogany louvered doors with 14K solid gold handles. Row upon row of teak drawers came into view, each with ten velvet-covered compartments holding an outrageously expensive bottle of the finest vintages available. Each drawer was on roller ball bearings with two solid gold handles apiece. Jonas pulled open one of the middle drawers and selected a vintage 1996 bottle of Dom Perignon. Opening a stainless steel door to a large refrigerator/freezer situated beside the wet bar, he withdrew a bag of ice. Grabbing a silver wine bucket, he poured enough of the ice into it to fill it halfway. He placed the bottle into the bucket and grabbed an elegantly carved piece of Waterford crystal stemware from a shelf in preparation of the tasting.

While waiting for the wine to chill, Jonas crossed over to the centerpiece of the room which was an over sized cherry desk. Easing himself into a regal chair situated behind the desk, he removed his $800 shoes and allowed himself to stretch prior to turning on his state of the art computer and color printer. As the computer was warming up, Jonas made his way back to the wine bucket and examined the bottle's external temperature. Deeming it suitable, he opened the bottle with a few deft movements of his practiced hand, revealing its contents. The succulent golden liquid was poured into the crystalline vessel, and he reveled in the color. Drawing the glass to his lips, Jonas' olfactory senses were delighted by the bouquet, as he breathed in deeply to gain maximum pleasure from the heavenly fragrance. Parting his lips he allowed a small amount to trickle into his mouth. Swishing it around, Jonas couldn't help but think of the phrase "Nectar of the Gods." He swallowed it, and silently praising the vintner's skills he began to sip in earnest. Walking leisurely across the room, Jonas seated himself behind the desk and took a remote control out of one of the drawers. As he did so, his eyes swept the room.

An impressive mahogany bookcase dominated the eastern wall. It stood almost to the top of the twelve-foot high ceiling. Each shelf was filled with hard backed books by many of the world's most renowned authors. An old-style gliding ladder was attached to the bookcase to allow easy access to even the highest shelves. Flanking the bookcase was a pair of medieval knights in suits of armor. Each knight held a gleaming upraised broadsword in the hand as if it were ready to do battle. The western wall had a row of long necked trumpets protruding from the top portion of the wall with pennants hanging down from each trumpet. Beautiful matching tapestries depicting life in the middle-ages were hanging down from the ceiling on each side of this wall. Each tapestry occupied an area 6 feet wide by 12 feet high. The remaining center portion of this wall was a stunning painting of the knights of King Arthur's round table seated around that famous piece of medieval furniture. The painting was done on the mahogany paneling. This gave it a dark rich background and provided a vivid contrast to the artist's bright bold use of colors. The word CAMELOT was emblazoned in gold with red trim at the top of the painting.

The real highlight of the room however was to be found on the northern wall. The center of this wall was a chessboard with each square trimmed in 14K gold, set against a black illuminated background. The chess pieces themselves were solid ivory and were each 6" to 12" high depending on the rank of the piece. The respective queens were fitted with stunning jeweled tiaras whose brilliance cast a soft glow on the board. This board was a working game with each piece capable of being moved and locked into place on each square of the wall. Faux torches on either side of this chessboard added to the medieval theme.

Jonas pushed a button on the remote control that he had been holding, and both fake torches began to slowly revolve 180 degrees into the wall itself. In their places were now illicitly obtained Renoir and Manet artworks that, although they didn't really match the theme of the rest of the room, were magnificent to behold in their own right. As a true aficionado of the arts, Jonas appreciated the two paintings for both their artistic merit, and the place that their master painters held in the art-world. However for a man like Jonas Trina, the real attraction to their possession was the fact that both had been heisted from a world renowned gallery expressly for him by a world class art thief whose services Jonas had secured. At this very moment in fact, there were a number of detectives across the globe still working on the case of the missing masterpieces, which Jonas was confident they would never solve.

Pressing the button again, the paintings retreated back into the wall, replaced by the torches. Jonas sat down at the computer, and after typing for almost 3 hours he hit the print command that activated the high-speed printer. The printer spit out a few short paragraphs of introductory material and then got into the main purpose. Exactly one hundred and twenty three lines were printed after the introduction. Each line held the name of a victim of Legionnaire's disease on it, along with the deceased's age, and whether or not that person was a Pharmacor retiree. After all of the lines had been printed, Jonas tripled the size of the font on the computer. With that Jonas printed out the final word.

SUCKERS!

Jonas took the printed pages off the printer and opening a drawer in his desk, he took out a three-hole paper punch. Carefully positioning the papers in the punch, he punched out the round holes and replaced the punch in his desk. Next he walked over to the chessboard. He moved three pieces to new locations on the board in a precise manner. Upon completion of the third move, an amazing thing happened to the chessboard. The bottom portion of the middle section began to slide down the wall towards the floor while the upper portion of the middle section slid up towards the ceiling. The remaining side sections also retreated away from the center of the board. As the four sections slid apart from each other, a wall safe came into view.

When the four sections came to a stop, Jonas advanced to the safe, papers in hand. Twirling the dial on the safe to match the combination, the door of the safe slowly swung open. Reaching in, Jonas removed an elegant looking oversized golden ring binder notebook from the safe's interior. Opening the notebook he saw numerous pages, which had been put in before. Each page held the name or names of people who had been eliminated either by Jonas Trina or at his direction by others.

The entries were arranged in the precise order that the deeds had been done, and a running tally was being kept on the last page of the gruesome journal. Jonas pulled open the rings and placed these latest entries into his notebook. With a smug sense of satisfaction Jonas removed a page from the gold-embossed binder that had the word Legionnaire's and the number 104 on it. That had been his estimate of the death toll placed in the binder 2 weeks ago, so he had not been very far off at all. It was just a little game he played with himself. Next he added 123 to the previous tally, which gave him a new total of 198. "Now we're getting somewhere," he thought to himself, as he closed the notebook and put it back into the safe. Jonas closed the safe door. When he performed the three chess piece moves in reverse order, the board sections retreated to their proper places as the sections of the wall chessboard rejoined each other, once again concealing the wall safe.

Jonas reacquired his drink, and as he finished sipping, he made a final visual sweep of the room to assure that all was as it should be. As he did so his eyes took in a plaque hanging on the wall. He had commissioned a skilled woodworker to rout his favorite saying in teak and he liked to gaze upon it occasionally, lest he forget the place that it held in his life. The Latin equivalent of "Never give a sucker an even break" was the phrase immortalized in teak. It was a saying that Jonas Trina C.E.O....Captain of Industry.... Consummate Murderous Bastard lived by. Turning out the lights he closed the oak doors, and left his bastion as he had found it.

CHAPTER 3

Holland Brittainy Matthews gazed out of her office window at the azure blue sky spotted here and there with cotton puff clouds on this glorious spring day. The fragrance of freshly cut grass wafted through her window as a bumblebee jitter-buzzed outside. The bee purposefully hovered down to a dandelion in search of nectar. Dipping its antennae into the flower's center, it recreated that symbiotic scene that had been played out between bees and flowers for untold eons. A pang of wanderlust briefly entered Holland's thoughts as she subconsciously reflected on how nice it would be to dangle her bare feet in a cool brook on a day like today, instead of being stuck in her office. An involuntary sigh left her lips as she conceded to the reality that duty must take precedence over desire. DAMN WORK!!! Holland thought to herself.

Holland (or Holly-Brit as her friends and family called her) shifted her attention to a humorous act that was being played out before her. A pair of gray squirrels, who had moments ago been playfully leapfrogging over one another at the base of a weathered brown telephone pole, suddenly became utility linemen as they shot up the pole in rapid fashion. This in and of itself would have been of limited interest had it not been for the flock of pigeons spaced out on the taut telephone wires like bulbs on a string of Christmas tree lights. Upon reaching the top of the pole, the lead squirrel raced pell-mell across the thick black wire, followed closely by its bushy tailed friend. The pigeons, not wishing to be bowled over by the headlong rodent rush, arose en masse from their high wire perch squawking their displeasure at being so rudely disrupted. The squirrels, which were seemingly oblivious to the chaos they had caused, continued to scamper along the wires. This comedy of nature brought a smile to Holly-Brit's face. The smile was abruptly replaced by a look of abject horror as the comedy suddenly turned into a life and death drama.

As the squirrels were playing, a hawk was following their every move. Suddenly, it swooped silently down to seize its prey. The hawk's talons dug deeply into thick gray fur as the winged creature initiated an attack upon one of the startled squirrels. It was at this moment that fate and friendship joined forces to intervene on behalf of the beleaguered rodent. Upon snatching the squirrel, the hawk attempted to fly straight up into the air to affect its getaway. Underestimating the amount of effort needed to compensate for the weight of the squirrel, the hawk temporarily lost altitude. It dipped below the top of the telephone pole, from which its victim had been plucked, and upon which the other squirrel was still perched. Seizing the opportunity, this squirrel reacted.

Without hesitation, the second rodent hurtled itself through the air to come to the aid of its stricken friend. Landing squarely on the back of the laboring hawk, the rescue squirrel launched an attack of its own. It buried two sharp front teeth into the upper back of the furiously flapping foe in an effort to allow its bushy tailed buddy to regain freedom. The combined weight of both squirrels was simply too much for the hawk to overcome as the combative opponents made a rapid and raucous descent to the ground, accompanied by flying feathers and fur. Holland could barely breathe as she watched the struggle unfold in front of her.

The plummeting trio hit the ground with an audible thud, and all three creatures were flung apart by the impact. Shaking off the effects of the rough landing, and livid that its plans had been thwarted, the hawk whirled to regain sight of the prey and to resume the attack. It was met by a united pair of gray squirrels standing on their back legs with teeth bared and claws upraised in front of them. Sizing up the situation, the hawk made a show of tremendous flapping and shrieking. However, recognizing the rodent's ability to defend themselves, particularly in view of their superior numbers, the hawk made no effort to close the distance between itself and the squirrels. Realizing that further attempts were futile, the hawk turned and with one final defiant cry flew into the air in search of easier prey.

The squirrels now focused upon themselves and began licking and grooming each other in a loving manner to ease the pain of their wounds and to reaffirm their affection for one another. Holly-Brit could barely contain her joy at the outcome of the battle and she closed her eyes to savor what she had witnessed. Her restive moment was shattered by an authoritative voice barking out in drill sergeant fashion the name;

"HOLLAND BRITTAINY MATTHEWS!!"

Startled, Holland spun around in her chair, all senses at attention as she looked apprehensively up at her supervisor, Daniece Davis who had a stern look upon her face.

"Lordy girl, what in the world had such a grip on your senses that I had to scream to get you to come back to our little piece of paradise here at Pharmacor. I've been standing here for two minutes trying to get your attention!"

"Oh Daniece you should've seen it. There were these two squirrels and they shooed away these pigeons and they ran across the wires and they got attacked by this hawk and they all landed on the ground and they...."

"Whoa, slow down young lady before you have a heart attack," counseled Daniece. "Now, I understand that you were allowing yourself to be distracted from your duties by something outside these lovely four walls. As to what that distraction was and how it ended, well my dear, I can only say that you have mistaken me for someone who gives a rat's, or should I say a squirrels' ass? Anyway, after you compose yourself and finish whatever it is you are supposed to be working on, come see me in my office. I've got an assignment that I'd like to discuss with you, if it's not too much of an interruption to your obviously busy workday!" With those words Daniece Davis, 38-year old daughter of a black Baptist Minister, turned on her heel and proceeded to make her exit back towards her office.

Holland was dumbstruck by the tongue lashing which had just been administered to her. She could feel her fair skin turning crimson as she painfully turned back to her workstation for what she knew was going to be a difficult few minutes as she attempted to gain control of her emotions. "Be strong!" she muttered to herself, but it was no use, as she could feel the tears beginning to form in the corners of her beautiful hazel eyes. Just before the tear duct dam burst, Holland became aware of a pair of gentle dark skinned hands softly grasping her upper arms. Slowly turning in her chair, Holland came face-to-face with Daniece whose compassionate understanding look had replaced the stern countenance from moments ago.

"Wasn't that something the way those two squirrels fought off that damnable harpy hawk," Daniece gushed. "Thank goodness that other squirrel helped his little buddy escape. And those pigeons, were they pissed or what! Anyway, I think you and I ought to get together after hours real soon and reminisce over some drinks about what we saw. Sound good?"

"Oh Daniece, thank you, thank you, yes, yes I'd like that very much" stammered Holland in gratitude. "Daniece thank you for understanding," Holland said while dabbing her eyes with a tissue.

"Don't mention it sweetie, after all, just like the squirrels found out, what are friends for? Oh, don't forget about that meeting later O.K.?"

With those final words Daniece departed in the direction of her office. Holland let out a sigh of relief as she shifted her seat to position herself in front of her computer. She said a silent prayer to thank God for

Daniece being her boss, and she got back to checking over reports that she was supposed to have been working on all along. Twenty minutes later, Holland was finished with her mundane task, and she made her way across the room to Daniece's glass enclosed office. Mrs. Davis was on the phone as Holland tapped lightly on the door. A brief but cheery "C'mon in" beckoned her to enter. She went in, and was directed by hand signals from Daniece to be seated in a chair by her desk. Daniece soon freed herself from the phone call and smilingly turned toward Holland.

"Thanks for coming so quickly Holly-Brit," Daniece said. "Can I get you a glass of ice water, a soda, or something?"

"No, I'm fine right now, although that after hour offer you made a while ago would sound pretty good later on," Holland replied.

"It's a date then," Daniece countered. "Shall we say sixish at Johnny's, and if you're the first one there, see if you can get a table for six. I'd also like to have Jane, Jennifer, Joan, and Ernesto join us if you don't have any objections."

"No objections here chief," Holland replied borrowing a phrase she'd once heard in a Superman movie.

"Good, now let's get down to business," Holland's supervisor retorted as she closed her office door.

"As you may have heard through the office grapevine, some changes are coming our way. From what I understand, the driving force behind these changes appears to be our relatively new C.E.O., Sir Jonas the Unfriendly. I don't know what his game is, but I just can't seem to get a read on that man. I suppose its human nature to be somewhat suspicious of anyone who never ever smiles, don't you think," offered Daniece.

"I can't say that I've really had any contact with him in my position, but from what I hear, he's never going to be voted in as Mr. Congeniality," Holland responded truthfully.

"The scuttlebutt is that the Board of Directors was made some type of proposal by our man Jonas which caught their good ear. My understanding is that the illustrious Mr. Trina made them some type of deal that he would guarantee them a 10% increase in profits this year and a minimum 10% increase in sales if he got to keep a sizeable portion of the increase in his own grubby little paws. I've got a good friend on the Board who told me that they established last year as a base year. They then projected 3% growth per year on sales of last year's numbers to set some projections as to where they would normally expect to be after each of the next 5 years. Jonas convinced them that if he could raise sales and profits both by ten percent this year, then he gets 10% of the increase. Furthermore any increases above ten percent he is to keep 15% of the increase," Daniece said confidentially to Holly-Brit.

"Wow, that could make him one of the highest paid C.E.O.'s on the planet" Holland stated.

"Let's see, last year's sales were 2.1 billion. If we do 10 percent better and he gets 10% of the 210 million dollar increase he makes 21 million dollars. If we somehow do 15% better, he would make an additional 10.5 million dollars. That's some hefty pocket change," admitted Holland.

"You betcha," agreed Mrs. Davis. "However, increases of those sizes are difficult to attain in an industry such as ours, unless you invent a new wonder drug or something, which by the way is not part of the equation. The folks on the Board may be dumb, but they're not stupid. Sales and profits from all new products are not to be included in Trina's compensation package deal. That makes it a bit more of a challenge. Now remember, all projections are based off last year's figures, not the higher figures that would result from a successful year this year. The reason that I point this out is that if in fact, Jonas Trina has figured out some way to get substantial increases this year and that same formula works year after year, he could end up joining the $100 million plus club after his 5 year deal. H'mm, now that I think about it, maybe I better see if I can get to know him a little bit better," Daniece joked.

"Knowing what you and others have said about him, I don't suppose that he's been spending the majority of his time researching charities to support with his potential windfall," Holland contributed.

"You're on the money there honey. The numbers he has to beat will be finalized in a couple weeks when our fiscal year is put to bed. Now that I've given you a little bit of the background, here is where we all fit into the mix. I've been put in charge of a departmental task force designed to lower costs and increase productivity by, you guessed it, at least 10 percent. With your background, intelligence, creativity, and intuitiveness I thought that you just might fit into the team that I'm looking to put together to achieve our fearless leader's goals.

The work will be hard, the hours will be long, and the thanks will be nonexistent, but it will insure that you will be insulated from any cuts which I'm sure will soon follow. I'd like to consider you as my "right hand woman" who will work very closely with yours truly, and who will serve as my liaison with other members of the team. By the way, if you accept, I have already worked out the details to get you a five percent raise based on your additional responsibilities. I realize it's not much, but it's better than nothing. I've also arranged an exemption for all members of my team from having their medical payroll contributions increased. That's something I'm sure will be on the agenda for all of the others. I realize that I'm not talking about some high paid glamour assignment here, but it would be good experience. You'd also get to rub elbows with all of the bigwigs, and it wouldn't look too shabby on a resume if need be in the future. So, what do ya say Holly-Brit. Can I count on you to help in the noble goal of helping to make smiley Jonas a really, really, really, rich bastard?" Daniece amusedly implored.

"Oh what the hell! Why not? I wasn't planning on doing much this year anyway," Holland said obligingly. "Besides, where else could a girl get to hobnob with the filthy rich while wearing discount store threads and bringing granola bars in for lunch because that's all she can afford."

"That's my girl!" Daniece delightedly exclaimed. "Let's go celebrate by grabbing a couple of those ¼ lb solid fat frankfurters we love from one of those street vendors, and chase 'em down with a couple pieces of "happy cake" from Lou's bakery across the street, my treat!" With that the duo exited Daniece's enclosure and strolled through the main office giggling like a couple of schoolgirls as they made their way out of the building and into the bright sunshine, to the bewilderment of the rest of the staff.

The twosome sauntered back into the main office nearly 90 minutes later wearing oversized grins and bearing three long nut rolls or "happy cakes" from Lou's bakery. The delicious aroma of the fresh baked nut rolls sprinkled with powdered sugar permeated the office. Soon the pair was surrounded by a bevy of moochers begging for "just a little piece" of the tempting treat. While the staff dug into the happy cakes, Daniece retreated back to her office to check her messages.

The first two messages there were of little consequence. These she deleted immediately. However, the third and final one was of such import and urgency as to elicit an involuntary "DAMN" from Daniece's lips. Grabbing a notebook off her desk, Daniece bounded out of her office and made a beeline for Holland. Pulling her aside from the rest of the munching group, Daniece informed her that she had just learned of an impromptu meeting that had been called. All department heads were required to attend, and if they hurried they would almost be able to still make it on time. Muttering an apologetic "We'll fill you in later" to her staff, Daniece shooed Holland out the door of the main office, and the twosome scurried down the hall in the direction of the corporate auditorium. Racing down the corridor, the ladies made record time to the auditorium. As they approached the room, Holland heard Daniece curse under her breath as she realized the door was closed. This could only mean that the meeting had already begun and they would have to suffer the ignominy that accompanied being tardy to an upper level gathering. Taking a deep breath Daniece grabbed the handle and pulled the door open, ushering Holland in at the same time.

"The projections for the first and second quarter which...." The speaker, an impressive looking middle-aged man, paused in mid sentence as he allowed his eyes to stalk the two newcomers who had interrupted his briefing.

"Good afternoon ladies. Gee Mrs. Davis, I hope that we haven't interfered too much with your afternoon plans by holding our silly little meeting," Jonas Trina snarled.

Clearing her throat to offer an explanation Daniece was able to get out an "I" before she was forcefully subdued by the C.E.O.'s next verbal assault.

"I can assure you Mrs. Davis, that neither myself, nor the rest of this meeting's attendees are in the least bit interested in excuses for you and your companion's tardiness. We would however appreciate it if you would not allow yourselves to distract our meeting anymore during the remainder of our time together today, UNDERSTOOD?" A meek nod of the head signaled her compliance and Jonas Trina picked up where he had left off.

"As I was saying; the projections for the first and second quarter's sales and profits which have been presented to me are pure unadulterated horse crap! You people have grown so lazy and complacent over the years that you accept mediocrity as the norm, and lackadaisical growth as excellence. I realize that I've only been C.E.O. of Pharmacor for a few short months, and that I don't know everything here. However what I do know is that this company is not hitting on all cylinders and that poor performance and excuses are not the expectations I have for this company. This is the third company that I have headed as C.E.O. in the past 9 years, and just like the other two, I want to impress upon you that we are not here to just collect a paycheck. I am a winner, and I intend to surround myself with winners. We will have no losers, no whiners, and no quitters on my watch. If anyone here is unsure of what I mean please speak up! …. No? … Very well then! For the next twelve months we here at Pharmacor are going to do something that hasn't apparently been done for quite awhile around here. We are going to work! We are going to work hard, we are going to work smart, and we are going to work with more productivity than most of you ever imagined possible. Furthermore we are going to accomplish more with less. During my time here, I have identified certain areas of, shall we say, negligible benefit to our overall corporate strategy for the upcoming fiscal year. These areas will be scaled back, and/or totally eliminated depending on a variety of criteria. An example of this would be in research and development. Mr. Schultz, would you please stand for our guests." Thomas Schultz, Vice President in charge of R&D silently did as commanded, unsure of what would come next.

"Mr. Schultz, it is my understanding that you have been gainfully employed by Pharmacor for 21 years, and you now occupy the top position of what usually is the lifeblood of a corporation, which is new product development. Grow or die is a cliché that has always had, and will always have, relevance in the business world. New product development of very successful companies runs about 7-10% per year, with many companies routinely exceeding these figures with ease. To the uninformed this means that in a given year 7-10% of these company's sales and profits come from products they didn't have the year before.

Mr. Schultz, from what I have been able to ascertain, since you became department head four years ago, R&D has been rocketing along at less than a 2% pace of all sales being attributed to new products each year. To what do you owe this phenomenal record of growth and achievement? I suppose that we could wait for an answer, but from what we've seen of your record, we might be waiting for quite some time for anything substantive to emerge. Rather than submit all of us to a futile attempt to explain your incompetence, I prefer that you gather your things and leave this conference room at once so that all of us here who are still employed by Pharmacor may get back to our business. Oh and Mr. Schultz! When you get back to your office and begin to clear out your personal items, please inform the rest of your department that their services will also no longer be required. Be informed that there are 3 armed security personnel who will accompany you and your staff off the corporate grounds, and your final paychecks will be mailed to all of you at the end of the month. Good day Mr. Schultz," Jonas Trina contemptuously spat out with a degree of finality.

As Thomas Schultz dejectedly made his way towards the exit, an undercurrent of murmuring began to grow throughout the conference room. The murmurs were cut short as Jonas Trina began to walk around the room in perfect command of the situation.

"For those of you who think they have just witnessed one of the cruelest dismissals they've ever seen, let me ask you to pause and reflect on a couple of things. Is there anyone here who would let someone work, either with you or for you who was not pulling their own weight? Do you think that by acquiescing to incompetence we improve company morale or stifle it? Furthermore, recognize that this purging will allow us to bring in fresh minds with fresh ideas. I am confident that this will result in a stronger more vibrant corporation in the long run. That I'm sure you will agree will benefit us all. Regarding Mr. Schultz and his associates, they appear to have retired four years ago. I just made it official today so that they may begin to receive their benefits!" This last line must have struck Jonas Trina as particularly humorous because one corner of his mouth turned up in the hint of a smile. That was something Jonas was rarely ever witnessed doing.

"As I said at the beginning, new products are the lifeblood of a corporation's long term livelihood. We at Pharmacor believe in R&D and are committed to R&D, just not with that particular staff, and not for this coming 12-month period do we feel it to be a necessity. On a positive note, I plan to take $2,000,000 of the $8,000,000 that had been allocated in the budget for R&D this year and turn it over to you department heads. You may utilize your share in whatever manner you wish so long as it allows you to achieve the desired results. Speaking of the desired results, our new national sales manager Ray Titus will now fill you in as to what is expected for the next fiscal year." With that the C.E.O. handed his portable microphone to the sales manager in a well executed baton exchange fashion and took a seat at the front of the assemblage for all to contemplate.

Ray Titus cleared his throat before commencing his part in the meeting. Those who were closest to him could detect beads of perspiration on his upper lip and forehead, signifying his anxiety level at being forced to follow such a tirade.

"As our new C.E.O. Jonas Trina has just made clear, there are going to be some sweeping changes within the organization which are going to herald a new day for all of us here at Pharmacor. Change is not to be considered a bad thing. Rather, the changes that we envision should be embraced by one and all because they are going to take us deeper into the twenty first century as a much stronger and more committed company. We will have a new and clearer focus on what our duties and responsibilities are, and we will share in the rewards that peak performance makes possible." Ray paused to let the assemblage digest his introduction before jumping into the meat of his presentation.

"I'd like to now lay out for all of you the strategic corporate goals for the next fiscal year. Sales are to increase a minimum of 10% and I repeat the word minimum. We actually are looking more towards a 15-17% increase, but will accept 10% if we feel that an all out effort was made on each and every employee's part. Nothing under 10% will be acceptable, and as we have just witnessed with R&D, such performance will not be tolerated. Calls will be increased, selling methods will be "tweaked", and no stone to increase sales will be left unturned. Each of the regional managers will be submitting their plans to me within a week on how they are going to increase business within their respective regions by 20%. By striving for 20% we should easily attain the 10% plus growth that is minimally acceptable. The inside sales staff which we feel has been underused in the past will be expected to achieve 25% growth due to the fact that the previous years' numbers were so low. You will all be given enough selling "ammunition" by upper management to make these challenges obtainable. However, it is going to require commitment and hard work from everyone to achieve our strategic goals.

The other major strategic corporate goal for this year is focused on improving our relatively dismal profit picture. Over the years we have allowed ourselves to lose a bit of our lean and mean attitude, and we have become a bit complacent. **This ends today!** Profits will rise, and they will rise dramatically! Cost cutting and cost containment will be the words we live by for the next twelve months and beyond. Profits will be expected to rise minimally by 15% and that figure is non-negotiable. If we enter the final quarter of this fiscal year with that figure in jeopardy of being attained, you can expect to see budgets and departments slashed immediately. Department heads will be expected to submit their initial plans to upper management within a week, detailing how they intend to meet the strategic goals for this year. These plans will be reviewed and discussed during the following week, with final plans cast the last two weeks of this month.

There you have it ladies and gentlemen. One month from today we will be sailing on a new corporate course. It will be a charted course with a definite destination and a strategic map for all of us to use as a guide on how we are going to arrive at our destination. This charted course will not be for the weak! It will not be for the lazy! It will not be for the incompetent! It **will be for** the strong, the bold, the innovative, and the achievers! They will share in the rewards of their efforts both financially and with a renewed sense of pride both in themselves and in their company!" With those words, Ray Titus' talk ended and he handed the microphone back to Jonas Trina as he took a seat beside him.

"People, this concludes our festivities for today." Jonas stated as some shuffling of chairs and closing of notebooks began to take place. "A few final thoughts are in order as you are preparing to leave. Be forewarned that the short notice given for today's meeting was not by accident. There will be future meetings with little or no time given which will also be of great import and all members of management in the building at that time will be required to attend, regardless of previous plans. This will serve to make sure that we are always current with how our strategic goals are being adhered to, and to help all of us to maintain our focus. I thank all of you for coming today, and we look forward to reviewing your plans next week on how we are going to make this company great!"

As those closest to the door were about to exit, Jonas' voice was heard one final time. "Oh people, I almost forgot. Next week when you submit your plans, please also give me a list of any individuals you are aware of that have been released from your departments within the last few months who, in your estimation, might possibly be capable of aggressive or hostile action toward this company or it's employees because of their dismissal. We've all seen over the years numerous examples of former employees coming back to do harm to their previous co-workers and bosses. At Pharmacor we will do everything within our power to identify those individuals and keep those types of incidents from occurring. Your help in this matter would be greatly appreciated. Goodbye and good luck." With those final words Jonas walked to the rear of the auditorium and disappeared through a door built into the wall much like a judges quarters in a courtroom. The assemblage wasted no time exiting the conference room by the main entrance, doing so almost as a crowd seeking to escape an overcrowded theater after a matinee in search of fresh air.

"Well Holland, what do you think of your first up close and personal view of our esteemed leader?" Daniece knowingly asked.

Holland pulled Daniece to the side of the hallway, and into a secluded section away from the departing crowd so that no curious passersby could hear her response. "I think that he is the rudest, most arrogant, most conceited, cruelest, son-of-a-bitch that I've ever had the unfortunate experience to see in action. As far as I'm concerned he can rot in Hell. Furthermore, how in the world did he ever get to become C.E.O. and why in the world would ours or any company tolerate his type to lead an organization." They resumed walking back towards the office as Daniece formulated her response.

"Child, unfortunately there are men out in the real world like Jonas Trina who, while they are not pleasant, they are effective, and therein lies the answer. The boards of major companies such as ours are concerned with results and results only. They don't care so much how a company grows, so long as it grows. Jonas Trina has a track record of enviable growth with the previous two companies he led, and our board of directors is confident that he can perform his managerial wizardry here so that the company can regain its past ranking in the industry. Pharmacor will shoot ahead, which makes the board look good while making all of those bluenoses even wealthier than the smug bastards already are. The methods employed to achieve the growth are inconsequential. More often than not, when it comes to corporate America the ends truly do justify the means.

And do you know what? It's a pity, but there ain't a damn thing that you or I can do about it. If I can give you some advice, for the long term just do your job to the best of your ability and keep your mouth shut. For the short term though Holly-Brit, let's just concentrate on keeping our jobs, which begins with you getting the staff assembled for our meeting at Johnny's tonight. Make sure to inform Jane, Jennifer, Joan, and Ernesto, and feel free to have any one else that you deem necessary to put together battle plans there also." With that Daniece opened the door to their department's office and departed at a brisk pace back to her own enclosure where she would begin to make some sense of the daunting task now laid before her and her consorts.

CHAPTER 4

"We would like to welcome all of you to Mercurio Enterprises!" the cute young blonde hostess gushed to the small group. "Today's tour will start here at the reception area. On the wall you will note many of the plaques and awards earned by Mercurio over the years that signify the esteem with which we are held in the pharmaceutical industry. Our company celebrated its 95th birthday last year, and we look forward to reaching our centennial stronger, more prosperous, and with even a greater, more diversified product offering than the 247 different products that we currently have. Our total sales for 2011 were $9.3 billion. That makes us one of the world's largest companies in our field. We are involved in many different aspects of medicine, and we enjoy a dominant position in several areas such as high blood pressure medications and AIDS related products. We employ over 30,000 people worldwide and have 11 different manufacturing plants, 4 of which are in the United States, as is our corporate headquarters here in Columbus, Ohio. Next we will proceed through these double doors to our office area where orders are processed and where corporate management maintain their offices."

The tour group dutifully followed behind the guide looking duly impressed with the power and prestige that seemed to radiate from the very walls of this multinational conglomerate. The tour group was composed primarily of budding pharmacy students, although it was not limited to just students. There were several middle aged and in fact a few senior citizens who helped to comprise the group. One individual in particular stood out from amongst the older crowd. This was due in part to his athletic 6'5" frame and piercing blue eyes, but also in his keen interest in absorbing everything about Mercurio Enterprises.

"Ladies and gentlemen, if there are no further questions regarding order processing or management functions, we'll visit the research and development area next," the guide said as she moved towards another set of double doors. Ike Steele took note of the security cameras as he shuffled along with the rest of the group into the R&D area. After a walk of about 75 yards through a long hallway the group came to the research area. Determining that the majority of the group was within earshot, the guide began to speak again.

"As I'm sure you can all understand, the research area must maintain a sterile environment, free from any source of potential contamination. For that reason, we will not be allowed direct access to the rooms where the researchers are conducting their work. However if you will all look through the large window to your right, you can see several of the researchers engaged in various stages of experimentation." All eyes turned in unison to the right where they were rewarded with a view of masked and gloved workers in white lab coats performing their assigned tasks.

The last areas the tour group would visit were those that were the most important to Ike Steele. These were the labeling and bottling area, and the shipping area. As the group approached the bottling area, large overhead containers could be seen dispensing a steady stream of various capsules, caplets, and pills down numerous slides. From the slides the medications would land on rapidly moving stainless steel tables which would vibrate, moving the meds towards their appointed destinations. With the divine guidance of computer intervention, somehow sense was made of all the moving and shaking. The proper pills, arrived at their specific tables, and were then placed into the correct bottles. From there the bottles received accurate labels, and were then placed on trucks for shipment to designated distributors. They in turn got the medication into the hands of the retailers whose pharmacists dispensed the properly prescribed pills to the correct customers. Naturally, a licensed physician had prescribed the medication.

"Over here ladies and gentlemen, is where we make the labels that are affixed to the bottles. Each label contains a wealth of information such as the product name, active ingredients in the product, the date it was manufactured, and the batch number for tracking purposes. I see where the printer is running off a series of Zenophol labels. This is our number one selling pain pill containing the active ingredient acetaminophen. Here you can easily see the manufacturing date and the corresponding batch number. Also...."

While the tour guide was explaining the labeling procedure, Ike had slipped away into the nearest men's room. Checking to make sure that the room was empty, he quickly pulled out a cigarette lighter and used it to set a few paper towels on fire. He threw the burning towels into a covered receptacle, threw a thick wad of other paper towels on top of them and quickly exiting the washroom, he returned to the back of the group. Within three minutes of his return, smoke detectors sensed the smoke now issuing from the trash container and fire alarms began sounding throughout the building.

Offices throughout the plant began clearing out as employees implemented practiced fire drill procedures. "We need everyone to stay calm and please follow me toward the emergency exit." cautioned the guide. Thin wisps of smoke now were becoming visible as they wafted out of the restroom area. Someone yelled "FIRE", which was what Ike had anticipated. Amidst the ensuing confusion and screaming, he made his way over to the labeling equipment, removing a strand of Zenophol labels in one deft movement that he slid into a notebook he had brought along for just such a purpose.

"PEOPLE PLEASE TRY TO STAY CALM," admonished the guide as she fought valiantly to regain control of the situation. Ike moved rapidly to her side to lend his imposing figure to her efforts.

"LISTEN TO WHAT SHE SAYS EVERYONE!" Ike's commanding voice boomed out. "THE GUIDE KNOWS THE FASTEST AND SAFEST WAY OUT," he bellowed. With that, the group regained their composure, and within two minutes the guide had them all on the exterior of the building.

"Thank you for your assistance in there mister," the guide gratefully said to Ike.

"Glad to help. It's funny how easily panic can set in, even in a relatively safe situation," replied Ike.

"You can say that again," the guide responded. "Well I'd better get back to my sheep."

"Yes, you'd better. In the meantime I'll just drop off this notebook in the tour bus. I've got a sneaking suspicion that our departure is going to be delayed because of this little fiasco, and I don't want to carry this bulky thing with me for the next several hours." With that, Ike turned and began to make his way in the direction of the silver tour bus that was scheduled to take the tourists back to their original boarding location in twenty minutes.

Ike looked over his shoulder to make sure that he wasn't being watched and he made his way around the side of the bus. Continuing past the bus, he nonchalantly strolled across the remainder of the parking lot and entered a row of pine trees flanking the long drive. Hoping to exit over a barbed wire topped fence that surrounded the entire corporate campus, Ike first thought to test for electricity. He threw a twig at the wire and was only half surprised by the ZZZT sound made when the twig contacted the wire. Another way out would have to be found. Briefly studying the guard post at the entrance to the drive, Ike decided upon his course of action.

Jogging rapidly through the tree line, Ike approached the gate. He could see two uniformed guards in the guard post and a couple police cars stationed in the street for both security and traffic control purposes. He could also make out the sound of sirens from approaching fire trucks. He observed that he would have concealment to within twenty yards of the guard post by staying in the trees. His plan was to put a fire truck or two between himself and the guards. To accomplish this, he would also have to cross the drive, which he estimated would expose him an additional fifteen yards. On top of that, he had another fifteen yards to the gate, ten additional yards to the sidewalk, and then he would have to somehow deal with any curious police on security duty. He decided to take a chance on human nature being what it was to buy himself a few precious extra seconds for his plan to work.

A loud blaring disrupted Ike's thought process as two long bright red trucks rounded a corner and came into view of the guards. They turned to take in the sight and sound that always seems to serve as a mesmerizing attraction to both children and adults. Seizing the moment, Ike emerged from the tree line. He walked at a steady but not overly rapid pace that might arouse suspicion. As expected, both the guards and the police had their attention on the approaching fire trucks as Ike came even with the guard post. Timing it perfectly, Ike was concealed from view by a corner of the guardhouse itself as the trucks swung into the drive. As the front of the first truck came abreast of the guard post, Ike broke into a semi sprint, knowing that he had to get as close to the sidewalk outside the gate entrance without being seen for his plan to work. Fortunately the trucks had slowed significantly to turn into the drive, and were only moving about 10 mph as they hid Ike from view of the guards. By the time the second truck had passed the guardhouse Ike was within a step of the sidewalk, well outside of the gate. With his heart beating wildly, Ike forced himself to drop to one knee to affect a shoe-tying pose.

"HEY YOU OVER THERE, WHAT ARE YOU DOING?" barked one of the policemen.

Feigning the mannerisms and accent of an English gentleman that he could easily pass for, Ike answered. "I believe I'm tying my shoes kind sir."

"Where did you come from? I don't remember seeing you there a minute ago."

"Why from my villa over there." Ike said pointing in the direction opposite that which the trucks had come from. I've had you gentlemen and those fine red trucks in view ever since I rounded the corner there, as I've been engaged in what you Americans refer to as a power walk.

Amazing how much distance one can cover in a relatively short time. It appears we have a regular little circus going on here, what with all the horns and sirens and trucks, wouldn't you say? Jolly good entertainment!"

With that the officer in charge told Ike to move along. That was exactly what he had in mind. Saying a silent prayer that the police would not notice that he had on dress shoes, Ike proceeded past the officers at a brisk pace.

"Hey Winston Churchill or whatever you call yourself, hold up there a second," hollered one of the officers. Scarcely daring to look back, Ike braked to a complete stop.

"You forgot this," the officer said as he bent to pick up the notebook with the illicitly obtained labels lying on the ground where Ike had tied his shoes.

Breaking into a cold sweat, Ike managed a smile and said "Silly me. Sometimes I think I'd forget to wear me knickers if I didn't have Mum to look after me."

As the officer handed him the notebook he advised him "Stay out of this area for awhile. Nobody's allowed in or out except authorized personnel."

"Yes Sir!" And with that Ike made his way down the block.

CHAPTER 5

Some men are born to wealth with a silver spoon in their mouth. A few find fame and fortune from pure dumb luck. Others achieve financial freedom through genetics. Perhaps they were born beautiful, or grew to be seven feet tall and could dribble. Perhaps they were blessed with a unique talent, or an I.Q. of 185. Most arrive at great wealth after years of hard work and applying life's lessons learned correctly. This is the same whether you are a famous actor, an entrepreneur, a stockbroker, realtor, athlete, or President of The United States. Then there was Jonas Trina.

One couldn't say that Jonas was part of a "type" because he was virtually unique in the manner in which he ascended to great wealth. He certainly was not born into money. Nor was he athletic. While he was attractive, his achievements were not attributable to his looks. Neither luck, nor an extraordinary work ethic, nor a Mensa intellect held the keys to his success. Rather Jonas' rise to the top was the result of above average intelligence, combined with rare cunning, persistence, a total lack of morality, sheer ruthlessness, and a love for the game of chess.

Jonas Trina came into the world in a small trailer in rural Indiana on a dreary March morning in 1959. He was the product of a loveless marriage between two of life's castaways. His father was an abusive alcoholic who tenuously maintained a low paying job at the local grain elevator and farmed a small acreage he inherited which provided a subsistence level of living for the family. The mother worked part time as a waitress at the local diner when not at home berating Jonas and his father for her miserable lot in life.

Jonas, being unloved at home, grew to be a serious and introverted youth who had difficulty making friends at school. He found his only solace in books at the local library. During the first semester of sixth grade, Jonas watched a couple of classmates playing chess at recess. He was instantly fascinated with the game and picked up all of the books on chess that he could find. By reading the books and watching his classmates play, Jonas gained a bit of early proficiency and was able to prove himself during the few matches in which his peers would allow him to participate. Entering junior high, Jonas learned that his seventh grade math teacher Kurt Stevens was an avid chess player and he hounded him until Mr. Stevens reluctantly agreed to give him a match. Kurt handily defeated his young opponent, but he was impressed with the eagerness and love for the game that Jonas displayed, and he took the wayward youth under his wing.

These were good days for both Jonas and Kurt, with the master being able to impart his skill and knowledge of the game to the willing novice, who in turn not only showed a real knack for the game, but also seemed to be coming out of his shell as a result of their afternoon chess matches. Kurt noticed an occasional smile cross the serious youth's face while playing, and a yelp of glee would be forthcoming on the rare moments when Jonas was able to capture an important piece during a match. Other teachers began to notice a change in Jonas' demeanor. He was becoming more attentive and productive in his classes. It appeared that Jonas had turned a corner in his life, and that he might yet be able to salvage some goodness and purpose out of his rough beginnings.

Kurt set up some school wide chess tournaments that were quite popular with the students. Oftentimes there would be a dozen or more matches going on simultaneously with others waiting their turn to "take on the winner." While Jonas continued to have trouble socially due to his overly serious nature, he did begin to gain respect due to his newfound chess prowess. Occasionally a classmate would stop him in the hallway at school to ask his advice on a certain move or a particular bit of chess strategy. Kurt felt a renewed sense of accomplishment in his profession for his part in helping Jonas find new meaning in his life. For after all, what greater achievement can a teacher realize than to witness a student blossoming due to their guidance and assistance? The next three years were filled with chess filled afternoons that for Jonas were some of the best times of his life.

Jonas came to revere Kurt for his both his grace and charm, in addition to his friendship. He soon began to adopt mannerisms and phrases that Kurt would often use in an attempt to emulate his idol. Kurt had a habit of pulling out a gold pocket watch, inherited from his deceased father who had been given it upon his retirement. Jonas was enraptured by the sight and perceived prestige imparted by the watch. Though in his impoverished state, Jonas could only dream of owning such an exquisite timepiece, the thought became ingrained into his psyche. He longed for the day when he too could have something valuable, like Kurt's gold pocket watch hold a meaningful place in his life.

As Jonas entered high school, the future began to look up for him. Though his parents were still quite poor, his own prospects were beginning to blossom due to his innate intelligence, ambition, and growing skills. With Kurt's continued work with the young man, Jonas was even showing signs of breaking out of his social shell and attempting to form interpersonal relationships with his classmates. Then, without warning, tragedy struck.

In addition to his position as a math teacher, and chess overseer, Kurt volunteered his services to the local high school as a groundskeeper to help keep the athletic fields in shape. Part of his requirements as such was to line the fields before the Friday night football game. On a chilly Friday night in mid October of Jonas' sophomore year, Kurt stayed to watch the game after having lined the field. Friends said he stayed around awhile after the end of the game, and didn't start for home until almost midnight.

On the drive home Kurt had an asthma attack, and he reached into the glove compartment for a bottle of medication that he always kept there for just such occasions. He opened the brand new package and administered a dose to himself as he continued driving. This time however, unlike the dozens of previous doses he had taken over the years, relief was not forthcoming. Unbeknownst to Kurt, due to a prank at a drug manufacturing plant in Ohio, the asthma bottle contained rubbing alcohol instead of asthma medication. As his asthma attack worsened, Kurt found it more and more difficult to breathe. As sweat began to stream from his pores, Kurt fought to force air into his oxygen-depleted lungs. In his desperate attempts to maintain consciousness, he neglected to slow down to negotiate a sharp curve in the road. Kurt's car was found Sunday morning upside down in the Wabash River where it had plunged down an embankment. He was still strapped inside the submerged vehicle when the rescue unit arrived.

Jonas learned of Kurt Stevens' death the next day at school. Crying out a hysterical NO, NO, NO, NO, NOOOOO!!! Jonas ran past a group of startled upperclassmen and fled out the double doors into the bright crisp Indiana fall morning. He was found wet and shivering beside a haystack two evenings later by a farmer 33 miles from his school. When found, the farmer reported that the boy was glassy-eyed and mumbling incoherently. It took several days before Jonas returned to any semblance of normalcy.

An ensuing investigation into the accident revealed the rubbing alcohol in the medication bottle to be a prime contributor in the cause of death. The manufacturer of the asthma medication swore that there was no way that they could be held responsible for Kurt's tragic death. A lawsuit was filed on behalf of the Steven's family and both parties appeared in court on successive days to argue their case. During these hearings, a steely-eyed Jonas sat at the back of the courtroom silently glaring at the defendants and their attorneys. His glares were not even noticed by either the defendants or their counsel. Such was Jonas' insignificance in their eyes. Jonas' sense of his own powerlessness gnawed at his very core. A seething hatred of all things outside of his command and control began to fester within him. As each court day dragged on, the young man's goals began to change and crystallize with each and every word and phrase. Someday someone would pay for the injustice taking place right before Jonas' very eyes. He would see to that! The company eventually paid an out-of-court settlement of $10,000. However, the company never admitted to any wrongdoing or being at fault, nor did they ever issue any type of apology to the family.

For a long time afterward, Jonas Trina the chess protégé no longer existed. He was replaced by a person who, though he came to school, stared vacantly at the blackboard with no communication whatsoever with teachers or classmates. He did do his work, both in school and homework, and got A's and B's, but it was all done in silence. Some said it was a tribute to Mr. Stevens. Others said he was still somehow in touch with Kurt, who was directing him from beyond the grave. All that was certain was that he was silent and serious, and that his chess playing days appeared to be over. In his junior year another tragedy overtook Jonas.

At twilight two days before Thanksgiving, police were called to investigate sounds of shooting coming from the direction of a trailer in the countryside outside of town. When they opened the rusty trailer door they discovered a grim scene. In an apparent murder/suicide, Jonas' parents lay dead of gunshot wounds to the head. An empty whisky bottle lay on the trailer floor and the place stank of cigarettes and stale beer. Shortly after the police arrived Jonas was seen approaching the trailer. Two officers intercepted him and as gently as possible broke the news of his parent's deaths to Jonas. Shaking his head and screaming for his mother, Jonas bolted for the trailer door. It took 4 policemen to restrain him and to keep the boy from viewing the carnage inside the trailer. Jonas was given a sedative and taken to the local hospital for the evening. He was placed under constant watch, as authorities feared a possible suicide attempt was a distinct possibility in view of the circumstances.

The funerals were held several days later. They were sparsely attended due to the reclusive nature of both of the deceased and the lack of popularity for Jonas himself. One of those in attendance was Kurt Steven's older brother Kent, whom Jonas had met numerous times while with Kurt, as well as at Kurt's own funeral. The two brothers had shared many common traits. Both were local men who had stayed in the area after college, and both had made a career in the teaching profession. Kent was one of the twelfth grade science teachers at the high school. Like Kurt, Kent also felt sorry for young Jonas Trina, whom he felt had not gotten a fair shake in life. Another trait they shared was that they were both men of action. If they saw something that wasn't right they didn't talk about it, they did something about it. Once again this would prove very fortunate for Jonas. Kent approached Jonas to offer his condolences.

"Jonas, I can't begin to tell you how very sad I am for you, and I wanted to offer my most heartfelt expression of sorrow to you." Jonas accepted the kindness as he blinked away the tears that were once again beginning to form. "Son, I don't know if now is the time or the place to bring this up, but have you given any thought as to where you're gonna live and where your life is headed from here?" Fighting back tears, Jonas admitted that he had been too distraught to look very far ahead, and beyond staying at the hospital the next few days, he wasn't sure of what his future living arrangements would end up being.

"You know son, my house is really way too big for just one person, a cat, and a couple of hamsters. It gets pretty lonely coming home to an empty house all the time with no other person to share the events of the day with. Jonas, you and I have always gotten along pretty well, and seein' as you're kinda down on your luck at the moment, I'd like to extend an invitation for you to consider. Why don't you give some thought about movin' in with me? I don't think the cat would mind too much. I've always got plenty of food in the 'fridge, and I'd like to think that this arrangement would be a fitting tribute to the memory of my brother Kurt for whom we both cared so deeply. What do ya say partner? Is it a deal, or do you have a better offer from one of the frisky fillies at the high school?" chided Kent.

"I don't know what to say Mr. Stevens. It's all so sudden, what with my parents dying and everything. I don't know if I would be fit company for people for quite some time," countered Jonas.

"Don't you go worrying about my feelings son," shot back Kent. "I'm a big boy and I can handle mood swings. Hell, I know you've just experienced one of the most traumatic things that could happen to anyone. Naturally I would expect that you're going to require some time to put this terrible tragedy behind you and be able to think about the future. That's part of why I'm offering this. I'm not only a teacher, but I also serve as a guidance counselor. Jonas I can help you work through all of this and get you back on the road to recovery while acting as your guardian and making sure your physical and financial needs are being taken care of. The way I look at it, it sure beats eating hospital food and answerin' a bunch of stupid questions from a flock of fat ole' nurses like I always see at Community General. Besides, I'd like to see if you are ready to take on the one who taught Kurt everything he ever knew about chess," Kent teased.

"That's a real generous offer Mr. Stevens," replied Jonas. "As you may have seen from the sparse turnout here at the funerals, I really don't have a lot of kinfolk beating down the door for the honor and privilege of taking care of Jonas Trina. If it's alright with you, could I take a few days to get my affairs in order and then perhaps have you come out to the trailer after school Friday so that I could haul my gear over to your place?"

"Fine Jonas," Kent responded. "It'll take me a few days to alert the authorities and get the proper guardian papers drawn up and all that legal mumbo-jumbo out of the way anyway. We'll talk during school this week and iron out some of the other details, O.K.? And by the way, call me Kent. Mr. Stevens is my father," Kent said good-naturedly.

"Yes Sir! Oh and Kent, I'd just like to say that this is the nicest thing that anyone has ever done for me," Jonas thankfully added.

And so it came to pass that Kent Stevens became the legal guardian for Jonas. This arrangement had many beneficial and long lasting effects upon the life of young Jonas. True to his word, Kent was a big help in counseling Jonas on not only how to put his life back in order, but also in helping him set a course for the future. Shortly after moving in with Kent, Jonas appeared to have overcome the trauma of his parent's death and seemed to actually be thriving under the tutelage of his new mentor. His grades improved to straight A's, he was more responsive in class, and he even began to gain some new acquaintances. Many a night was spent with the master pitting his chess skill and experience against the now formidable upstart as Kent and Jonas matched wits and strategy into the wee hours. Most important of all was Kent's charisma, and his connections in helping Jonas gain a foothold to a promising future.

As a lifelong member of the teaching profession, Kent had made friends and connections throughout the state of Indiana at all levels of education, including the collegiate level. An old friend, Randall Talley, was on the staff of the engineering school at Purdue University in West Lafayette, Indiana. On a beautiful fall weekend during Jonas senior year, Kent and Jonas traveled to West Lafayette to view the campus, and to meet with both Professor Talley and the dean of the prestigious engineering school, Dr. Thomas Bryson, for an interview that had been arranged by the professor.

Kent had spent many hours coaching Jonas on what to wear, how to act, proper posture and etiquette, and what to say and not say during the interview. In the end it proved to be time well spent. Jonas was the perfect gentleman and Kent the perfect spokesperson as he persuasively pleaded young Jonas' case in an effort to secure admission to the college the following year. He also hoped to line up scholarship monies to help ease the financial burden college life would entail. The interview concluded on a positive note with the dean coming away very impressed with Jonas' demeanor, as well as his ability to overcome extreme hardship in an attempt to persevere. Normally extracurricular activities, which Jonas was lacking, weighed heavily on scholarship considerations, Jonas' grades, coupled with his circumstances, along with Kent's charismatic presentation, secured a pledge from the dean. He would assist Jonas in being admitted to Purdue the following year with at least a partial scholarship, provided Jonas kept his grades up the remainder of his senior year, and that he would engage in some extracurricular activities.

Upon their return home the twosome immediately began plans to resurrect the chess club that had been such a hit in junior high. Jonas now had an incentive to make it part of his life again, as it would be an extracurricular "feather in his cap," particularly if he founded the club. The club's founding was announced during homeroom the following week, and eager participants were soon applying for membership with Jonas and Kent. Many of these were the same ones who had previously defeated Jonas years ago. To their utter surprise they now found in him a wizened and skilled opponent with abilities and strategies heretofore unseen. His daring, cunning, and unique talent to discern an opponent's next moves earned Jonas the nickname "King Fox," a moniker that he wore proudly.

As Jonas' prestige grew, so too did his confidence. He was no longer the shy and serious introvert. Now Jonas began to exude a swaggering almost arrogant nature when amongst his peers. While still respectful and somewhat reserved with teachers and authority figures, Jonas truly played the part of "King Fox" with his classmates, expecting and getting both accolades and respect. Sporadic reports of his arrogant demeanor would occasionally filter back to Kent Stevens. These were dismissed as normal jealousy on the parts of those whom Jonas had bested at one time or another. One aspect of his life that remained constant was a lack of friends. Whereas before it was primarily due to his serious introverted manner, the reason now was the boastful, aloof style of his new persona.

Jonas' senior year flew by with him garnering honors both for his chess playing ability and his scholastic achievements. His performance during this final year made his acceptance into Purdue University a foregone conclusion. Dean Bryson was so impressed with his academic achievements that he bumped up the partial scholarship to a full scholarship for Jonas' freshman year at Purdue.

Jonas entered Purdue in the fall of 1977. He hit the ground at West Lafayette in full stride making Dean's List each quarter his first year. This was largely due to the fact that he had none of the usual distractions that often seduce young adults away from home for the first time. Having seen first hand what alcohol can do, drinking at that time was not even a consideration to Jonas. Furthermore his aloof reclusive nature kept most of his matriculating classmates at bay. That effectively limited his partying to a minimum. The only recreation that Jonas had was going to movies and joining the student chess club.

As opposed to the high school club, which Jonas had jumped into with both feet and quickly dominated, his entrance into the Purdue club was subdued with a minimum of actual matches that he allowed himself to be drawn into. Jonas preferred to stay on the sidelines of the matches as he chose to observe the style and strategies of his soon-to-be new opponents. His reservations about going full bore into the club was deliberate, and reflected a well thought out strategy on the part of the young man. Jonas knew that the majority of club members were both upperclassmen, and more often than not were some of the best and brightest students on campus. Indeed Jonas knew that the competition level was certainly much more advanced than he had encountered in the past. Though confident of his own abilities, Jonas felt that time spent scouting the opposition would offer him the best chance to gain the upper hand in future matches head to head with these new adversaries. Six weeks after joining the club Jonas felt that he had gathered enough background on each person's game that he was ready to participate in the club in earnest.

His initial plunge into the club came with his inclusion in a single elimination tournament that was composed of 64 matches in the first round based on a format paralleling that of the NCAA basketball tournament. The 32 winners of the first round matches proceeded to the next round, with the winners of those matches advancing on to the "sweet sixteen." The winners of those matches would be among the last 8 in the tournament. It was at this stage in the tournament that Jonas finally tasted defeat. His conqueror was a third year chemical engineering student from San Francisco named Li Wei, who would go on to eventually win the tournament. Jonas derived little satisfaction at having been defeated by the winner. While he was able to accept his loss outwardly, and offered congratulations to Li upon the conclusion of their match, inside he fumed. He had to find out how he had been compromised so convincingly and how his opponent seemed to always be three steps ahead of him and everyone else during the tournament. The answer was not long in coming.

At the end of the tournament came the awards presentation with both trophies and monetary prizes being given out. In addition to the large trophy that he received for winning first place, Li also received $500 as a monetary prize awarded to the winner. Correctly guessing that a celebration of sorts would probably follow for Li, Jonas chose to trail him from a distance following the awards presentation. He was rewarded for his efforts shortly after as Li entered an off campus bar. Pulling a cap out of his pocket to effect a change of appearance, Jonas waited three minutes and then discreetly entered the smoke filled bar to discern Li's whereabouts.

Adjusting his eyes to the dim light, he was barely able to make out Li's face. He was seated at a small table in a corner of the establishment with two companions seated beside him. These two looked vaguely familiar to Jonas. This he thought rather strange in view of his limited contacts in West Lafayette. Following a hearty laugh, and a lengthy pull on a draft beer, Li produced the award envelope from his pocket. Counting out several bills from the envelope, Li proceeded to give a portion of his winnings to each of his two friends. From his vantage point, Jonas couldn't make out exactly how much, but he did see enough to figure that he had just witnessed some type of payoff. Since the monetary split had come from the awards envelope, it made sense to Jonas that the payoff was somehow connected to the tournament, but for what purpose?

Remembering some large bushes near the entrance of the bar, Jonas devised a plan. Half an hour later Jonas saw the three men begin to reach for their coats in preparation of leaving. Hurriedly downing his drink, Jonas abruptly left the bar and hid behind the largest of the overgrown bushes outside the bar so that he would have a good vantage point to see those leaving without being detected. A minute later Li and his associates emerged from the bar and lingered under a light outside as they said their farewells to one another. The overhead incandescence offered a much better view than that inside the bar, and it was here that Jonas remembered why the companions looked familiar. They were a couple of part time chess club members who really didn't seem to take it too seriously or want to get involved. Neither had participated in the tournament, and Jonas had dismissed them early on as people that he needn't concern himself with. The trio parted company and they disappeared into the darkness as they went their separate ways back to their respective dwellings. Jonas waited a full five minutes before deeming it safe to come out of the bush and begin his own trek back to his dormitory.

As Jonas made his way across campus in the cool night air he concentrated on the relationship between the threesome he had observed this evening. What possible connection could they have between each other that it would be of value to Li? Suddenly it hit him. Thinking back on his match prior to his competition with Li during the tournament, he vaguely remembered one of the men being very interested in all of his moves, while at the same time the other man was very interested in his opponent's moves. Jonas had dismissed it as meaningless at the time, but in light of what he had seen tonight, their interest level took on new significance. That was it! These two were scouts for Li! They would report back to Li on his next opponent's strategies, tendencies, and style, so that regardless of who won the match, Li would have a dossier on his next adversary. That type of info, as Jonas well knew from his own previous weeks' surveillance, was invaluable in chess. Over the next few months Jonas devised a plan to avenge his defeat.

At the beginning of the next quarter Jonas called home to tell Kent Stevens that he had been robbed and that he needed money to buy food and books that were not covered by his scholarship. Kent wired him $400 to replace the money that he said had been stolen. Owing to the fact that no robbery had taken place, Jonas now had the funding to put his plan into effect. Shortly after the quarter had begun, the chess club voted to have another 64-person tournament. Jonas wasted no time in signing up to participate in the event. This time however, he planned to make sure that the scales were tipped in his favor.

Prior to the tournament, Jonas made a trip to a bar in town known to cater to local blue-collar workers. It normally was populated with factory workers and farmers who had little love for the "pampered pretty boys" of Purdue. Here Jonas had no trouble finding a couple of recruits to help him implement his plan. On the first day of the tournament Jonas had his recruits, a couple of large muscular Indiana farm boys stationed outside of the entrance to the tournament hall. By means of some prearranged hand signals, Jonas alerted his recruits as Li's scouts were about to enter the hall. The farmers intercepted them, and utilizing some force, they steered them to the side of the building. Here the boys informed them that it would probably be better for their health if they stayed away from the tournament this time. They made it very clear what the consequences would be if they chose to ignore this sage advice, and gave each of Li's minions a stiff shove to the ground as a sample of what they could expect. Jonas watched the proceedings with amusement from a vantage point in the hall, as Li's underlings scurried away from the hall at a brisk pace in an effort to put as much distance as they could between themselves and the farm boys as quickly as possible. Part two of Jonas' plan was about to begin on a much more subdued and indirect basis, but it was to prove equally as successful.

Jonas had signed up to be a tutor towards the end of the previous quarter as a way to pick up some extra cash. One of the students assigned to him for math help had been a former head cheerleader at some high school in the Midwest. Her name was Candy Kane (her parents just couldn't resist the temptation), and she had the most incredible body that Jonas had ever seen. Furthermore she was very fond of showing off her assets with a wardrobe of short skirts, tight tops, and painted on jeans. Jonas made a deal with her to handle her tutoring fee if she would agree to attend the tournament and follow his instructions.

At the beginning of his first match, Li looked up to discover a pair of round firm corn fed breasts perched atop his left shoulder as he was about to make his opening move. "Are you Li Wei?" gushed the pretty co-ed as Li was able to divert his gaze from her breasts to her eyes just in time to avoid being slapped with a leering charge by the campus police.

"Yes, yes I am," Li stammered as he tried to regain his composure.

"I've heard so much about you that I wanted to make sure that I got a place nearby where I could watch your match. I understand that you won the last one of these tournaments and I'd like to learn how to play from the very best," she admiringly cooed.

"I'll do my best to show you," responded Li. His face and ears were flushed with a combination of embarrassment, excitement, and bewilderment, as he attempted to make sense of all the attention being lavished upon him by this comely co-ed.

As Li and the rest of the onlookers attention was focused on Candy, a mousy disheveled fellow took up a position amongst the group directly behind Li's opponent. He was one of those nondescript people that are easily overlooked and often ignored by the subconscious of many people as not being worthy of consideration. This built-in anonymity was an advantage for the timid appearing Sergei Stepanovich, a Russian exchange student whom Jonas had bribed into acting as his own chess spy. Behind the meek exterior lurked a brilliant mind, one that had been ingrained with chess, which was Russia's national pastime, at an early age. From his vantage point Sergei was able to easily view all of the moves of each participant in Li's match, and he took mental notes of each player about which he would report back to Jonas.

Between Candy distracting Li, and Sergei scouting him, Jonas figured that he would be able to overcome any advantage that Li had over him in skill and he would be able to gain his revenge. The strategy proved to be off to a good start. So much so in fact that Li almost lost his opening match due to his preoccupation with Candy's charms, and the bewilderment he displayed as his eyes swept the room in search of his scouts who were nowhere to be found. This against a very mediocre player no less! Jonas on the other hand disposed of his opponent in almost record time. Jonas met with Sergei and Candy individually later that week in a secluded area of the library to discuss match schedules and make battle plans for the remainder of the tournament.

Although Li continued to struggle in his matches, due in large part to Candy's interruptions which Li seemed powerless to ignore, he did advance to the "Great Eight." Here once again he would meet up with Jonas who had swept aside his outmatched adversaries to this point. Jonas kept an eye out to insure that Li had not replaced his scouts with new ones, and he seemed pretty confident that Li had been unable to groom replacements on short notice. This grudge match was only in Jonas' mind, as Li seemed to only vaguely recall having defeated Jonas among the multitudes he had vanquished within these hallowed halls.

Armed with fresh information from Sergei on Li's strategy up to that point in the tournament, Jonas started the match off aggressively. Feinting with his knights, parrying with his rooks, thrusting with his queen and bishops, and taking full advantage of his sacrificial pawns, Jonas soon had gained the upper hand in the match. Li's irritation with how the match was proceeding was evident in his terse replies to Candy's deliberately inane questions which Li was periodically accosted with, and which was part Jonas' strategy. Finally Li had had enough of Candy's interruptions. Red-faced and fuming, Li turned and screamed at her to please let him alone so that he might be able to concentrate. In an acting performance worthy of Oscar consideration, Candy broke into tears and ran from the hall sobbing hysterically. All in attendance turned as one to view the spectacle of Candy's exit. As she departed, all eyes turned to Li as he sat with both fists clenched, visibly shaking from shame and embarrassment. The hall was totally quiet as everyone awaited the next act in this human drama.

With a show of tremendous mental effort Li stopped shaking and unclenched his fists. Next he closed his eyes for a full 30 seconds as the assemblage silently looked on in anticipation. Taking a deep breath, Li finally and reluctantly opened his eyes. He pushed his plush chair from the table and slowly stood up facing Jonas. Reaching slowly and deliberately towards his own side of the chessboard, Li took hold of his king. He turned the king on its side in the traditional act of surrender in a chess match. Reflecting the value of honor in his heritage, Li bowed deeply to his opponent. He slowly turned and stoically walked out of the hall's oaken vestibule. Each footfall made a resounding din amidst the utter silence that shrouded the room like a cloak. The silence immediately gave way to a crescendo of murmurs as the crowd discussed amongst itself exactly what had just been seen, and the reasons behind the drama that had been witnessed.

A few of the chess club members approached Jonas and offered him their congratulations on his unexpected victory. While Jonas was not exactly the most popular guy in the club, Li's growing narcissism had begun to wear thin with many club members. This made Jonas a bit of a celebrity for the moment and it could have been used as a springboard to catapult him into a much more accepted social situation. However, by this point in his life, Jonas had wearied of even the pretense of trying to make friends. The metamorphosis that had begun so many years ago was now complete. As the skillful use of his cronies in engineering Li's defeat had proved to him, friends were not necessary. Interpersonal relationships were irrelevant. People were pawns to be utilized for advancing one's self, nothing more. That day Jonas crossed a line within his own psyche from which there would be no return.

Jonas went on to win the tournament. Shortly afterward, Li submitted his resignation from the club. Jonas was acknowledged as the preeminent club member from that victory on until his graduation a few years later. His skill level grew to such a degree that often he would take on 10 matches at once, moving from board to board, making move after move, and defeating foe after foe. Due to his increasingly vitriolic nature, there were no accolades, there was no applause, and each victory represented merely another "notch on the gun belt," nothing more. Other than his professors who had to tolerate him, the only person with whom Jonas had any type of relationship was the steadfast Kent Stevens. Even Kent had to admit that Jonas had grown a hard shell around himself since he'd entered college.

CHAPTER 6

Upon graduation in June of 1981, Jonas put his engineering degree to use by going to work for Sutton Industries, a weapons manufacturer based in Chicago. During his first couple of years there, Jonas helped develop improvements to the guidance system of a hand held rocket launcher that the company had introduced in 1980. These improvements went into production in the fall of 1983, in the third year of the Soviet war with Afghanistan Soviet invasion of Afghanistan later that year. Initial tests of the improved rocket launcher dubbed "The Seeker" were very successful and accolades were given to Jonas and the rest of the engineering staff for their part in the weapon's development.

Immediately after the Soviet incursion into Afghanistan in 1980, the U.S. made their displeasure known as they implemented sanctions against the U.S.S.R. Not the least of these was boycotting the Olympics that were held in Moscow that year. The U.S. supported the Afghanistan mujahideen both publicly and clandestinely. Part of the un-avowed support for the Afghan people came in the form of smuggled shipments of U.S. armaments that made their way into the country and into the hands of the rebel fighters. Seeker rocket launchers to combat the Soviet helicopters were an important part of these shipments. However, almost from the very first shot, the Seeker fell into disfavor with the mujahideen. This was causing a serious rift between them and the U.S. policy makers, who were hoping to curry favor in order to gain them as allies in the battle to thwart Soviet expansionism.

It seemed that in the hands of the mujahideen, the Seeker was an extremely unreliable weapon. Almost 70% of the launches missed their target, which had the accompanying adverse effect of alerting Soviet helicopters to the whereabouts of those who had just fired upon their gun ships. A trail of smoke from the rocket's exhaust was like a long white finger pointing to the shooter. The helicopters followed the smoke trail of the rockets back to their source and eliminated whoever had fired the shot. The mujahideen took to sarcastically referring to the weapon as "The Peeker" because it allowed the helicopters to "peek" in on those unfortunate enough to have launched the errant missile. Something had to be done, and done fast! Otherwise Afghani independence would soon be a thing of the past.

It was decided by the U.S. hierarchy that it would be necessary to sneak a handpicked team into Afghanistan to help the mujahideen "get the bugs" out of the Seekers. A team of four men was selected and smuggled into Afghanistan through Pakistan. The leader of the team was Major Donald Garner, U.S. Army. Donald, the only son of a southern Ohio schoolteacher, had distinguished himself in covert operations in Vietnam. The second member of the team was Captain E.B. Bankston, selected for his ability to speak the native language of Afghanistan in addition to both weapons superiority and martial arts abilities, which he was noted for. The next was a 6 foot 5 inch, supremely confident 22 year-old Army Ranger named Isaac "Ike" Steele, who was a marksman with everything from a blowgun or crossbow, up to and including Seekers. The last member chosen for the team was a civilian engineer from Chicago named Jonas Trina. He was chosen in large part due to his familiarity with the weapon system itself, and partly because he was the only person in the Sutton Industries' engineering staff who wasn't the head of a family.

While it would've been admirable of Jonas to volunteer for the hazardous assignment when the request came to his company from the government, it was not the case. As one after another of his colleagues were eliminated from consideration for one reason or another, Jonas could see the direction the selection process was taking. While he argued as best he could against the government agents sent to gain his enrollment on the team, he knew that all things being considered, he was the obvious choice. His appointment to the team was secured after a half hour meeting in a room alone with an Army colonel, during which time it was made expressly clear to Jonas how miserable the government could make his life were he to continue to resist. The colonel also showed Jonas how this adventure, should it prove successful, could return him to the U.S. as a hero, and propel him on his way to a truly illustrious career. Convincing Jonas of the wisdom in accepting the assignment with a positive attitude, rather than being taken kicking and screaming, the duo emerged from their meeting with arms figuratively around each other, and broad smiling countenances.

The team entered Afghanistan in early February of 1984 and a meeting with several mujahideen leaders was quickly arranged. The meeting took place in a cold, dark, dimly lit cave in a mountainside near Kandahar. When Jonas was introduced to the members of the mujahideen as representing the Seeker's manufacturer, one of the fighters pulled out a curved sword and attempted to rush Jonas. Though he was quickly subdued before he could do any real harm, the reason for the attack remained. In questioning, it was learned that his twin brother had been one of those killed due to a Seeker miss. Several minutes of angry taunts and accusations followed. The meeting eventually got back to order, with the net result being that the American team was prone to blame operator error for the Seeker's dubious record thus far, while the mujahideen insisted that there was something wrong with the weapon itself. It was decided that Ike Steele the marksman, and Jonas Trina the weapons expert, along with two mujahideen freedom fighters, would perform a Seeker attack on a Soviet gunship at the earliest opportunity to give the Americans a front row seat to the rocket launcher's battlefield performance.

Three days later, Jonas found himself on a windswept ledge of a mountain pass 10,000 feet above sea level with Ike Steele by his side. Ike had a pair of binoculars to his eyes as he scanned the eastern opening of the pass in search of Soviet Hind gun ships known to favor this pass as a shortcut between bases.

"Does it always have to be so damn cold in this Godforsaken country?" Jonas blurted out between spasms of shivering.

"What do you expect up here halfway to son-of-a-bitchin' outer space? Hell I was talking with those two goat jockeys they sent along with us for the ride, and I got the impression that they were glad it wasn't as cold as it usually is around here," Ike replied.

"Sure coulda fooled me," Jonas shot back.

"Where you from?" Ike queried.

"Chicago now, by way of Indiana as a kid. How about you?"

"Beaver Falls, Pa., home of Joe Willie Namath, and they tell me another fella named Kelly from my town might turn out to be even better than good ole Joe Willie. You are a football fan aren't you?" Ike returned questioningly.

"Of course," Jonas lied. "Hey how did you ever get to be such a good shot?" Jonas said in an attempt to change the subject.

"I've been hunting all over Western Pennsylvania since I was eight, and I was shootin' at trees and cans and things in the woods around our house since about five. Hell with all the shots I've taken over the years, it was just a matter of time before I actually started hitting something!" Ike replied jokingly, his breath visibly issuing forth from his icy mustachioed lips.

Jonas opened his mouth to continue the discourse, but his words were cut short by a "whup, whup, whup" sound as a pair of Hind gun ships entered the pass. They were flying at an altitude which would put them about 500 feet above the pair when the reached their location. The spot they had chosen for the ambush offered ample concealment amidst several large boulders, but it was by no means impregnable.

"I sure hope our Afghani buddies are paying attention to our visitors," Ike shouted above the growing din of the Hind's rotors.

"Ready with that Seeker?" Jonas yelled back.

"Ready as I'll ever be," answered Ike.
Jonas and Ike both knew that the Seeker Ike held in his hands had been examined excruciatingly over these past few days, and it should be in perfect working order.

"I'm gonna let both of these redbirds fly by, and when the rear one gets about a quarter mile past I'll let loose with our calling cards," Ike stated matter-of-factly.

"You're the hunter, do what you think is right," Jonas replied.

The sounds grew louder and louder as the gun ships had almost pulled abreast of Jonas and Ike's perch. Jonas felt an icy shiver run down his spine that he knew was not in any way related to the cold, as he hunched down even further between two large boulders. "Steady, steady" Ike said to himself as the Hinds noisily whipped past. Five seconds later Ike calmly spoke "Ready, aim, FIRE!" A white trail of smoke leaped from the ledge as the Seeker initiated its attack run. For 200 yards the rocket proceeded in the direction of the trailing helicopter. Suddenly and inexplicably it veered 75 degrees left and began to gain altitude while it shot past the helicopters as though they were hovering. Jonas peered out from his hiding place and with his own binoculars he could see the excited expression of a rear facing Soviet gunner pointing directly at the rock formation occupied by the now endangered duo. The white rocket exhaust trail was like a ghostly finger pointing directly at them.

Ike quickly reloaded the Seeker as the Hinds employed evasive maneuvers designed to throw off his aim as they rapidly turned to commence an attack of their own. Jonas had a fleeting thought of a pair of angry hornets charging to stop a bear from raiding their hive as he watched the Hinds approach. His thoughts were interrupted by the whooshing sound of a second Seeker missile being loosed from the weapon Ike held firmly in his grasp. This rocket once again began the journey headed directly towards the target. Fortunately for Jonas and

Ike, the pilot of the foremost helicopter saw it coming right at him and he too proceeded to take extreme evasive action. It was fortunate for Jonas and Ike, because this rocket proved to be defective also. In one of those strange quirks of fate, the Soviet pilot's rapid and extreme course change coincided with the errant path that the Seeker rocket now elected to pursue. The result was a staggeringly bright red, white, orange, and yellow fireball, followed by voluminous thunder as the explosion reverberated off the surrounding mountainsides.

The second gun ship now unleashed a pair of rockets at the ledge that the telltale white exhaust indicated should be the focal point of their attack. Ike got as far as "Our Father who art in Heaven" when the rockets hit the ledge with an earsplitting roar. A large portion of the ledge disintegrated with pieces from the size of tennis balls to Volkswagens flying off in every direction. The other rocket hit a boulder just to the right of the two that Jonas was hiding behind. This boulder split in two with each 5-ton piece flying upwards before commencing their downward plunge to the valley floor.

Not satisfied that the rockets had accomplished the task, the remaining Hind now let loose with 20mm cannon and machine guns. The straight on angle of attack that the Hind had chosen gave Jonas and Ike just enough room behind the remaining boulders to be concealed from the opening round of gun and cannon fire. However, with the helicopter's hovering ability, it was just a matter of seconds before the Hind found an angle of attack suitable for the kill.

Suddenly a different noise of heavy gunfire erupted in the distance. The sound was the heavy throated staccato burping of a .50 caliber machine gun as its rounds stitched themselves large holes across the front fuselage of the Hind. From a position 500 yards east and 400 feet above them, Jonas and Ike's mujahideen friends were now making their presence known. The gunship pilot attempted evasive action, but the mujahideen were excellent marksmen in their own right and they adjusted their aim to send a line of tracers flying directly towards the helicopter blades. One of the blades was sheared off, sending the Hind out of control. The helicopter went plummeting towards the side of a nearby mountain, and the ferocity of the ensuing crash, explosion, and subsequent fire was sufficient to insure that another crew of Mother Russia's finest would never reach the homeland again.

Jonas' knees were quaking as he slowly began to take stock of his body to determine whether he had been hit, and if so, how badly he was injured. Ike also was doing a two hand touching exercise over his own fuselage to ascertain if he had any holes in it or not.

"You alright over there Jonas?" inquired Ike.

"I'm having a tough time keeping my knees from knocking together, but other than that and a hell of a ringing in my ears, I guess I'll live. How about you?" Jonas queried back.

"Seems as though all of the pieces parts are still attached, so I guess it could have been worse. Thank goodness that our two Afghani buddies remembered how to pull the trigger on that fifty when they did. Otherwise that Hind would've had our hinds! Remind me to get them a round of yak milks or whatever the heck it is they drink around here to celebrate," Ike exclaimed.

Their conversation was disrupted by the sound of the mujahideen gunmen and their accompanying pack goats making their way down the mountain to check up on Jonas and Ike and determine if their efforts had been in time to stave off disaster. Ike came out onto what remained of the ledge and gave out a cry in the direction of the rapidly descending fighters to let them know that all was well. Another ten minutes brought the allies together on the ledge where an impromptu spirited celebration of sorts took place as they congratulated one another on their good fortune in being able to overcome the superior firepower of the two Soviet gun ships. At least that is what Jonas and Ike took away from the celebration in that neither pair could speak the other's language. By the smiles and the boisterous antics of the Afghanis, Jonas could tell that they were pleased with the way the confrontation had gone. And why shouldn't they be? After all, not only had they achieved a confirmed kill on a Russian helicopter, but also they had witnessed the failure of the Seeker, thus justifying what their countrymen had been saying about the weapon's unreliability.

The quartet began the arduous trek down the mountain to report back to their superiors on the results of the confrontation. As nightfall approached, they came to a cave that offered protection from both the elements and from any prying eyes attempting to locate those responsible for the elimination of the two helicopters. The wind had begun to increase, and the stinging, drifting snow was making further descent in the dark a very risky proposition at best.

The group entered the cave and unpacked. The mujahideen tended to their goats, making sure that they were fed and made as warm and comfortable as possible in the harsh conditions. Following a light meal of prepackaged meals ready to eat for Jonas and Ike, and dried yak jerky for the Afghani's, the men once again began to rehash the day's events. One of the mujahideen joined the discussion by reaching into the pack that held the remaining Seeker rockets and pulled one out. He nudged his compatriot to watch him and then turned to insure that the Americans were paying attention also. He held the rocket slightly above his right shoulder and made a whooshing sound to mimic the firing of a Seeker missile. Moving the rocket in a fashion not unlike a child playing with a paper airplane, the mujahideen moved the rocket in a straight line for 10 feet. Suddenly he began waving the rocket around in a wild zigzag pattern to signify the whimsical wanderings of each of the day's launches. The two mujahideen laughed uproariously at the playful gesture, much to the chagrin of Jonas and Ike.

As quickly as the laughter had begun, suddenly it stopped as the rocket toting Afghani, without warning, turned and glared at Jonas with eyes burning like hot coals. With a primal scream and a look of fury and contempt, the likes of which Jonas had never seen on any man before, the crazed freedom fighter whipped his rocket holding arm toward the cave floor. Fortunately, for all in the cave, the warrior had the presence of mind and self-preservation to not release the missile from his viselike grip. With the scream still echoing around the walls of the cave, the mujahideen slowly raised the rocket in front of his face and spat on it with a show of utter disgust. Gently placing the rocket back in the pack, he next picked up the launcher itself and shook his head from side to side. Holding the launcher horizontally in front of his body, the fighter propelled it in the direction of Jonas like a chest pass in basketball. Thankfully for Jonas, Ike leaped to his feet and intercepted the launcher from colliding with Jonas' forehead, for which it was aimed. His anger spent, and with the hatred slowly ebbing from his eyes, the mujahideen turned his back on the two Americans and walked slowly back to his countryman whom he joined on the cave floor, deliberately facing away from Jonas and Ike.

Borrowing one of Shakespeare's more famous lines, Ike said, "Methinks he doth protesteth too much. After all, didn't we knock one of those Russky birds out of the sky with our little spitball shooter."

"Yeah we did." countered Jonas. "But don't kid yourself. They saw the flight path of the rocket just like we did, and they know we were just plain lucky, nothing more. I sure as hell wish I could figure out what in the world is making these weapons malfunction like they're doing. They almost never failed in the extensive tests we gave them back in the states."

"Well even though it appears that we can't rely on the rockets, one thing that we can depend on is that tomorrow it's once again going to be colder than the proverbial witch's bosom here. We'd better get some shuteye so that we're up to the task at hand, which is haulin' all this gear down the mountain in the snow," Ike frostily muttered.

"I'm with you there," Jonas said. With that both men rolled out their thermal lined sleeping bags and proceeded to make ready to bed down for the evening. The sound of snoring coming from farther back in the cave indicated that the mujahideen were already asleep. Half an hour later Jonas sat up bolt upright, prompting Ike to follow suit and reach for his weapon.

"What is it Jonas, did you hear something?" questioned Ike.

"No, nothing like that," Jonas replied.

"Then why the hell did you scare me half to death by jumpin' out of your sack like you did! You didn't wet the bed did you?" Ike inquired amusingly.

"Ike let me ask you something. How cold would you say it was today? Ten below or maybe a couple degrees warmer?" queried Jonas.

"About that I'd say," responded Ike.

"How about the day before?"

"Little bit colder I'd say," Ike shot back.

"Day before that was colder still wasn't it?" Jonas continued.

"I reckon so," Ike obliged. "Now that we've had the replay of the weather in central Afghanistan, would you mind telling me if there is a point to all of this?" asked Ike.

"When I mentioned that we had done testing on the Seekers I was serious. We had them tested in all types of weather, temperature, fog, elevations, etc. Anything we could think of that might come up out in the field that could affect the Seeker's performance. However, I don't think that we ever tested how they would perform in temperatures where they are forced to go for months on end without ever getting a chance to thaw out as has been the case here," Jonas stated matter-of-factly.

"You know, you might be on to something. Got any ideas on how we can warm these rockets and launcher up short of sendin' them on a Bahamas cruise?" asked Ike.

"I just might." said Jonas. "Grab two of the rockets and bring them back to your sleeping bag, and I'll grab the launcher as my par d'amour for the evening that I'll be bedding down with. Hopefully the combination of being protected from the elements by the bags, combined with our body heat, little as it is in this Godforsaken place, will be enough to straighten them out if that is indeed what is causing the problem."

Moving slowly and quietly so as not to awake and startle their Afghani hosts, Jonas and Ike noiselessly commandeered the weapons and brought them back to their respective sleeping bags.

"Damn these rockets are colder than the jugs on this frigid chick from Slippery Rock I took out a couple of times!" Ike kidded.

"My date's a little on the cold bony side herself, but remember it's all for a good cause. Now shut up and let's get some sleep," retorted Jonas. Within fifteen minutes, four sets of nostrils were issuing twin streams of frosty exhalations into the frigid mountain air at regular intervals to attest to the day's exhaustive efforts.

In a dreamlike state Jonas imagined that he heard the sound of small arms fire. His subconscious assured him that it was a replay of yesterday's encounters. However the sounds persisted. Opening one eyelid halfway, Jonas peered through his awakening mental fog and thought he saw two or three figures on their stomachs nearby. Snapping out of the haze, he suddenly remembered where he was and the mission at hand. Crawling on his hands and knees, he joined the other three members of his team at the cave entrance.

"Well look who's up! Welcome back to our little mountain retreat." chided Ike.

"What's the early morning ruckus all about?" inquired Jonas.

"As near as we can tell, there appears to be a firefight going on a little ways down on the mountainside. Unfortunately we can't quite see through the haze to determine exactly what's happening," explained Ike.

Their conversation was cut short by the far off sounds of approaching helicopters. "Unless our Afghani hosts have gone into chopper production overnight, I think it's safe to assume that our Russian flyboy friends are back," said Jonas. On cue, a pair of Soviet gun ships emerged from the mist a mile away, heading in the direction of the shooting far below. Their path would take them past the cave, and 2000 feet below their position that offered a perfect target for the Seeker, if it was up to the challenge. Racing back to the sleeping bags, Jonas grabbed the launcher, and freshly warmed rockets and returned to the cave entrance.

"Well Annie Oakley", are you ready for round two? " Jonas said handing the weapons to Ike.

"I'm always ready for some target practice, I just sure as hell hope that putting these birds in the oven last night has helped because my heart can't take too much more excitement like we had yesterday," retorted Ike.

"You do your thing. I'm going to see if I can recruit the goats into helping to warm up the rest of the ammo." With that Jonas grabbed the rest of the rockets, and put them under the warm bodies of the goats, who proceeded to perch on them like a couple of hens attempting to incubate their brood.

Ike rammed a shell in the launcher and took aim on the foremost helicopter. A satisfying whoosh signified that the first shot had taken place. This time the missile made a beeline to the target and exploded against the front of the gunship, producing an obscenely large fireball which sent the flaming wreckage hurtling toward the snow filled valley below. Not wishing to stand upon his laurels, Ike was already taking aim upon the second Hind helicopter. Squeezing his trigger finger, Ike sent another white trail flying off in the direction of the enemy. Like the first round, this one also found the mark, with the end result being another flaming hulk plunging downward.

Jubilant cheers erupted from the Afghani's and Americans alike as the warmed weapons proved themselves a huge success. The celebration was cut short by a high-pitched scream followed by tremendous explosions to the right and left of the cave entrance. A shower of shrapnel flew in all directions, and the concussion of the twin blasts knocked everyone to the ground.

"What the hell was that?" yelled Jonas to no one in particular. The answer was immediately forthcoming as a MIG29 roared past, machine gun blasts tearing huge chunks out of their rocky enclave.

Jonas and the mujahideen fighters dove for cover in the relative safety of the cave's interior. "Ike, what are you doing? Get your butt back in here before that MIG returns. Now is not the time to play hero!" screamed Jonas at the figure of Ike lying prone at the cave entrance. Seeing no response from Ike, Jonas raced back to the front of the cave, arriving at Ike's side the same time that twin lines of machine gun slugs began marching themselves up the mountain side as the MIG made another pass.

Jonas pulled the unconscious Ike away from the entrance, and flattened both of their bodies to the side of the rocky wall just as the MIG found the correct elevation to put several rounds through the cave's opening. The men were unscathed by the rounds, but one of the goats had been killed. As the jet rocketed by to loop and set up for another pass, Jonas sprung to action in their defense. He grabbed two of the rockets from under the dead goat and ran back to the cave opening to reload the Seeker. Removing his heavy gloves to make loading easier, he realized that the rockets had not been under the goat long enough to warm up very much, but he would have to take a chance that the rocket would perform correctly, still cold.

As the MIG returned for its next run, it was greeted with a Seeker missile launched from the cave front. The Soviet pilot immediately took evasive action, performing a high right turn. This, as it turned out, was totally unnecessary because the rocket took a 90 degree angle straight down and exploded harmlessly against a rock formation far below. "Damn" muttered Jonas. "The son-of-a-bitch is still too cold." At least the shot had the effect of keeping the MIG from firing on the group during this pass, so the launch was not totally without effect.

"I've got to find a way to warm these damn rockets up fast, otherwise we're toast." Jonas thought to himself. With his mind racing, Jonas suddenly hit on an idea. Grabbing a knife he ran to the dead goat. He cut open the abdomen of the dead animal. Next he grabbed four large plastic bags that they had for keeping gear dry and placed rockets in each. These he stuffed back into the still hot abdomen of the goat. The Afghani's watched in surprise as Jonas finished his task and proceeded to wipe the gore from his gloves onto some nearby hay.

The MIG had not made any more attempts, but Jonas figured that meant the pilot was running low on fuel and would be notifying his buddies to come finish the job. The Afghani's began setting up the .50 caliber machine gun by the cave entrance to return fire. While this was a laudatory effort, Jonas knew that their best chance for survival from the next onslaught lay in accurate rocket fire. Although the men did not speak each other's language, each knew they all shared a common hope, which was that the Russians would not return until the rockets had warmed up.

As they waited, Jonas examined Ike to see if he was still alive, and if so, how Jonas might be able to help keep him on this side of the daisies. Bending low over him, Jonas noticed a nasty bruise on the forehead, and a deep cut on his left arm that was seeping blood at an alarming rate. An involuntary moan escaped Ike's bleeding lips as Jonas pulled the thick jacket from Ike's arm in order to apply a tourniquet to slow the blood loss. Jonas completed that task as quickly as possible and put Ike's jacket back on him. Then he covered him with blankets to reduce the risk of shock.

Within an hour, their Russian foes had reappeared with a vengeance. Two MIG29's roared through the mountain pass, and made straight for their cave. In an attempt to buy more time, Jonas now fired the last missile which he had taken from under the goat earlier which had not had a chance to properly warm. Once again the shot went astray, but again it disrupted the attack as the MIG closest to the rocket's trail broke off their advance and took evasive action. The second MIG bore in on the stalwart defenders, machine guns and cannon blazing. The overmatched Afghani's attempted to return fire with their machine gun, but the jet was simply too quick for them to get a good bead on it. Double puffs from the underside of each wing announced the ignition of incoming missiles. The mujahideen fighters flattened themselves as best they could for protection against the fiery death winging their way at Mach2 speed. The missiles hit in unison with a deafening roar, and explosive fury collided with the mountainside just 15 feet below the cave front. The force of the explosions tore virtually the entire cave entrance off and catapulted one of the Afghani's over the edge along with the .50 caliber gun. The other mujahideen fighter was luckier, being blown back into the cave's interior alive, though bloodied and bruised. A similar fate would have been Jonas,' had he not had the foresight to retreat to the dead goat with the Seeker in tow after firing his previous round. Though the blasts dazed him and knocked him down, he was very much alive as the MIG began a second attack, this time to be accompanied by his friend.

Reaching into the goat's belly, Jonas extracted two of the rockets. Tearing open the plastic, he hurried back towards the front of the cave, loading as he ran. Saying a silent prayer that the weapon would work, Jonas took aim and fired just as the MIGs were beginning to start their next run. This time the rocket ran true and disappeared into the turbine opening of the lead MIG resulting in a fiery disintegration of the jet in front of his partner's eyes. The pilot had never made even the faintest attempt to evade, which prompted Jonas to think that they felt the rocket launcher incapable of ever firing a reliable round. Arrogant fools! Jonas could almost taste the bile of the remaining pilot's hatred as the second jet shot ahead to extract revenge for its fallen comrade. Unfortunately for this pilot, Jonas had been busy since immediately after loosing the first missile. He had accomplished a reload in a matter of seconds, and took aim standing on what remained of the cave floor entrance.

Like a pair of gunfighters in the old West, both combatants fired at once. This time the MIG pilot did immediately commence changing both direction and altitude, as he made his best effort to escape his compatriot's fate. However, the Seeker, as it was born and bred to do, followed suit and trailed the MIG through all the course changes. It disappeared up the tailpipe of the second MIG and ended the encounter with a huge explosion. The MIG's missiles were aimed badly and struck far up on the mountain, posing no threat to Jonas, who stood ramrod still after launching the second missile, and thus took in the entire life ending drama of his triumphant shot.

Pausing briefly to savor the thrill of both victory and life, Jonas turned and made his way back to the cave's interior to check up on the other two men. The Afghani, though in significant pain from his injuries, put his huge fur lined arms around Jonas and proceeded to lift him off the ground in a crushing bear hug. Releasing Jonas from his grip, he gave him a big gap toothed smile and walked over to the dead goat. Reaching into the goat's belly, he removed the other two rockets. He took the plastic off one of them, put it to his lips, and gave it a resounding kiss. Next he grabbed the Seeker and both hugged and kissed it also. As Jonas was about to turn away and attend to Ike, the Afghani yelled "Hey!'. Tapping his index finger to his temple in the universal sign of intelligence, the mujahideen alternated between pointing at Jonas and pointing at his temple to drive his appreciation home.

Slightly embarrassed, Jonas made his way to where Ike was laying unconscious on the cave floor. Checking his pulse, Jonas determined that Ike was still alive and breathing regularly. However, medical attention was urgently needed if Ike was to survive, and the sooner the better. Jonas became aware of a presence nearby and looked up to see the Afghani towering over him with a resigned expression on his face. Seeing that he now had Jonas' attention, the mujahideen man gazed down at Ike and sadly shook his head. Next he alternated pointing his finger between himself and Jonas, while interspersing his pointing occasionally with a shooting gesture at Ike. His meaning was all too clear! Jonas leaped to his feet and began to vehemently protest against the mujahideen's idea that Ike was too badly injured to travel and thus should be shot and left behind. The Afghani warrior, though he appeared to empathize with Jonas, would not be deterred from his original plan. With slow deliberate steps he started to work his way back toward his rifle. Guessing what he had in mind Jonas turned and raced toward his gear where he had a handgun stored.

Arriving at his pack, Jonas found the gun, slapped in a clip, and wheeled, just in time to see the huge Mujahideen warrior pointing his rifle at Jonas' head in a menacing fashion. The air inside the cave was thick with tension as the two men faced each other, weapons ready. Neither wanted to make the first move, but neither dared to be caught making the last one either. Both men gestured for the other to drop his weapon, but this came to no avail. The two men glared intently at each other.

The deadly spell was broken by a voice from the front of the cave saying sarcastically "Is this a private party, or can anybody join in?" The face of Captain E.B. Bankston was peering around the side of the cave entrance taking in the drama that was playing itself out in the caves interior. Simultaneously the command to drop weapons was issued both in English and in the native tongue of the mujahideen as Major Garner and the ranking mujahideen leader made their presence known. Doing as ordered, both men lowered their weapons to the ground, each supremely happy that the responsibility for Ike had been lifted from their shoulders.

"Man I've never been so glad to see anyone in my whole life" a relieved Jonas exclaimed.

"We've been climbing to get to your position for the past hour since we made our way through a little Russky patrol halfway up the mountain." Maj. Garner said. "We figured that anybody doing such a good job disposing of all that Soviet hardware couldn't be all bad. Actually when you didn't make it back to the base last night, we thought that maybe you were in dire need of some assistance and figured we'd stop in to lend a hand."

"Well I'm glad that it didn't take you a minute longer because my mujahideen friend and I were just about to re-enact the gunfight at the O.K. Corral between ourselves over what to do with Ike."

For the first time, the major and captain took notice of Sargeant Steele lying on the ground. "How badly is he hurt?" inquired Major Garner.

"He's pretty tore up major," offered Jonas. "I've applied a tourniquet to his arm to stem the bleeding, and he's probably got a concussion from the looks of his forehead. With proper medical attention though, I'm sure he can pull through, as opposed to the second opinion offered by Dr. Afghani over there who was opting for a bullet through the head as the proper course of treatment."

"I guess that explains the showdown we saw when we crashed the party," suggested Captain Bankston.

"Captain Bankston! Get a couple of mujahideen fighters to help you rig up a litter so that we can assist Sargeant Steele out of this hole, and off this rock pile. Mr. Trina, I'd like to congratulate you and extend to you our thanks on behalf of Sargeant Steele and the entire U.S. military for a job well done. By the way, I assume that Ike was hit at the end of the jet attacks, in that so many Soviet aircraft went kaput that it must have been his superior marksmanship accomplishing the deeds," said Major Garner.

"Actually major, Sargeant Steele was knocked unconscious by the first MIG rocket attack," spoke Trina.

"You mean to tell me that not only did you save the life of a valued member of this team, but you also single handedly disposed of two top Soviet fighters and chased a third one away? There goes the need for all of that so-called military training," laughed the major.

"I had help from a damned good weapons system in the Seeker, and also considerable help from two of the bravest men I've ever known, one of which who has gone to meet his maker," said Jonas as he looked in the direction of his mujahideen compatriot.

"Speaking of the Seeker, it looks like it performed flawlessly in the hands of capable people, just like we thought it would," Captain Bankston contributed.

"I'm afraid that's not quite correct sir. Early on, the weapon performed very poorly. Had it not been for some incredibly good luck, and the timely and accurate shooting by our Afghan hosts, Sargeant Steele and I would not be making any return trips, except in body bags. This will all be forthcoming when we get back to base and I can write my report, which I'm sure that our accompanying host will verify, as will Sargeant Steele when he is able." said Jonas. "Let me say this. If this weapon is going to perform acceptably in this theater, a way must be found to keep the system from the effects of intense and prolonged cold." With that the conversation ended, and the men made the final preparations to begin the trek back to their base.

Jonas spent another month in Afghanistan helping to teach the mujahideen how essential it was to keep the Seeker weapon system warm enough in the field to operate adequately. At each stop he was treated like royalty by the grateful Afghani freedom fighters. He was always accompanied by Captain Bankston to offer interpretation, and the huge mujahideen fighter who regaled his countrymen with tales of Jonas' exploits on the mountain. He was particularly fond of describing Jonas' idea of using the goat's insides for added warmth that made the mujahideen howl with laughter, particularly after several pints of fermented brew. In spite of himself and his normal personality Jonas found himself a bona fide hero and celebrity to the Afghan people. It was during this time that Jonas was befriended by an Islamic mullah.

In a show of admiration and respect, he gave Jonas the name The Lion Seeker in honor of his help to their cause. This bonding between the Islamic leader and Jonas would surprisingly be maintained via correspondence even after Jonas' return to the United States.

The entire American team, including the recovering Sargeant Steele, was spirited out of the country and into Pakistan for the return trip home. As they awaited their flight, Ike Steele pulled Jonas aside and thanked him for the umpteenth time for saving his life. Jonas looked Steele squarely in the eyes and said: "I'm glad to have been able to help, and it was a pleasure to serve with you Ike. This time it was my good fortune to be in a position where I could help you. Who knows, in the future there may come a time when I may need a man of your unique talents and abilities. Let's stay in touch." Both men knew that Ike owed Jonas now. It was just a matter of time before repayment would be sought.

Though Jonas had shown on the mountain that he could be cordial and decent, it repulsed him that he had to be accommodating. He went along with it due to the fact that unfortunately, if he was to get back alive, he needed each and every one of these people, and he didn't see any benefit in alienating any of them. But, oh how he hated to have to need them, and he could barely wait to get back to the States where he could dictate the time and place when he would exude grace and charm, or release the venom that was more befitting his nature. The good deeds of Jonas Trina had now officially come to an end.

CHAPTER 7

"Hey shark face, you gonna pass some of those potato skins down this way, or are you planning on devouring them all yourself?" Daniece asked hungrily.

"Mine all mine," sneered Jennifer as she opened wide to slide another cheddar, bacon, and chives stuffed skin past her grease smeared lips.

"You know that something just isn't right in the universe when a size 6 like Jenny can scarf down food the way she does," moaned an envious Jane.

"Eat your hearts out while I eat these skins up," quipped Jenny as she eyed up yet another piece of palate pleasing potato perfection.

"And as for you my little Puerto Rican party boy, go easy on those brewskis OK?" insisted Daniece. "Who knows, I might need some input from that cute curly cranium of yours tonight," added Daniece.

"Aw c'mon boss lady, it's only my second beer," replied Ernesto innocently.

"Yeah your second 32 oz. honey lager draft microbrew with a-seven percent alcohol content!" contributed Joan.

"Mind your own business you tee totaling tattle tail!" Ernesto retorted.

A perky young waitress headed in their direction carrying two steaming platters of hors d'oeuvres. "Here are the garlic chicken fingers and special recipe wings you ordered Miss Davis," said the waitress as she placed the platters on the oversized round table. "Enjoy!" Ms. perky said as she made her way back towards the kitchen carrying away the empty plates from their table.

"You don't have to tell me twice," giggled Jenny as she reached for the cornbread coated, butter fried, garlic chicken fingers.

"Remember to stop eating when you get to the platter Jen, I'd hate to see you chip your teeth," joked Holly-Brit.

"Alright everyone it's time to get down to business," announced Daniece in an authoritative voice. "To borrow a phrase; you're probably wondering why I asked you all here this evening. As you may or may not have heard through the company grapevine, some major changes are in the works for good old Pharmacor, and you people are to be at the forefront of them. All departments have been requested to submit plans on how to raise profits while trimming overhead. I have selected you five to be our departmental task force. Your challenge will be to come up with innovative ideas on how to get more out of less.

Your rewards will be longer hours, fewer potty breaks, and the opportunity to have yours truly riding each of your derrieres if I don't get some substantive results. Actually, there will be some benefits to each of you, starting with an immediate 5% raise. Additionally you will be insulated from any departmental cuts which may come about, and your $40 per week contribution to our fabulous health care plan will be picked up by the company effective with tomorrow's paychecks, so financially it should be a nice increase in each of your take home amounts. But that is where the perks end.

In order to meet corporate goals, you will be asked to consider everything. There are no untouchable programs within our department, and you are to leave no stones unturned in our mandated order to improve profitability. Just for the record, this order comes down from the C.E.O. himself, so be assured that all departmental units worldwide are being asked to do the same things and will be undergoing the same scrutiny. Holland Matthews, whom you all know, will be serving as my quote unquote right hand man. Holland and I met this afternoon and she now will give you the guidelines and logistics on how this will all play out over the next few months. Holland if you would please..."

Holland stood up and cleared her throat. "Thank you Daniece. As Daniece has so eloquently pointed out, the times they are a changin', and as such we have no choice but to change along with them. However this is not something to be feared, but rather to be looked upon as a good thing that in the long run will make Pharmacor a healthier company, one that can insure our livelihoods far into the future. Our department here in human resources must achieve an increase in profitability of 15%. To do this we must identify areas where costs can be reduced. This can be accomplished through reductions in material costs from our vendors, scaling down or eliminating programs, streamlining our tasks to become more efficient, or reduction in staffing. By the way, the last part regarding staffing is to be viewed as a last resort. I'm not comfortable throwing people out on the streets and I would hope that we would achieve the stated goals without having to consider layoffs as an option. We do expect that we will end the year with a reduced staff, but it is our intention that it be accomplished through retirements and those voluntarily leaving to pursue new careers. We will meet at my apartment Saturday morning at 9:00 A.M., yes I said Saturday to begin ironing out the details. If any of you had plans for this weekend, cancel them."

This announcement was met with frowns and cries of indignation, as both Holland and Daniece knew it would. "Look people." continued Holland, "Neither myself nor Daniece are trying to be bad-asses or anything, it's just that this is the timetable that has been laid down to us. The C.E.O. is expecting initial plans to be on his desk one week from today, and that doesn't leave us a whole lot of time to work with. As Daniece and I saw today, you don't want to have anyone from our department in front of Mr. Trina next week pleading with him for more time, because then we'll all be gone. Trust me on that. So please, apologize to your family and friends for any inconveniences this entails, and show up Saturday with ideas and a productive attitude, so that we can make the best of it," Holland said in closing.

As an afterthought she added, "If there are any questions please write them down and give them to me tomorrow. Also, I know that most of you have grown accustomed to calling me Holly-Brit. Well due to my recent elevation in stature within this department, I would appreciate from now on being referred to as Lord and Master of Human Resources or simply Omnipotent One." Holland flashed a mischievous grin after this last line.

Hearing that, Ernesto involuntarily spewed a mouthful of honey lager in Holland's direction, drenching her face. Flushed with embarrassment, Ernesto rose to help dry off the results of his social faux pas. Motioning him to sit back down, Holland grabbed a napkin and wiped the offending liquid from her lovely countenance. With a huge grin Holland said; "I guess in light of the circumstances, continuing to call me Holly-Brit or Holland will be just fine!"

An hour later, with all of the chicken consumed, and numerous beverages laid to rest, the group finished saying their goodbyes in the parking lot of Johnny's and headed for their respective vehicles.

"Hold up there a second Holly-Brit," requested Daniece. "So how do you think it went?"

"In my opinion I think things went pretty good after the initial shock wore off," said Holland.

"Me too." concurred Daniece. "Thank heavens for Ernesto; and you girl! The way you threw out that Omnipotent One B.S., and then took that beer-in-the-face thing in stride broke the ice that was starting to settle over the group at that point. I guess we'll find out Saturday if we've got the right people or not," continued Daniece as she opened her car door.

"Oh we've got the right people all right. Everywhere but the top of the company...everywhere but the top," muttered Holland as Daniece started her car and began to pull away.

70

CHAPTER 8

The fire at Mercurio had been contained very quickly, and other than some minor smoke damage, the plant was basically unfazed and back in operation two days after the mishap that was attributed to negligent smoking. A few internal alterations were planned in the near future, such as cameras focused on the entrances of the washrooms to record the comings and goings of employees, but for the most part it was business as usual.

"Hey Ed, I understand that you guys at Mercurio found a new way to liven things up around here a few days ago," said Dan Randle as he backed his truck up to the loading dock to receive today's shipment.

Ed Somerville, the loading dock supervisor, took the good-natured ribbing in stride. "Yeah, the boss told me to turn up the heat on some of these workers to see if I could improve productivity around here, and I guess I overdid it," he joked.

"Who's this big pallet for?" asked Dan as he pointed to a shrink-wrapped pallet noticeably larger than the others.

"That's going to MailMed, that new mail order pharmaceutical house that opened up in Topeka awhile back. We're starting to get some real good business out of them. Hope we don't do something to screw it up," Ed said in an off-the-cuff-fashion.

"As long as you guys remember to hold your weinie roasts on the outside of the building instead of the inside, you should be just fine," Dan replied with a smile.

A short while later the truck was loaded, the bills of lading were filled out and Dan was ready to continue with his part in the American chain of product distribution. "See ya next week ya old sack-a-shit," kidded Ed as Dan's wheels began to roll toward the exit.

"Takes one to know one!" Dan shot back. "See ya in a week." With the niceties having been exchanged, Dan put the truck in gear and commenced out the gates and on to the roadway.

After making a few more stops in the Columbus area, Dan decided to break for lunch at Mabels, a well known truck stop specializing in oversized sandwiches, fresh hot coffee, reasonable prices, and ample parking which was always of prime concern to truckers. Dan pulled his rig into the lot, and chose a spot towards the rear to park. He climbed down from his Peterbilt, and sauntered across the gravel lot towards the front entrance of Mabels, adjusting his Levis as he approached the door. Unbeknownst to him, his every step was being followed by a tall man with black hair, a moustache, and blue eyes, who had been following Dan since he pulled out of the Mercurio Enterprise driveway.

Ike Steele pulled into Mabel's parking lot and parked in the rear, not far from Dan Randle's rig. He got out of a late model Ford Taurus, and while casually adjusting his cap to better shield his eyes from the midday sun, Ike walked into Mabels. As he entered, he quickly located Dan seated with two other men who appeared to be truck driving acquaintances. His mark was seated in an area of the restaurant that did not afford him a view of his rig, which was ideal for Ike's purposes. In addition he was studying the menu carefully, which indicated that he was probably grabbing more than a quick cup of coffee. That was another plus. A full lunch would provide Ike with at least 45 minutes to accomplish his task, which was more than enough time. Ike continued past the cashier to the public restroom. After washing his hands, Ike slowly walked out the front door.

Strolling back through the parking lot, Ike made his way back to his car and opened the trunk. He took out a role of plastic shrink-wrap, a utility knife, a small flashlight, some packaging tape, and a roll of the labels he had made off with from Mercurio earlier in the week. Closing the trunk, he gazed around the lot to make sure that he wasn't being watched. Satisfied that there were no interested observers, he stole to the back of Dan's rig.

Fortunately for Ike, the driver had not bothered to put a lock on the doors for daylight running. Although he was perfectly capable of picking most standard commercial locks, that would have used up precious minutes. Ike opened the large rear doors and jumped in, closing the doors as best he could from the inside, leaving a small crack between the doors. Switching on his flashlight he began to search the numerous pallets in the interior for one from Mercurio. Within a minute Ike had located the pallet that was destined for the mail order house in Kansas. He used the utility knife to slice open the shrink-wrap and ran his flashlight over the boxes of various drugs until he found one of the products he had been instructed to look for. Ike picked up a cardboard box labeled Keldrane, which was an antihistamine. He quickly sliced open the top of the carton and peeled away the now useless packing tape. Ike peeled the labels off of the two-dozen bottles in the carton as quickly as he could, using up almost ten minutes in the process. He had begun to perspire from the close dank air in the truck, coupled with the fear of discovery that lurked in the back of his mind. Not that he was fearful of being able to handle anyone who might stumble upon him, but discovery would entail complications, and complications were not a good thing in Ike's present line of work.

Ike replaced the Keldrane labels with the Zenophol pain killer labels on the twenty four bottles. Placing them back in the box, he re-taped it. Now he removed the Keldrane label from the outside of the box and replaced it with a large Zenophol label, brought along to complete the ruse. He put the box back on the pallet in the exact position from which it had been removed. Making sure that all of the previous shrink-wrap had been taken off, Ike proceeded to rewrap the pallet. He directed the flashlight beam all around the pallet to insure that he picked up all of his "tools" in addition to the shrink-wrap and tape he had cut. Satisfied that he had everything, Ike made his way back to the truck doors and slowly opened them a bit wider. Seeing no one in the immediate area, Ike hopped down and re-closed the large double doors. Doing his best to appear nonchalant, he walked back to his Taurus and deposited an arm full of items into the trunk. As he closed the trunk and walked around to the driver side door, he glanced at his watch. Thirty six minutes had elapsed since he had first opened the truck's doors.

Pulling out of the lot, Ike could see Dan Randle standing by the cash register waiting to pay his bill. Dan wouldn't be the only one who would be made to pay because of his lunch, mused Ike as he removed the baseball cap and donned his sunglasses for the drive back up I-71 north to Cleveland.

Days later, at the MailMed warehouse in Topeka, Kansas, a nineteen year old warehouse worker absent mindedly plays with the middle of three earrings on his left ear while checking in the Mercurio order which arrived earlier that day.

"Hey, Darryl, what do you make of this?"

"What do I make of what, Donnie?"

"Well, here on the bill of lading it says we were supposed to get two boxes of Zenophol and we got three, and one of the boxes doesn't even look like the other two. I opened it up and the bottles are even a little bit different."

"What do I look like, Mercurio Man or something! Hell it's probably one of those deals where they're changing packaging. Companies do that all the time with little or no warning. The label on the box and the labels on the bottles all say Zenophol right?" asked Darryl.

"Right." answered Donnie.

"Well if it waddles like a duck and it quacks like a duck, it must be a duck. Just put them all on the rack in the proper Zenophol location, and since the one that doesn't match the other two is more than likely the old packaging, put that in the front so that we ship it out first. It'll probably expire before the other two," suggested Darryl.

"OK." responded Donnie. "Also I think they shorted us a box of something called Kelbane or Keldrane. I'll bet they screwed up at that Mercurio place and sent the Zenophol in place of the other stuff by mistake."

"Yeah probably." answered Darryl. He continued, "Well just fill out the WTF form and tell them they owe us a case of Keldrane or whatever it is, and don't mention anything about the extra Zenophol. Got it?"

"Got it." said Donnie as he placed the innocuous looking Keldrane/Zenophol on his stock cart to wheel to its shelf location.

CHAPTER 9

At G. Donsky and Associates in Cleveland, which was a third party administrator of pension funds, Ken Kalista sat at his terminal reviewing data from client companies as he sipped his second cup of coffee in the past half hour. Some mornings it took just a little bit extra to get going. A light knock on the side of his cubicle was followed by the appearance of pixie faced Christine Stanton peeking apprehensively around the corner. A transplanted Californian with an impish smile and an engaging personality, the arrival of Christine was usually a welcome break in the office drudgery. This visit would prove to be that and so much more.

"Got a minute?" Christine asked.

"For you Bright Eyes certainly! Have a seat," Ken said as he pulled up an extra swivel chair he had in the corner of his cubicle. "Can I get you a cup of coffee or something?"

"No thanks Ken, but I appreciate the offer. A true gentleman as always!"

"So what can I do for you this morning?" inquired Ken.

"It's probably nothing, but you know how we've got the computers programmed to run reports on any unusual changes in our client's pension portfolios."

"Yes, I'm aware of that being one of the many fantabulous things that our new supercomputer is supposedly capable of, among it's many other talents. So what's up?"

"Last night it spat out a report on Pharmacor, a local pharmaceutical company that I think you should take a look at." Christine proceeded to place a lengthy computer generated report on Ken's desk.

"Why?"

"Well, according to this report, 264 fully vested people have been removed from their pension account due to death in the past four months, which for a company their size is highly unusual."

"Christine, how many fully vested retirees do we show as being on the books for Pharmacor as of now?"

"Approximately 12,000."

"That is way above the ordinary expected number of deaths for that period of time according to any actuarial table. Hey wait-a-minute.

wasn't Pharmacor the company that had that big problem with some retirement party awhile back? A bunch of people got sick and died from something they caught at the party, Legionnaire's disease I believe."

"Very good Ken, you're absolutely right. Here and I thought you were just another pretty face. Beauty and brains too! However, that accounts for only 123 of those dropped. That still leaves 141 more in four months, which is still way too high, especially when you look at the average ages of those who have died, which is 67.8 years old."

"Have you run a back-up report indicating the cause of death, which should be in the computer?"

"Sure have, and that shows only 95 of the 141 have died of natural causes. That on top of the 123 dubiously dubbed "natural deaths" from Legionnaire's disease strikes me as rather disturbing. Of the 46 unnatural deaths, we run the gamut as far as causes of death. We've got hunting accidents, boat accidents, drug overdoses, suicides, fires, and car accidents, with a few murders occurring during robberies thrown in for good measure. To me it looks like the most dangerous occupation in the country right now is to have retired from Pharmacor!"

"Whoa, slow down a minute there. While I admit that the figures are sufficient to warrant some concern, let's not go jumping to any far-fetched conclusions," admonished Ken.

"I don't think that I am jumping to any far fetched conclusions, nor am I about to go off making any wild accusations about somebody targeting Pharmacor. I just think that it is a situation that perhaps needs to be looked into."

"I wholeheartedly concur. Why don't you get in touch with the contact person at Pharmacor, and see if you can set up a meeting so that we can air our findings. Then we can see if they feel threatened in any way by these statistics. If they feel the circumstances suggest foul play in any way, we can put together an action plan. Remember, we are just the program administrators. We are to follow their direction, not vice versa."

"O.K., KK!"

"Let me know what you find out, and what did I tell you about calling me KK?"

"Righto, Mr. Kalista SIR!" With that Christine gathered up the report and coquettishly sashayed out of the cubicle flashing a big smile at Ken as she departed.

"Now I know what the French aristocracy felt like waiting for their turn at the guillotine back during the days of the French Revolution," Holly-Brit stated apprehensively as she and Daniece waited for their assigned turn to present their initial profit plans at Jonas Trina's office.

"Not to worry Holland, today is only the day to submit the plans. This will probably be more of a social occasion than anything else. He might ask us a basic question or two, but he doesn't have time to grill us today. No, that will come in the next few weeks, after he's had a chance to read and digest all of the plans. That's when the official reamings will take place. Not to worry though. From what you showed me in my office this morning, and the sheer volume of paper we've got here, at least even Jonas has to admit that an honest effort has been made. My hat's off to Jane, Joan, Jenny, Ernesto, and of course you Holly-Brit for a job well done."

With that the door to Jonas Trina's office opened and the back of a middle-aged Caucasian man with glasses filled the doorway. "Remember what I said Mr. Robinson. Here at Pharmacor we're interested in results, not excuses," spoke Jonas Trina in a succinct manner.

"You can depend on us," said Hank Robinson, the plant manager of the Cincinnati manufacturing plant. "We'll get this thing turned around."

"See that you do Mr. Robinson, see that you do."

With that Hank Robinson, red faced and perspiring heavily, closed the door. As he turned and walked rapidly away from Trina's office, he appeared to be visibly relieved to be getting away.

The intercom on Jonas Trina's secretary's desk buzzed. "Miss McKinney, would you please show Mrs. Davis and Miss Matthews in now."

"Follow me please," requested the leggy Miss McKinney to Holland and Daniece as she rose from her desk and proceeded towards Jonas' office.

"Into the lion's den we go," muttered Daniece as she opened the door to the C.E.O.'s plush office

"Please have a seat ladies," said Jonas without looking up. He was perusing a report on his desk, more for effect than content.

"Thank you," said Daniece and Holland in unison, as they settled into two serviceable but hardly plush armchairs.

Several interminable minutes passed during which time Jonas Trina continued silently reading to himself without regard to the staff members directly in front of him. Holland began to fidget nervously, uncomfortable with the impolite silence that they were being forced to endure, no doubt to stroke the ego of the man before them. Finally the C.E.O. lifted his eyes and began to speak.

"My, my Mrs. Davis, it seems you and your people have been busy little beavers this past week by the amount of dead tree material you have brought in with you. I trust that it is both grammatically correct and not written in ancient Sanskrit," said Jonas in an attempt at witty repartee`.

"My assistant Holland Matthews and her staff have worked very hard every day of the past week to put together the best plan they could," Daniece said positively.

"Time will tell, although one thing that I'm sure of is that it will beat hands down the sorry five page affair that I was just presented from our flunkies down in Cincinnati, but I digress. Miss Matthews, I don't believe that I have had the pleasure of formally meeting you, although I've heard a lot of good things from Mrs. Davis about you."

The abrupt flip in demeanor took Holland by surprise, but she tried to do her best to accept Mr. Trina's words as a genuine compliment. "It's a pleasure to meet you also Mr. Trina!" Holland said, praying that she sounded sincere. "I also have heard a lot about the outstanding success that you had with the previous two companies that you were the C.E.O. of sir, and I join in welcoming you to Pharmacor."

"Oh Miss Matthews, I'm sure you've heard plenty about where I'm from, and who or what I am. I have no illusions on that, so let's not kid each other shall we? All that I ask of you or anyone here at Pharmacor is that when you are at work, you give your best effort. That shouldn't be too much to ask of anyone should it?"

"No," responded Holland and Daniece on cue.

"Good, then we are in agreement, are we not ladies?" politely asked Jonas.

A double "Yes" came from the women.

"Wonderful. Now Mrs. Davis, if you would be so kind as to enlighten me with a brief overview of what is contained within these reams of paper you've both brought with you, I would be very grateful," Jonas said engagingly. Years of giving presentations brought Daniece automatically to her feet.

"Mr. Trina sir, we've identified several areas where we are going to put the squeeze on in order to exceed corporate profit expectations for our department this year. To begin with we have put a freeze on hiring. Any employees who retire, leave, or are fired will not be replaced for at least the next twelve months. Their workload will be incorporated into the remaining staff's tasks. We will be reviewing all key vendors contracts, and using our volume leverage to negotiate favorable price adjustments and to stave off attempted price increases. In a related vein we will be reviewing insurance contracts that fall within my department's jurisdiction, and requesting new quotes from numerous insurance companies. This we expect will result in a substantial reduction in premiums. We will also be accelerating our efforts to go "paperless" where possible, thereby reducing space requirements, paper costs, filing clerks, etc. Also...."

"That will be enough. As expected, I see you have truly done your homework. I look forward to reading your whole report over the next several days. Ladies, that will be all for now, and you may leave the door open as you depart. Good day." With a show of finality, Jonas' eyes once again returned to his desk further signaling the meeting's end.

"There now, that wasn't so bad was it?" queried Daniece to Holland as they walked back to their department.

"I suppose." Holland admitted. "But why does he have to be so impolite and arrogant? And what's with this Mrs. Davis and Miss Matthews stuff! I get the feeling that he just likes to toy with people, and that what he really enjoys is being petty and making people miserable."

"Just the nature of the beast I guess. Just remember, you only have to put up with him for short infrequent times. Try to grit your teeth and get through it when necessary and maybe you can live a long prosperous Pharmacor life. If that's what you want."

As they walked back into the human resource dept., Daniece stopped to get her messages from her secretary. "Anything urgent for me Teri?" asked Daniece.

"Mostly stuff that can wait, although there was one call from a woman named Stanton that she said was pretty important. It was something about our company pension-plan. The message is the third one down I think."

"Thanks Teri. I'll give her a call in a few minutes." Turning back to Holland, Daniece said: "Holland, how about if you get the other members of our little departmental task force together for lunch tomorrow; my treat. I think you all did a wonderful job and I want to show my appreciation for all of the hard work, and sacrifice each of you gave to make it happen. Pick someplace nice." With that, Daniece disappeared into her office to make some calls.

"Hello, Donsky and Associates? I'd like to speak to Christine Stanton. You can tell her that it is Daniece Davis returning her call from earlier today." A minute later a new voice came on the line.

"Daniece Davis? Hi this is Christine Stanton, thanks for returning my call. As you know, we are the third party administrators for Pharmacor's pension plan. One of our duties as such is to serve as a watchdog, and to alert our clients if and when any anomalies show up in their pension plan demographics."

"Christine, I appreciate that you have given me some insight as to what your company does, but how does this have any bearing on our pension plan at this time?"

"My supervisor, Ken Kalista and I have identified what appears to be some disturbing statistics showing up when comparing your plans mortality rates to the norm and we would like to present our findings to your company for your consideration."

"If you're referring to the Legionnaire's disease tragedy, yes we are aware that a lot of former employees were involved, which is naturally going to skew the numbers. However, an inquest was done and any wrongdoing was dismissed, if that is where this is headed."

"Actually there is more than that involved Mrs. Davis, which we are somewhat reluctant to get into over the phone. Could we please set up a meeting at your convenience so that we could make a full disclosure of all of the information which has come to light?"

"Unfortunately Christine, your timing couldn't be worse in that we have just been hit with several mandates from the top which require my personal attention at this time. However, I could have you meet with my personal assistant, Holland Matthews, who has the full confidence of this department. I'll have her get back to you with an appropriate meeting time and location. If Holland deems the information to be noteworthy enough we'll proceed further, fair enough?"

"Fair enough," agreed Christine "I'll await Holland's call."

"I'll have Holland call later this afternoon. Good day Christine."

With that concluded, Christine prepared to leave her seat in order to report back to Ken Kalista on how the call had gone. She was startled when she turned to see Ken already standing behind her.

"Well, how'd it go?" he asked.

"Good, I think. I'm supposed to hear from someone this afternoon to name a time and a place for the meeting."

"Keep me posted, and by the way the new number in the past four months for Pharmacor is 265, not 264. They just said on the radio they found a probable suicide out in Strongsville. Some guy named Thomas Schultz blew his brains out this morning. He was described as a recently fired V.P. for Pharmacor."

CHAPTER 10

Jonas returned to the United States as a hero, albeit a closet one, due to the fact that assistance to the mujahideen was officially not being provided by the U.S. Therefore all of the team member's actions went unreported to all but a handful of the governmental hierarchy, which included the President. In a private ceremony, he was awarded a medal by one of the Joint Chiefs of Staff for his part in helping the Afghani people, and a special dinner was held to honor all four members of the team.

The management and engineering staff at Sutton Industries, though sworn to secrecy by the government, also honored Jonas upon his return. He was given a raise, and a management position in research and development was created for him, which effectively put him second in command of R&D. However most of this was window dressing, done to appear grateful, but at the same time not expecting or planning on Jonas doing much. Upper level members of management at Sutton were aware of what an accomplishment like the one Jonas had just pulled off in Afghanistan could do to catapult one's career. They were a bit jealous of his success, and more than a bit worried that he might replace one of them in due time, so they planned to stonewall him in R&D. The idea was to have the head of R&D, Ralph Weldon, sidetrack any marginally good ideas that might come from Jonas or his staff. Any really good ideas were to be usurped from Jonas and he was to be discredited if he protested, with all of the managers sticking up for Ralph Weldon, should that prove to be necessary. Unfortunately these men did not realize the depths of Jonas' ambition, nor his willingness to stop at nothing to achieve his goals. They also underestimated Jonas' ability to think through all of the possible scenarios of a situation, which playing chess had taught him to do.

By this point in his life, Jonas had determined that in order to live life on his own terms, he would have to become the top dog. That was to be his goal, and nothing or no one would be permitted to stand in his way. This meant that peers, managers, even the C.E.O. himself were to be viewed as either pawns to be used, or opposing queens and kings to be overcome. In the short term, he felt that his best chance to "rise up the corporate ladder" would be to overwhelmingly succeed at his current position. Thus he set to work to grab the limelight for any good ideas or products which came out of R&D, which put him on a collision course with the plans of Ralph Weldon and the other managers. Something or someone had to give.

Within two months of his return to Sutton, Jonas had developed a couple of lightweight polystyrene prototypes for packaging to help keep the Seeker and its rockets warm and protected in the harsh climate of Afghanistan. Tests were successful and he presented his findings to his boss Ralph Weldon. Not only was Weldon not impressed, he ridiculed everything on the packages from their color to their vulnerability, and would not permit Jonas any type of rebuttal to defend his prototypes. Next he surprised Jonas by ordering him to leave the prototypes and the file concerning them in Weldon's office. He would look them over when he had more time, but he doubted if it would come to anything. Telling Jonas to get out of his office and come up with something good, Weldon slammed the door in his face.

Stinging from the rebuke, Jonas retreated back to his office and spent the remainder of the day trying to make sense of what had happened. While he knew that he and Weldon were not the best of friends, still they maintained a decent working relationship, at least until today, so a personality clash had to be ruled out. While it was possible that Weldon might be just "having a bad day," that didn't explain the virtual total scrapping of the prototypes that he called for, so that was not it. In turn Jonas eliminated financial gain or loss, product performance, or product cost as reasons to have the idea thrown out without even seeing it perform.

In the end, Jonas tried putting himself in Weldon's shoes and considered both the product and Jonas from his side. All he was able to come up with was jealousy, but what was there to gain by reacting as he had? Angry and confused, Jonas shut down his office and drove his BMW home to Naperville, an upscale suburb of Chicago favored by many of the employees of Sutton. Opening the door to his condo, Jonas hastened straight to the liquor cabinet. Grabbing a bottle of Chivas Regal he kept on hand for emergencies, he did something totally out of character. He poured himself two fingers of the light golden liquid and downed it in a swallow. He indulged himself twice more, before replacing the cap on the bottle and walking over to grab the remote control to turn on the TV. The set flickered on, but as soon as the bleach blonde newscaster on Channel four appeared in focus, he clicked the TV off. He couldn't get his mind off the incident in Weldon's office, Although Jonas wasn't much of a drinker at this time he had adapted since college, and had discovered that a few drinks could sometimes be helpful.

The scotch was helping him to relax, and in turn it helped him to eliminate distractions. Focus damn it, FOCUS, Jonas told himself. People tend to act in their own best interests he reasoned. How could the events of the day have helped to serve Ralph Weldon's best interests? Suddenly an idea came to him. It hit him so abruptly and so logically that he couldn't help but take his right hand and whack the meaty part of his palm into his forehead for being such an idiot. That's it, he thought as he grabbed his keys and flew out the front door to his Beemer.

Racing back to the office, Jonas squealed to a stop not far from where Ralph Weldon's car was still parked. Even though the luminescent dial on Jonas' Seiko watch said it was 7:49 P.M., Jonas tried the front door, but it was locked. He could see a light on upstairs in his second floor office, conspicuous in that no other lights were visible on that floor. He pushed the buzzer that would bring a security person to the entrance. As the guard could be seen coming down the corridor towards the front door, Jonas noticed his office lights went out, and he thought he saw a face look briefly out from the blinds, but he wasn't sure. The security man reached the front door and began to unlock it.

"Forget something Mr. Trina?" asked Walter, the retired policeman who handled late afternoon and early evening security.

"Yeah Walt, I forgot to take a file home with me. Is anybody else still here that you know of?"

"I saw Mr. Weldon a little while ago. He said he'd be finishing up pretty soon, had some odds and ends to take care of he said. Oh look here he comes now."

"I'll be leaving now Walt. Trina what are you doing here? I thought you left hours ago," said Weldon

"I did, but I forgot a file. What kept you here so late this evening if you don't mind my asking?"

"I had a report I had to get done. Also I'll be going on vacation in a few weeks and I'm trying to get a leg up on some things so you guys don't fall on your face while I'm gone."

"I thought I saw a light on in my office when I pulled up," Jonas said as he looked hard at Weldon.

"Oh, that was probably me trying to catch that damn mouse." replied Weldon, not very convincingly. "I saw it run down the hall as I was leaving, and it ran into your office, so I thought I'd try and find it and kill the little pest. However, as you'll probably find out tomorrow, I was unsuccessful. You know, you really ought to lock your door like you're supposed to before you leave. I'll let it slide this time, but I'll have to report you next time. I locked it on my way out. Goodnight gentlemen!" With that Ralph Weldon proceeded to his car and quickly began to back out of his assigned spot prior to heading out of the parking lot.

"Mr. Trina did you want to come in and grab that file?"

"Yes Walt, I'll only be a couple minutes." With that Jonas entered the building and hurried up the stairs to his office, fearful of what he may or may not find. As he unlocked the door, he had a sense of foreboding. Turning on the light he felt a brief moment of relief as he scanned the room and didn't detect anything noticeably out of place. As he reached for the bottom drawer of his file cabinet though, he realized that the drawer was open a couple of inches, which was highly unusual for himself. Jonas prided himself on his neatness, and it just wasn't his nature to leave his office with something even as minor as this out of place. Apprehensively he opened the drawer and reached for the file marked Seeker/Poly/Packaging. As he feared, the file was now empty. It had contained his only other copies and notes on the polystyrene packaging since he had left the original in Weldon's office as ordered.

Panicking, Jonas searched all of the files close to that one, in a vain hope that he had somehow misfiled them, knowing all the while that he had not. As he checked his desk drawer, in a last gasp effort, Jonas heard Walt outside the door.

"You about done in there Mr. Trina?"

"I'm coming out right now Walt," said Jonas as he turned off the light and rotated his key in the lock.

"Didn't need that file after all?" asked Walt.

"It wasn't there. I must have left it in someone else's office by mistake. I spent a lot of time in Mr. Weldon's office today. I'll bet we can find it in there," said Jonas hoping that Walt would honor his implied illegal request.

"I'm sorry, Mr. Trina, but I can't allow you to go in there without Mr. Weldon's permission. You know that."

"But Walt, you just heard him say that he was in my office; what's the difference?"

"You also heard him say that your door was unlocked, and he was just chasing a mouse. Although, if I had happened to be in that corridor at that time I would've shooed even him out because nobody is supposed to be in anyone else's office after hours. Are we done now?"

"Yeah, I suppose so. Let me out the front door so that I can go home."

"Yes sir Mr.Trina."

Jonas awoke late the next morning somewhat thick tongued and bleary eyed from the effects of the scotch. He really wasn't much of a drinker he reminded himself as he hurriedly went through the paces of his morning routine, scurrying out the door 10 minutes faster than it would normally take him. He arrived at the office 25 minutes late. Ralph Weldon happened to be going by the front entrance as Jonas arrived,

"You are aware Mr. Trina, that we start at 8:00A.M., are you not?" Weldon said contemptuously.

"Yes I am. I'd have been here earlier, but I was trying to find a missing file that seems to have disappeared from my office in the past day."

"Well, if it has anything to do with what you showed me yesterday, it's just as well. I consider that subject closed." With that, Ralph Weldon turned and walked to his office, closing the door behind him.

Weldon's door flew open and in came an agitated Jonas Trina. "I am about to reopen that subject Weldon!" barked Jonas. "You and I both know that you took that file when you were in my office last night. At first I couldn't figure out why, but now I have. You're the type of manager who makes a name for himself by stealing the ideas of those under him and claiming them as his own. By doing so, you eliminate potential rivals and make yourself look good at the same time, suggesting all of these good ideas have originated from yourself. What is it Weldon, fear of being caught up to by your peers? Perhaps it's jealousy or extra bonus money? What is it?"demanded Jonas.

"I don't have to answer any of your ridiculous accusations Trina! And by the way, just who in the hell do you think you are to come barging into my office this way. Just because you appear to have done a decent job in Afghanistan, doesn't mean that you can come back here like God's gift to engineering or something. Yes I took your damn plans, and you should be thankful that I did! I've been working on polystyrene packaging for months, and all of a sudden you pop into my office like it's your idea. Just exactly how were you able to get hold of my plans, you sneaky little S.O.B. I was going to just let this whole thing slide, because it does none of us any good to have the "Golden Boy" exposed as a petty usurper of other's ideas, but it seems that you're not willing to let that happen," Weldon countered.

Jonas was momentarily shaken, but he quickly went back on the offensive. "Oh, so you've been working on the polystyrene for months huh Weldon? Well then it shouldn't be too difficult for you to answer a couple of simple questions concerning stress tolerances, or temperature gradients, etc. concerning the prototypes. You know, some of those basic engineering types of questions that both of us had to concern ourselves with when we were designing our packaging. How about us going up to President Stewart Jones' office right now and presenting our cases, since we're both experts on the subject?"

"I've got a better idea," Ralph Weldon shot back. "Why don't you just get the hell out of my office right now, and maybe, just MAYBE, I'll let you keep your job!"

Both men stood glaring at each other for a full five seconds before Weldon shattered the silence by speaking into his intercom; "Miss Williams, this is Ralph Weldon. Please have security come to my office immediately."

As he backed to the door Jonas said; "Since it appears that we won't be going to Jones' office together, I guess I'll just have to go alone." With that, Jonas slammed the door to Weldon's office and proceeded back to his own to arrange a meeting with the company president.

"Miss Williams, this is Ralph Weldon again. Cancel that security call, and get me Stewart Jones on the phone."

Jonas picked up the phone in his office to dial Stewart Jones' extension, but he replaced the receiver back on the hook, prior to dialing. "Damn," muttered Jonas as he contemplated his situation. Without his original plans, his copies, or prototypes, which Weldon may have stashed anywhere by now, Jonas had no physical proof of his idea with which to present his case. Furthermore, with the camaraderie that Weldon shared with Jones and the other members of Sutton Industry's upper management, Jonas had to have an airtight case before they would ever side with him in a head-to-head battle against Ralph Weldon. Reluctantly, Jonas came to the conclusion that he had to get back to Weldon's office, and hopefully, there might still be some evidence he could get his hands on to bolster his chances.

As he approached Weldon's office, Jonas could see that the door was open just a crack. It probably hadn't totally shut when he'd slammed it earlier. This was very fortunate for Jonas, in that it allowed him to both see and hear into the office without being detected. From his viewpoint he could see Weldon talking on his phone, with his back to the door.

"That's right Stewart he just left my office in the past five minutes. I hate to say it, but those prototypes looked pretty damn good. I tried to deflect him by telling him that I'd been working on the same idea, and that he'd stolen it from me, but I could see he wasn't buying it. Look Stew, you guys have got to cover me just like we agreed. You and Smitty in manufacturing, Cassidy in accounting, those two plant managers, and Marsden in sales. What's that? Yeah, I've got his copies right here in my desk, and his originals back at my place. It shouldn't be too tough to get some prototypes of my own made up in a couple days. I'll talk with Carter in production. Yeah he's the same guy that Trina had to be working with to make the prototypes of his. We'll have to bring him into the loop also. Whatever we do, I need all of you guys to swear that I had the idea before him. If we don't all stick together on this stuff, we might all be answering to this S.O.B. down the road, and I know none of us relishes that thought. OK, I've got it. Alright, see that you do."

Jonas was virtually in a state of shock over what he had just heard. Not only was Weldon trying to steal his idea, it also appeared he had the backing of upper management to do so, and in fact it had all been planned. He contemplated what to do next. He didn't want to let anyone know what he'd just heard, but he still had to get his hands on his plans. His decision was made for him as Weldon opened his desk drawer and took out several sheets of paper. As he laid the papers on his desk, Jonas could see that the top sheet had the word Polystyrene written on it. He chose his course of action.

Bolting into the office with his right fist cocked, Jonas shouted; "Weldon, you piece of..." Ralph Weldon lifted his hands in front of his face in a defensive posture to ward off the coming blow. The blow was never struck, as Jonas forcibly snatched the papers off the desk. Verifying that these were in fact his plans, he raced from the office.

As he shot down the hallway, Jonas fled toward the front entrance that led to the parking lot. He needed time to think. What to do? Where to go? Who to see? Who can I trust? Not desiring to speak with the security at the front desk, Jonas detoured down a side corridor. Here he was able to exit, although he would have to walk around much of the building to get to his car.

Meanwhile Weldon, having composed himself, called Jones on the phone. "Stewart, Trina just attacked me in my office and took the plans back. It looks like he's going to go for his car. Should I have him stopped at the front gate?" asked Weldon.

"Let him go," said Jones. "Who can he really go see that would help him? There's nothing that he can take to the police. Let him go blow off some steam. He'll be back after he realizes that he's got nothing. Soon we can begin building a united case against our Mr. Trina, and have him dismissed from the family. In the meantime, may I suggest that you occupy yourself with getting some prototypes made up so that you can counter his accusations! Call Carter in production right now and make sure that he understands the situation. Feel free to put some pressure on him if it appears that he might go to bat for Trina as far as whose prototypes came first. We've got to make sure that we're all on the same page on this. Understood?"

Jonas drove out the entrance of Sutton Industries, half surprised that he wasn't challenged at the front gate. He turned onto the highway and commenced driving with no particular direction in mind, just a desire to put distance between himself and Sutton. His mind was spinning. It sounded from the conversation that he overheard that everyone was against him throughout Sutton. Wait, Carter might be able to help. Kevin Carter had helped him to get around the manufacturing schedules and enabled him to run the prototypes through production. Not once had Carter ever mentioned that Weldon or anyone else had been involved in something similar to Jonas' project. Seeing a payphone by the side of the road, Jonas abruptly changed lanes, cutting off a construction worker in a pick-up truck, who responded to Jonas' move in horn blowing, one-fingered fashion. Leaping from the BMW, Jonas dialed the number to Sutton Industries, and requested to speak to Kevin Carter. A pleasant female voice responded: "I'm sorry, but Mr. Carter is in a meeting right now, may I take a message?" Recognizing the voice of Triste, Carter's secretary, Jonas said "Triste, its Jonas Trina. It's imperative that I speak with Kevin right now if at all possible."

"Mr. Trina, I would let you if I could, but Mr. Carter is in a meeting with Mr. Weldon, and Mr. Weldon said that they were not to be disturbed for ANY reason, or I could consider where else I would like to work, other than Sutton."

"I understand Triste. Maybe it's best that you not tell anyone that I called. I'll talk to Kevin later." Jonas replaced the receiver back in its cradle. Who to call now? Who? Was there anyone who could make a difference? Jonas took some change out of his pocket and deposited it in the payphone slot.

"Sutton Industries." answered the feminine voice at the other end of the phone.

"May I please be connected to C. Gerald Dilley, the C.E.O. of Sutton Industries?" requested Jonas.

"I'll connect you with his office."

"Mr. Dilley's office."

"May I please speak to Mr. Dilley?"

"I'm sorry sir, but Mr. Dilley is out of town at the moment."

"May I ask when Mr. Dilley is expected back in the office?"

"He's expected back in the day after tomorrow. May I take a message Mr...."

Jonas hung up and slowly opened the door to the phone booth. He walked the short distance back to the car and leaned on the driver's side door as he weighed his options. If he couldn't speak to the C.E.O., then there was a chance that neither would Jones or Weldon until Dilley got back in the office. He had to get to Dilley first if there was any prayer for his cause. Unless he could somehow convince the C.E.O., not only of his innocence, but also the righteousness of his case, all hope would be lost. Marshalling all of his cunning, experience, and logic, Jonas began to formulate a plan that even his old chess adversaries would have had to admire.

The electronically controlled gate swung open, allowing the limousine access to the long winding drive leading up to the grand estate of C. Gerald Dilley. It was almost twilight, and the setting sun cast a beautiful reddish hue on the waves of Lake Michigan that served as Mr. Dilley's back yard. The long black limo pulled to a stop on the rose-colored brick semi-circular drive in front of the mansion's entrance. The driver's door opened, and a large middle aged man who seemed to exude culture emerged and made his way to the passenger door.

"Shall I take in the clubs sir?" asked Nelson the chauffer.

"By all means Nellie, and while you're at it, give my two-iron a big wet kiss, and break my sand wedge into five pieces. One piece for every shot it cost me at Merion today! Just kidding Nellie, just kidding," said C. Gerald.

A solitary figure emerged from behind a large sculpted shrub in front of one of the mansion's 8-foot arch top windows. "Would you care to have me clean the clubs sir?" said this interloper.

"Who are you?" demanded Dilley as he strained to make out the figure in the approaching darkness.

"Shall I call the authorities sir?" asked Nellie.

"Wait, please Mr. Dilley. I desperately need to speak with you," said Jonas as he came into view.

"Do I know you?"

"Well, yes and no sir, we met several months ago at an award banquet in my honor. My name is Jonas Trina."

"Why yes, I do recall us having met. Now Trina, just how did you evade my security system, and just what is so terribly important that it won't keep until we could meet in my office."

"How I evaded security is not important, let's just suffice it to say that I'm both an electrical engineer by trade, and that I've had some special governmental training to prepare me for the role for which I was honored. As for the reason I'm here, may we speak in private? On the night we met at the award ceremony you said that if there was ever anything you could do for me, that I shouldn't hesitate to ask. Well, sir I need your help, and we need to speak tonight. Tomorrow would be too late."

"Alright, if it is that critical, I'll give you a few minutes, but mind you, it is only because of your service to both this country and Sutton, which you performed so admirably that I will grant you a brief audience this evening. Nelson, take the car around if you would please, and don't forget about those clubs."

As they approached the massive front door, almost as if on cue, the custom designed portal opened, revealing a butler who eyed Jonas warily. "It's alright Mason, He's a business associate." spoke C. Gerald.

"Are there any bags which I can retrieve for you sir?" asked the butler.

"Not at this moment Mason. However if you could you be so kind as to bring us a decanter of sherry, we'll take it in the study."

With that both the C.E.O. and Jonas strode through the three story foyer and entered a stunningly well-furnished library/study off the main hallway. Jonas was given a brief tour of the room, during which time the butler reappeared with the sherry in an elegantly cut leaded crystal decanter, replete with matching glasses. The butler poured a generous amount of an exquisite sherry into each glass, and awaited further instruction.

"That will be all Mason."

The butler's response of "As you wish," coincided with his closing of the double doors that led to the study.

Handing a glass to Jonas, C. Gerald Dilley initiated the discussion. "Mr. Trina, today I shot the poorest back nine in the last ten years within my golfing memory. I lost my footing and stepped in mud calf-deep while looking for one of my errant shots. I haven't had a decent night's sleep in a week, and tomorrow I have a board meeting with a bunch of surly old fogies who would like nothing better than to have my ass handed to them on a platter. Therefore, for expediency's sake, won't you please tell me why you are here?"

"Yes sir, and sorry to hear about your troubles also," replied Jonas. The next fifteen minutes were spent with Jonas recounting the events of the past few days at Sutton, occasionally being interrupted by the C.E.O. who would require clarification on some point or other. At the end of the recitation Jonas produced the copies of his plans as the only physical proof to offer for his side of this tale of corporate intrigue.

"Let me see if I understand this correctly," said C. Gerald. "You would have me believe that virtually all of the upper management at Sutton has joined forces against you, Mr. Trina out of a sense of jealousy and perhaps apprehension? They fear that someday they may have to answer to you, which is something they all find a bit distasteful, is that essentially correct?"

"Put in those terms sir, I guess it does seem awfully farfetched," admitted Jonas.

"And yet, desperate times call for desperate measures. Certainly your story, along with what you undertook to get tonight's audience with me cannot be dispelled lightly. I should think that only a man not only desperate, but also sure of his convictions would go to the lengths which you have in order to prove their cause is just. It's either that, or a man would have to be an exceedingly clever person. Are you Mr. Trina?"

"I've spoken the truth as I know it sir."

"Well then, where does that leave us? When we arrive at Sutton tomorrow, I assume there will be two sets of plans, two sets of prototypes, and you will be outnumbered something like ten to one insofar as whose idea came first. Since he has had a few days to bone up on your plans, I suppose that it wouldn't do much good to quiz both you and Weldon on technical aspects of the prototypes. Did you note that I said YOUR plans? I am inclined to believe your story Jonas, because not only of the measures you took, but also because I've witnessed this closing of the ranks on a corporate level many times before. Although, it is generally done to cover a group of derrieres when a screw-up occurs. This personal vendetta they appear to have undertaken to "keep you in your place" as it were is rather extraordinary to say the least. Are you dangerous enough to be so feared Jonas? I wonder. Ah, but I digress. Do you have any thoughts on how we should proceed into the mouth of the lion?"

"With all due respect sir, yes I do. I grew up studying the game of chess from the time I was eleven until I graduated from Purdue. A couple of important lessons that chess taught me were the values of examining a situation from all sides, and anticipating all of the consequences of one's moves or the moves of one's opponent. I realize that for the company's sake and the shareholder's sake, it is truly very unimportant who is right or wrong in this corporate infighting. The overriding concerns to them are profitability, market share, assurances of a solid corporate future, etc. These are the types of issues that you Mr. Dilley, in your role as C.E.O. must concern yourself with. While I would love to win this battle, and see justice served, I recognize that I must bow to the greater good in order to help Sutton achieve their goals. However, surely it must irk your sensibilities to see an injustice such as this occur.

Also you know that this is probably just the tip of the iceberg compared to all of the corporate shenanigans that may be going on at this point in time. I mean, let's face it, if they are willing to go to these lengths to discredit someone who only has a couple of prototypes of a potentially decent new product, to what lengths would some, or all of these people go to get a really big payoff. Or are they already skimming? Perhaps even something worse? Who knows, corporate espionage happens everyday. I'm sure that there are lots of foreign nationals willing to bribe corporate insiders for a plan here, or a drawing there. What would the U.S.S.R. give for a way to overcome the "Seeker?" Anyway, here is what I propose: You should have both sides tell their stories. You weigh the findings, and in a decision that even King Solomon would be proud of, you decide that it truly was a simple case of both men working on the same design at the same time, unbeknownst to each other. Therefore as far as the rest of Sutton knows, there are no good guys, or bad guys. There is merely a coincidence to blame. Weldon and I share the accolades and split the bonus money.

However, since we have already identified probable bad guys, they should, and must be dealt with. And they should be dealt with in such a way that the company is not jeopardized. I realize that you still may have some misgivings about whether I'm telling the truth or not. I propose the following: You initiate a program whereby each department head and manager up to and including the company president begin to train a successor. The successor is to be trained in all aspects of the job with no holds barred. It could be announced as being done merely to implement sound corporate policy, so that when a management change takes place, the new person can hit the ground running. This will eliminate the need to waste months "growing into the job" and significantly reduce the amount of poor decisions made by personnel who are still learning the ropes.

At the same time I will keep you abreast of any promising new products on the horizon, and who is responsible for them. For instance right now another engineer named Ray Chang and myself are working on an anti missile system which shows a lot of promise. When it comes time, I'm sure that Weldon and Jones and the others will attempt to discredit Chang and myself for our parts in this also. Then you would know that I speak the truth. The usurpers could be dealt with properly and their successors would already be able to step right in ready to make us a stronger company with greater integrity not only for our employees, but also for our stockholders. In addition you would have the satisfaction of knowing that justice had been served."

"Well, it certainly looks like you've thought this thing through Mr. Trina. You are absolutely correct in what you said initially about my responsibilities and concerns being for the stockholders, and not whether you or Weldon, or whoever, comes out on top in this mess. However there is a great deal of merit in what you say. Tomorrow when I finish with my board meeting, which should be early afternoon, I will arrange for a meeting between you, Weldon, and Jones in my office. I'll listen to both sides and do as you have suggested, declaring a coincidence that you should not be too pleased with in order to keep up appearances. Then we shall await further developments in the near future. Fair enough Mr. Trina?"

"Yes sir."

"It might not be a bad idea for you to make yourself scarce tomorrow until we convene, O.K?"

"Got it Mr.Dilley"

"Good, I'll have Mason show you to the door. Goodnight Mr. Trina."

"Good afternoon gentlemen, I trust that you haven't been waiting too long. Sometimes those board meetings can become insufferable. My apologies," spoke C. Gerald Dilley as he entered the waiting room to his office. Won't the three of you follow me into my office so that we may commence with the proceedings?" Stewart Jones, Ralph Weldon, and Jonas did as instructed, with Jonas closing the door to Mr. Dilley's private office upon clearing the threshold.

"Let's get right to it, shall we?" said the C.E.O. "I'd like to begin this hearing of sorts by bringing everyone here up to speed. I'm already aware of Mr. Trina's side of the story. He claims that his plans and prototypes for new rocket and Seeker launcher packaging, have effectively been stolen by Ralph Weldon, and he feels that it was with the knowledge and approval of Mr. Jones here. Is that right Mr. Trina?"

"That is correct sir," acknowledged Jonas.

"And you Mr. Weldon claim to have been working for a longer period of time on essentially the same type of new product ideas, without the knowledge that Jonas was duplicating your efforts. Is that right?"

"Well yes and no sir," responded Weldon. "Since I was working on mine for a significantly longer period of time than Trina, it baffled me that he should, on his own mind you, come up with almost an exact duplicate to my plans. Thus I feel that he must have somehow been able to tap into my work and basically try to steal my idea. I've got Stewart Jones here who can attest for the amount of time I've been working on this, as well as Kevin Carter in production, the person who built the prototypes, and several others who can vouch for my side of the story," stated Weldon, as Jones nodded his head in agreement.

"Yes Mr. Weldon, I'm sure you've got all of your supporters lined up in order to plead your case. That won't be necessary. I've decided to call this a draw and award bonus money and credit mutually to both of you should a viable product result from your efforts. My reasons for this are as follows. I do not wish to bog down this company in a bitter internal dispute causing hard feelings and lost productivity. Additionally, like it or not Stew and Ralph, there are an awful lot of people in the Pentagon right now who look upon our Mr. Trina as a bona fide hero of sorts. Now just how would it look if we were to have to present him in a negative light, and vice versa, how would it look if Sutton Industries was found to be attempting to steal a brilliant idea from Jonas? You are all aware, are you not, that our number one customer is the armed forces of this great nation of ours? I don't know about you gentlemen, but I can think of no reason why either ourselves, or our stockholders would like to see us do anything to disrupt the partnership that we currently enjoy with the Pentagon. I could go on, but I believe you can see the direction in which I am headed. Regardless of whether any wrongdoing or not has taken place, the safest course of action for this company is the one which I have chosen, and that is the one which will be followed. Is that clear?" All three men nodded silently.

"Good, then we shall consider that matter closed, except for this. This will be the last "coincidence" of this nature, understood? Any future disagreements like this will be met with the immediate termination of ALL parties concerned. Now let's all shake hands and part amicably. I do not expect that this unpleasantness will in anyway affect your working together to the best of your abilities from this moment forward. Good day gentlemen."

With that the three men shook and departed the office. Jonas followed the other two out, with his shoulders slumped a bit in a show of dejection. As the men made their way down the hallway leading away from Dilley's office, Weldon abruptly wheeled around and faced Jonas. "Regardless of what happened in that office just now Trina, make one thing damned clear! I still don't like you, and I'd watch my back if I were you." With that, both Jones and Weldon quickened their pace, and Jonas was content to let his adversaries lengthen their distance from him as he stopped to ponder what he had been told.

The next several months passed without incident as a type of peaceful co-existence settled in between the combatants as they both went about their business, sidestepping each other unless it was unavoidable. However, both men were once again on a collision course. The Seeker polystyrene packaging had proved to be a big success that had driven both men even further apart as Jonas fumed that he had to share the spotlight with Weldon. Furthermore, Ray Chang's anti-missile missile was looking to be a viable defensive weapon system which Jonas had made some small but significant contributions to, and for which he could reasonably expect more kudos. This upset Weldon and the other members of management who continued to fear Jonas' rising star within the company. Jonas could see a showdown approaching and he knew he needed help. While he had been keeping C. Gerald Dilley apprised of the progress of the anti-missile system, he knew that Mr. Dilley could ill afford to take sides in any corporate politics. Also, for what Jonas had in mind, he needed assistance from someone with a rare combination of skills and courage. He had just the person in mind.

"Steele residence, it's your dime and I've got the time so start talkin' or I'm walkin'," spat out Ike Steele upon picking up the receiver at his parent's home in Beaver Falls, Pa.

"Ike this is Jonas Trina."

"Jonas you old corporate ass kisser, how the hell are you?"

"I'm well Ike, and I hope you are the same. It's good to hear your voice. I really didn't expect to catch you here, but it was the only place that I knew to start looking for you. I assume that I caught you on leave from the Army or something."

"Not quite Jonas. My association with the Army has come to an end in the past few months. Turns out they have some type of regulation against beating the crap out of a superior officer, even those in desperate need of a knuckle massage on their chin. If it weren't for my stint in Afghanistan, and my fairly decent record prior to that, I'd be receiving my mail at Leavenworth. Anyway what can I do for you, my old mountain buddy?"

"Ike I need a favor from someone, and you came to mind first. In your training with the Army Rangers, I'd imagine that they taught you some pretty specialized and extensive training, perhaps even espionage type training. Am I correct?"

"You'd better believe it."

"Ike, are you working at this point in time?"

"Not unless you consider flipping burgers and flipping channels working. I just got back in town a month or so ago, and there ain't a whole hell of a lot going on in Beaver Falls, so I took a part time job serving burgers and brew at a local bar. You got something in mind?"

"How soon could you arrange to fly to Chicago? I'll make all of the arrangements and set you up at a local hotel for a week. Do you think you could see your way clear to make that happen in the next few days?"

"Say the word and I'm there."

"Alright Ike I'll advise you later this evening as to the flight and lodging arrangements. I'll fill you in on the details of why I need a man of your particular skills when you get here."

CHAPTER 11

"Here's to your health, Ike," said Jonas as he raised his glass of stout ale.

"Back at you my old compatriot!" returned Ike lustily as he wiped the foam from his own ale off his lips with the back of his hand. "So Jonas, are you going to explain what this cloak and dagger assignment you've got for me is all about, or should I just start breaking into places until you tell me to stop?"

"One place I have in mind should suffice Sir Isaac. As you know, I work for Sutton Industries. Some bad blood has cropped up between some members of upper management and me, since my return. Jealousy has reared its ugly head." With that Jonas detailed the past many months activities and problems up to the present.

"Call me stupid, but I don't get it Jonas. What is it that you need me for?" asked Ike.

"In a couple of days we are going to reveal the anti-missile missile as a successfully tested, ready for final approval, weapon system which is all set to go into production. My enemies fear that if I get any credit for the success, it will boost my standing within the company so that I may become a rival for power in the organization. Many of them are aligned against me and will do whatever they can to discredit me, or worse. I've got to know what their plans are, and in order to do that I need an extra set of eyes and ears. But not just any eyes and ears my friend. I need someone to break into a couple of offices at Sutton and plant bugs and wiretaps so that we can ascertain without a doubt what they are up to in order to effectively counter any schemes they may be brewing. This is where you come in. I'm hoping that in your Ranger training you may have picked up the necessary skills that would enable you to take on such a mission. Have you?"

"Let's just say that some of the training sites I was at in the Army weren't exactly on the map. The breaking in shouldn't be too difficult. Hopefully I can secure the electronic equipment needed to accomplish the electronic surveillance. In a town the size of Chicago I should be able to find enough pieces/parts to Rube Goldberg something if I have to."

"So you'll do it?" asked Jonas imploringly.

"What are old friends for? Besides, things were getting kind of boring back home, and this should serve to liven things up. Not to mention the fact that I'm still kind of beholden to you for what you did for me in that cave. Count me in."

"It's settled then," said Jonas as he reached into the inside pocket of his jacket. He pulled out an envelope and handed it to Ike. "There's three thousand dollars there which should be plenty for the electronics, with a good bit left over for you considering that your room and flight are paid for, including room service dinner each night. You may start procuring your equipment tomorrow. Rent yourself a car, and pay cash for it. I'll reimburse you at the end of the week. Make all of your calls from pay phones so there is no record of them tied to you. I'll call you at 7:00 P.M. tomorrow evening here at the hotel to check on your progress and to see if you need anything. Oh and Ike, I'll drop off a tape recorder for you to record the wiretaps for evidence in case we find something worthy. In an emergency, you may leave a message at my home phone and I'll get back to you. Here's the number. Do you have any questions for me?"

"Not that I can think of at the moment."

"Good, then I guess there is just one more thing, Thanks Ike."

"I'll talk to you tomorrow Jonas."

The next two days were productively spent with Ike buying the necessary electronic equipment. The next evening Jonas and Ike met for dinner.

"Do you have everything that you'll need Ike?" asked Jonas

"Everything I can think of."

"Good. Then we'll plan on planting the bugs and wiretaps tomorrow night around 7:30 P.M. I'll arrange to work late and then when I get out to the parking lot, I'll see to it that I have a flat tire which should hopefully encourage Walt the security guard to come out and offer assistance. That will make your job all the easier, but of course I can't say for certain that he'll help me, so be prepared to deal with all eventualities. With the decision on the anti-missile system scheduled to take place Thursday morning, the airwaves should be full of any juicy tidbits that our friends may be concocting. If not this week, certainly next week I would expect. Would you be able to stick around through next week if need be Ike?"

"Sure, no problem! Let's see what happens."

"Excellent. How long do you think it will take you to place the equipment in Weldon and Jones' offices?"

"From the time I break in until the time I leave, I don't expect to be there much more than 20 minutes."

"Alright then, let's plan on meeting in the lounge at your hotel at 9:30 which should give you ample time to get back. You'll be on your own tomorrow, so good luck and I look forward to seeing you at 9:30, tomorrow night. Good hunting Ike."

"See you then Jonas."

The planting of the eavesdropping devices went without a hitch the following evening. Even Walt cooperated by being a gentleman and insisting on spending half an hour helping Jonas change his tire. In the hotel lounge at 9:30 two glasses were raised in salute to a mission accomplished.

"To a job well done," toasted Jonas.

"And to you my friend," offered Ike. "Here's hoping that it catches the no doubt nefarious scoundrels in the act of planning some dastardly deed," Ike deadpanned as he took a long pull on his ale.

"Time will tell my friend, time will tell."

"C'mon in Ralph and close the door behind you" requested Stewart Jones as Ralph Weldon cruised past his office. "Ralphie boy, it's a great day to be an American, and a great day to be part of Sutton Industries."

"If you're referring to the approval of the anti ballistic missile, I'm not so sure that I share your enthusiasm," replied Ralph.

"Of course that's what I'm referring to. Great product, great exposure for the company, should do great things for the price of our stock, and it can't hurt the way the resident head of R&D and the president of the company look either."

"Yeah, I suppose, but you know it also takes that son-of-a-bitch Trina up another peg too."

"Are you still worried about him? Look I told you we'd take care of him once and for all and we will."

"I'll feel more comfortable when I don't have to share a department with him anymore. I was hoping he might be gone before this project was approved. Even though Ray Chang was responsible for the majority of the concept and design, Trina had enough input to attempt to share the spotlight with him."

"As of next Tuesday evening your problems with Mr. Trina will be a thing of the past."

"Oh really? How so?"

Throughout this project, I've had Kevin Carter making up microfiche film of every plan which Chang and Trina have been showing him as they worked on putting together the prototypes. Next Tuesday we will plant these microfiches in Trina's car. As he leaves to go home, he will be stopped by security at the main gate and his car will be searched. Naturally the microfiche will be found, which of course will beg the question of why in the world would Jonas Trina possibly want to smuggle super sensitive missile technology out of the company that he's working for. If he's lucky he'll be found guilty attempting to do it for one of our competitors. If treason enters the picture, there's no telling what might be in store for him. Either way, I think you can safely say that we would no longer have to worry about Jonas the Wonder Boy anymore. Hell, just the negative publicity will be enough to get him drummed out of Sutton. You know how C. Gerald Dilley Bar feels about bad press."

"That'll be a relief. The sooner the better if you ask me."

"You can take it to the bank. Just make sure not to be sick next Tuesday, because I'd hate to have you miss all the fun."

"Well Ike what did I tell you?" said Jonas as they listened to the taped conversation between Jones and Weldon later that evening in Ike's hotel room.

"I must admit that I had some doubts about us actually getting anything of any real value. I thought that you might be just a little bit paranoid. Now I can see why you were so concerned. I guess the question now is, where do we go from here?"

"The answer to that question lies in your answers to the next question or two which I'm about to throw at you."

"Fire away."

"Isaac Steele would you like to go for a ride?"

"Sure, where are we going?"

"Not a physical ride, I mean a life changing ride. I mean a ride that will take you places in your life that you've never even dreamed about."

"Hey pal, remember I've been to Afghanistan, and Lebanon, and a few other places compliments of Uncle Sam, so I've been around," Ike said feigning that he'd been slighted.

"Let me put it another way. How would you like to make more money than you ever thought possible? I'm talking 6-figure type income. I can make that happen for you Ike, and I'm talking within the next year, perhaps sooner."

"Sounds good. When does the course in bank robbing start, and will I need a notebook to take notes. Seriously Jonas, of course I'd like to make that type of money. Who wouldn't! But just how in the world do you propose to do that for me?"

"I'm already proceeding on phase one of my plan. What we found out today on tape forces me to move up my timetable, and alter my plans a bit, but I was already working on becoming president before I called you in Pennsylvania. Ike, what would you say if I told you that within the next month, I will become president of Sutton Industries, and within 6-9 months after that I will become C.E.O."

"I'd say let me have a toke of whatever it is you're smoking."

"You can be part of it, and in fact you can stick around for the long haul and have yourself a fantasy life."

"Does this mean that I couldn't go back to flippin' burgers in Beaver Falls?"

"Only on the weekends."

"Alright, let's get down to the nitty-gritty. Just exactly what would I have to do for this fantasy life, because certain things I draw the line at! I mean I am a card carrying heterosexual, and that ain't gonna change. I don't do windows, and I'm not very good at shining shoes since they drummed me out of the Army."

"Could you kill?"

"Could I what?"

"Could you kill? Let's say the situation called for it and those in question were worthy of it?"

"How much money did you say again?"

"More than you'll make in ten lifetimes playing it straight."

"Well, I have killed before," said Ike matter-of-factly

"Yes, I know, in Afghanistan."

"No, before that." .

"Earlier in the military then."

"No, before that. At home."

"You mean in Beaver Falls?"

"Yeah, I was 17 and me and some buddies got into a fight with some jerks from a rival school after a football game. They roughed up a friend of mine pretty good. Put one of his eyes out with a busted beer bottle. We swore revenge on them. A few weeks later we got up a few guys and set a trap for them. My buddies knew what a crack shot I was so they had me be the shooter. One night they went to a bar in this other town where they thought they might find those punks. Sure as hell they were there. My buddy Tommy sucker punched one of them and took off out of the bar where they had a getaway car all set to go. Little Joey was driving I think. Anyway, the assholes fly out of the bar and come after my buddies like bats out of hell. I'm positioned in some trees right before a curve and I've got a good view of both cars coming my way. When my buddy's car flew past where I was hiding, they gave me the thumbs up, meaning it was a go on the car in back of them. I put two slugs into the driver's windshield at a distance of about 60 yards. The car kept coming straight, but never made a move to negotiate the curve. They flew over the edge of about a 100-foot embankment at 75 m.p.h. I counted six of them in the car as it went past. They didn't see me, but I flipped them the bird right before they took the plunge. Had a big smile on my face with each new crashing sound their car made before it hit bottom. I got all six of them."

"Didn't the police come looking for you guys?"

"Sure they did, but they couldn't prove anything. Tommy was only in the bar a minute before he sucker punched the guy, so nobody really got a good look at him. Then they took off so fast that the only ones who got a good look at the car were the six stiffs."

"Surely, people from both schools knew about the fight between your guys and theirs. Didn't they put two-and-two together?"

"They tried to, but they had no evidence. My buddies all hung together on their stories, I cleaned up after myself at the sight, and the gun I used was one that had been stolen out of a farmer's house a year before by one of my buddies. The police found out that I was a good shot, and came over to my place to try to match the recovered slugs to one of my rifles. When they tested each of my registered rifles and came away without a match from ballistics, they had nothing. Sure they suspected there was a connection, but they couldn't prove it. Plus, these jerks that died had a nasty habit of picking fights with every school their team played, so it turned out there were all kinds of people who they'd pissed off. AND let's face facts! Hunting is a pretty popular pastime in the hills of Western Pa., so it's not exactly like I'm the only one who can handle a rifle around those parts. You know the funny thing about the whole affair?"

"No, what's that."

"I liked it. I mean I really enjoyed sending those six jerks over the cliff. I still get goose bumps every now and then just thinking about it. It wasn't only because of the kind of scum they were either. I think it has to do with the power that killing imparts. I mean to know that you have the ability to do the ultimate to your fellow human being is a damn intoxicating feeling, once you've sampled it."

"If I'm reading you like I think I am, I believe that you have just answered my previous question in the affirmative."

"Yeah, I think I could kill again if the situation called for it."

"Mr. Steele, I believe that this could be the start of a very prosperous relationship. One final question, do you have, or can you get a working hand grenade?"

"I made a few contacts when I was with the Rangers. Let me see what I can do."

"Alright, but time is of the essence. For what I have in mind, we need one here in Chicago before next Tuesday."

"I'll make a few calls."

"Assuming you can get one, let me tell you what I have in mind...."

The following Tuesday, Jonas showed up at Sutton at 6:30 A.M. which he knew was the earliest that he could get through the gates. Parking in his assigned spot, Jonas took his briefcase out of the BMW and proceeded to the door. Peter Fleming, the morning security guard, let him in and dutifully checked the contents of his briefcase prior to letting him proceed. Jonas took the briefcase to his office, and then reappeared at the front door a few minutes later. "Peter, could you be a good man and open the door for me, I left my gym bag in the car."

"Your gym bag?"

"Yes, it was such a beautiful morning that I thought that I'd bring my running gear and take a jog around the perimeter of the fence before we get started for the day."

"Oh, another one of those health nuts. As for me, give me a cup of coffee and a donut, and finishing them is all the exercise that I want to perform at this time of day. C'mon I'll let you out, and hold the door while you get your gear."

Jonas opened his trunk and produced the gym bag. Peter checked the contents and allowed Jonas to re-enter the building. There was standard jogging apparel, running gear, and a gold watch with a gold chain attached to it.

"Why the watch?" asked Peter.

"Just brought it along to see how long it takes me to finish my run," Jonas lied.

 Jonas changed into the running gear in his office, complete with baseball cap, and jogged back to the front door. "Peter, so that I don't have to bother you, and also to save me the extra half mile jog around the building, which I really won't want to do half an hour from now after running two miles, would you please unlock the rear door by Section B1?"

"Now Mr. Trina you know that there is only supposed to be the main entrance opened for security reasons."

"Peter, do I really look like much of a security threat? You're not afraid that I'm going to turn my jockstrap into a slingshot and pull a David and Goliath number on you, are ya?"

"If you did, I'd be a little curious as to what you might plan on using for your slingshot stones, but we probably don't want to go there. All right, I'll open that door, but don't let anyone know. Notify me the moment you get in so I can re-close it before anyone else finds out and I get reprimanded or something. OK?"

"You betcha, Goliath!" With that Jonas commenced a leisurely paced loosening up type jog across the grass in front of the building. He continued straight until he reached the security fence that encompassed the property. Turning right, Jonas began the trek down the one-mile long fence that ran along the perimeter of Sutton Industries. He checked his watch. It was 6:48. After following the perimeter at a relatively slow pace for several minutes, Jonas heard an unusual bird whistle. Looking back over his shoulder, Jonas could not see anyone in sight. Taking off his hat and wiping his brow, Jonas looked in the direction of the whistle. Hearing the word "Catch," he saw an oversized dirt clod arcing over the fence in his direction. Jonas only had to move a couple of steps to make a nice over the shoulder reception. He put the dirt clod in the hat and continued on his jog.

As he reached the far end of the property, Jonas came to an underground storage bunker. He checked to see if he was being observed. Feeling confident that he wasn't, Jonas reached into his shorts and took out a key to the storage bunker that he had taken home the previous evening. The key opened the padlock on the bunker door, and Jonas stole inside making sure to take the dirt clod with him. Turning on the light produced a dim glare. The dull luminescence reflected off the tiled hallway that ran for thirty yards. At the end of the hallway was a padlocked metal door. Jonas took out a second key and opened this door. Flicking on the light, Jonas could make out a large, cool, somewhat dank room, fitted with row upon row of wooden shelving. Each long set of shelves had numerous berths which served to section off each thick shelf. Many of the berths held rockets in them, although some were empty.

Jonas got on his hands and knees and took the dirt clod out of his hat. Gently brushing the caked dirt off the clod revealed a hand grenade with a duct taped pin and lever. Gingerly removing the duct tape, Jonas took the grenade and put it to the nose of one of the rockets on the bottom shelf. The rockets were facing with their noses pointed toward the wall as a safety precaution. He secured the grenade to the rocket detonator with the duct tape. Next, he removed a small tube of clear adhesive from his shorts. Keeping the tube in his hand, Jonas went back into the tiled hallway, walking back to the entrance. He bent over and began running the adhesive in a thin bead along the joint where the wall and the floor met. In the dim light it was barely discernible. When he had applied the sticky material all the way back to the storage room door, Jonas went back to the hallway entrance where he'd first began to lay down the adhesive bead. Reaching once again into his shorts, Jonas took out two spools of strong thin eggshell white thread. He pushed one end of each thread into the bead and proceeded to imbed the threads into the glue along its entire length, working his way back to the storage door. He ran the threads under the door and spooled out a sufficient amount of thread so that it would reach to the duct-taped grenade. Satisfied that the thread lengths were essentially correct, Jonas bit through the thin threads. He took the end of one and wrapped several loops around the grenade pin. The other thread he wrapped around the lever several times. He checked to insure that the pin was firmly, but not too firmly seated, in the grenade, and gave a gentle test tug on the thread to check the amount of slack.

Now he turned his attention to the gold watch. Jonas walked to the rear of the storage bunker and took the gold watch out of his pocket. He opened the watch and once again admired its inscription. A wry smile crossed his lips as he took the watch and hung it by the chain upon a wooden post.

Deeming that all was in order, Jonas examined the interior of the room to make sure that the grenade was not readily visible unless one got on their hands and knees. He brushed some loose dirt under the shelves. Satisfied that all was in place, Jonas replaced all of his equipment back in his shorts, put on his hat, and turned off the light. Padlocking the room back up, Jonas hurried to the entrance of the storage bunker. He peered out of the bunker's entrance, and breathed a sigh of relief that no one was as yet visible. Crouching, he snuck out, and reapplied the padlock to the heavy metal door. He began to run across the dew-covered grass, rapidly working his way back to the main building. He raced to the backdoor and was relieved that it was still unlocked. Once inside he hustled back to his office, trading a few good-natured barbs regarding his running attire with fellow employees on the way. Opening his office door, he immediately dialed the front security desk.

"Security, Peter." a voice answered.
"Goliath, David has made it back to the promised land."

"Hell, I forgot all about you. What the heck took you so long?"

"I didn't realize that I was so out of shape, and when I got back I was so exhausted that I plum forgot to call you. Sorry Peter."

"That's all right I suppose Mr. Trina. Just don't let it happen again or my ass could be grass. I'll head back and relock the door as soon as my relief arrives in a minute or two."

Satisfied that all was in order with the initial phase of his plan, Jonas grabbed a towel and headed for the men's locker room for a much-needed shower before putting the rest of his plan in motion.

By 8:30 Jonas was all freshened up and back in his office. Jonas commenced to make the first of his many fateful phone calls for that day.

"Hi, Kevin? This is Jonas Trina. Hey Kevin, Weldon asked that you meet me and a few other people at the reserve storage bunker out near the back fence later today, say around 11:30. He thinks he's got an idea for missile storage that you're going to like, especially with those new anti-missile missiles coming on board soon. Think you can get away for a few minutes? Good, we'll see you then." "Hi Chang? Jonas here. You know how we've been trying to come up with a place to store those anti-missile missiles? Weldon thinks he's got an idea that you'll be interested in seeing. I'll stop by your office about 11:15 and pick you up for a short tour of what he has in mind. OK? Good, 11:15 it is." "Ralph, Jonas Trina here. Kevin Carter, Ray Chang, and I are taking a look today at a storage possibility for the new missiles. They'd like to get your input on what they have in mind, if your schedule permits. Say around 11:30 at the old storage bunker, near the back fence. Do you know the one? Good, we'll see you there at 11:30."

At 11:25 Ray Chang and Jonas were approaching the underground storage bunker. As they came closer to it, the face of Ralph Weldon could be seen in the shadow created by an overhang of the bunker. At 11:33 Kevin Carter came, half jogging the last 50 yards, to complete the quorum.

"I assume one of you has a key to get us into this underground palace." muttered Ralph Weldon.

"Right here." acknowledged Jonas.

As he put the key into the padlock, a strange sounding bird cry was heard, which brought a wry smile to Jonas' lips, as he removed the padlock and swung the metal door open.

"Just follow the yellow brick road to the end of the hallway gentlemen, if you don't mind," requested Jonas acting as the host.

"Kinda dim in here," grumbled Weldon as he and the others made their way down the hallway.

Upon reaching the storage room, Jonas produced key number two and quickly gained the group entrance to the rocket storage area. Turning on the light he said;

"As you can see, this area has already been found suitable for long term storage of munitions such as these rockets, which are circa 1950's and 60's for the most part."

By this time the other three had entered the storage room. "If you would all please move to the rear of the room, I'll show you why we're here today," said Jonas. Ralph, Ray, and Kevin co-operated, moving to the back of the storage area, passing by Jonas in the process. Chang and Carter were understandably confused because they thought that this was Weldon's idea, but each remained silent, not knowing what each had been told. Jonas was inexplicably making his way towards the door. When the threesome reached the rear of the room, Weldon saw the gold watch hanging on the post. He placed it in his hand and pressed the small button to open the exquisite timepiece. He read the inscription aloud to Carter and Chang. "So long suckers!" was all it said.

"Is this some kind of joke Trina?" Weldon said in an irritated manner. A second later the door was closed and the light turned off, plunging the room into total darkness.

"Very nice Jonas, what do you for your next act?" Kevin Carter said somewhat sardonically.

"Trina this isn't funny. Get some son-of-a-bitchin' light in here pronto mister!" demanded Weldon.

The next sounds that the three men could make out were somewhat muffled, but they appeared to sound like the snapping of a padlock, followed by footsteps proceeding down the hallway away from the room. Another set of footsteps could be heard advancing from the hallway entrance towards the room.

"Everything go alright Jonas?" Ike Steele asked as he and Jonas met at the halfway point in the hallway.

"Like clockwork my friend. Good to see you made it here with no problem yourself. Do you think you'll have any problem getting off the grounds after the big show?

"Not really. Especially since I've got my magic carpet parked outside."

"Beautiful. I guess I'll be going to lunch then. Give me about 30 minutes before you start the fireworks. That should allow me to reach the main gate to establish my alibi. By the way you do have the videotape of them planting the microfiches in my car last night do you not?"

"Sure do! The original is in a safe deposit box, and one of the copies is in your trunk."

"Excellent. I've arranged to have our other ally positioned where he can come to our aid at the proper time. We'll reconvene at 7:30 P.M.

this evening at the usual place. If you don't hear from me, stay put for two more days. After two days, drive back to Pennsylvania and have a nice life. I fully expect however, to see you this evening. Make a safe clean getaway Sir Isaac. Oh by the way Isaac, pull the top thread first. That's the one attached to the pin."

"Gotcha! Tell the boys at the security post up front that I said Hi."

Jonas left the bunker and began to make his way in the direction of the parking lot and his BMW. Ike proceeded down the hallway to the storage room where he could faintly hear voices through the thick steel door.

"Trina, this little stunt of yours will cost you your job. You can count on that you bastard. I'll make it so that you never work in the city of Chicago or the defense industry for the rest of your hopefully short natural life," scowled Weldon.

"Jonas if you can hear us, please let us out," pleaded Ray Chang.

"Yeah Jonas, this isn't funny anymore. Let us out," implored Carter.

These and subsequent pleas were met with total silence as Ike sat placidly outside the storage room door, picking his nails and occasionally glancing at his timepiece. In the meantime, Jonas had arrived at his car and in view of Stewart Jones' office he reached for his keys to get into his black BMW. Stewart dialed Weldon's extension to alert him that the show he'd been waiting for was about to begin, but he got no answer. He dialed the number to the security guard post and notified them that Trina would soon be coming and reminding them of their duty. Satisfied that all was in place, Stewart sat back to enjoy the show, only wishing that he had brought a pair of binoculars so that he could see the reaction on Jonas Trina's face when the incriminating microfiches were found and he was taken into custody.

Precisely 30 minutes after Jonas had left the bunker, Isaac Steele began to walk purposefully back to the bunker entrance. At the doorway he bent down and probed with his fingers the joint between the wall and the floor. Within two seconds he had both thread ends between the thumb and index finger of his right hand. A laconic smile turned the corners of his mouth upward. The smile soon turned into a chuckle. The chuckle transformed itself into a laugh with sinister overtones, as the huge ex-Ranger's demonic howls of glee reverberated off the tile and walls of the hallway, well within earshot of those about to die within the storage room. At the absolute height of his rapturous bellows, Ike began running towards the bunker's entrance. As he was about to exit the bunker, he tugged on the top thread, pulling out all of the slack. Next he pulled the bottom thread taut. Satisfied that his job had been accomplished, Ike plunged through the bunker door to the outside and ran like a frightened antelope toward the far side fence.

The demonic laughter, though easily discernable through the storage room door, would not be the last sounds the three storage room occupants would hear in this world. A light metallic plinking sound as the grenade pin was pulled out was followed immediately by a heavier metallic clunking sound within the darkened room as the grenade-arming lever fell to the floor. "What was that?" asked Ray Chang.

"I don't know, but after that Vincent Price imitation, I don't like whatever it was," said Kevin ominously.

Weldon remained quiet as his memory banks tried to place where he'd heard those two sounds before in close succession. Suddenly realizing it reminded him of something he'd heard numerous times decades ago and half a world away on the Korean Peninsula in 1952, Ralph Weldon involuntarily blurted out Oh MY G...

The rest was drowned out by the noise and fury of the grenade blast setting off the attached rocket's explosive power resulting in a chain reaction of every bomb and rocket in the underground bunker. The effect was literally volcanic as the ground above was rent wide open by the sheer force of the initial explosions. Fiery projectiles shot skyward as the Vesuvian spectacle spewed its raging force in all directions.

"Mr. Trina, I'm going to have to ask you to step out of the car please," the head security guard stated forcefully.

With a somber look on his face, Jonas did as requested, trying his best to keep up the charade of pretending not to know what was happening. With a performance that showed a lot of forethought, the guard managed to take six or seven minutes to "discover" the secret hiding place of the microfiches. He'd obviously been well coached not to find them too quickly, or that might appear suspicious. The guard removed the microfiches from the car and began to walk toward Jonas with a triumphant look upon his face. His moment of glory was cut short by the arrival of a long black limousine, flanked by two police cars. Out of the rear of the black limousine emerged the C.E.O. of Sutton Industries, C. Gerald Dilley.

"Officers, please arrest that guard for his part in this shameless affair," the C.E.O. said authoritatively. "Next we'll be taking a trip inside the building to arrest several..." His words were lost in the din of the underground bunker ripping itself apart in explosive violent upheavals. The earth split open to reveal white-hot tumultuous blasts and a ceaseless roaring, as it attempted to simultaneously shower both heaven and earth with its fury. Huge chunks of terra firma were lofted skyward by the cataclysmic explosions. Although they stood almost a mile away, an occasional bit of shrapnel would zing past, causing them to keep their heads down until the bunker's contents were completely destroyed.

After what seemed like hours, but was in fact minutes, the bunker's rage was spent with everything that was able to explode having already been cooked off. All that was left was a huge hole in the ground filled with debris and multiple blazes burning furiously. The police were busy contacting emergency units to advise them of the situation. They also arranged reinforcements to come and cordon off the area so that no one would be allowed into or out of the area until some semblance of order had been brought upon the scene. As emergency vehicles began to arrive, C. Gerald persuaded one of the initial police officers to accompany himself and Jonas to the main building to find Stewart Jones.

When they finally tracked Jones down, to his credit he was engaged in attempting to coordinate standard emergency operating procedures throughout the building. As the threesome approached Stewart, a look of relief came across his frenzied countenance. Totally ignoring the presence of Jonas, Stewart said; "Boy, am I glad to see you Mr. Dilley! As you can see, all hell has broken loose here. Something set off explosions in an old underground storage bunker in the far end of the complex, and I'm implementing emergency procedures by the book to secure the plant."

"That's all well and good Stewart. What is left to be done from your end?"

"So far damage control is reporting that the main buildings have received very little damage. Fortunately, most of the buildings on the complex were far enough from the blasts that they escaped with only superficial damage. However we will continue to get reports in via crisis teams from all sectors until we determine the full extent of damages. As for the cause of the explosions, it's too early to know.

However, we believe that it is due to some type of system malfunction."

"It seems to me that your continued presence here is not a life or death matter to the security of this facility. All emergency systems are being adhered to and help is arriving even as we speak. Therefore, I can in good conscience do what I came here to do, which was to relieve you from your duties, effective immediately."

A look of disbelief came across Jones' face as he realized the meaning of what he'd just heard. "Mr. Dilley sir, surely you can't be serious? I realize that the explosions..." At this point C. Gerald stopped Stewart and dismissed the policeman so that they could converse privately.

"The explosions are a bona fide disaster, and they occurred on your watch Stewart. That in its own right is certainly enough to warrant your dismissal. However, that is only a part of the reason. The bigger reason is your part in the attempted framing of Mr. Trina here. Please don't embarrass all of us and try to deny it, because I heard a tape of you telling Ralph Weldon last week how and when you were going to get rid of Jonas. Then I watched the entire charade go down right before my very eyes. Oh, and by the way, I don't like to be referred to as C. Gerald Dilley Bar like you said in the recording. Additionally, I have been made aware of a video whereby the planting of the microfiches took place last night at Mr. Trina's residence. It shouldn't be too difficult to get a guilty conviction with the evidence stacked as it is against you Stewart.

Perhaps these explosions might in fact prove to have an unintended benefit for you. I spoke with Jonas on the way to your office, and he seems to think that if you were to step down because of the explosions, there would be no need to bring up this sordid microfiche affair. He would be willing to forgo prosecution if you resign, and recommend him as your successor, which I believe is an outstanding idea. I believe I could also convince the board to accept your resignation in lieu of criminal prosecution. Naturally, you could not expect to receive your full pension after something like this, but we would see to it that you don't go away totally empty-handed. I'll expect to hear from you tomorrow with your final decision. Furthermore, be forewarned Stewart that should you decide to fight this in the courts, you will still be gone due to the explosions having occurred with you running the show. If I were you I'd choose the resignation. Now, if you would please, just get out of my sight. You disgust me."

The following day, Stewart Jones agreed to resign and did suggest in his outgoing news conference that Jonas Trina would be an excellent choice as his successor. C. Gerald Dilley was on hand to reluctantly accept his resignation and to wish him well in future endeavors. During the following weeks, extensive investigations were conducted as to the cause of the explosions. However, because virtually all of the evidence was destroyed in the blasts, no conclusions could be drawn. Several theories were bandied about, including a shelf giving way, an ill-fated trip by one of the men in the bunker dislodging one of the munitions, or an electrical malfunction of some type. In the end, it was all conjecture. One month after the explosions occurred, Jonas Trina was installed as the new president of Sutton Industries.

Not wishing to rest on his laurels, Jonas got to work immediately applying every waking moment to learning as much as possible regarding company operations on all fronts. He immersed himself in the financial aspects of the business, and held late night meetings with the comptroller, more often than not to pick his brain rather than going over reports. The same could be said in regards to his meetings with manufacturing. He seemed more interested in how things "ticked", rather than the actual production figures, schedules, or forecasts themselves. Additionally, he was constantly badgering C. Gerald Dilley to meet together, in order to glean as much wisdom as he could from those private talks. Mr. Dilley took great pride in Sutton Industries and he was extremely pleased with the attention and dedication that Jonas devoted to his new position. He was always ready to mentor Jonas in any way possible believing that by so doing, he could further the interests of the company. Therefore, it came as a great shock when Jonas proved to be a treacherous, blackmailing, bastard. The cruelest blow to C. Gerald was that he had inadvertently given Jonas all the ammunition that he needed to bring about his own ruination. He had been checkmated.

During their talks, C. Gerald had conversed with Jonas on a wide range of subjects, including family, personal interests, and on occasion, even vices. C. Gerald treated Jonas almost like the son he'd never had. And Jonas for his part played the eager student and confidante, seeming to dwell on Mr. Dilley's every word. Nine months after installing Jonas as president, it became all too clear why he was so interested in Dilley's life, as well as the obsessive interest Jonas had in Sutton as a company.

Dilley had shared with Jonas a lifelong penchant he'd had for women. "I like 'em eight to eighty, blind, crippled, or crazy," C. Gerald confided. He and Jonas had enjoyed a long laugh after that cliché, and in fact Jonas had related some trysts of his own to the C.E.O. over a few cocktails. During these bonding conversations Dilley mentioned a young niece of his named Patra whom he doted on, and would do virtually anything to please. Armed with these bits of information, Jonas formulated a plan. It would prove surprisingly simple to topple the incumbent, and bring about a changing of the guard. All that was required was a couple of down-on-their-luck teenage runaways, some drugs, booze, professional camera and recording equipment, and some background information on a ten year old named Patra Collins.

A couple of weeks after Dilley and Jonas had swapped stories of their romantic interludes with the opposite sex, C. Gerald strolled into Jonas' office with a large smile on his face. "Good morning sir," said Jonas. "You seem to have a bit more bounce in your step this morning. What'd you do, get laid last night or something?"

"Jonas my boy, you wouldn't believe me if I told you," Dilley said smugly.

"Try me!"

"Do you remember a couple weeks ago when I said I liked all women, eight to eighty and all that stuff?"

"Sure do."

"Well, it turns out some of us in our sixties have still got what it takes."

"What are you talking about?"

"I was driving home last night, and we get to a stoplight by a Catholic girls high school. Two little lovelies in plaid skirts and saddle shoes knock on the window of our limo and ask us for a ride. They told me how they just love older men, and expensive cars. Nellie and I just couldn't resist, especially in lieu of my schoolgirl fantasies that I shared with you a fortnight ago. The girls directed us to a local motel where they had a friend who would let us have a room. Anyway, these two minks were the wildest two creatures that it has ever been my pleasure to bed. Naturally, being the generous sort, I had Nellie enjoy their company prior to leaving us."

"C. Gerald, you dirty dog!"

"And you young bucks think you have all the fun! Some of these young girls can appreciate the values of maturity and experience. Indeed, we've arranged for a discreet round two at my estate tomorrow."

"Be careful, and make sure that you don't catch anything that might be harmful to your health and wellbeing."

"Catch anything! Hell at my age, to catch anything would be a badge of honor! Besides, I'd probably be dead before anything that I would catch from them would begin to manifest itself, you spoilsport."

"O.K. but don't say that I didn't warn you. Enjoy yourself you lucky stiff."

The following week, Jonas requested a meeting with C. Gerald. "Well Mr. Dilley, I certainly don't have to ask how round two with the ladies went the other night."

"And just why is that Jonas? Am I still grinning?" Dilley said with a self-satisfied smirk.

"Nothing quite so mundane as that Dilley. I was actually referring to these." Jonas flipped a manila envelope on the desk. With a quizzical look, Dilley picked up the proffered package and began to remove the contents. Detailed photos of the two girls and him from their trysts at the hotel, and later at his estate, tumbled out of the envelope.

"Where did you get these, and just what in the hell is the meaning of all this?" barked Dilley.

"You know C. Gerald, you really are very photogenic. And you're not in bad shape for a man of your age. Good staying power also, at least according to one of the fifteen year old girls in the picture with you. Of course at fifteen, how much experience could she really be expected to have for comparison purposes? You know it just occurred to me; are the laws in Illinois the same as they are in Indiana regarding adults seducing fifteen year olds? Notice that bottle of brandy, and the funny little rolled up cigarettes on the nightstand there in the corner of that picture. What is that all about? Oh, and by the way, get a load of this," Jonas produced a pocket-recording device that he turned on. There was no mistaking C. Gerald's impassioned voice intermingled with that of a young girl at the peak of a sexual encounter.

"Look Trina. I don't know what your plan is, but if you're planning on some sort of blackmail..."

"Mr. Dilley, you surprise me. This isn't just some sort of blackmail. This is the ultimate sort of blackmail! And from now on don't call me

Trina. The name is Mr. Trina to you, you lecherous **FORMER** C.E.O.!"

"Get out of my office before I have you thrown out."

"Soon this will no longer be your office. I have some demands that I will now lay out before you. If you do not agree to each and every one, two very disagreeable things are going to happen to you. To begin with, I have arranged to have prints of these photographs sent to ten major newspapers two days from now unless I put a hold on it. There is an accompanying letter detailing the girl's names and ages in addition, of course, to your own name and personal info. Secondly, the wellbeing of a certain ten year old named Patra Collins would no longer be assured. By the way, I understand that when she arrived at Visalia Academy this morning at 8:26, she had a pink ribbon in her hair to match her pink stockings and book bag. You may call and verify that if you like, or you can take my word for it. Trust me C. Gerald, my people have been, and will continue to be, experts on the whereabouts of Ms. Collins."

"If you so much as harm a single hair on her head I'll..."

"**SHUT UP!** You're not the one calling the shots around here anymore Dilley Bar, **I AM!** The following demands are non-negotiable: First of all, you will step down from the position of C.E.O. citing health issues as the reason. Next you will recommend me as your replacement. Furthermore you will address the board detailing my strengths and praising my virtues, and you'd damn well better be convincing, for Patra's sake! Only, and I repeat only if I am selected as your replacement, will you and Patra be off the hook. Also, if at anytime in the future something should happen to me, I have a plan in effect whereby the photos will automatically be sent, so I wouldn't try any funny things down the road either. Oh, and one final thing. I've recently become a bit of a car lover. However I just hate haggling with those obnoxious car dealers. Thus I've hit upon the ideal solution. Once a year you will arrange to procure for me the gift of a new automobile of my choosing. I'll let you know the make, model and color. I'll of course send you a nice thank you card to let you know that I appreciate your thoughtfulness."

"You ungrateful bastard! When I think of all I've done for you.."

"Admittedly you've been a worthwhile pawn for me, but nothing more Dilley. Your usefulness to me is now at an end. I'll expect to see confirmation of our little arrangement within 48 hours, or the proverbial fecal material will begin to hit the fan. Remember, anything other than full compliance with my demands will put in motion some exceedingly unpleasant developments for both you and your niece. I'll await word of your resignation. Oh, by the way, you might wish to get in touch with your physician now to verify that your health is being seriously compromised by your job. I have a sneaking suspicion that your blood pressure at this moment might just be a tad elevated and you could use that to bolster your decision to resign. Good day Dilley Bar!" With that Jonas walked out of the room leaving a red faced sputtering executive powerless to do anything more than to spew epithets at his back.

The next afternoon, a hastily called press conference was convened, at which time C. Gerald Dilley announced his retirement, effective immediately, and put forth the name of Jonas Trina to be his replacement, pending board confirmation. After an impressive performance by Dilley in front of the board, Jonas stood one vote short of being approved as the new C.E.O. That situation was rectified three days later when 68-year old board member Kathryn Crowley, who had cast a dissenting vote, was found dead in her bedroom of an apparent heart attack brought about by a rare air bubble embolism in her bloodstream. Two weeks later on Jonas' birthday, March 15th 1987, he became the new C.E.O, of Sutton Industries. He had just turned 28 years old, and was thus the youngest chief executive officer of a Fortune 500 company in the country at that time. His timetable for revenge was slightly ahead of schedule.

CHAPTER 12

"Christine and Ken, I'm Holland Matthews. Sorry about the wait. I had a departmental mini-crisis to referee." Christine Stanton and Ken Kalista, who were seated in the reception area of the Pharmacor lobby, rose in unison at the approach of Holland. Christine took the lead.

"No problem Holland. We have our own interoffice squabbles to officiate from time to time ourselves. It is a pleasure to meet you. May I introduce you to my department manager, Ken Kalista."

"It's a pleasure to meet you Ken."

"It's very nice to meet you as well Holland. I trust Christine gave you a brief synopsis as to why we were interested in meeting with you?

"Yes. She mentioned that there were some statistical irregularities which your company thought that we should be made aware of regarding our pension enrollees."

"That is correct. Is there someplace where we may continue our discussion in private?"

"Certainly! Won't you follow me?" Holland proceeded out of the lobby in the direction of a first floor conference room that was unoccupied at the moment.

"May I get you some coffee, tea, or perhaps a soft drink?" offered Holland.

"None for myself," responded Christine.

"Me neither," said Ken.

"Then I suppose we should get started immediately," stated Holland as she opened the conference room door.

"Would there happen to be a projector screen in this room upon which I could show some computerized slides?" asked Christine.

"Yes there is," Holland said as she walked to the front of the room and pulled down the screen.

Christine and Ken seated themselves at the front of a long table, and Christine began to set up her laptop computer for the video portion of their presentation. Holland took a seat across the table from the others.

In a few minutes Christine had set up the computer and was prepared to begin her presentation.

"Holland, our supercomputer at G. Donsky and Associates is programmed to monitor anomalies in any of our client company's pension portfolios. Several days ago the computer emitted a report showing that life expectancy for Pharmacor retirees has recently taken a distinct turn for the worse. In this first graph that I will show on the screen, you will see the normal amount of deaths that could be expected for the retirees of a company your size in a twelve month period of time. Now I will superimpose on the graph the lines indicating the mortality rate of Pharmacor in the past several years. As you can see, everything was proceeding normally until the past six months, when this abnormally large spike in the numbers has taken place. The next graph I will present shows the expected unnatural deaths for a company your size over a twelve month period. Now superimposing Pharmacor's figures of unnatural deaths over that same period, you'll note a larger discrepancy than in the previous graphs we compared. Even allowing for the 123 deaths that were involved in the Legionnaire's disease tragedy, these graphs represent a disturbing number of Pharmacor fully vested retirees that have departed this earth in the past several months. Were you or perhaps others in your department aware of any of this?"

"I myself was not," admitted Holland. "As for others within my department or company, no one has brought it to my attention, and I would expect that I would've heard something if anyone had any indication that we were experiencing this level of retiree mortality. Do either you or Ken have any idea why the numbers are so high?"

"While Pharmacor's mortality rates are abnormally high, they are not the highest we've seen among the hundreds of companies that we keep tabs on," offered Christine. "In some cases there have been disasters, be they natural or manmade, which have caused great loss of life, thereby skewing the mortality numbers skyward. Also, there can be political upheavals such as that seen a few years ago in Rwanda that can have an adverse effect on the rates. Of course there can be such a thing as just plain bad luck, which though rare, can I suppose occur to explain figures such as Pharmacor's. However as you know, insurance deals with statistical probability, not happenstance. It is statistically unlikely that so many of Pharmacor's former employees should have met with their untimely demise in so short a time. Either your company is experiencing an extremely unfortunate set of occurrences, or some force or forces are at work to enhance the numbers," finished Christine.

"Are you implying that it's possible someone may be going around eliminating Pharmacor retirees?" asked Holland.

"I'm merely stating that it is one of the possibilities which could account for the statistical abnormalities. At this point it is a possibility which I would not rule out," stated Christine.

"But who would want to kill ex-employees and what would they have to gain?" inquired Holland.

"You'd be surprised why some people do what they do," said Ken.

"Hatred, revenge, jealousy, greed, etc. all can rear their ugly heads at some time or another as motives for murder. May I suggest that we supply you and your staff with the personal data of all those who have died recently? With copies of their files, perhaps your people could examine the cause and circumstances of death to see if any glaring patterns or similarities can be discerned. If a pattern is found, it would lend credence to the possible existence of someone who is actively targeting your company. For all we know at this point, it probably is merely an extended case of very bad luck. However, we at Donsky and Associates felt it was our duty to alert Pharmacor to the real possibility of foul play. I've taken the liberty to put together a list of all of the 265 deaths in the past four months detailing names, addresses, and causes of death which your people might find of interest"

"Have either of you had a chance to examine the causes of death that have been responsible for the unnatural early demise of so many," asked Holland.

"We have, and it runs the gamut from car accidents to hunting accidents to murders committed during the course of robberies," answered Christine. "Because of the variety of circumstances surrounding their deaths, we are inclined to believe that it probably is coincidence that so many happen to occur to Pharmacor ex-employees. After all, I should think it would take an extremely gifted set of professional assassins to accomplish so many murders in such diverse ways in so short a time. On the other hand, it really is an extraordinary number of unnatural deaths to have occurred without the numbers getting at least some help. Regardless, the prudent thing to do would be to look into the matter as Ken has suggested," said Christine in closing.

"I'll take your proposed course of action under advisement, and I'll see if I can get a task force together to discern a pattern. We'll also investigate possible current or former employees who might have an axe to grind against our company. If there is nothing further, then I believe that this will conclude our meeting for today. Christine and

Ken, on behalf of Pharmacor I'd like to thank both of you for your diligence in advising us of this information. Also, please keep us abreast of the mortality rates in the future to let us know if this disturbing trend is continuing" said Holland as she arose from her seat and offered her hand to both Ken and Christine in a parting gesture.

"We certainly will," said Christine as she commenced to begin packing away her presentation material and computer while Ken sought to be of assistance by wrapping up an extra extension cord.

"Thank you again for coming. I'll have one of my assistants escort you out" Holland said as she opened the door to the conference room.

"You needn't bother, we can find our own way," stated Ken.

"Very well," said Holland as she began the trek back to her office.

"C'mon in," Daniece said in response to a light knock on her office door.

"Got a minute?" Holly-Brit asked as she glided past the threshold and directed herself toward a chair in front of Daniece's cluttered desk.

"For my trusted right hand, always," said Daniece obligingly.

"As you know, I met with the people from Donsky this morning and they brought some interesting points to light. They presented me with some very intriguing facts and figures concerning Pharmacor pensioners and..."

"Let me guess" Daniece interjected. "They feel that there are a few too many dying and that we have a boogey man running around the country bumping everybody off or something like that. Holland, do you know how ridiculous that sounds? They tried to get me to bite on that bit of hogwash the other day myself, but I cut them off and delegated them to you figuring that you would be able to send them on their way without us wasting too much of our limited and valuable time. Don't tell me that you see any reason to pursue their wild goose chase?" asked Daniece sarcastically.

"Umm, uh, I kinda sorta..."

"Well what is it Miss Matthews, is there some relevance to their charges or isn't there?" demanded Daniece.

"I guess maybe not," Holly-Brit dejectedly muttered as she prepared to turn and exit the office.

"Of course there is some relevance!" Daniece shouted. You don't find the unnatural deaths of 155-160 people in a short time of any interest, especially when all of them just so happened to work for us at some time or other? I find that damned interesting. That's why I had you meet with them in the first place. If I hadn't been tied down with all this unholy paperwork, I'd have met with them myself. The only reason that I gave you such a hard time is that I wanted to give you a taste of what you might have to go through with our boy Jonas down the road.

"Darn you Daniece, I wish you would quit doing these kind of things to me. Sometimes I don't know whether you are kidding with me or not," Holly-Brit responded.

"Trust me, there's a method to the madness hon. I'm trying to get you to trust your own instincts and to learn to stick up for yourself. Holly-Brit, you're a bright young lady with a lot on the ball, but sometimes I've noticed that you don't always have the courage of your own convictions. I want to get you to have confidence in your own abilities. It's an asset that will serve you well both in your career and your own personal life. Learn to be assertive. Let's face it, it's a dog eat dog world we live in, and throughout your life you're going to run up against people who are out to derail you for whatever reason. Holly-Brit, you are the expert on this matter. Be assertive and stick to your guns. You'll like yourself better in the long run, and you'll gain a lot of respect from your peers. Now, please detail for me what they told you about our pensioner's mortality rate."

The next ten minutes were filled with Holland's version of the Donsky Co. findings coupled with the suggestions offered by Christine and Ken.

"How do you think we should proceed from here?" asked Daniece earnestly.

"I think it was sound advice that they gave us to attempt to discern a pattern. Also, I agree that we should have some of our staff in personnel put together a list of unhappy former employees. Chances are that if someone truly is killing our retirees, it would be someone who worked for us and left on a bad note," offered Holly-Brit.

"I concur, but don't lose sight of what our main goals and objectives are during our basic 9 to 5 day. I would propose that the majority of this effort be done either before or after regular hours. May I suggest that you try to interest some of our staff to help you get to the bottom of this? You might find that you could enlist a core of volunteers eager to help you crack the case if there proves to be some credence in the

"Boogey man" aspects of the mystery at hand. Please keep me informed of your findings, and if it is warranted, I'll be more than happy to help take anything of substance up the corporate ladder for further consideration. Now unfortunately, it is time for us to both get back to our jobs. Happy hunting Holly-Brit and here's a hope that you don't turn up anything other than bad luck, because that may open a can of worms that we really don't want to open, you dig?"

"I dig boss lady! We'll let you know what we find," Holly-Brit said excitedly as she made her way towards the door.

CHAPTER 13

Fifty two year-old Jeannie Wellman threw open the curtains adorning the bedroom windows of the seaside villa. This allowed the radiant golden rays of the newly risen sun to burst forth in splendor upon the rumpled sheets and bed spread of the four-poster which she shared with her husband George. A light breeze fluttered the curtains and brought with it the pleasantly salted fragrance of the Atlantic surf into the sanctuary of their St. Augustine, Florida abode.

"Wake up little rosebud, wake up" Jeannie whispered sweetly into George's ear as she gently attempted to coax him back to consciousness from the Captain Morgan induced stupor which was a remnant of the previous night's beach party festivities. Jeannie's attempt at arousal was rewarded by George's self-administered ear scratch, an involuntary groan, and a half-hearted effort at raising his left eyelid.

"Can't an old seadog like me get some well deserved shuteye without an ungrateful wench, left over from the night before, buggin' the bejeebers out of him?" he rasped. "Now, why don't you join the other tarts and sirens and go down to the beach to lure some ships onto the rocks, or some other useful pastime, and let this poor wretched soul rest?"

Jeannie switched strategies and slid under the cool sheets to put her still taut, lithe figure in close proximity to that of her mate. She began a slow gentle back massage, lightly kneading the tight muscles of George's back as she slowly worked her way down to his buttocks. Having reached the pleasure area, she began to softly caress each cheek in a method that she knew pleased him.

"C'mon, wake up Blackbeard and service your wifely wench in the manner to which she is accustomed," Jeannie playfully cooed into his ear as she seductively brushed her nipples against his shoulders.

"Arrgh, alas a man's work is never done!" responded George as he struggled to a sitting position, still attempting to raise his eyelids. A slight throbbing at the temples alerted him to the need for some painkiller to help dispel the effects of the alcohol, and a persistent throbbing in the groin area alerted him to another need which required addressing. He let out another involuntary moan as he flipped his legs over the side of the bed, and silently padded off to the master bath in search of relief.

As he stood over the gaping mouth of the toilet letting nature take its course, George was a bit puzzled. He had indulged in a decent amount of rum last night, but not overly so. In a lifetime of non-temperance George had long ago learned his limits, and rarely exceeded them when it came to imbibing. He had also learned over the years that taking a few pain-killers before going to bed would allow him to wake up hangover and headache free the next day. Following that regimen the previous evening, he'd downed a couple of Zenophols before retiring. This was the first time George had ever tried Zenophol in that he had decided to buy them on sale at the local drugstore earlier that week. They appeared to have had a minimal effect at best. Chalking it up to maybe he had drank more than he thought, George reached for the bottle of Zenophol and swallowed two more as he turned on the water faucet while reaching for the mouthwash.

"Don't neglect to wash off that tool of yours before you come back in here lover boy," called Jeannie. "You know it's been awhile since I've let you sample my fruits and I don't want any cobwebs on that thing," she teased.

"Fear not you little spider, no webs shall there be. However, I need some assurance from you, my black widow woman, that you won't eat me after my usefulness here is ended," George joked.

"That all depends on how I rate your performance! So, for your sake I hope that you put some effort into it. Also, don't forget my after sex affection, or who knows how much of you I'll leave undigested."

George sauntered back to bed feeling a bit refreshed and in fact glad that his wife of six years had persisted in pursuing an amorous A.M. Their busy lifestyles didn't leave many opportunities for unscheduled mornings, and when the chance presented itself, it certainly should be taken full advantage of. Getting back into bed, George pulled Jeannie into his arms and forcefully kissed her fully on the mouth, pleased that her breath tasted as fresh as his own. After a brief period of foreplay, they were both ready for the main event. George plunged into Jeannie's womanhood with lustful vigorous strokes, and was thrilled by her enthusiastic response. Their ardor became more and more vocal as their grinding loins began heading them toward the mutual spasmodic release that they both knew and loved so well. At the height of their passion, Jeannie detected an unusual movement in George's thrusts. Suddenly George ceased altogether which was both unusual and disappointing to Jeannie, so much so that she opened her eyes to lovingly protest. Her loving gaze was met by a look of tremendous pain etched upon George's face as he clutched his right hand to his chest. The color seemed to drain from his face as his eyes closed tightly in a vain effort to fight off that which was afflicting him from within.

"What is it honey?" Jeannie implored.

Unfortunately, by this point George was incapable of speech, or anything other than focusing on the pain and the fervent desire to make it go away. A half-minute went by before the distressed look began to ease from his face. As George began to slump forward, she thought she heard him mumble the word "hospital" before he passed out. Struggling to get free from his inert body, Jeannie frantically half-wiggled and half-pushed her way clear. In a panic she tried to recall what she had seen and read about how to perform CPR. Beads of cold perspiration began to form on Jeannie's upper lip as the stark reality of what exactly was taking place hit home.

Dial 911...**DIAL 911!!!** Jeannie's subconscious screamed as her brain fought for control over the hysteria that threatened to overwhelm her senses. Leaping for the phone, Jeannie rapidly punched in the numbers, and was imminently grateful when the call was answered halfway through the second ring. The well trained emergency person soon had an ambulance on the way to George's aid, and gave Jeannie a crash course in cardio pulmonary resuscitation technique, which she proceeded to put to use immediately. The ambulance arrived nine minutes after the call was placed as the ambulance crew, recognizing the urgency of the situation, roared through the streets of St. Augustine with lights blazing and siren blaring. George was quickly strapped into the vehicle for the trip to the hospital where the serious business of saving his life would continue in earnest.

Thanks to the efforts put forth by the hospital emergency staff, the ambulance crew, and Jeannie, George pulled through, and was expected to make a full recovery within a few months. Tests performed at the hospital on George initially cast question marks on the cause of George's close brush with fate. He had suffered near fatal heart abnormalities of a rare nature. Being a non-smoking, athletic vegetarian with low blood pressure and no genetic predispositions towards heart problems, George would be one of the last people normally expected to have experienced this type of attack. Acting on a hunch, one of the doctors, a Dr. Moodt, suggested the possibility of a drug interaction that had been known to produce symptoms such as George's. The only drug George had taken recently was Ceramin, an antibiotic containing erythromycin that he had been prescribed to take for a sinus condition. As an afterthought George mentioned the Zenophols he had taken the day of the attack, and the previous evening. Sensing a possible connection, Dr. Moodt sent Jeannie back to her home to retrieve the bottles of Ceramin and Zenophol for analysis.

Arriving back at the hospitals with bottles in hand, Jeannie sought out Dr. Moodt. Finding him at a nursing station in the intensive care ward, Jeannie handed the doctor the two plastic containers. As soon as Dr. Moodt opened the Zenophol bottle his eyes grew wide. Pulling out a tablet, Dr. Moodt placed the pill in Jeannie's hand.

"Mrs. Wellman, does this look like a "Z" to you? I would say that it is more likely a "K" offered the doctor.

"It most definitely looks like a "K" to me," responded Jeannie.

"That it is I can assure you," said Dr. Moodt. "I'm quite familiar with Zenophol pain killers, which this is not. I'm also quite familiar with a product made by Mercurio Enterprises called Keldrane which this almost certainly is."

"Is that a problem, and is it possible that was a contributing factor in my husband's illness?"

"Not only is it possible, but in my estimation it was highly probable. You see Jeannie, Keldrane contains the antihistamine terfenadrine. When terfenadrine is used in conjunction with the antibiotic erythromicin, fatal heart rhythms are a likely result. Numerous studies have confirmed this deadly pairing, and many medical journal papers have been written warning of the dangers of combining these two chemicals at the same time within a patient's metabolism. Do you know where the mislabeled Keldrane was purchased, because not only should the product be removed from their shelves, but perhaps even a nationwide recall might have to be initiated to keep the public safe?"

"I'm not sure where the bottle was purchased because George bought it, but my guess would be the local drugstore a half mile from our home".

"Naturally I'll have the lab test the pills, but I'd be willing to stake my house on the outcome being that pill is Keldrane," said Dr. Moodt with an air of righteousness.

"Does this sort of thing happen often, that is are drugs found to be mislabeled very much?" asked Jeannie.

"Although it does occur, there are checks in the pharmaceutical industry and their distribution network which keep them at a minimum. Also, it normally is not associated with products that can have such a devastating effect."

"Do you think that we should talk to a lawyer about pursuing some type of legal action?" inquired Jeannie.

"That would be up to yourself and George, but one thing that definitely must be done, is that we must find out from George where he bought the pills," re-iterated Dr. Moodt.

Lab analysis confirmed Dr. Moodt's suspicions of the mislabeled pills being Keldrane instead of Zenophol. The local drugstore was alerted to the problem, which initiated a chain of events as standard operating procedures went into effect to handle situations of this nature. Naturally the drugstore's supplier, a company from Topeka Kansas named MailMed was notified, along with the manufacturer, Mercurio Enterprises. Mercurio, being a responsible corporation, but more importantly being a company, which wanted to limit their potential legal exposure while limiting their sales loss, did the almost right thing. They quietly commenced a total recall of the product Zenophol from their customer's shelves. Unfortunately for four unlucky souls, a press release followed by a public announcement detailing the problem and its inherent dangers, was not immediately forthcoming. It was thought by upper management that such a step was not necessary in that only two of the recalled bottles turned out to be mislabeled with Keldrane in them. Left unsaid was the unspoken truth that a press release with it's associated negative connotations to millions of unsophisticated consumers could be bad for sales which would be bad business practice, and surely unwarranted at this time.

Of the bottles that Ike Steele had mislabeled, 22 reached the unsuspecting public. Four others besides George Wellman would experience the causal effects of combining erythromicin with terfenadrine. George was the only one to survive. Of the other four, only one of the deaths was correctly tied to the fatal drug interaction. The resultant lawsuit along with one brought forth by the Wellman's was quietly settled out of court with Mercurio neither admitting guilt nor wrongdoing, but merely settling to avoid bad publicity. All of Mercurio's problems related to mislabeled Keldrane would probably have ended right there had it not been for the fact that Ike Steele still had over 100 Zenophol labels and he was still quite adept at gaining entry to an eighteen wheeler's trailer.

Jonas Trina learned of the product recall that Mercurio underwent, which was expensive. However he was disappointed that they were not forced to put out a press release that would've hurt them much worse. Jonas called to mind the old adage "Fool me once shame on you/ Fool me twice shame on me!" He surmised that Mercurio's customers might let them slip up once on a faux pas of this magnitude, but if it ever happened again they would lose all credibility and hordes of customers. This would be especially true in light of Mercurio's assurances to their accounts of all of the safeguards now in place to insure product reliability. With this in mind Jonas and Ike formulated a plan.

Two months after the initial label switch at the truckstop, Ike once again surreptitiously followed Dan Randle's truck from Mercurio Enterprises. Though it was difficult and nerve wracking, Ike managed to keep Dan's rig accounted for the entire day without him becoming suspicious that he was being trailed. In the early evening the rig pulled into a $40 a night motel in Western Indiana. Ike noted which room Dan brought his gear to, and jotted it down in a notebook for referral. Ike checked into a nearby motel, where he paid cash and went to his room. After finishing a quick light meal, Ike set his alarm for 2:00 A.M and went to sleep. At 2:15, Ike quietly left his room. He went to his vehicle and took out an athletic gear bag filled with the Zenophol labels, shrink-wrap, utility knives, handgun, flashlights, and assorted pens and markers. He also had a professional lock pick's tools to make short work of whatever type of lock he knew he would encounter on the back of Dan's rig. Ike was dressed in a dark loose fitting casual outfit replete with dark sneakers. This outfit would provide comfort, concealment and speed should the need for flight occur.

Pretending to be on a casual late night walk, Ike sauntered the quarter mile from his motel to Dan's. Nonchalantly lighting a cigarette, Ike glanced at Dan's room to make sure the light was off, indicating that Dan was probably in dream world. Strolling slowly across the parking lot, Ike bypassed Dan's truck, puffing on his cigarette as he surveyed the lot. "Good" he thought, not a soul in sight. He noted the position of Dan's trailer, and that the rear doors backed up to a stand of trees that would reduce the chance of him being spotted while at work. Taking another complete look around, and once again looking at Dan's room, Ike was convinced that he was not being observed. He took a deep breath and slowly circled to the rear of the trailer. Removing a flashlight and the lock picking tools from his bag, Ike went to work on the $15 lock that he found in place as the sole security to the rig's contents. In a matter of minutes the lock was off and Ike was inside the trailer.

Once again the prime target would be Keldrane in that this would have the biggest impact with Mercurio customers. Playing the flashlight beam on one pallet after another, Ike soon had identified two pallets that contained cases of Keldrane and he set to work replacing the labels with the stolen Zenophol labels. He decided to use all of the remaining labels rather than save any, should a third attempt at discrediting Mercurio be considered. They would probably change labels after the second batch hit the street anyway he figured. It took Ike almost three hours to accomplish the task, due to the number of labels being slightly over one hundred. Also, Ike had to stop every 15-20 minutes to check on Dan's hotel room to insure that he was still sleeping. Being careful to pick up every piece of scrap as he'd done before, and checking to see that he'd done a proper job of rewrapping the pallets with shrink-wrap, Ike felt satisfied that all was in order.

He put all of his tools back into the athletic bag and cautiously opened the door to the trailer. Slowly easing his way out, Ike once again lit up a cigarette and innocently strolled around the motel parking lot. He glanced at the luminescent dial on his watch that showed the time to be 5:15 A.M., still well before dawn, but a time when a trucker with lots of miles to cover might soon be heading for his truck to begin his day. Not wishing to tempt fate, Ike began to head back to his motel, pleased that once again his mission had gone off without a hitch. Ike jauntily crossed the darkened street and took a circuitous route back to his hotel to throw off any onlookers as to his final destination. Arriving back at his vehicle after a 2-mile trek, Ike flipped the bag in the trunk, and got into the car. He pulled slowly out of the motel's lot softly whistling a tune from "The Phantom of the Opera" as he hit the eastbound onramp to the interstate, pulling the visor down to ward off the orange yellow rays of the rising sun bursting over the horizon to beckon in a new day.

It took several weeks for fate and circumstances to take their course, but soon telltale signs of a widespread medical problem began to manifest itself across the country. Thanks to an article published in the American Medical Assoc. Journal, submitted by a Dr. Moodt reminding the medical community of the dangers of intermingling erythromicin with terfenadrine, doctors were prepared to look for this possibility when facing heart irregularities of an unusual nature. Cases began to pop up across the country with numerous deaths being reported, listing the probable cause as drug interaction. Subsequent investigations into these cases eventually established the erythromicin/terfenadrine connection.

When Dr. Moodt in St. Augustine learned of these new cases, he anonymously notified a local newspaper, The Saint Augustine News Herald, that they might wish to contact the Wellmans for a possible medical story. The story would center on some disturbing similarities between their experience and some unusual heart deaths that appeared to be happening around the country. The Wellmans were not at liberty to speak freely due to conditions related to the out of court settlement with Mercurio, but they suggested that the newspaper contact Dr. Moodt at a local hospital who might be of some assistance. Dr. Moodt was subsequently asked to relate the current widespread medical problems to a case that he had handled a few months before. Now the good doctor was able to open up to the press. He divulged the facts behind the Wellman case and the connection to Mercurio Enterprises, which up until now remained hidden from the public.

The News Herald, smelling a possible Pulitzer in the offing, flew two investigative reporters to four different cities to see if they could establish a Keldrane/Zenophol connection to cases identified by Dr. Moodt as some of the suspicious ones. They were able to establish without a doubt in three of the four cases that mislabeled Keldrane was in fact present in the households along with products containing erythromicin, both of which had been used by the recently deceased. Armed with that information along with Dr. Moodt's testimony on the Wellman case, The News Herald approached Mercurio Enterprises for their side of the story. Receiving a swift rebuke from Mercurio via their use of a curt "No Comment", The News Herald felt they had no choice but to go public with the story. Four days later the following News Herald headline hit the wires: "Is your Zenophol painkiller killing you?" Reporters from around the country descended on Columbus, Ohio to attempt to get the story directly from the horses' mouth.

Under the intense media scrutiny, Mercurio was forced to acknowledge a possible connection between their products and an increase in deaths due to fatal heart rhythm abnormalities caused by improper drug interactions. A press release was forthcoming detailing what appeared to be a case of erroneous labeling occurring on a relatively small number of Mercurio products that were being recalled at this very time. Mercurio stated that they had interviewed all employees who could possibly have had any connection to the problem, and they were at a loss to explain how such an occurrence could take place. The press release alluded to a theory concerning corporate sabotage, but they were unable to explain how competitors could make such a thing happen or who might be behind such evil deeds. Mercurio Enterprises might have been able to wiggle out of this mess, but when it was learned that this was the second occurrence in approximately three months, all hell broke loose. By the time all consequences had run their course, both the C.E.O and the president of Mercurio had resigned in disgrace, Mercurio stock had plunged 42%, and both Keldrane and Zenophol had been pulled off the market resulting in sales losses of $277 million/year for Mercurio. Furthermore, a class action lawsuit was being put together which would keep Mercurio's battery of lawyers busy for quite some time.

"I think that will do it for today gentlemen. Keep up the good work, and don't forget to stay on your guys so that we can gain as much market share as we possibly can out of that Mercurio screw-up. Remember, nature abhors a vacuum, and since Mercurio has temporarily gotten out of the painkiller and antihistamine markets, there's a helluva big void that is just demanding to be filled. Let's make sure that we get the biggest share of the spoils. We're off to a damn good start, but we've got to make sure we keep the heat on. Comprendez? Very well!"

With those final words the sales meeting broke up as the regional managers in attendance pushed away from the oversized conference table and began to stuff papers and files into their briefcases. As the managers filed out of the room, Ray Titus, the national sales manager for Pharmacor, allowed a brief smile to cross his lips. He couldn't believe his good fortune. While he had gotten the fiscal sales year off to a good start with some aggressive programs, he knew that in order to meet corporate objectives of a 15% minimum increase, he was going to need some breaks. Then this Mercurio fiasco happens and drops tens of millions of sales dollars in his lap for the taking, virtually assuring that his department would exceed their figures for the year.

He would've liked to have been able to shove this increase up Jonas Trina's nose and taken credit for it all, but unfortunately that was not the case. In fact Jonas had been more than instrumental in helping to bring about the increase. He had approached Ray two months ago suggesting that they put together a major sales promotion featuring their Blockaid brand of pain killers along with their Nostrilatum antihistamine product. Customers were alerted to extra discount possibilities, and production on both products was increased to meet anticipated increases in demand. The sales force had been out spreading the word for weeks hounding customers to turn business their way. When word of the Zenophol/Keldrane problems got out, the related Pharmacor products were still fresh in the customer's minds. Since then the phones had been ringing off the hook as the drug stores, discounters, etc. sought to fill their shelves with suitable substitutes to ease America's ailments. Thanks to Jonas' foresight they had the right promotions, the right products, and an ample supply to take full advantage of the situation when it presented itself. It was almost as if Jonas knew that something like this was going to happen. "Oh well, sometimes you just get lucky," thought Ray as he closed his briefcase and turned out the light to the conference room.

CHAPTER 14

"Thank you Mrs. Davis. And you also Miss Matthews, for your report on the progress being made within the human resource department" said Jonas Trina. "I believe that we have now heard from everyone, is that correct?" All of the departmental managers and vice presidents in attendance at this impromptu meeting nodded in the affirmative.

"Very well" continued Jonas. "As you all know, we have just finished the first quarter of the current fiscal year. I must admit that from what I've seen, and from what you've all shared with each other today, we are making significant strides towards meeting our corporate objectives. However I must caution you against becoming complacent and resting on your laurels. As you know, in order to win the race, first you must finish it. Let's make sure that we all end up this year like the tortoise and not the hare that gets sidetracked in the middle of the race. That will do it for today people. You may all get back to your duties, and keep up the good work," With that Jonas unhooked his microphone and briskly departed out the door of the oversized conference room heading back in the direction of his plush office.

Daniece and Holly-Brit were at the back of the line as the attendees departed from the conference room and made their way back to their respective offices. "Well that was certainly not as difficult as I thought it would be. Mr. Personality almost seemed human today," said Holly-Brit.

"Why shouldn't he be in a decent mood?" answered Daniece. "Sales are up 24% and growing stronger everyday, profits are up 21%, costs are down, and virtually every department is reporting good tidings for the future. From where I sit, Jonas Trina should be a happy camper, because if this all keeps up he's gonna be one rich dude. Remember what I told you about his incentive program?"

"How could I forget," replied Holly-Brit. "That's probably all that S.O.B. ever thinks about is his money, and how to make more of it. He's probably on his way back to his office to count his money and check up on his financial portfolio. I doubt if he has any hobbies, vices, or even pleasures that he spends his money on, so what good is it to him?"

"Don't be too sure about that sweetie. Remember, still waters run deep. Just because none of us here at Pharmacor seem to know anything about his background or personal life doesn't mean he doesn't have any interests. Who knows, he might be a world class skeet shooter or something, in addition to being a world class prick."

"Anything's possible I suppose," replied Holly-Brit as she opened the door to their department and gestured for Daniece to enter.

"Miss McKinney, hold my calls for the remainder of the week. You may leave messages of an urgent nature only on my voice message system. I'm going to take a little vacation and I shall be incommunicado until I return. No, I shall not tell you where I'm going or what I will be doing. I will let you know next week what day I shall be returning, but as of right now, that is undecided. I shall have need of the company helicopter that I have arranged to be flown out today. There you have it my dear. Have a pleasant week and give my regards to all of those who will no doubt be in tears at my abrupt departure. Good day Miss McKinney". As Jonas picked up his briefcase in preparation of leaving he spoke once again. "Oh, Miss McKinney, for those who insist on pestering you regarding my whereabouts, you may inform them that I have gone for a little ride in the country." With that Jonas Trina turned and strode out of the office grinning like the proverbial Cheshire cat.

The bright full moon shined down through a wisp of cloud as it illumined the cool Wyoming flatland. The baleful cry of a lonesome coyote pierced the 3:00 A.M. silence as it protested its solitary existence to the heavens. The high pitched whine of tires singing under the strain of an 18-wheeler's load as it approached the tiny town of Rozet was the only other sound at the moment in this out of the way portion of Americana. The serene peacefulness was suddenly shattered by the rapidly approaching reverberations of a helicopter flying at maximum speed on a westerly heading over interstate 90. The helicopter was shining an unbelievably bright light down on the highway as it zoomed forward.

"Birddog to Snakecharmer, Birddog to Snakecharmer, do you read me Snakecharmer?"

"Snakecharmer to Birddog, I read you loud and clear."

"You're clear for the next 15 miles with the exception of a couple of widely spaced Peterbilts, so why don't you put the pedal to the metal and let's see what that set of wheels you're sittin' on can do."

"Why don't you drop down a few hundred feet Birddog, so you can eat my dust when I blow by you!" shouted Jonas Trina into the receiver.

"Catch me if you can big fella, but don't forget the purpose of my being here is to act as your forward eyes, so you don't have to wipe a wolf's ass off the windshield of your little pet snake."

"Roger" said Jonas as he applied more pressure to the foot pedal of the 560 horsepower Dodge ACR Viper. The response from the vehicle was throaty and instantaneous as the Viper leaped forward with the speedometer advancing from a sedate 95 m.p.h. to 150 m.p.h. in a matter of seconds. As the Viper rocketed down the black ribbon of highway Jonas pushed the pedal to the floor. The needle on the speedometer made a sweep past 175 m.p.h. as both the Viper and driver sought to test their limits. Jonas let out a howl of exhilaration as he flew by a truck doing 80 m.p.h. as if it was standing still. He was past the truck long before the trucker could even begin to shout the first of 20 expletives at the Viper's rapidly disappearing backside.

The obsidian colored Dodge with silver trim was approaching the almost 200 mile per hour barrier as Jonas took aim on another truck in his headlights. This driver veered to the shoulder of the road upon Jonas' rapid approach. This allowed maximum passing distance in case the maniac behind the Viper's wheel should lose control. Jonas executed the pass flawlessly and left another driver in his wake.

Looking back over his shoulder, Ike Steele in the helicopter could make out the halogen headlights of the swiftly moving Viper trailing him. He returned his glance forward just in time to pick up a couple of specks on the highway in the distance. As he came nearer, his 50,000 candlepower lights picked up the forms of two large animals standing in the center of the highway.

"Birddog to Snakecharmer, we've got an emergency slowdown approximately seven miles in front of you. It appears to be two large deer or elk, or hell for all I know they might be moose or even elephants out here. All I know is that they are big and they are in the roadway. Suggest you cool your jets and approach under the yellow caution flag. Do you copy?"

"Understood Birddog. May I suggest you drop down and use your whirlybird powers to remove the offending creatures from the playing field?"

"I'm way ahead of you Snakecharmer. I was already dropping down to see what effect my wind breaking might have on 'em, but just wanted you to understand the situation. I'll advise, over and out."

Ike dropped the helicopter down and made for the elk in the highway. The sudden appearance of the chopper startled the beasts. Initially they panicked and ran in circles, but with the assistance of Ike's herding, the animals were soon 200 yards from the highway and moving farther away with each bound.

"Situation handled Snakecharmer, you may resume normal cruising speed which appears to be just slightly less than an F-15."

"Thanks for your help Birddog. Please keep me apprised of any additional impediments to my amusement ride."

Ike climbed up to 1500 feet and resumed his high-speed westerly reconnaissance patrol as Jonas began accelerating past 150 m.p.h. again. "I wonder if we've got any county mounties up ahead" said Ike nonchalantly into the mouthpiece.

"It is of little consequence whether we do or do not in that I have my get out of jail free card, if you remember?" answered Jonas.

"Oh yeah, that's right, I'd forgotten about that," Ike responded.

Jonas had nothing to worry about in regards to police interference. He had seen to that with a $45,000 donation to the campaign fund of the governor who had by agreement sent out a directive effectively giving Jonas free rein to take this high-speed journey without fear of police involvement. Almost as if on cue, Ike flew past a couple of Wyoming's finest who were shielded from his view by the side of a gas station they were hiding behind.

"Whew, that chopper is sure headed somewhere in a hell of a hurry." observed officer P. J. McClintock.

"Sure is alright. Wonder if he's out joyriding, or if there's a method to the madness," responded his partner Tony Zemla.

"Don't know, but get a load of this. That pair of headlights that just shot over the bluffs has got to be coming our way at 150 m.p.h. minimum. Should I turn on the siren and call for backup?" asked P.J.

"Not so fast. Remember that directive that came down from the chief yesterday about some hot shot with a black viper who is supposed to be ignored if he happens to be observed breaking the speed limits. Let's see what the car is before we make our play," said Zemla.

"I'll get the spotlight ready to shine on him as he flies past us so that we can make a positive I.D. on the vehicle. At the speed he's approaching, we're gonna need all the help we can get," observed P.J.

"Whatever you do, make sure you don't blind him and have him wrap whatever he's driving around a tree or something," cautioned Zemla. "I've got a hunch that if this is Viper Boy, he has the clout to make life pretty miserable for a couple of guys like us if we mess up his little joyride."

Jonas bore down on the trooper's position at 190 m.p.h., concentrating intently on maintaining control while at the same time relishing the exhilarating experience of truly living life on the edge. He shot past the gas station, a black blur against the moonlit Wyoming landscape. Jonas was startled by the sudden appearance of a bright light in his rear view mirror, which had his Viper as its main target. Jonas experienced a sudden intense flashback, unconsciously trying to recollect what this unexpected spotlight reminded him of. The bright glare disappeared as suddenly as it had materialized.

"Black Viper it is my friend, let's let it be and get back to prairie dog observing," said officer Zemla.

"Fine by me," answered McClintock.

Jonas continued on at breakneck speed, still contemplating what the light had reminded him of, and why his mind for some reason wouldn't let it go. As he sped onward, he could see the faint reflection of the helicopter's red taillight in the distance as he gained on Ike. At his current 200 m.p.h., he would overtake Ike regardless of whether or not Ike thought it to be prudent.

Jonas' memory banks suddenly kicked in, flooding his brain with bright spotlights, and a distinct remembrance of their origin. AFGHANISTAN! Soviet gun ships had a nasty habit of appearing out of nowhere and bathing the cold, bleak, desolate Afghani mountainsides with banks of floodlights mounted on their undercarriage. Fortunately, Jonas had never been caught directly in their harsh glare, but he had seen countless remains of Afghani fighters who had been discovered and consequently slaughtered. Jonas attempted to return his full attention to the high-speed task at hand, but his mind wouldn't shake the images of Afghanistan. Why? WHY is this so damned important to some part of me, and why now of all times? As the Viper flew on, a plan began to crystallize in the gray mists of Jonas' subconscious. It was a plan born of faraway experiences, combined with current world events, and intermingled with Jonas' own personal desires.

An earsplitting high-pitched screech of tires shattered the still night as Jonas hit the brakes hard. Luckily the roadway was dry, the brakes were good, the tires were first rate, and the Viper and its stabilization components were some of the world's best. All of which meshed to enable Jonas to get away with his foolhardy move of bringing a mass of metal moving at 200 m.p.h. to an emergency stop by applying heavy brakes. Lights from surrounding houses began to dot the countryside as the dying echoes of Jonas' abbreviated stop echoed off the nearby hills.

"Snakecharmer to Birddog, come in Birddog."

"Birddog here."

"Turn your chopper around and head for home. We've got work to do."

"That's it then, just like that?"

"Just like that."

"Will do, over and out." Ike immediately did as instructed. He knew from years of working for Jonas that an order was never to be disobeyed or questioned, even one as abrupt and confusing as this.

An evil sneer formed on Jonas countenance as he started the Viper moving again, making his way to an exit a mile up the road so he could turnaround and head back to Ohio. Once back home he would begin to fully develop the possibilities of his newly formed idea. The summertime full moon bid farewell to the eastbound pair as Ike and Jonas began their journey back home to wreak havoc on an unsuspecting populace.

CHAPTER 15

"Jane, have you had any luck on finding patterns concerning our retiree situation?" asked Holly-Brit.

"Funny you should ask, assistant boss lady. Just last night Ernesto, Jenny and I stayed late to compare notes. Most of the cases gave us very little in the way of witnesses or anything out of the ordinary to go on. However in three cases, there appears to be a possible connection. In two of the murders that occurred during robberies at the victim's homes, neighbors reported seeing a tall middle-aged stranger in the vicinity the day of the murders. Also in one of the car accidents, witnesses stated that the victim had been deliberately sideswiped by a large man. This was based on how high his head was in the vehicle. In all three cases the witnesses stated the man was a tall Caucasian male in his mid to late 40's with dark hair and a moustache. We asked around the office as well as several other departments such as maintenance, and we came up with three possible suspects who left the company on a very sour note, and who would somewhat match the witnesses descriptions."

"Good work Jane. Get me a list of the names, and current addresses if possible and I'll take it from there. Oh, and tell Ernesto and Jenny I said thanks for a job well done."

"Come on in Holly-Brit," said Daniece, as she acknowledged the light knock on her office door. "To what do I owe the pleasure on this fine morning?"

"You had asked me to report back to you if we discerned any patterns or connections in the retiree deaths, and I think that our staff has uncovered something."

"Why don't you show me what they've come up with?"

Holland related the findings to Daniece with her recommendation that they take the information directly to Mr. Trina to determine what steps he would wish to pursue in order to best protect the company.

"I concur," agreed Daniece. "But don't be surprised if Jonas doesn't share your enthusiasm for the hunt. In addition, you might want to prepare yourself for a bit of an interrogation. Jonas Trina doesn't strike me as one who is willing to go out on a limb to initiate an investigation without being pretty damn sure there is significant substance to warrant such an action. Make sure you've got your ducks in a row, and make sure to anticipate any possible questions so that you can handle any objections he might throw at you. I'll be willing to go with you to lend moral support, and also because I happen to agree with you that something is going on here. However, as far as I'm concerned, this is your baby. I suggest that you get in touch with Jonas' secretary and set up a meeting for next week when he is supposed to be back in town, and we'll see what he has to say."

"How was your trip Mr. Trina?" inquired Holland.

"It was a welcome break if you must know Miss Matthews. Now I assume that you and Mrs. Davis have some pertinent business related topic for the mutual discussion, which you by the way requested."

"We believe we do sir," offered Daniece in an effort to buy Holland some time to mentally shrug off the rude Trina response. "Holland, would you please show Mr. Trina what you and your staff have discovered?"

"Mr. Trina, you may not be aware of this, but in the past 6 months almost 270 of our former employees have died. Of that number, most have died from something other than natural causes. According to Donsky and Associates, the third party administrator responsible for handling our retiree's pension fund, this is an alarming number of deaths for a company the size of Pharmacor. While there is nothing concrete at this time, both the people at Donsky, and several members of our human resource department who were alerted to these statistics, feel that this number of deaths may be more than just bad luck. There is concern that an individual or perhaps even a small group is going around eliminating former employees of Pharmacor for some unknown reason. Over the past few weeks our staff in the personnel department has done some investigative work to come up with a list of possible suspects who might bear monitoring. This list was based in part upon physical characteristics which we have reason to believe might be relevant, and also those who left the company on a bad note and who may hold a grudge against Pharmacor."

Before Holland could continue, Jonas shattered the mood in his office with three well-spaced resounding claps of his hands. These were accompanied by a decidedly annoyed look on the face of the C.E.O., and a deep breath that foretold of unpleasantness about to be unleashed.

"Bravo Miss Matthews! What you have just informed me is that you have arbitrarily decided to divest the personnel department of their regular Pharmacor duties, so that they may pursue the more exemplary goal of engaging in your self avowed witch hunt to ferret out some nefarious evildoer. At what point did you come to the conclusion that I, or any member of management, would appreciate you using the resources of this company for any purpose that does not advance the stated goals of Pharmacor? Mrs. Davis, were you aware of these activities within your department?" Daniece responded with a meek affirmation. However, she quickly regained her composure and commenced to deflect the verbal onslaught that she knew was imminent.

"Mr. Trina, on behalf of both Holland and myself, I'd like to mention a few things in our defense. First off, none of this investigation was done on company time. Furthermore, there weren't any company funds utilized in order to gather any information. All participation was strictly voluntary, and if I daresay, the volunteers were in fact most eager to lend a helping hand. Also, weren't we directed months ago to submit lists of potential troublemakers who might cause harm to Pharmacor? We all thought that we would be providing a direct benefit to the company if we uncovered someone willfully eliminating both former and current staff members. The information provided to us by Donsky and Associates led us to believe this may be a very real possibility."

"I see. Ladies, let me ask you a question. What in your mutual backgrounds, or the backgrounds of your staff, would lead you to believe that any of you are qualified to be private detectives? Also, why do you think that we asked you to give us the names of potential evildoers? Did you believe that we would take those lists and round file them? I can assure you that in the past few months I have had a special task force examining the backgrounds of those individuals identified as causes for concern. They have all been behaving themselves, and we shall continue to monitor their activities to insure that they commit no foul play. Furthermore, regarding the numbers of deceased retirees brought to your attention by Donsky, it comes as no shock or surprise to myself, or my immediate staff. We are quite aware of the numbers, and no we do not currently find them as cause for alarm. After all, the majority of those deaths occurred at the ill-fated retirement party due to Legionnaire's disease. The remaining deaths simply indicate a streak of unusually bad luck that I'm sure will soon cease and desist. Speaking of ceasing and desisting, it would be a great relief to this office if both of you would stop playing detective, return to your posts, and reacquaint yourselves with the duties for which you were hired and upon which your future employment depends. That will be all. Please close the door on your way out." The thoroughly dumbfounded ladies meekly did as instructed and left the office.

A morose silence accompanied Daniece and Holland as they made their way back to their department. The browbeating that Jonas had laid on them had been both unexpected and undeserved, and a period of psyche recovery was proving to be necessary. As they reached the outer office door to the human resource department, Daniece broke the silence by quipping, "Well I guess that's gratitude for you!"

"That arrogant son-of-a-bitch!" responded Holland. "How dare he dismiss the deaths of all those people with a few snide comments and a shove out the door to those of us who are genuinely concerned about their deaths? I don't buy any of that crap about his appointing a special task force. He doesn't strike me as the kind who would be overly concerned about the welfare of anyone other than himself. As far as I'm concerned, this matter is not over, and I shall continue to search for answers on my own time to the best of my ability, with or without anyone else's help!"

"A couple words of caution Holly-Brit. Jonas is a very powerful and arrogant man who I'm sure doesn't like to be crossed or second guessed. If he finds out that you are continuing to pursue this matter in direct defiance of his authority, being on the outside and looking in at Pharmacor may be the least of your problems. Also, what other possible reason could he have had months ago in asking us for lists of problem people? Chances are that he really does have surveillance on them to keep abreast of what they are up to. That strikes me as being very much in character for an elitist bastard like Jonas Trina."

"Perhaps," acknowledged Holland. "But I'm still not buying it. If he had any concern about this company's employees both past and present, I should think that he would welcome our findings and vow to not let any stone remain unturned until something definite was determined regarding all of these deaths. To me his arbitrary manner convinces me that either he knows more than he's letting on, or that he just doesn't give a rat's ass about those people. Either way he's wrong and I'm not going to just let this rest."

"Tread lightly then my dear and be careful not to step on the snake's head because you just might get bit."

Ike Steele's private line rang at his home. Before answering, he already knew the caller. Picking up the receiver Ike uttered a simple "Yes"

"We may have to bump up the timetable on the Hughes plan."

"If the subject is positioned properly, I'll begin tomorrow."

"Very well, that's all for now."

After replacing the receiver Ike reached for the lustrous velvety Persian that was caressing his calf with fur. As he picked up the large feline and began stroking it softly, a fiendish smile crossed his lips. This is going to be fun Ike mused as he and the Persian made their way toward his well stocked liquor cabinet.

Jonas Trina replaced the phone in the back seat holder of his limo and pulled into position a fold down laptop built into a tray table that was designed as a backseat workstation. Turning the computer on, he wasted little time in getting to the task at hand. Composing an e-mail, he typed in the electronic address of someone he had not seen in well over two decades, but someone with whom he had kept in touch with over the years. The terse message read as follows: Greetings! Hope all is well. I am now positioned to help your cause. Request a meeting ASAP. You name time and place. Western Europe would be nice. Regards! The Lion Seeker.

Jonas hit the send button and initiated the sequence to shut down his laptop. As he did so, half a world away a computer positioned at the entrance to a cave on a mountaintop straddling the border between Afghanistan and Pakistan received his e-mail. Awaking at daybreak an hour later, the recipient, a high-ranking Imam in the embattled Taliban read the message and carefully considered his response. After due deliberation and consultation with others, the Imam replied thusly: Greetings also Lion Seeker. Agree to meet, although I cannot get away. Will send emissaries. Western Europe is good. One week from today. Will send address of location within 48 hours after security details arranged. Be well! IKM3.

Jonas checked his e-mail just prior to retiring for the evening and read the Imam's reply. He was pleased that a meeting would be arranged. If all went well, the end result of this meeting should be suitable to help him further his needs. Satisfied that all was proceeding as planned, Jonas shut down the computer and smugly smiled as he turned off his bedroom light.

CHAPTER 16

The 11:00 A.M. Cleveland sun felt warm on Ike's face as he continued his surveillance on the working class bar to which he had followed Danny Hughes. Danny had been in there almost an hour, so he should be off and running on his daily quest to bring on cirrhosis of the liver. Deeming the time was right, Ike opened the door to the beat up Ford he had picked up for appearance's sake. With an act of great effort he extricated himself from the driver's seat, and slowly ambled across the street towards a ramshackle building with a discolored sign hanging precariously on the wall. The sign proclaimed this establishment to be O'Malley's Bar and Eatery. The amount of food actually partaken of on the premises however was certainly an infinitesimal percentage of the owner's take here. Cheap beer, cheap whisky, big talk, and thin wallets were the everyday realities behind the tattered facade. Ike slowly pushed the heavy creaking door open and pretended to stagger some to feign a slight bit of tipsiness.

"Drinks are on me barkeep for everyone in the house, yerself included." This line was delivered with as fine an Irish accent as you'd find anywhere on the Emerald Isle. The speech classes Jonas had insisted Ike take years ago were once again paying dividends.

"You heard the man, gents! Belly up to the bar and be quick about it so as I can be havin' my refreshment too," stated the owner/bartender/bouncer/waiter. "What's yer name and where ya from lad? I don't recall yer darkenin' me doorstep before now."

"Kevin's me name, drinkin's me game, and from Cinci's where I came! That is unless ya got a few shapely lasses around here, in which case wenchin's me game."

With that the bar filled with hearty laughter as the handful of late morning drinkers made their way in front of the proprietor to refill their glasses and mugs. Ike endured several good-natured pats on the back from the semi-inebriated patrons. The most boisterous smack was administered by a good-sized middle aged man that Ike recognized as being his pigeon, one Danny Hughes.

"What brings ya to town, Kevin me boy?" asked the owner.

"Me dear sweet old mother has taken sick and I've come to provide her some solace in her infirm condition. That, and the fact that as of a month ago I got no more work, which frees me to travel a bit if the cause arises."

"Oh, out of work are ya? My condolences! Where did ya work, if I might ask?"

"Here I'll show ya." With that Kevin/Ike unbuttoned his shirt to reveal a t-shirt with bright lime green letters that emphatically stated "PHARMACOR SUCKS."

Seeing that, the owner shouted out in Danny Hughes direction, "Danny Boy come here quick, ya gotta be seein' this."

As Danny leaned forward to rise from his barstool, a loud belch emanated from his core. Ignoring his social gaffe, Danny made his way over to where Ike and the owner were conversing. Taking one look at the lettering on Ike's shirt, a dumbfounded expression came to Danny's face.

"Sure and BeGorra lads, I've died and gone to heaven! A stranger comes to me favorite pub, buys me beer, and now reveals he's sportin' a shirt with the two words I live by! Mister O'Malley, get us a pitcher of yer finest for me newfound friend and I. We'll be takin' up that corner table over there where we can catch up on old shoptalk, if you don't mind."

The pitcher was brought forth in short order, and Ike and Danny made their way over to the table. "Me name's Danny Hughes, and yours?"

"Kevin, Kevin Michaels." answered Ike.

"Well Kevin Michaels. it's a pleasure to be makin' your acquaintance. Tell me, what's with the shirt?"

"If it's the "Pharmacor Sucks" shirt that you're referrin' to, I'll tell you me tale of woe right here and now. I worked at their Cincinnati plant for 21 years. Yep for over two decades I gave me heart and soul to those fine purveyors of pills and potions, and what thanks do I get? A swift kick in the pants, and not even so much as a thank you, for two decades of sweat! All because of a little nip of Jameson's a little too often, least-wise accordin' to the fine gentleman whose duty it was to advise me of my terminated employment status. Hell, as anyone knows, a man with a little extra fire in his belly is more productive, not less."

"Hear! Hear! I'll drink to that! How long has it been since the ungrateful bastards showed yerself the door?"

"Well as I told the owner, it's been about a month now. I gather from the way we were introduced that you used to work for Pharmacor at some time also."

"Sure did. In fact me story's pretty much the same as yours. Trumped up charges of drinkin' on the job, when in reality it was that ferret-faced supervisor I had that done me in. I'll never forget that bastard, Tom Chauncy he was. That no good S.O.B. had it in for me from the very minute he took over my department. I'd sure like to even the score with that bastard. I wouldn't mind bringin' down some of the other jerks that I worked with as well now that I think about it."

"That's too bad yerself Danny. How long has it been since they gave you the boot?"

"Nine months, and I ain't been able to find a decent job since. I'm sure that Pharmacor's got me blacklisted or something, because everywhere I go I don't even get an interview. Seem's strange for a man who's had steady work all his life until now."

"Did you leave on a sour note?"

"If you call spittin' in Chauncy's face and referrin' to his wife as a pig-faced whore a sour note, then I guess you could say I did."

"Hear! Hear! yerself Danny Hughes! That must've caused quite a stir when Chauncy found himself with a face full of spittle. Did he come after you?"

"Naw, Chauncy's much too clever to approach me as a man would face to face. He knows I'd wipe the floor with the likes of him. No he prefers to do his dirty work in a more secretive manner. That's why I think that it's hisself with maybe the help of some of his superiors who are workin' behind the scenes keepin' me in this downtrodden place, not gettin' no interviews and such."

"Listen my friend, how'd ya like to get back at those miserable pukes who've done ya so terribly wrong?"

"Luv to Mr. Kevin Michaels, what do ya have in mind?"

"Don't know yet, but I hate to see bad deeds to good people go unpunished. Let me ask ya, do you know any personal habits of Chauncy and his buddy's?"

"Well, I know that every Wednesday night they like to play poker at the Pharmacor recreation center which is kind of a gatherin' place for company retirees to socialize here at the corporate headquarters in Cleveland. Chauncy was always braggin' how easy it was to fleece those sheep that he played with."

"Any idea how many people would be at the center on a Wednesday night?" asked Kevin/Ike.

"Countin' Chauncy's ilk, the socializin' retirees, and those who just drop by after their shifts, there are probably anywhere from fifty to eighty at any given time."

"Let me ask ya this, have ya ever hurt a man?"

"I've seen me share of scuffles," replied Danny with a bit of braggadocio thrown in for emphasis.

"I mean REALLY hurt a man! Hurt a man so ya thought he might never be gettin' up again?"

"I split a man's skull with a piece of concrete in a street brawl once. I thought at the time I mighta done him in for good. I just dropped the rock, and left him lying bleedin' in the street while I ran away, afraid to look back for fear that either he was dead or his buddies might be catchin' up to me. I didn't see no mention of the affair listed in the paper the next couple of days, so I've always figured that he lived."

Ike focused his steely blue eyes on Danny so intently that they bore directly into his very soul as he slowly asked the final question. "Danny Hughes, do you think you could ever kill a man if he had it comin'?"

"I believe I could Kevin, I believe I could." Danny said as he slowly nodded his head several times.

"That's me boy Danny. Between us I think we can teach Tom Chauncy, his buddies, and that whole damn company a lesson they'll remember for a long time. Drink up Danny boy we've got work to do!"

"Aye, Aye, Mr. Michaels! That we do, that we do!" Danny replied agreeably. He drained the last half glass of ale from his mug in one pull while he pushed away from the table with his meaty right hand, already savoring the vindication which he was sure would now be forthcoming for Mr. Thomas Chauncy and friends.

CHAPTER 17

Holland entered the deli and her nostrils immediately flared wide to drink in the pungent aroma of the savory corned beef and garlic pickles, for which Ira's deli was renowned. As usual the establishment was packed as the midday crowd arrived to hurriedly grab their sandwiches to go. Some chose to join the patrons at the counter when a seat became available. Earlier in the day, Holland had made the decision to indulge in a thick hot corned beef sandwich, complete with a side of potato salad, and the obligatory garlic laced kosher pickle. Upon paying for her purchase, Holland quickly made her way out the door. Rather than taking her lunch back to the office cafeteria, Holland decided to take advantage of the ample sunshine and join scores of other office workers who were lunching outside this day. Finding an unoccupied bench half shaded by a building, she sat down and began un-bagging her delicacies. As she took her first bite, she became aware of an approaching presence.

"Ira's corned beef is good, but Manny's around the corner is better," said a tall suit-clad hunk, with a great tan and laughing green eyes. "And if you'd like a real treat, try the reuben, it's like a little kraut-filled taste of heaven!"

"Excuse me, but do I know you?" Holland asked as she eyed up the stranger warily.

"No."

"Then why, of all of the people in the world that you could be verbally accosting on this beautiful day, have you chosen me?"

"It's because you happen to be sitting in my seat."

"I beg your pardon."

"If you would be so kind as to get up for a second, I'll prove it to you."

Mildly perturbed, but slightly curious, Holland did as requested. Looking down she noticed a small rectangular section of the bench had been routered partway out of the wood. In this recessed area, a typed note had been placed and then lacquered over. The note stated that this space was reserved for John Kazek F.B.I. "Are you serious?" inquired Holland.

"Yes and no."

"What's that supposed to mean?"

"That means yes, that is my seat as the note states, and no I'm not going to ask you to relocate."

"Well, that's a relief, because then I'd have to ask you for some I.D. to prove you are this John Kazek fellow. Next I'd have to flag down a policeman to arrest you for defacing public property."

The stranger produced his F.B.I. photo credentials and verified his identification. "Sorry to disappoint you on all counts Miss. Not only am I the person for whom the seat is reserved, but also this does not happen to be public property. If you will look at the brass nameplate on the side of the bench..."

Feeling for any evidence of a nameplate on the side of the bench, Holland's lips sarcastically and involuntarily muttered the words "Brass plate my..." Her fingers ran across a smooth cold metallic surface with screws at each end. With her curiosity piqued, Holland swung her head over the side of the bench in order to discern the truth. Reading upside down, she still had no difficulty making out the words etched upon the brass plate. They read: "Bench is property of John Kazek F.B.I." A droll smile crossed Holland's face as she stated, "Pretty taken with ourselves aren't we Mr. Kazek, or should I say Mr. Kazek F.B.I.?"

"Actually, you may call me John, and as for being taken with myself, I'd like to set the record straight. This whole bench thing is in reality the result of a bet I lost in a free throw shooting contest with some of my colleagues. They had been complaining forever of always having to sit on the wet grass, or having to stand when we ate outside. I told them that rather than complaining, they should do something about it, like build or buy a bench. Things kind of escalated from there, fueled by a few after hour drinks, some macho talk, and a penchant for competition. This bench is the byproduct of that evening. I figured that if I was going to have to provide the bench for all of those cutthroats I work with to enjoy, the least I could do was to lay some type of claim to having provided it for them and future F.B.I. members. Hopefully you believe at least some of that so that you don't think that I'm some type of egomaniac or something."

"The story you've just given me is too farfetched to be anything but the truth, so John Kazek F.B.I., I'll defer to your good deed of providing this bench, and offer you the chance to share it with me for lunch."

"Why thank you Miss, uh..."

"Matthews. Holland Matthews."

"It's a pleasure to meet you Holland. That's an unusual name. I don't think I've ever met a girl named Holland before," John said as he sat down and produced one of Manny's marvelous reubens from a brown paper sack he'd had in tow.

"I guess my name is unusual," Holland said between bites of her sandwich. "I was always the only Holland in any of the schools I attended. My parents said it was kind of a compromise. It was the first name of over 200 they bounced off each other, which they both agreed was acceptable."

"That's amazing. I assume that your friends probably all call you Holly."

"Not quite. My father didn't care for the name Holly, but he did like the name Holland, so he kind of discouraged me from suggesting that people call me Holly. I have though, over the years, come to be known by my closest friends as Holly-Brit, after my middle name of Brittainy. This seems to be palatable to my dad. Well, that's enough about me and my many names. So you're with the F.B.I.?"

"Why yes I am, how did you ever guess?" John laughingly chided. "I've been in the bureau for a little over three years now."

"Are you from Cleveland?"

"Not originally. I grew up in Virginia, not far from where the F.B.I. headquarters are. When I was growing up, it was always an ambition of mine to join the bureau and to bring the bad guys to justice."

"And now here you are, fighting evil and buying benches by being bad in basketball!"

"I believe you're rhymin,' Simon."

"That's what we in Cleveland call a little alliteration."

"I hope that doesn't mean that you are alliterate!"

"That's illiterate, and I'll have you know that me can wead and wite vewy well, thank you vewy much Mr. John Kazek F.B.I.!"

Both of them chuckled at the irreverent wordplay that had taken over the conversation, and Holland found that she was enjoying herself very much. It had been eons it seemed since she'd had as interesting, and yes flirtatious, a discussion as this, and she was determined to keep up her end of it to see where it would lead.

"So, Miss Holland Matthews, do you work around here, or just passing through?"

"I work at Pharmacor."

"Oh, where's that?"

"You don't know where Pharmacor is from here?"

"Can't say that I do, M'am."

"If you will direct your gaze to the other side of the street and look that way two blocks, our building is the three story one that takes up most of the block. Don't tell me you work in this big building here and you never heard of Pharmacor?"

"I'm afraid they don't let me out to roam the streets very much. Also, I rarely head in that direction for anything. What kind of business is it, and what do you do there Holland?"

"Pharmacor is a large pharmaceutical company, and I work as an administrative assistant in the Human Resource department."

"How do you like it?"

"I like it a lot, although there is a substantial amount of tedious recordkeeping to be done, which is sometimes a drag. But I work with a bunch of really nice people and my boss and I get along real well. We often get together after hours for socializing or business meetings."

After downing a swig of his drink, John continued the discourse. "After hours business meetings sound like a bit of a downer to me. What sort of things does the human resource department need extra hours to discuss exactly? How to correctly file computer discs left-handed instead of right handed?"

"I'll have you know Mr. John Kazek F.B.I. smarty pants, that we discuss a good deal of wide ranging topics at our meetings. We talk about cost cutting, employee evaluations, insurance concerns, and sometimes we branch off into areas that are really interesting like the one we're looking into right now."

"And just what would that be?" asked John with an eyebrow raised to denote his piqued interest.

"Oh my goodness, Just look at the time! I've really got to be getting back to the office. It's too bad that I don't have time to finish our conversation. Not only is what we're working on exciting, but it's something I'm sure you'd have a professional interest in also," said Holland coyly as she wrapped the remaining half of her sandwich and began to rise from the bench.

"Hey wait a minute! You're not going to just leave me hanging are you?"

"That depends, Mr. John Kazek F.B.I., on whether you'd like to resume our discussion later."

"You name the time and the place, and I'll be there. After all, in my professional capacity, I have to develop all of my sources so that I can to keep the information flowing in from the street." John chuckled.

"The Raging Bull bar on West 6th Street, shall we say sixish Friday night?"

"You're on Miss Holland Matthews. I'll be looking forward to it. Let's exchange cell phone numbers, just in case something unforeseen comes up O.K?"

"Good idea."

An awkward moment ensued a minute later as both grappled with the slight problem of exactly how to say goodbye after this brief but somewhat intimate initial meeting. John solved the social dilemma by offering his hand in friendship with a vow to be on time for their rendezvous later that week. After shaking hands they both turned to walk back to their respective offices. Holland had taken perhaps 30 steps when the uncontrollable urge to peek back in John's direction proved to be simply too strong to resist. She was rewarded with a slowly backpedaling F.B.I. agent admiringly gazing in her direction. Both smiled and waved goodbye from afar, as they turned around for good.

As Holland waltzed into her department, Daniece and Jenny couldn't help but notice the joyful glow radiating from her. As Holland approached the twosome, Daniece observed the way she fairly floated towards them.

"Jenny, if I didn't know better, I'd say that our little Miss Holly-Brit just got some on her lunch hour. Wouldn't you say that she has that just-screwed look about her?"

"Indubitably so! Yes indubitably so!"

"You two are just jealous."

"Did you notice, Jenny that she did not deny it."

"It's impolite for a lady to kiss and tell," Holly-Brit volleyed back.

"Sounds to me like she did get some! All right young lady spill it! I want names, places, positions, and a lover rating from 1 to 10," Daniece playfully ordered.

"Well, if you two must know, I did happen to meet someone new over lunch. He's tall, dark, and gorgeous, and he works for the F.B.I. We're meeting later this week to pick up where we left off."

"Would that be your tongue in his mouth, or his in yours!" laughingly blurted out Jenny as she burst into hysterics.

"For your information my immature co-worker, I believe that I may be in the opening stages of recruiting a strong ally in our effort to determine whether or not someone is bumping off our pensioners. It doesn't get any better than the F.B.I. when it comes to investigating, and this way I can casually feel my new friend out regarding if we're on to something or not, as opposed to having to request help directly."

"Did you say feel him out or feel him up?" replied Jenny impishly.

"Jennifer, you are impossible."

"All right you two, let's get back to work," said Daniece as she unsuccessfully attempted to repress a smile.

Jenny headed back to her cubicle giggling all the way, while Holly-Brit resumed floating towards her office, a faraway look in her eyes that spoke volumes.

"Miss McKinney, I would like to make you aware of my schedule for the coming week. There has been a change of plans. I will be jetting off to Germany on Tuesday to take a look at a company that I've had my eye on for sometime. They would be a good fit for Pharmacor, and I've just learned that they may be amenable at this time to enter into acquisition discussions. I'll call you from Europe with my hotel arrangements once I arrive. Due to the somewhat delicate nature of these talks, I'm not at liberty to divulge the name of the German company at this time. Please do your best to forestall any curiosity seekers in my absence on that matter. For regular affairs you have my e-mail address that I'll be checking twice daily. For emergencies, and I stress the word emergencies only, you may contact my cell phone. Good day Miss McKinney and I wish you a pleasant week." And with that, Jonas Trina took his next step toward his life's remaining goal.

CHAPTER 18

"That's better Danny boy. Just squeeze the trigger, don't jerk the trigger. A nice light touch is all you'll be needin' with a weapon like this. Fire off a few more rounds at the target and let's be havin' a look-see at yer fine Irish marksmanship."

Danny complied with the request, and after three more shots were fired, Ike retrieved the target via the wire pulley method at the indoor shooting range they had visited.

"Not bad, not bad at all," Ike half-lied as he held the barely damaged target in his large hands. Twenty rounds had managed nine blemishes on the target, but only 1 round had pierced anything but the target periphery. Ike knew that from the 40-yard range they had been shooting from, he would've been dead center with no less than 18 rounds on an average day. However, marksmanship was not totally important for the purpose Ike had in mind for his Irish mark.

"I could do better with a pint of Guinness under me belt."

"Tis well enough what you've shown me here. Yer a veritable Audie Murphy already me boy. Now what say we retire to that little pub I saw around the corner for a couple of pints, and a final review of the battle plans we've been discussin' these past few days."

"Yer on Mr. Michaels!"

The twosome retrieved their personal gear from a locker at the range and strolled out the door into the waning sunlight as the warm summer sunset cast a reddish glow on the western horizon. After a leisurely three-minute walk they arrived at the pub. A compact disc entertainment system was blaring loudly as they entered the smoke filled, dimly lit establishment. The loud music and the sparse crowd were perfect for their purposes. While Danny negotiated two pints of stout ale, Kevin/Ike laid claim to a secluded rear booth befitting the privacy requirements he had in mind for their conversation.

"Yer a good lad Danny Hughes, for fetchin' us these sweet swills. Here's hopin' the wind is always at yer back, and that yer in heaven an hour before the devil knows yer gone!" After the men toasted, Kevin/Ike took a healthy swig from his bottle to match that of his compatriot. "Now Danny let's review our plans for this comin' Wednesday, startin' from the top."

"Yes sir, Cap'n Michaels," shouted out Danny as he offered up a mock salute to Ike. Leaning forward so as not to shout and still be heard, he began to recite the particulars concerning their vengeful plans. "At 5:00 P.M. we meet at my place to assemble the necessary gear and armaments. We double check the gear and load up in my van. At 6:00 P.M.we leave for the thirty minute trip to the Pharmacor Social Center. We park in front of the building and stay out of sight as we observe the parking lot for the arrival of one Mr. Thomas Chauncy and friends. After their arrival, we wait for the sun to go down. Once it gets dark we carry the gear to the side of the building keeping a sharp eye out for police, loiterers, or cars entering the grounds. You go back to the van and park it around the next block where we'll make our getaway. When we are sure the coast is clear, we padlock the doors and then the fun begins. Is that right?"

"That's right Danny."

"With me on one side of the building and you on the other, Chauncy and the boys should have their work cut out for them wouldn't you say Kevin?"

"You betcha."

"To borrow a phrase, next Wednesday it looks like there's gonna be a hot time in the old town tonight!"

"You can say that again Danny my boy!"

"Waitress, get us two more ales 'cause we got some celebratin' of the future to do this evening," hollered out Danny to a passing server. Continuing on Danny stated; "Tis a bit of a pity that some innocents will have to share their fate."

"There are always collateral casualties in war. And remember Danny! This is a war that they started. We're just having them reap their just rewards. Payback, as they say, is truly a bitch."

"Yer right as rain there, Kevin, yes sir."

"Well drink up lad! It's Friday night and since last time I looked, neither of us has to be to work tomorrow, we might as well enjoy ourselves!"

"It looks like the final countdown for that miserable S.O.B. Chauncey and his buddies has begun."

"Yes it has." answered Kevin/Ike as he took a long swig on his bottle of ale. "For them and one other, them and one other," he thought.

As Danny and Ike traded toasts on the workingman's side of town, another meeting was taking place across town amidst more posh surroundings, as Holland and John finished dinner at the upscale Raging Bull saloon. Soft subtle lighting, the sweet pulsing sounds of an accomplished jazz band, and the after effects of a couple of snifters of Sambucco had done their parts to continue the evening's discourse.

"Well Holly-Brit, I think that you now know more about me than any human being with the possible exceptions of my mother and some snoops in the F.B.I. Human Resource Dept. Now, how about you? Who exactly is this alluring creature I find myself with this evening? From what royal lineage does she come from?" Holland shifted slightly in her seat and flashed a bit of an impish grin before she began.

"I hail from a small mining town just vest of Vladivostok dahling," said Holland with a coquettish smile and a fake Russian accent. While naturally, I could have stayed in Mother Russia, and quickly climbed the communist success ladder to become a high ranking member of the Politburo, I chose instead to emigrate to America. I vanted to see how you capitalists live, and to someday take back to the old country all of the secrets on how to overthrow you imperialist dogs! John and Holland both had a good chuckle over the ridiculous story and Holland's quick-witted acting ability.

"Actually John, my life has been a tad more mundane than that. I was born in the Greater Cleveland, Ohio area somewhere between twenty and thirty years ago. My mother, who I adore to this day, is one hundred percent Hungarian, and my dear father has English, Welsh, German, Irish, and Swiss ancestry with a little Cherokee Indian thrown in for good measure, somewhere along the line. I have one older brother and a younger sister. I went to a state university where I studied business and literature and Pharmacor is the first bonafide business job that I've had since I graduated from college. I enjoy tennis, swimming, jogging, and reading cheesy romantic novels. Also I love to play with my parent's Berniece Mountain dog Baxter when I stop over at their house, which I do every couple of weeks since they don't live too far away. And that Mr. Snoopy Dog F.B.I. agent is all you're going to get out of me this evening without a warrant." John laughingly said that for starters this would be just fine. However he did admit that he might have to get together in the future for more interrogation depending on how the rest of the evening went.

"One thing which I still don't know though is the subject that you alluded to the other day which you and your co-workers had found so interesting."

"Oh that. It's nothing really John. I doubt that you would find it very interesting."

"Try me."

With the hook set, Holland began to reel in her catch. "Well you see, in my position at Pharmacor, a lot of personnel information comes across my desk. This applies to retiree information as well. Awhile back, the third party administrator responsible for handling our pensioner's accounts came to us with some disturbing statistics. It seems that Pharmacor retirees are dying off at a tremendously accelerated rate compared to normal expected death rates for a company of our size. This prompted both the administrator and us to do some investigative work as to the causes of death in these cases. We found a very high number of retirees having died in ways that would not be classified as natural causes."

"When you say not natural causes, could you enlighten me as to what some of the causes were?"

"Sure. Many died in car accidents. There were a few boating accidents. A couple deaths were hunting accidents. Several others were killed during the commission of crimes. And the biggie, over 120 perished due to a Legionnaire's disease outbreak at a company sponsored retirement party."

"How many people are we talking about, and in what timeframe?"

"Approximately 160-165 people have died un-natural deaths in a six-month period."

"Wow that does sound like a lot. Have you talked with your superiors about this deadly aberration?"

"We've tried."

"And what was their take on the matter?"

"Our C.E.O. Jonas Trina is inclined to chalk it all up to a short term run of bad luck which will correct itself soon without any interference."

"I take it you don't concur with that rosy outlook."

"Absolutely not! I can't at this point prove it, but several of us at Pharmacor feel strongly that someone is going around bumping off our pensioners. We don't know why, but we do have some suspects in mind. In a few of the deaths, witnesses said that they had seen a tall, middle-aged Caucasian male with a moustache shortly before the deaths occurred. I had our personnel department review the files of former employees who left on a sour note with the company. We came up with three who matched the previously mentioned description."

"Did you mention that to your Mr. Trina?"

"I sure did, and he dismissed it. He said he was well aware of the death rate, and that he had been monitoring disgruntled former employees to make sure they wouldn't "go postal" on us as a company. Instead of thanking us for our diligence, he made us feel that we've been abusing our job performances and that we should cease looking into the matter if we knew what was good for our continued employment at Pharmacor."

"Is it possible that he in fact has been keeping an eye on possible threatening types?"

"Unfortunately, it is a slight possibility. When he first became our C.E.O. he asked all department heads to submit a list of possible candidates who might have an axe to grind against Pharmacor."

"As I see it Holly-Brit, I'm afraid that from what you've just told me, you don't have a leg to stand on in this matter. It sounds like your C.E.O. is on top of things and has acted in a more than responsible manner to do all he can to head off trouble before it starts. My advice to you would be to drop your investigative activities and focus on keeping your job."

"But that's just it John. Jonas Trina is one of the least caring people to ever walk the face of the earth. People are dying on his watch and he's dismissing the whole thing as a passing fad that will just fade away like a puff of smoke. I'm not buying it. Furthermore it strikes me as damn peculiar that these abnormal statistics just so happened to manifest themselves shortly after he became C.E.O!"

"You didn't tell me that."

"It's true. Within a couple months of his taking over, retirees started dropping like flies."

"Now wait a-minute Holland. You're not suggesting that your own C.E.O. has been running around knocking off retirees. That's absurd!"

"Is it?"

"Of course it is. Ignoring the fact that a captain of industry doesn't have the time or the criminal acumen to pull off crimes of this magnitude, what possible motive could he have for doing this?"

"How about millions of dollars in bonus money?"

"Pharmacor pays a bonus to their C.E.O. based on the number of ex-employees they bump off? Doesn't sound like much of a company recruitment incentive plan to me if that info ever hits the streets." Even Holland had to smile at that retort.

"That's not exactly the way it works John Kazek, F.B.I." said Holland as she lightened the mood herself. "My understanding is that Jonas negotiated a contract that tied a substantial amount of his compensation to his statistical performance. If he increases our profitability by a certain amount, he stands to pick up millions in incentive pay. I hadn't figured this out until the past couple of days, but do you know that with the number of dead retirees we no longer pay retirement benefits to, our profitability has gone up almost 2 million dollars. That could very well be the amount needed to insure that he hits his incentive clause numbers and reaps the windfall."

"Whoa there Holly-Brit. Even assuming that what you just said is true, we only have a small number of actual crimes thus far, don't we? I mean I've got to believe that the local police checked out these deaths, and except for the killings involved with robberies and such, it sounds like the majority have been attributed to accidents and the Legionnaire's disease incident. Your C.E.O. could very well just be benefiting from some extraordinary circumstances. I'll tell you this! I sure as heck wouldn't want to be the one to accuse him of wrongdoing on the scale you've drawn up here based on what you've told me so far. If you were lucky, you'd just lose your job. If he chose to press the matter, he very possibly could have the makings of a strong case of slander against you. Furthermore, depending on the man himself, your life could be put in danger if he is in fact involved with foul play in the abrupt demise of these pensioners, as you seem to think. Anyway you look at it, I'd advise you to leave well enough alone and concentrate on your human resource duties."

"But if I do that, then he gets away with murder! Plus the lives of innocent people will continue to be in jeopardy."

"It sounds to me like you've already tried and convicted this man, without the benefit of due process of law. You might want to cut this guy some slack considering that as of now you've very little proof that crimes have actually been committed. Not to mention the fact that you can't tie him to anything even if crimes have been committed."

"You don't know him like I know him."

"That is true, but I do know the law, and right now I don't see where he has broken it. Now why don't we change the subject and get back to enjoying ourselves. In my humble opinion, it would be a terrible waste of good food, good spirits, good music, and great companionship to not join the crowd on the dance floor. Are you game?"

Feigning a pout, Holland stuck out her lower lip to let John know that she still disagreed with him. Then she brightened up a bit saying; "I suppose that I could be persuaded to get out there and do a little "Funky Chicken" or something, on one condition."

"And just exactly what might that be?"

"That you would agree to assist me in looking into this matter further if I can supply you with more credible proof of wrongdoing."

"You really do intend on continuing with this don't you."

"There are too many unanswered questions for the matter to be resolved at this point."

"All right Holland. I'll give you a definite maybe. If you can come up with more substantial evidence of some criminal involvement in this matter, then I'll do what I can on a personal level to get you some investigative assistance. However, don't misconstrue this to mean that the F.B.I. is going to become involved with this in any way. Our rules of engagement are pretty cut and dried. Only if it falls within our jurisdiction can we join the fray. However, I can use my contacts with the local police to solicit some aid on your behalf. Also, I could do some snooping around on my own in an unofficial capacity to help if that might be beneficial. Now, enough of this, let's boogie!" With that the couple rose as one, proceeding arm-in-arm to the dance floor to add their own stylish steps to fellow romance-seekers swaying to the hypnotic beat and soulful sax.

Hours later the twosome strolled leisurely up the walkway to Holland's apartment building. Holland had told John that it was unnecessary for him to follow her from the nightclub back to her apartment, but he insisted, citing that one could never be too safe with all of these evil types such as Jonas Trina lurking about. They had shared a good laugh over that and Holland had reluctantly acquiesced to allow John to accompany her. Arriving at her apartment complex, the twosome began walking up a long walkway to the front of Holland's building. As John stopped to admire the twinkling stars radiating their luminescence, Holland slipped her hand into John's, and joined his skyward gaze. The warmth of his touch coupled with the feverish emotions racing through her body was heightening her desire. As they silently stood focusing on the celestial wonders, the urge to kiss and be kissed was almost overwhelming to Holland. As if by extra sensory perception, John suddenly shifted his expressive eyes to gaze into Holland's and slowly, wordlessly brought his lips to meet hers. Spasms of pent up emotion cascaded through her veins as Holland opened her lips to return the kiss with a fervor that surprised both of them. John responded to Holland's opened lips by opening his, and was rewarded by an eager inquisitive tongue, jousting with his own in an impassioned unrehearsed duet. Holland's senses were swimming in pleasure as she greedily drank up the electric sensuality of the moment. John also was experiencing vibrations, too delicious to let go as he ground his lips to Holland's and returned her ardor.

The kiss lasted almost a minute. Holland was the first to regain command of her faculties, and she lightly, but insistently began to draw back from their embrace. John slowly opened his eyes to meet Holland's.

"Wow," both of them exhaled in unison as they savored the moment and the residual sensations coursing through their bodies.

"I'd better be getting inside before my neighbors start even more rumors about me than they already are spreading," said Holland as she took a hesitant step in the door's direction.

"You're probably right, we're probably better off not rushing things. At least that's what my brain is telling me. Other parts of my body are admittedly sending contradictory signals," returned John. "May I call you tomorrow?"

"Do you think I'll let you live if you don't?" giggled Holland as she took another step toward the door. "Remember John Kazek F.B.I., I know where you park your butt for lunch, and I'd hate to see anything bad happen to your bench."

"Just remember young lady, I have a couple friends in the F.B.I. who are pretty good at solving crimes, and they would probably apprehend the culprit very quickly should my bench run afoul of some evildoer."

The couple separated more with Holland making a solitary path to her building's entrance. As she unlocked the door, she whirled around and rushed back to John, kissing him lightly on the cheek and lips before beginning a slow backpedal back to her building.

"Call me," she silently mouthed as she entered her building, leaving John breathless in anticipation of their next rendezvous.

The special private phone line rang at Ike Steele's residence and it was answered on the second ring with a simple "Yes".

"Do you remember a certain favor you did for me in the office of one Stewart Jones years ago?"

"Of course"

"I need you to perform that same favor for me in a couple of Pharmacor's offices next week. I've sent you an e-mail with explicit instructions. I'll be out of town this coming week. Is everything set for the festivities next Wednesday evening?"

"All set."

"Good. I shall look forward to reading about the results sometime Thursday. Remember, you are not to contact me this week under any circumstances! My European trip must serve as an airtight alibi should the need arise. I've arranged a substantial bonus to be credited to your account in anticipation of your completion of this coming week's events. I hope you don't mind."

"Much obliged."

"Very well, that will be all for now. Happy hunting! And I wish you success in all of your endeavors. Have a pleasant evening."

"You too."

CHAPTER 19

The miles on Autobahn E48/70 flew by effortlessly under the wheels of the E class Mercedes sedan. Jonas gazed admiringly at the Bavarian countryside as he sped past rolling hills speckled with countless stands of evergreens that were native to this part of Germany. Though the calendar said it was the last week of July, the temperature was a rather cool 18 degrees Centigrade that paled in comparison to the 95 degrees Fahrenheit he had experienced in Cleveland the day before his departure. A road sign showed Bamberg to be only 25 kilometers further, which reassured Jonas that he was making excellent time. He did not wish to be late in arriving at his final destination, the town of Bayreuth that lay just to the east of Bamberg. This was the home of Richard Wagner the famous nineteenth century German composer, whose works were celebrated every year in Bayreuth during this particular week. Wagner was a particular favorite of Jonas, and he was thrilled when the meeting with the Imam's emissaries was scheduled to coincide with the Wagnerian festival in Bayreuth. He had procured a seat at the Festpielhaus in Bayreuth for performances of Wagner's romantic opera Tannhauser on both Tuesday and Wednesday evening. He had no intention of inviting the emissaries to join him due to the possibility of their detracting from the experience that Jonas was anticipating.

Bamberg came up on the right, and Jonas could make out the spires of the Karmelitenkloster as he approached the town. This was a 12th century hospital-abbey belonging to the Carmelite order. Established atop seven hills ala ancient Rome, and situated at the confluence of several branches of the river Regnitz, Bamberg boasted a rich heritage for both artistic and brewing skills. For a brief moment Jonas contemplated detouring off the Autobahn and visiting downtown Bamberg. The travel guide at the Frankfurt airport had spoken glowingly of the beauty of the Domplatz that was the center square of Bamberg. Numerous impressive historical sites such as the Baroque Bishop's Palace built in 1763 or the stately cathedral of St. Peter and St. George could be viewed here.

Jonas however, was a man on a mission, and he was not one to be sidetracked. Continuing on past Bamberg, he soon came to Autobahn E22 which would lead him into Bayreuth. While appreciative of the rolling hills and omnipresent evergreens, Jonas was amazed by the vast numbers of red tiled roofs on the residences he whisked past. He deduced an abundance of red clay indigenous to this region must lay behind the propensity to finish one's roof in such a manner. Distracted by the scenery, Jonas came upon Bayreuth quicker than he had expected. Pulling off to the side of the roadway, he reviewed his directions to the hotel. Satisfied that he had his bearings, Jonas resumed his drive and soon arrived at the Therese Haus hotel.

The Therese Haus was perched atop a large hill with a backdrop of conifers and a small lake that made for a very picturesque setting. The hotel was actually based in a large 200-year old fieldstone villa that featured old world charm coupled with upgrades to provide guests with every modern convenience. In addition to two restaurants and a lounge, the villa boasted a sauna, solarium, and an Olympic size swimming pool.

After checking in under the prearranged alias of Jonathon Saxton, Jonas made his way to the smaller of the two restaurants to quench the ravenous hunger he had worked up on the drive from Frankfurt. Requesting a window seat, Jonas had a beautiful view of the town of Bayreuth below. Hordes of tourists were already wandering the streets searching for souvenirs, landmarks, and refreshments. Jonas hated crowds, but he was mentally preparing himself to stoically endure the masses he knew he would encounter these next days. Such he knew, was the price to pay in order to experience Wagner the master, in his element.

Jonas made his menu selections, and soon a large tray of delicacies was forthcoming via a fair-haired maiden outfitted in traditional garb. The maiden's bodice featured an ample bosom that was threatening to overflow its linen constraints. He couldn't help but be reminded of some beer labels he'd seen over the years for which this young lady certainly could have served as the model. The platter was set down in front of Jonas, and the server disappeared to dispense her charms elsewhere. Set before him was a large bowl of Leberknodelsuppe and a plate of Kartoffelsalat. The suppe's liver dumplings were both aromatic and filling, as was the Bavarian version of potato salad. A steaming cup of kaffee with an apple charlotte accompaniment provided a fitting end to the repast. His hunger assuaged, Jonas now turned his intentions toward taking in the sights before preparing to attend this evening's opera performance.

His first destination was the Villa Wahnfried. This was the final home and resting place of Wagner and his wife Cosima. Though the home was destroyed during World War II, it was lovingly restored in the 70's. After paying his respects at the tomb of Wagner in the garden of Villa Wahnfried, Jonas went in search of the Franz-Liszt Museum that was also located in Bayreuth. Liszt was another accomplished composer of the nineteenth century, and in fact it was his daughter whom Wagner married. A half hour was all that was needed to peruse the museum, and now Jonas set off in search of the piece de resistance of this afternoon's impromptu tour.

Situated less than a quarter mile from the Liszt museum, was the Markgrafliches Opernhaus. This remarkable opera house was world-renowned for its baroque beauty. Upon entering the opera house, Jonas was overcome by the sheer grandeur and opulence that had been handcrafted into this 1740's masterpiece to produce such a magnificent edifice. From the rich wooden railings which separated each individual booth, to the golden lighting, to the breathtakingly beautiful painting on the vaulting, to the immense size and scope of the grand hall itself; the Markgrafliches was perfection personified. Jonas felt a sense of inadequacy as he tried to imagine the genius of Giuseppe Galli Bibiena and his son Carlo who had designed this revered structure.

Jonas spent over an hour examining every nook and cranny of the impressive structure. He would've liked to spend even more time, but having glanced at his watch, he knew that he must return to his hotel and get ready to attend the evening's operatic performance. Following a short walk, he arrived back at the Therese Haus. As Jonas entered the villa, he proceeded to the concierge's desk to inquire if there were any messages. Not surprisingly he was presented with a large envelope that had been delivered for him. Opening the envelope, he pulled out a green handkerchief, and a brief note. The note stated that he was to meet his two emissaries at the Bayreuth Bistro restaurant tomorrow at noon, and that he was to wear the green kerchief in his breast pocket.

Jonas subtly began to take note of his surroundings to see if he could detect anyone examining him. However, except for a pair of elderly matrons, and a young couple with their preschool twins in tow, the area was deserted. The envelope had a Turkish postmark on it, so it was entirely possible that the emissaries had mailed it a couple of days ago and that they would be flying in tomorrow to meet with him as scheduled. However, that would not be the way he would do it, if the roles were reversed. He would want to be assured that his subject was not being followed and that he was not being set up if in fact he was a terrorist, as he figured the emissaries were.

Assuming that he was being watched, and that he in fact had been under surveillance since he arrived in Germany, Jonas proceeded to his suite. He was not unduly concerned about being watched, because his mission was a sincere one. He had not done anything to warrant suspicion, nor would he during his stay, because his goals meshed with the goals of those whose partnership he sought. He was quite impressed with whoever was coordinating the assumed surveillance. He had not detected even the slightest hint that he was being observed throughout the entire day.

Arriving at his suite, Jonas changed into an exquisite Italian suit and glanced around the room to be reassured that all was in place. He noticed one of his suitcases was on the bed at a bit of an angle. To an ordinary person, this would not be noticed. However Jonas, as was his nature, always laid his suitcases with the handles exactly parallel to the edge of the bed. It was one of myriad obsessive habits he had developed over the years. Since the room was fully prepared prior to his arrival, there would have been no reason for the suitcase to be moved by any hotel staff. Jonas smiled as he considered the implication. It appeared that perhaps the hotel staff was in fact a part of the surveillance team, and that his luggage had been examined. These people were pro's and they had influence. Both of which were good and necessary things in their business.

Hours later Jonas returned to his lodging, the power and majesty of Tannhauser still fresh in his mind. His ears were still ringing from a combination of the performers singing and the boisterous applause from the appreciative audience. The opera was all that he had hoped for and more. He was especially taken with the scene of the minstrel's contest in the singing hall. All in all it was a memorable occasion, and he was already looking forward to tomorrow's repeat performance. While he didn't detect any surveillance this evening, he still had the feeling that he was being watched. It would be good if he were being watched, because that would help assure his soon-to-be benefactors that he had indeed come alone. Quickly undressing, Jonas got into bed still mentally enjoying a replay of the opera's highpoints. He would allow himself this one evening of recreational indulgence before getting back to the tasks at hand. There would be plenty of time in the morning to finalize his preparations for the all-important meeting with the emissaries.

The midmorning sun peeked above the tops of the conifers, forcing Jonas to squint as he finished his breakfast on the veranda. The sun's reflection off the small lake made the greenish blue water sparkle and shimmer, adding to the beauty of the Bavarian setting. He downed the last of his kaffee, and pondered taking one more bite of his Reibekuchen. Though the potato pancakes were scrumptious, he declined more, knowing that in a few short hours he would be eating again with his new hoped for benefactors. Replacing a notebook and jeweled pen back into his luxurious briefcase, Jonas made his way back into his suite to finish dressing.

As he closed the door to his suite, Jonas began a mental review of the most important topics on his meeting agenda. While he recognized the need for cordiality and diplomacy, he knew that he must gain control of the meeting if it was to be brought to a satisfactory conclusion. Unless his demands were met on certain criteria, there was no sense in bringing the proposed partnership to fruition. However, the talks must be conducted with an air of respect so that both parties were satisfied of their needs being addressed and met. He felt confident that he could pull it off as long as a deep-seated sense of mutual trust and need was established.

He arrived at the restaurant precisely ten minutes early, as was his custom. A lovely hostess seated Jonas at a choice table. Her sense of profound nervousness lent credence to the distinct possibility that she was working on behalf of the emissaries. Correctly surmising that several minutes of final scrutiny would now take place prior to the actual meeting, Jonas readjusted the green kerchief and opened the world newspaper to affect a casual demeanor. A half hour later, two distinguished looking Middle Eastern types approached his table. Jonas stood up to greet the two men.

"Ahlah Wa Sahlan," said the taller of the two emissaries as he offered his hand in friendship to Jonas.

"Ahlah Wa Sahlan," returned Jonas in a traditional Arabic greeting to both men as they exchanged handshakes. In impeccable English, the leader of the emissaries introduced the duo.

"Mr. Saxton, my name is Tariq Al-Salem. This is Nishil Najir. We are pleased to make your acquaintance. You have traveled far to meet with us. I trust you trip was a pleasant one."

"The trip and the accommodations have been most satisfactory. Was your journey here also acceptable?"

"Most agreeable I assure you. Let's all sit shall we?"

As the trio seated themselves, Jonas took stock of his potential partners. Tariq was slightly over six feet tall with a thin moustache, perfect grooming, and a slender but wiry strong type physique. He appeared to have stepped right off the front page of "Gentlemen's Quarterly" with his striking good looks and expensive suit that smacked of stylish London tailoring. His supremely confident air told of a man who knew what he wanted in life, and was used to getting it. His partner was at least four inches taller than Tariq, and had an exceedingly thick lustrous black mane. He gave the impression of extreme physical strength and Jonas guessed he was probably the bodyguard type sent to assist Tariq should the need for protection arise. He too was nattily attired. Both men appeared to be in their late thirties to early forties.

"What do you recommend for lunch?" inquired Jonas.

"All of the dishes are exemplary here. I particularly enjoy the Sauerbraten, but really you can't go wrong with any of the entrees," said Tariq.

"Excellent! Now, are we at liberty to speak freely here in the restaurant?"

"We are amongst friends."

"That's reassuring. I've had the feeling that I've been amongst your friends ever since I arrived in Germany."

"Have we been that obvious?"

"On the contrary, your friends are excellent at what they do. I've detected nothing." Rather it was a feeling and a supposition. If I was in your line of work, and I had a similar type of proposal to meet, I would have me followed. If I could be so bold, at what point did they begin?"

"When you landed, and if I might add, you have not been without our companionship since."

"You must maintain a large staff in Germany."

"We have many sympathizers here who believe our cause is just. Tell me, did you enjoy the Tannhauser opera last evening?"

"It was all that I had hoped for and more."

"Excellent! I'll let you in on a little secret. In addition to two of our people in the audience who had you under surveillance, one of the performers was keeping tabs on you as well."

Just then a male server appeared to recite the daily specials and to take the food orders of the trio. Once the selections were made, he disappeared, which allowed the conversation to resume.

"Mr. Saxton, do you believe our cause is just?"

"Mr. Al-Salem, if I had any problems with your cause, do you believe that I would've made contact with the Imam?"

"The Imam spoke very highly of you. He said that you were a great benefactor in the Afghani war against the Soviet aggressors. I believe they gave you the title of the Lion Seeker."

"Yes. I valued the Imam's friendship while in Afghanistan long ago when we shared some common bonds. We have maintained correspondence over the years, and I know the Imam to be a person of supreme intelligence, great integrity, and devotion to cause. I propose we work together in order to assist each other in furthering our mutual goals. This time the battleground would be within the United States. I am now in a position to be of significant help to your cause, both financially and strategically. I can personally provide significant funds, and assist you in having easy access to soft visible targets in America along with a safe haven to conceal your people's whereabouts. I have the power to get your people into places they would have difficulty gaining access to on their own."

"That is most generous of you Mr. Saxton. To what do we owe this newfound offer of assistance?"

"Let's just say that my own interests would also be served at the same time if I could select the targets, at least in the early stages."

"Your proposal is most interesting Mr. Saxton. How could we be assured that you are not setting us up to hand over to your authorities in a counterterrorist sting operation?"

"I appreciate your concern in this matter. I suppose that I could point to the assistance I gave to the Afghani people as proof of my sincere intentions on your behalf, but I realize the weakness of that. Therefore I have arranged a dramatic demonstration. Very soon I will prove my devotion to my own cause, and show your people the seriousness that I bring to the table today. In less than 24 hours, there will be a great tragedy in Cleveland, Ohio which I have set in motion. Over fifty people will be killed. The majority of those killed will have ties to my company which is named Pharmacor. Hopefully this will convince you of both my sincerity and my own organization's abilities. I should imagine that your local television news or the newspapers would report on a disaster of this magnitude at least by the end of the week. Believe me. I have no interest in doing anything other than working together to achieve common goals."

It was at this point that the server reappeared, along with a helper. Each was carrying a large platter of Bavarian cuisine. The emissaries had chosen the sauerbraten with sides of kartoffelklossen and apfelmus. Their roast beef entrees gave off a pungent aroma that contrasted significantly with the potato dumplings and apple puree accompaniments. Jonas' salivary glands involuntarily began to moisten as his pichelsteiner was placed in front of him. He had chosen this combination meat/potato/and vegetable dish for its relatively low caloric content, and the fact that he felt it would not offend his Islamic host's culinary sensibilities. This also would allow him to feast upon a piece of kuchen for dessert without guilt. As the men began to eat, the lead emissary resumed the conversation.

"Mr. Saxton, you speak of our helping you to further your own goals and objectives. Tell me if you would please, what would cause a man to turn against his own countrymen?"

"In answer to your question, I'll choose to reserve most of the reason at this moment. Let's suffice it to say that my life has been dedicated to a singular purpose for approximately three decades, and now with your help and my direction, I can readily see a successful conclusion forthcoming."

"It sounds to me as though you've given the matter a good bit of thought."

"Mr. Al-Salem, may you be the judge."

With that Jonas reached for his briefcase. That prompted an instantaneous reaction from Najir as he picked up his steak knife and brandished it in a threatening fashion. Recognizing the intent behind the powerful man's quick defensive posture, Jonas slowed his movements as a smile crept across his face.

"No need for that my friend, I'm merely going to grab a plan set from my briefcase for you gentlemen to peruse at your leisure."

Najir eased slightly, but he still remained vigilant, watching Jonas' every move as he slowly extracted the prepared documents from his leather valise. "Here you will find a detailed workable plan to make a significant statement for your cause within the United States heartland. This will strike fear into America as they begin to realize that you are even more capable than they had envisioned. I assume that at this time you have operatives in deep cover within America who are only awaiting orders to commence an attack. You don't have to confirm or deny this, but I would also assume that your operatives have caches of explosives that they could utilize to pull off a mission, if the operation were deemed worthy. I believe that you will find that my plan would generate a great deal of trauma to the American psyche. If the American populace begins to feel like the hunted rather than the hunter, they may begin to pressure their leaders to adopt a new stance in the Middle East."

"You appear to be very committed to your cause also Mr. Trina."

"As I stated before, this is my life's mission."

"We will take your offer under advisement with our superiors and shall give you an answer when a decision has been reached. I will tell my people that the opinion I have of you is that you are both truthful and sincere in your desire to help us. That cannot hurt your chances. You will be staying at the Therese Haus until Friday morning I believe?"

"Doubtful. I imagine at some point early tomorrow morning I will be contacted by my company's officials and made aware of the tragedy. At that point I shall be required to show proper concern and return immediately to the United States."

"We shall try to secure an answer for you prior to your departure. If the answer is yes, we will have someone call your room and ask for Mr. White. If we will not join forces with you, the caller will ask for Mr. Black. If an answer cannot be arranged before you leave, we will e-mail you with our decision. Do you understand?"

"Yes"

"All communication after this week will be conducted via e-mail. Should we decide in your favor, I will, at that time, furnish you with all necessary e-mail addresses. This will conclude our discussion for today. Your meal has been provided, and you are now free to go Mr. Saxton."

The trio arose as one, and after perfunctory handshakes were exchanged, the two Middle Easterners made their way out the door and disappeared into the crowd of Wagner enthusiasts. As Jonas made his exit into the bright July midday sun, he replayed the events of the past hour. He felt good about how the meeting had evolved and he was confident that the proposal would be given serious consideration by the decision makers within Tariq's organization. There was a lot at stake for both parties. While his offer represented an opportunity to breech America in ways heretofore inaccessible to his Arab hosts, it also opened them up to an appreciable element of risk should Jonas be attempting to perform a sting operation on behalf of Western governments to expose the terrorists. However, the Cleveland tragedy should allay their concern in that regard. Time would tell if they deemed the risk worth taking.

Jonas opened the door to his luxurious suite at the Therese Haus and clicked on the light. After hanging up his suit coat, he undid his tie and draped it over a hanger, all the while humming a tune from Tannhauser. This evening's performance had been every bit as enjoyable as the first, and as usually happens with operas, he had gained some additional insight from the second viewing. Unsnapping his Movado, he placed the watch on the nightstand beside his king-sized bed. He gave a brief glance in the direction of the telephone to see if the message light was lit, and was gratified to see it was not.

After a short stint in the restroom, Jonas returned to his bed and finished undressing. As he turned down the blanket and sheets, he glanced once again at his watch which showed the local time to be midnight. Turning off the bed stand light plunged the room into total darkness. The drapes on the suite's French-doors that opened to the veranda were slightly parted. He could see across the lake that some revelers had built a bonfire amidst the conifers. By the light of the fire, he could make out dancing figures whose sounds of merriment carried across the water and could be easily heard even through the closed doors. A brief thought entered his mind that across a much wider expanse of water another party of sorts should be just about ready to begin. However, there would be no dancing and certainly no cause for merriment. He'd wished that he could've arranged to have a trademark gold watch placed at the scene, but in this case, that was too risky. Jonas closed his eyes, and within ten minutes subconscious visions of costumed minstrel singers had blotted out all vestiges of reality from his mind.

CHAPTER 20

"Didn't I tell ya Chauncy and his boys would be showin' up this evenin'? Just look at him struttin' like a rooster he is. Well Thomas Chauncy ya won't be struttin' so high and mighty for much longer, right Kevin?"

"Yes sir, right as rain Danny."

Kevin checked the traffic on the street for the twentieth time since they had parked their van across from the Pharmacor Social Center. He was relieved that no police cars were in sight. The midsummer sun was continuing to make its downward arc, and within an hour it should be nothing but a reddish orange afterglow on the Western horizon. Another fifteen minutes beyond that and it should be dark enough to commence operations.

"Ya know Danny, I'm havin' second thoughts about just sittin' here waitin'. I'm feelin' kind of exposed. What if someone's takin' a gander at us right now and wonderin' why two guys would be sittin' and swelterin' in a muggy van on a hot July night for almost three hours? They might get a little nosy and call the police to have a little look see at what we're up to. I thought there was an ice cream place a mile or so back the way we came. What say we go and get a couple of cones or somethin' to pass the time and not look too conspicuous! We can always look for Chauncy's car before we begin, ta make sure he hasn't taken off while we're gone."

"Sounds good by me Kevin, let's do it."

An hour later the men had once again taken up position across from the Social Center. Having verified that Chauncy and his boys were still on the premises, they began to unload their equipment. Two wheelbarrows were pulled out of the van. One was filled with what appeared to be spraying equipment for bug infestations, two gasoline cans, some mason jars, strips of cloth, chain and two heavy duty locks. Into the other wheelbarrow were two AR-15 rifles, ammunition clips, a couple of Glock 9mm handguns, a basketball, and two duffel bags. This wheelbarrow was covered by a canvas tarp. Ike had on work gloves that he'd worn for several hours. They wheeled the supplies across the street, and set up shop on the covered porch that ran around the perimeter of the structure. Ike could see through the windows that a bingo game was being conducted in the main hall. Through the window of a side room he could see that a couple of card games were in progress. The men began spraying the outside of the building. Shortly after they'd begun their spraying, the front door opened, and out stepped a couple of men about to enjoy a cigarette break. Ike, with a spray gun in hand, took the lead.

"Gentlemen, ya wouldn't want to be doin' that right here right now if ya don't believe in self-immolation. We've already begun sprayin' fer termites and such, and the chemicals we use are highly flammable. So, if ya don't wish ta be a human torch, I suggest ya refrain from smokin' fer a wee bit and go inside ta spread the word to yer companions. We should be done in about 15 minutes or so, and another 15 minutes after that the chemicals should be dry enough so's a dropped cigarette shouldn't bother anything. But not right now!"

With that the two men begrudgingly obliged and disappeared back into the building. Looking into the side room window, Danny could see that the two would be smokers had gone up to Chauncy and were discussing something with him. Chauncy, looking irritated, arose from his seat and headed for the door.

"Hell Kevin, here comes Chauncy. No doubt he'll be comin' to raise some kinda stink with our sprayin' at this hour. What are we goin' ta do. We'll be screwed fer sure if he recognizes me."

"Danny, you go hide around back. I'll take care of the honorable Mr. Chauncy. Now begone with ya." With that Danny took off around back, and ten seconds later the front door opened.

"What the hell's the meaning of spraying for bugs at 10:00 P.M. on a weeknight? My friends tell me that they can't even catch a smoke out here because of your screwin' around. Who the hell authorized this little spraying party of yours anyway? I certainly wasn't made aware of any order to spray for bugs, and if there was to be any spraying, I sure as hell should've been notified!"

"Well my good man, I've got a work order back in the truck that says you folks were in need of our services. Somethin' about a termite infestation I think. As far as sprayin' late at night, that's the best time ta catch the little buggers in their nests so's that you can get the whole mess of 'em at once insteada havin' ta repeat applications of our termite love potion here."

"I'm going back inside to make a couple of phone calls. You can start packing up your gear buddy, because your spraying has just come to an end for this evening." With that said, Chauncy wheeled around, and reentered the building.

As soon as Chauncy disappeared, Danny returned. "Kevin, what are we to do now?"

"Danny! Get one of the gasoline cans, and start sloshin' it round the buildin' on the other side. I'll do the same here. Then fill one of the jars with gasoline and stick a strip of cloth in it. Light that like we practiced, and throw it in the back door. Close the back door, then chain it and lock it so's they can't open it. Then grab a rifle and some ammo and go back ta yer side of the buildin'. Shoot anyone that try's to get out the windows on yer side. I'll do the same on my side, and I'll send a little flaming callin' card in the front door and lock that way out meself."

Both men sprung into action. As Ike sloshed gas around his side, he could see Chauncy on his phone. His red-faced histrionics meant that someone was getting a tongue-lashing. Little did Chauncy know, but this would be the last verbal whipping that he would ever give to anyone. When Ike was satisfied that he had sufficiently wet his side, he filled a jar with gasoline and put a strip of cloth in it. He lit a match and threw it onto the side porch. A gigantic whoosh and a rapidly expanding flame pronounced his efforts a success. A second whoosh moments later around the other side of the building told of Danny's results. Screams from the rear of the building assured Ike that the back entrance had been taken care of by Danny. Ike moved to the front entrance and lit the cloth strip. He opened the front door, and threw the gas filled jar into the empty vestibule. The flaming liquid immediately set some curtains ablaze, and the eager flames began to march across the wooden floor devouring everything it its path.

Almost immediately screams and shrieks of panic began to issue from within the hall. The simple predictability of the reactions of those trapped inside the building would've been somewhat humorous if the end result of their collective efforts were not to ultimately prove so utterly tragic. Those nearest to the rear entrance when the first firebomb was thrown in raced for the front entrance. Those towards the front of the building who saw the firebomb thrown in the front entrance raced for the rear. Those in the side rooms who witnessed the "whoosh" of the porch fire on their side of the building bolted for the safety of the center hall. This gave the pandemonium within the Social Center the appearance of the proverbial "Chinese fire drill" with groups of panic-stricken victims bypassing each other in their futile efforts to escape.

Ultimately the sheer impossibility of a safe, controlled escape sank into each and every person inside the now blazing Social Center. As the smoke and fire within the walls and ceiling began to gain ground on the perimeter of the edifice, it forced the group into a tight circle within the center hall. The howls of horror from within nearly drowned out the roar of the fire. One could almost taste the terror written upon the faces of those who were about to die amidst the growing conflagration.

Danny located Chauncy on the edge of the crowd. His calculating eyes were darting to and fro as they weighed the chances of one daring escape plan over another. Danny felt that he could read the innermost thoughts of that bastard Chauncy, as he would certainly try something drastic rather than simply succumb to the inevitable. Suddenly Chauncy broke from the crowd and raced back into one of the side rooms. He emerged from the room with a blanket and headed for the restroom. He came out a half a minute later with a soaking blanket that he wrapped around himself. A grim smile came over Chauncy as he headed at a trot towards one of the side windows. It almost appeared that he was deriding the others for not being as clever as he was in affecting an escape. His smile turned to confusion, then to terror as he recognized Danny Hughes just beyond the flaming porch. Hughes was behind the business end of an AR-15 he had pointed at Chauncy who was about to launch himself through the window.

"See ya in hell Chauncy!" screamed Danny as he loosed three shots into the torso of his nemesis. Chauncy's lifeless body slumped against the blazing wall and the wet blanket began to smolder. Next he fired several random rounds into the crowd within the burning building to let them know that there was no escaping death outside of the Center either. A feeding frenzy of power over life and death had usurped the mind of Danny Hughes, and he was incapable of overcoming it. The mind numbing screams and the terrified cries of those literally being roasted alive served only to amplify his bloodlust. Two flaming bodies simultaneously burst through adjoining windows as a couple of Chauncy's cronies sought to escape the inferno. Danny calmly fired two rounds at close range into each of the human torches as they lay blazing on the flame filled porch.

The nightmarish scene reminded Danny of a time long ago when he had poured gasoline down a ground hive of black bees and set it ablaze. He had been fascinated by the attempts of the bees to escape the burning hole. Their wings would shrivel and melt as they reached the flaming entrance, and they would either fall back into the flaming aperture, or flop down pathetically by the edge of the hive hole to be consumed in the blazing grass surrounding it.

Above the roar and crackle of the fire, and the screams of those trapped within the building, sirens could be heard approaching. Ike took cover behind an oversized bush just as a hook and ladder, and a pump truck came to an abrupt halt in the street directly in front of the Social Center. As the driver of the hook and ladder attempted to open his door, the driver's window and the windshield were shattered by gunfire. Within seconds, the same fate befell the pump truck. Obeying the commands of the now screaming drivers, the firefighters on both trucks scrambled behind the vehicles for cover as more shots rang out. Ike knew that he could've killed both drivers and probably a number of the firefighters themselves before they reached cover. Instead he chose just to scare them. He'd always had a reverence for the bravery exhibited by firemen, and he just couldn't bring himself to seriously injure or deliberately kill one of them unless absolutely necessary. His mission was merely to keep the firefighters at bay in order to let the fire continue its deadly work. As long as a standoff remained in effect, he was satisfied with the status quo and would not spill firefighter blood. Realizing that it would be only a matter of minutes before the police and S.W.A.T. teams showed up in force, it was now time to put the next part of the plan into effect.

Ike fired several rounds into each of the fire trucks to effectively keep the firefighters heads down. A window behind him exploded as a flaming body burst through the just created opening. Ike squeezed his trigger finger twice and the writhing screaming matchstick went inert. Next he emerged from behind the bush and crawled beneath the billowing cloud of thick black smoke to the other side of the building where Danny was keeping watch. He could hear sporadic gunfire indicating that his partner was doing his job. As he reached the other side, the visibility was much better. He noticed the screams had virtually ceased. They had been replaced by a sickeningly sweet odor that only the burning of human flesh imparts. He could make out Danny, eyes blazing like hot coals, demonically challenging Chauncy to come forth like a man so that he could plug him again. Recognizing that Danny had lost touch with reality, Ike cautiously approached him.

"Danny, Danny, easy boy, easy! We've done it lad! We've done it! They're all dead."

Slowly the crazed look eased from Danny's face, and humanity began to seep back into his being. A sense of confused reality replaced the demonic appearance of moments before. Ike had seen this reaction before on the battlefield, and he knew just how to manipulate it to bring his plan to fruition.

"Danny, can ya hear the next wave of sirens approachin'? Those would be the police, soon to be followed by the S.W.A.T. teams I've told ya about. I need ya to go to the wheelbarrow over there and get out the extra ammo clips and yer handgun. I think we're gonna need 'em."

As Danny turned in the direction of the wheelbarrow, he laid down his rifle. At that instant, Ike began to stealthily creep up behind Danny. They were shielded from view by the thick acrid smoke that continued to issue forth from the burning Social Center. Muttering a hasty "Forgive me lad," Ike pulled out his Glock 9mm and as he drew up behind Danny, he placed the weapon to his partner's temple and pulled the trigger. Satisfied that no further effort need be expended, Ike gently laid his slain comrade down. Removing Danny's gloves, he placed the gun in his hand to further the appearance of a suicide. Taking an envelope from his trousers, he stuffed it into Danny's rear pants pocket.

Now he rapidly made his way to the wheelbarrow. He took out one of the duffle bags, the basketball, and a couple of AR-15 ammo clips. As he raced back to where Danny's rifle lay, he could hear sirens pull up in front of the furiously burning building. Picking up the rifle, he emptied the clip through the smoke in the direction of where the siren sounds had come to a halt. Quickly slapping another clip into the rifle, he expended that clip also in the same direction. Satisfied that he had bought himself some needed time, Ike proceeded to the next part of his plan.

Grabbing the duffel bag he emptied its contents on the ground. The bag had contained a pair of shorts, a basketball shirt, two wet rags, some handy-wipes, a towel, and a pair of tennis shoes. Quickly stripping off his clothing that had consisted of a t-shirt, boots, hat, and a protective uniform type coverall, he shoved them hastily into the duffel bag. He wiped himself rapidly with the wet rags, and used handy-wipes to quickly remove grimy residue from his face, neck, and hands. Donning the basketball garb, he shoved all of the paraphernalia he had used into the duffel bag also. As he zipped up the bag, Ike ran towards the burning building. With a mighty heave he flung the bag into the middle of the white-hot inferno.

Figuring that he had better buy himself a bit more time, he raced back to the rifle and slapped in another clip. By now random shots were pinging their way through the smoke and chipping off pieces of asphalt from the driveway as the police sought to return Ike's previous fire. They were much braver now that Ike had not fired for several minutes. Sensing that he'd better be more protective on this, his final clip, he lay prone on the parking lot next to Danny's dead body and unleashed his last volley. Discarding the rifle, Ike crawled over to the basketball and picked it up. He raised himself to a crouched position, and began to make his way as rapidly as he could towards the rear of the parking lot, away from the street. He could hear bullets ricocheting off the asphalt in close proximity to where Danny's lifeless body lay. More sirens could be heard screaming their arrival. These would be the S.W.A.T. boys.

Ike found the hole in the rear fence that he had cut the previous evening, and made his way through. Because the area was strictly commercial for blocks in all directions, it was still virtually deserted in spite of the fire and gunplay of the past fifteen minutes. Keeping in the shadows of an abandoned warehouse that backed up to the Social Center's lot, he hurried to distance himself from the crime scene as quickly and unobtrusively as possible. He took off his jersey work gloves and hurled them onto the warehouse roof.

Ike froze as he reached the protective end of the warehouse. Under a streetlight 100 yards away was a group of five inner-city teenagers who were taking a casual interest in the fire. Torn between the desire to remain unseen and the desire to put as much distance as possible between himself and the police, Ike began to weigh his options. The dilemma solved itself as a police cruiser careened around the corner. The teens scattered in all directions, assuming the police were to complicate their lives. Ike took advantage of the ensuing confusion and slipped across the street as the police attempted to ascertain whether the teens were involved in the fire or not.

As he scaled a high fence leading into the property of a sheet metal fabricating plant, Ike could hear volleys of gunshots emanating from the direction of the Social Center. As he ran down the plant's driveway, Ike could feel his senses tingling. He had a distinct feeling that he was not alone. Suddenly a dark shape leaped out of an alley fifteen feet ahead of him. A low guttural growl warned Ike that his intrusion was not going to be easily dismissed. The three-year old Doberman watchdog advanced slowly and ominously upon Ike, measuring the distance to its victim. The animal's instincts, agility, and cunning had been honed by thousands of years of evolution. Advancing slowly, the Doberman sized up its prey as it prepared to strike. Unfortunately for the dog, its adversary had also learned much over the eons. In addition, the foe used tools and could think quickly. Ultimately these advantages would decide the outcome.

The Doberman sprang at Ike from a distance of seven feet. The animal had been trained to inflict maximum damage upon all who intruded on the property. With no other defense at hand, Ike thrust the basketball into the enraged snarling face hurtling at his throat. The maneuver, coupled with Ike's 220 pounds behind it proved sufficient to deflect the initial attack. The animal, though somewhat surprised by the tactic, was only momentarily compromised. Regaining the initiative, the canine sprang again. As before, its charge was met by a counterblow to the snout. Changing tactics, the Doberman attacked the intruder's legs. As Ike attempted to ward off this new attack, he brought the ball down to his knee level. The Doberman seized this opportunity and was able to nip the fleshy top part of Ike's left hand.

Realizing that he could be in serious trouble, Ike sought a new defense. The battle had backed him up to a metal fence along the perimeter of the property. As he retreated along the fence, Ike felt his foot brush against something short and solid. Quickly glancing down in the dim light being emitted by some nearby streetlights, he made out a metallic glint reflecting off the short solid piece. The dog charged again, and this time it came away with a bit of Ike's skin removed from his left calf by razor sharp incisors. Fueled by this minor victory, the dog prepared to press the attack.

Recognizing the precariousness of his plight, Ike feverishly weighed a desperate strategy. While the basketball represented a shield of sorts to thwart the dog's frontal assaults, holding it made Ike's movements clumsy and slow. That had allowed the dog to draw blood twice. As the growling beast darted in yet again, Ike made his decision. Raising the ball over his head, he brought it down hard on the skull of the Doberman as it attacked. He knew that the blow was not sufficient to stop his quarry, but it did cause the animal to pause, allowing Ike a chance to grab the solid object he had made contact with before. Reaching down, he picked up the object, and was rewarded with the feel of metallic firmness within his grasp. A PIPE! He had little time to relish his newfound weapon because the Doberman, seeing that its adversary had discarded that defensive encumbrance, now launched a full fledged assault upon what it thought was a defenseless foe. The hound's furious leap was met with a bone-crushing blow as Ike swung the heavy lead pipe in nightstick fashion, meeting the dog's skull just below its left ear. The sickening thud of hair, bone, and blood co-mingling resounded off the nearby walls. The beast let out a high-pitched yelp, and landed at Ike's feet. The body twitched several times as it went through its death throes. It emitted some gasping and gurgling sounds, and then it was still.

Ike recovered the basketball and made his way to the far side of the property, resuming his efforts to put as much distance between himself and the fire as he could. Making his way over the fence, he jumped down on a sidewalk and peered down the street just beyond. It still appeared to be deserted. After looking both ways to make sure no police cars were yet in sight, Ike raced across the street. He hoped that his calf wound was not bleeding sufficiently so as to leave a trail. He could hear sirens racing in all directions in the distance. Once across the street, he came to a rundown abandoned factory of some type. With the ball and the pipe in hand, he quickly made his way to the far end of this property. Glancing back in the direction he came from, he saw two sets of flashing lights racing down the street with sirens blaring. He could make out flashlights probing into the darkness he had traversed minutes before.

Quickly racing across the property, Ike came to yet another fence. On the other side of the fence he could see an embankment with twin metal strips on top. Railroad tracks. Beyond the tracks, he could see lights and hear a multitude of voices. That would be the neighborhood basketball court where he had parked his car earlier in the day, explaining to Danny how they would use it for their getaway. Ike scrambled over the fence and landed roughly on the ground. As soon as he did, a shaft of light pierced the darkness to his left, and began slowly proceeding in his direction. A police car searchlight beam was sweeping in an arc towards him. With his heart pounding, Ike bolted for the railroad track embankment. He had just made it over the tracks and pitched himself head first over the far side of the embankment, when the shaft of light blazed over the spot he had just vacated.

Sweating profusely, and bruised and scraped by his exertions in the past few minutes, Ike attempted to compose himself. Still holding both the ball and the pipe, he began to make his way through the darkness towards the basketball court. Looking for a place to discard the incriminating pipe, he came across a 55- gallon drum partially filled with rainwater. Dropping the pipe in, he resumed his trek toward the late night basketball game being played in earnest on the dimly lit court.

Two three-man teams were vying for neighborhood supremacy on center court, while a couple of teenagers were idly tossing up random shots on a side basket. Ike was relieved to see the rusted 12-year old Malibu parked on the street where he'd left it several hours earlier. It appeared that the $1000 deal he'd made earlier that day with one of the men now racing up and down the basketball court would pay off. Time would soon tell. He made his way around the main court and, joined the two younger shooters. As the players on center court flashed past, one of the men shot Ike a look, and gave him a quick thumbs-up. As they reversed direction on a steal, suddenly he came up lame and called time out. Feigning a twisted ankle, he hobbled off to the side. Looking over at Ike, one of the remaining participants shouted, "Hey, you got game."

"I can play a little," replied Ike as he slowly jogged to the court to join in the resumption of the game.

A knowing glance in the direction of the fallen player cemented their arrangement, and Ike tossed in the ball to get the game going again. Though Ike was at least twenty years their senior, his training regimen and devotion to fitness now paid-off, as he held his own in spite of his age and slight injuries. Within a few minutes, the real game began in earnest as two squad cars squealed to a halt in the street adjacent to the court. Four officers exited from the cars and proceeded towards the game.

"Hold up there men. Have any of you seen anyone suspicious heading this way? There's a possibility that armed fugitives may be trying to escape in this neighborhood."

The question was met with some shoulder shrugs and disinterest for the most part, with a couple of head shakes thrown in for good measure. The officer's attention turned to Ike as his whiteness on the court looked conspicuously out of place in these late night inner city surroundings.

"What about you there slick, seen anything?"

"I ain't seen nothin' out of the ordinary."

"What brings someone like you to this part of town tonight?"

"I like to play hoop."

Now Ike's paid off benefactor joined in the discussion.

"My man here and I work together and I invited him to join us tonight. Any problem with that?"

"No problem, but I want to stress that some real dangerous and desperate people may be at large in the area."

"Hey bro's you hear that? There may be some bad mutha's roamin' the hood tonight. Gee Mr. Officer, we ain't never seen no bad folks here in our little slice of heaven."

With that, the rest of the players started to laugh, and the police could see that they were wasting their time. As they prepared to leave, one of them took note of Ike's scrapes and injuries.

"How'd you get so nicked up buddy?"

"These guys play a little rough, and that asphalt ain't exactly jello when you slide on it. It's nothing that I can't play through though. Hey, we gonna play twenty questions all night or can we get back to our game?"

"Suit yourselves, but I'm warning you guys that you could be in real danger. If you see any suspicious people, you could do yourselves some good by letting us know." With that the officers went back to their cars and pulled away.

As the game resumed, Ike's acquaintance announced that his ankle was feeling better, and he'd like to get back to playing. As he and Ike passed, Ike whispered something to him before he went to reclaim his ball on the side court. The two men exchanged high fives and Ike grabbed his basketball. The two men went to Ike's Malibu and upon opening the car Ike lifted up the carpeting and pulled out a small stack of hundred dollar bills. He pressed the money into the black man's hands while shaking his hand at the same time.

"Good luck." said the man to Ike.

"Thanks for your help," responded Ike as he started the car and put it in gear. As he slowly began to start the Chevy down the street, he could once again hear sirens in the background.

CHAPTER 21

The ringing of the telephone startled Holland as she finished washing her face prior to going to bed for the evening. Picking up the receiver, she was surprised to hear Daniece's voice on the other end.

"Holly-Brit, you got the news on T.V?"

"No Daniece, I was just getting ready to hit the sack. Why?"

"Go turn on channel four RIGHT NOW!"

As Holland pressed the button on her remote, a somber looking male television reporter came into view in front of what appeared to be a charnel house. The picture changed and now the view was from a helicopter circling the smoking remnants of a charred building. Holland was so intent on the visual image that she almost missed the reporter's critical commentary:

"I'm standing in front of a horrific scene here in a commercial area of Cleveland. The charred remains that you see in back of me are all that is left of a Social Center owned by the pharmaceutical company Pharmacor. I've been told that it was a gathering place for both current and retired employees of Pharmacor where they could socialize amongst their peers. I understand that a bingo game was being held on the premises tonight and from the number of cars that still remain in the parking lot, it appears to have been attended by scores of people. The initial cause of the fire has not been released as of yet, but from what we've been able to learn from firefighters on the scene, it most likely was a case of arson. Tragically, there has almost certainly been a large loss of life. Reports of scores of gunshots associated with this tragedy give the distinct impression that this was a planned attack on the Social Center, rather than an accident. At this time it is too early to determine what really took place here this evening. Police, S.W.A.T. members, and firefighters on the scene have been extremely tight lipped, and we are being kept at a distance. However the aerial views have shown numerous body bags being assembled behind the building. That coupled with the ghastly sickeningly sweet odor emanating from the scene tells of a tragedy of disastrous proportions. We will be on the scene all night, and we'll make the viewing audience aware of developments as they unfold. I'm Hale Harden, Channel 4 News."

"Oh my Lord Daniece, that's horrible! Who could have done such a terrible thing, and why?'

"I don't know child. This is even worse than the Legionnaire's tragedy, because at least that was an accident. This sounds like cold-blooded murder. I'm going to put through a group call to everyone else in our department to let them know about this as soon as I hang up. Be strong baby. There are good people who will be investigating this, and I'm sure they'll bring whoever is responsible to justice."

"I hope and pray to God that you are right Daniece. Let me know if you need my help in anything."

"I've got our department on speed dial, so it shouldn't take me too long to get in touch with everyone. Go to bed and try to get some rest. I'm sure we'll have some very trying days ahead of us. Take care Holly-Brit."

As Holland hung up the phone, she realized her hand was trembling. Tears welled up in her eyes as she stared blankly at the television. The news crew continued to broadcast from the scene of the disaster, but in her grief-stricken numbness, she could not detect a sound emanating from the screen. The questions: WHO? HOW? WHY? WHO? HOW? WHY, continued to repeat in her mind. As she stared unseeing at the smoldering ruins, a vision began to take shape. Just as the Phoenix arose from the ashes in folklore, so too did this image in Holland's minds-eye begin to rise from the charred embers. The face she knew only too well, but the body was other worldly.

Though she shook her head in an attempt to eradicate the vision from her mind, her subconscious was not ready to let go of it quite yet. The body was that of a serpent whose being was on fire. Rather than being consumed, it instead seemed to draw strength from the blaze. The serpent had two arms. One arm contained a gasoline can and a pack of matches. In the other was a pitchfork. The face of the serpent was that of Jonas Trina with horns atop his head. The demonic serpent's eyes bore into Holland's as though it was trying to subjugate her very soul. Holland slammed her eyes shut and pinched her forearm drawing blood. Preparing to open her eyes, she found herself gasping for air, fearing the image would still be present. Raising her eyelids little-by-little, she let out a huge sigh of relief when the image was no longer visible. Holland tried to make sense of what her brain had conjured up, but temporarily she drew a blank. Suddenly it all became crystal clear as her focus and her resolve became one. To Holland the vision represented the answers to the WHO and the HOW? Now she was going to set a determined course to find out the WHY.

In Bayreuth Germany, Jonas' cell phone rang four times before he could re-enter from the veranda to answer it. Answering it, he heard his hysterical secretary Nancy McKinney on the other end of the line sobbing as she tried to blurt out something about a fire. Commanding Nancy to compose herself, Trina ordered her to begin again when she was ready. Seconds later, she slowly and with great effort, began to relate the details of the tragedy at the Social Club to Jonas. Properly exhibiting both shock and remorse, he asked a few questions as to how much was known of the circumstances and culprits behind this despicable act. Next he told her that he would catch the earliest return flight that could be arranged and fly back as soon as possible. He told her to spread the word that today and Friday would be declared days of company mourning at the Cleveland plant, and all employees should take the days off with pay. Also he instructed her to get in touch with the company press spokesperson, Barbara Collister to prepare a fitting tribute for those company personnel who had lost their lives.

Ending the call with a thank you, and a word to stay strong, Jonas hung up. As he prepared to resume his kaffee on the veranda, the phone rang again. As he picked it up, a male voice on the other end requested to speak to a Mr. White. Informing the caller that there was no Mr. White here, Jonas prepared to hang up. The caller repeated the request, saying that this was the number he had been given. The voice had a strong Middle Eastern accent. Politely reaffirming that there was no Mr.White present, Jonas hung up. He smiled as he arose to exit through the French doors. The reinforcements would soon be coming to help him finalize his plans.

Holland's car-clock read 5:27A.M.as she parked her car on the street two blocks from the still smoking remnants of the Pharmacor Social Center. Having found sleep impossible, she had felt compelled to visit the disaster site. For what reason or purpose, she was not sure. Getting out of the car, Holland began to slowly and unsteadily make her way in the direction of the tragedy. Huge bright lights such as those used for night work on highways had been brought in to help facilitate the recovery efforts. Pulling out a large handkerchief from her purse and putting it over her face helped quell the rancor wafting in her direction. Even from this distance, the rancid odor of roasted human flesh was almost overpowering. She gained a new respect for the professional firefighters on the scene whose job took them into this arena often. It was surprising how many people were currently at the scene at this time. Between firemen, newspeople, police, and investigative personnel, she estimated there were between 200-300 people on the job at this moment.

Holland was stopped by a policeman, as she got within a block of the site. He advised her that only emergency personnel were admitted beyond that point. Holland joined a group of onlookers who were milling around the area. From this distance it was difficult to get a good view of the recovery efforts, but the scene was a beehive of activity. She could make out men and women wearing black jackets with the letters A.T.F. and F.B.I. emblazoned on them. They had masks over their faces as well to help deflect the disturbing smell. One of them broke from a trio of F.B.I. agents and headed toward a car parked not far from her vantage point. Opening the car, the agent took off his mask to gulp coffee from a thermos. A sense of recognition came over Holland as the agent took another mouthful.

"John, John Kazek" yelled Holland.

The agent tried to pick out the face calling to him from the group of curiosity seekers, but they were clustered in the predawn darkness as opposed to him being silhouetted against the bright lights.

"John Kazek F.B.I., It's me Holland."

"Holland!" John cried out. Making his way past the security perimeter, John hustled through the smoky darkness in the direction of her voice. As his eyes adjusted to the darkness outside the lighted perimeter, he glimpsed a familiar face. "Hello Holland. God I've missed you." John said as he hugged her tightly.

"I'm sorry to have to see you again under these circumstances."

"I'm sorry too John. It's just terrible. All those innocent and defenseless people killed, and for what?" Tears began to flow involuntarily down Holland's cheeks as her emotions proved too strong to contain any longer.

"I don't know, but we certainly intend to find out exactly who was responsible and why this took place." John reached into his pocket and produced a handkerchief that he gently began to dab at the tears on Holland's cheeks. "I'm also sorry that I haven't been in touch since our date, but when I got back to my place that night, I had an urgent order to head out west on an assignment. I just got back yesterday afternoon, and then this hit."

"What were you doing out west?" Holland asked.

"Unfortunately I'm not at liberty to divulge that information to you at this time."

"A likely story!"

"Sad but true, that is sometimes the real deal with my job. There are cases that I cannot comment on even to my own family. In fact if you and I were married, I couldn't tell you about the case out west. But that's enough of that. Boy it's good to see you."

"You too, John Kazek F.B.I. Have you people learned anything about who might have done this, or shouldn't I ask?"

"Officially, I know nothing. However, from the scuttlebutt that I overheard from members of some of the other agencies on the scene, it looks like it could be a multiple murder/suicide case. My understanding is that an ex-employee with a grudge may be responsible. I can tell you that much only because we don't have official jurisdiction in this case. We have been asked to help in this investigation by the locals, due to the overwhelming size and scope of this tragedy."

"I hope that you are right about there being only one person responsible. At least that would mean the end of these killings that I've been telling you about. Please make sure that all the bases are covered, because if anyone else had a hand in this, who knows what they might be cooking up for the future."

"Couldn't sleep either huh?" said a sweetly compassionate voice. Holland turned around and was surprised to be staring into the inquisitive face of Daniece Davis.

"Daniece, oh it's so horrible. How could anyone do this?"

"I don't know Holly-Brit, but I've been talking to a couple of fire fighters I've gotten to know over the years who happened to be here. They indicated that this might've been the work of one guy. They mentioned that a suicide note was found on a body in back of the building. The body supposedly was unburned with a gunshot wound to the head. By the way, should I be telling you all this in front of this gentleman you're with here?"

"Oh it's quite alright. This is John Kazek. He's with the F.B.I. and he's helping on the case. John, this is my boss, Daniece Davis."

"It's a pleasure to meet you Daniece."

"Likewise, John."

"John is my new friend with the F.B.I. that I told you about last week. I was just telling John that they've got to make sure to apprehend all of the terrible people responsible for this, no matter who or where it might lead."

"If you're referring to our good friend Mr. Trina, I'm sorry to disappoint you Holly-Brit, but he's in Germany, where he's been all week. Pretty hard to tie him in with this seeing as he was around 3500 miles away while it was all taking place."

"Sounds pretty convenient if you ask me"" said Holland.

"Well ladies, I'd love to stay and discuss this further, but I see my superior looking around for something or someone over yonder, and I think I'd better get back to my duties. Nice to meet you Daniece, and Holland I'll call you in the next few days after we get things sorted out here."

"You'd better Mr. Kazek!"
As John rejoined the teeming throng of investigators, Daniece resumed her conversation with Holland.

"Have you seen anyone else from the office here Holly-Brit?"

"No. Were you able to reach everyone in our department and tell them what happened?"

"All of them except Jane. Knowing her, she probably just slept right through the fifteen rings."

"You're probably right. Did you speak with anyone else from outside our group?"

"Not directly, but I checked voice mail, and there was a message from Nancy McKinney, Trina's secretary. The message stated that per Jonas Trina, all Cleveland employees are to take today and tomorrow off with pay. I think that may be the first decent thing that man has done since he got here."

"What choice did he have? Let's face it, how much work do you think would have been accomplished under the circumstances?"

"Probably not much, but at least it was a shift in his normal way of operating. I'm willing to give him the benefit of the doubt that this is a genuinely humane gesture on his part to allow the employees time to grieve and to pay their respects to those who paid the ultimate price last evening. The sun is beginning to rise. Why don't we find someplace to get a couple cups of coffee? Then we can go to the company parking lot to help console anyone who might still come to work. Also I'm guessing that most won't have checked their voicemails, so they are probably not aware that they may take the next two days off."

"That sounds like an idea worthy of management Daniece. However, I'm still not ready to assume that Jonas is totally blameless in this terrible crime. I guess time will tell."

Daniece had started back in the direction of her car when she realized the meaning behind Holland's last remarks. She whirled around and glared at Holland who had just begun to follow her.

"Now listen here young lady! **DO NOT, and I repeat DO NOT** even joke with anyone about Jonas having any involvement with the commission of this crime. If you even so much as insinuate the tiniest possibility that he had anything to do with this then I'm afraid that neither I nor anyone at Pharmacor could protect you from the repercussions. Do I make myself clear?"

"Yes"

"I 'm not trying to be a badass or anything Holland, but if any scuttlebutt like that were to reach the ears of Jonas, my guess is that the bull in the china shop analogy would be tame compared to the reaction of our C.E.O. Let's just strike that thought from our minds, shall we."

"O. K." said Holland grudgingly.

As the twosome headed toward their respective cars, Holland made a mental note to exclude Daniece from future discussions of her suspicions unless she had definitive proof.

The myriad law enforcement agencies involved with the case spent the next few weeks sifting through the evidence and following up on leads in an effort to determine if Danny Hughes had acted alone or if there had been accomplices in the heinous crime. A couple of firemen on the first trucks to arrive on the scene were adamant that they distinctly heard shots coming from both the front of the burning building at the same time as they heard gunfire issuing from the rear of the structure. Others disagreed, saying they never heard multiple guns being fired at the same time. The responding police and S.W.A.T. members were unanimous in their opinion that from the time of their arrival, shots emanated from only one location at a time. Furthermore, the only prints on any of the four weapons found at the scene were those of Danny Hughes.

An extremely promising lead came in within the first 24 hours after the tragedy. A local bar owner named O'Malley told the police that Danny Hughes had been befriended recently by a tall dark haired man from Cincinnati who very well may have been involved in the case. O'Malley was even able to furnish a name, and the purported fact that the Pharmacor plant in Cincinnati had employed the man lent significant credence to the lead. The detectives had taken the information and followed through in true investigative fashion. Unfortunately the alleged co-conspirator's name of Kevin Michaels did not appear in any company records of Pharmacor. Fact finding field trips to Cincinnati proved fruitless, as did discussions with the patrons at O'Malley's bar. While a few regulars at O'Malley's thought they recalled a stranger making friends with Danny Hughes, they couldn't further corroborate any more of Mike O'Malley's story. Detectives eventually chalked it up as a dead end, especially in light of the lack of sobriety they encountered from most of those they interviewed at the bar.

Though the investigation would remain open, after three weeks the prevailing wisdom regarding the tragedy seemed to be that it was as it appeared. A horrible case of revenge/murder/suicide as found in the suicide note on Danny Hughes' corpse at the scene of the crime. Additionally, the note took posthumous credit for several other killings of former Pharmacor personnel during the previous months, though no motives for these were laid out in the letter. The final toll of victims including Danny Hughes was 86. That number and a brief descriptive note on each victim's backgrounds went into a beautiful binder in a lavish basement office in the exclusive Hunting Valley community of metropolitan Cleveland.

A group funeral was arranged for the victim's with smaller private funerals to be held depending on the individual family's wishes. Beautiful floral arrangements and personalized cards were sent to each victim's family, compliments of Jonas Trina. The community at large, recognizing the tremendous emotional hardships surrounding the smitten company, began doing their best to turn business their way. In the month following the disaster, Pharmacor sales would increase 280% over the previous year's sales for that month.

A cell phone rang on a beach towel lying on the dazzling white sand of Oahu. A tall silver haired man in his early 50s picked it up.

"Trevor here"

"Enjoying our well deserved vacation are we?"

"You betcha! Is the heat dissipating in your neck of the woods?"

"I would say the heat is getting more bearable in all aspects of life here. I wish to inform you that your assistance at this moment is not necessary, so you may continue to indulge yourself as you see fit. The additional personnel I alluded to are now on board for the next endeavor, so your services will not be required. However, do not get too comfy because I'm working on some future plans that will require your charm and talents. Rest well my friend. You've earned it.

"We'll be in touch."

Trevor/Ike switched off the phone and absent-mindedly ran his finger across his upper lip that no longer featured his trademark moustache. Running his hands through his now thick silver locks, he gazed out at an 18 foot roller making its run toward the beach with numerous tawny lithe bodies of both sexes hitching along for the ride. Life is good thought Ike, as he took a sip from a coconut shell drink and settled back onto his towel to continue soaking up the Hawaiian sunshine.

CHAPTER 22

"Alright people, let's settle down and get this meeting to order shall we?"

The speaker was Jonas Trina, and he was addressing a group of twelve handpicked staff members of which both Daniece and Holland were included.

"I've called you all here primarily because I'm tired of seeing the morose attitude which has permeated this organization since the event of three weeks ago. Yes it was terrible. Yes it was emotionally devastating to many. Yes, numerous friends and former coworkers were lost. Yes it was a horrific tragedy, and yes, I realize that most of the company has not fully recovered from the shock and anguish of it all as of yet. However, time marches on! In this case time will serve as your ally, for after all, isn't it true that time really does heal all wounds.

With all that being said, I'd like to thank each of you personally for your efforts these past three weeks. I thank you for your loyalty to Pharmacor and your devotion to duty during this exceedingly difficult time. I have chosen the twelve of you for an assignment because I feel that you have the pulse of the company and the wherewithal to pull off an attitude adjustment plan that I shall now present to you.

Sometimes we help ourselves more by helping others, and I'm hoping that what we discuss today may have that effect. You may or may not be aware, but for months now I have been attempting to get our operation in Cincinnati up to speed with the rest of the company. Every other Pharmacor facility is exceeding the corporate objectives, and yet our Cincinnati location continues to lag behind. I've threatened them, cajoled, fired, and threatened some more down there, all with minimal effect. Of course the five-week strike there didn't help matters either. I believe that the main obstacle lies in employee attitudes. I'm thinking of attempting a new course of action which I would like your input on, and your help in implementing if we all agree the plan has merit.

I propose to give the plant what I feel is a very nice gift, no strings attached. I am willing to pay for a riverboat cruise with my own personal funds for as many as 300 employees of our Cincinnati facility. I would like you twelve to coordinate the event, and to convince those in attendance at the cruise that Pharmacor is a caring company. I want them to know that we are truly interested in making them feel part of the Pharmacor family. I've given this a lot of thought, and in fact I've even gone so far as to come up with a theme for the event. I've also arranged for a catering company to handle the food requirements. I'm hoping that by offering this evening of entertainment, this plant may come on board with the rest of the organization and pull their oars in unison with us as opposed to the borderline defiance that I see now out of them. Unfortunately, with the end of summer drawing near, there is no time to waste if we are to pull this off while the weather is still nice enough to really enjoy an evening of dancing on deck. Any thoughts on the subject?"

"How quickly do you believe this could be put together'?" asked Ray Titus.

"I'd like to hold the event before the last weekend in September, which gives us slightly more than a month to accomplish the task at hand."

"You mentioned that you had a theme and a caterer for the event. May I ask what these are?" queried Megan Stewart head of marketing.

"The theme I would like to go with is entitled Mediterranean Breezes which I feel lends a certain romantic and enchanting duality to the evening. The caterer would be an establishment known as Moroccan Interlude. I was turned onto them by a rather well to do neighbor, and after sampling their fare, I feel they would do quite nicely. They handle only the most exclusive parties, and though they are in great demand, I have tentatively secured their services for September 21st. I've also been working on an invitation to personalize the affair. I expect that I should have that finalized by next week sometime. As you can see, I've given this a good deal of thought and would like to see it come to fruition."

"Mr. Trina, with all that you have accomplished thus far on the arrangements, what is left that you need our assistance on?" asked Nancy McKinney.

"Numerous details still need to be taken care of Miss McKinney. A band or bands must be selected, alcoholic beverages must be procured and delivered, the invitations must be addressed and sent out, the cruise vessel itself must be decided upon and secured, and scores of little details would need to be ironed out to make the evening a success. Most importantly, I need all of you to get your own people behind this to shake them out of their doldrums and set a purpose they can all get behind. Also, I would need you and your people to make phone calls to

Cincinnati to drum up support for the event so that a good turnout is guaranteed. I realize that my popularity with the Cincinnati plant is not what it should be, and if they feel the affair is being put together by the Cleveland facility, rather than myself, I think that would carry much more weight."

"No offense sir, but with all due respect, isn't it the Cleveland plant which was most affected by the tragedy? I can see where some members of the local Pharmacor organization might be a bit resentful about doing something of this magnitude for Cincinnati when they feel that we are the one's who are hurting."

All eyes in the room turned in astonishment at the boldness of Daniece's question, and they breathlessly awaited the response of the powerful C.E.O., whose ego could very easily be bruised by such an impertinent inquiry. Jonas' face began to turn a subtle shade of crimson as he formulated his response. Just before he spoke however, he seemed to harness his rising emotions, and when he delivered his answer, it was done without the slightest bit of anger or tension.

"I was wondering who might bring this supposed slight to my attention. I should have known that it would be the always ebullient and, dare I say gutsy, Mrs. Davis. Well Daniece, I was planning on keeping this a secret until the very end of the meeting, but seeing as my hand has been forced, I suppose that now is as good a time as any to let the cat out of the proverbial bag. As with the Cincinnati plant, I also was planning on doing something of an entertaining nature for the Cleveland location as well. It is my understanding that we have a good many music fans in our organization. Furthermore it turns out that a Cleveland band from the 70's is being inducted into the Rock and Roll Hall of Fame. Due to the group's roots being here, the induction ceremony is to be held in Cleveland in mid November. A later ceremony to honor the group will take place in New York also. Along with the ceremony, the group being inducted, "America's Song", has agreed to perform a concert. I have committed us to be a sponsor for the event, and have arranged to have 450 seats reserved for Pharmacor employees and retirees to utilize for that event. You may consider it kind of an early Christmas bonus if you will. Please convey this to your staff at your earliest convenience so that they may make their plans accordingly. Mrs. Davis, do you feel that this might serve as a balm to help soothe their feelings over Cincinnati's fete?"

"Why yes, I most certainly do sir, and if I may say, bravo to you! I think this will have a most positive effect on morale."

"Very good! Well then, may I see a show of hands to indicate how many of you think that what we've just discussed for our Cincinnati brethren is doable?"
Twelve hands shot skyward.

"I guess it's agreed. Let's get to work then shall we. I've got a list of riverboats that ply the Ohio River in that area. I'll leave it here for you to get started. You may organize yourselves and delegate responsibilities in any manner you see fit. We shall reconvene here in one week for an updated status report, and I will see that I finish the invitation which I will present to you at that time. You may utilize a bit of company time to accomplish this, but please do not lose sight of our stated corporate objectives, because they have not changed. Have a pleasant week." With that Jonas rose abruptly and departed the room with a broad smile on his not unhandsome countenance.

As Holland and Daniece strode back to their department, Daniece couldn't help but good-naturedly chide Holland on her previous suspicions. "Still think that Jonas is the Boogie Man?"

"I must admit that leopards don't usually change their spots quite so abruptly, but it does seem that perhaps our Mr. Trina may have a touch of humanity in him after all. However, I still think that the findings in the Social Club tragedy were a little too cut and dried for my taste. It seemed too easy for the crime to be solved so definitively at the scene. I mean the killer had spent month's covering his tracks during the other crimes and now he decides to chuck it all in one big final ghastly act. It just doesn't fit. And everything was wrapped up so nice and tidy at the scene that you could almost put a bow around it. How often does that happen with serial killers?"

"Just be glad that it did in this case, or else we'd still be worrying our heads off over when and where he might strike next. Anyway, I'm starving! What say we stop back at the office and check for messages, and then go catch a bite to eat? Maybe we could even stop at Lou's for some happy cakes on the way back."

"You're on."

The Ferrari 360 Modena F1 roadster squealed to a stop in front of a Middle Eastern bakery in a modest working class neighborhood within the Cleveland city limits. Jonas stepped out of the candy apple red Italian creation. As Jonas pulled open the screen door to the bakery, his senses drew in the enticing fragrance of warm baklava recently taken from the oven. The glass enclosed shelves directly before him held various Middle Eastern fresh baked delicacies. A handsome Arabic man, fittingly attired in white pastry chef garb, was finalizing a sale to the only other customer present in the shop at that time. As his customer exited the bakery, the man turned his attention to Jonas. His eyes began to smile almost before his mouth, as a sense of recognition came over him.

"Mr. Saxton my friend, it is a pleasure to see you again."

"Likewise Mr. Al-Salem. You appear quite stylish in your work clothes?"

"It is necessary to keep up appearances. Let me get someone from the back to take my place here, and then you can fill me in on how your meeting went today."

Tariq Al-Salem disappeared through a door into the baking area, and within a minute he returned with a dark eyed beauty in her early twenties who would take over the counter. The two men retired to an office in the rear of the building and Tariq closed the door behind them. Jonas politely refused an offer for a beverage and the two men got down to business.

"I trust Mr. Saxton, that all went according to plan today."

"That is correct. While numerous final arrangements must be ironed out, my staff has agreed to commence working on a riverboat cruise tentatively scheduled for the last weekend in late September. I told them that I would handle the catering arrangements, and they seemed satisfied with that. Should complications on that end arise, I can always utilize my position to enforce my decision, but it will be so much easier if I get no challenges to your people handling the catering."

"Agreed"

"Have you been able to procure the necessary amounts of substance to give our riverboat partygoers a proper sendoff?"

"Through a couple of our other company fronts, we are well on our way to stockpiling quantities sufficient to our needs. Thank goodness that Americans place such a high value on keeping their lawns in tiptop shape!" The two men shared a private chuckle between them at that comment.

"I have ordered my staff to update me one week from today as to how they are progressing with the cruise arrangements. If there are any major complications, I will e-mail you. I'd better be going now. It's been a pleasure Mr. Al-Salem. Let me know if you need my assistance for anything."

"I shall Mr. Saxton. Please help yourself to some pastries on your way out. I shall buzz my daughter at the counter to let her know you are coming. Good day."

Jonas left the bakery with a large portion of baklava in his arms and a tune from Tannhauser on his lips. He was quite pleased at the way things had gone today, and for good reason. While he didn't really expect to be challenged on his riverboat cruise plans, there was always that possibility. Also, it was reassuring to see that Al-Salem appeared to be every bit as capable here in the U. S. as he seemed to be in Germany. Both meetings today had gone off without a hitch, and Jonas was feeling very confident that his plans were well on the road to success. As he pulled quickly away from the curb in his Ferrari roadster, his meetings for the day had officially come to an end. However, as fate would have it, his meetings were not the only ones of interest to him this day.

"Come on in Jane, and close the door please."

"Thanks Holly-Brit. I'll apologize up front for being somewhat curt, but what was it that you wanted to see me about? As you know, I'm leaving on vacation tomorrow, and I've got a lot of odds and ends to finish before I can go."

"I appreciate your taking a moment of your valuable time Jane, so I'll be brief. I understand that you are headed to the Chicago area to visit your parents, is that right?"

"Yes it is. I haven't been home in almost a year and I guess I feel the need for some of mom's home cooking and some good old parental love and comfort. Is there something you need from me while I'm there?"

"Actually, yes there is. I was wondering if you could do me a huge favor. As you know from our past conversations, I have some serious misgivings about our C.E.O. Well. I was checking up on his background, and I found out that he got his start in the business world at a defense company in Chicago by the name of Sutton Industries. It turns out that in only about six years time, he went from fresh faced engineer trainee right out of college, to C.E.O. of that major defense contractor. I'm curious as to what momentous things he might have accomplished in such a relatively short amount of time to warrant such a meteoric rise up the ranks. I was wondering if there might be any possibility that in your travels around the Chicago area, if you could swing by Sutton Industries and do a little poking around. I know that you feel the same way I do about our corporate leader, and this could be an opportunity to find out what makes him tick."

"Well..uh..I don't know Holly-Brit. I mean we might get in trouble if he ever found out we'd been prying into his past. Also, what's the point? It's not going to change things. He's our C.E.O. for the time being and good, bad or otherwise, we just have to live with it."

"What if we found out that he's partly to blame for all these recurrent deaths that have been taking place here since he arrived?"

"Do you really think that's the case?"

"Let's just say at this point that I'm not discounting that possibility. Look at the facts. Right after he's made our new commander-in-chief is when people connected with Pharmacor started dropping like flies. Also, I have it on good authority that his compensation just so happens to be positively influenced by these unfortunate circumstances. He is in the process of making millions in bonus money, in part because Pharmacor's retiree benefit funding has dropped significantly, due to the early deaths of over 200 retirees. It reminds me of ancient times when Nero fiddled while Rome burned."

"Do you have any evidence to back up this theory of yours?"

"Not yet. Right now everything is just hypothetical. That was in part why I wanted to have his background checked out. It could turn out that he is just that damn good and fully deserving of everything that has come his way in the business world. On the other hand, there may be a few skeletons in his closet that may shed some light on the tragic events that seem to keep occurring on his watch here. Can I count on you to give Sutton Industries a try while you're in the Windy City?"

"Oh well, what the hell, why not! Who knows maybe I'll find out that Mr. Trina really is the devil in disguise?"

"Anything's possible. While you're at Sutton, you'd probably better go kind of easy with the questions, just in case he still has some loyal folk there looking out for him. I doubt it, but as I said; anything's possible. Oh, I almost forgot, all of this must be kept strictly between you and me. As you yourself stated, we can't let this get back to Trina, and thus the fewer people who know about it, the better."

"I understand Holly-Brit, or should I say I'm pickin' up what you're puttin' down oh Omnipotent One?! With a feigned salute and a gleeful giggle, Jane turned on her heel and playfully goose-stepped out of the room.

"We'll see if anything comes of that," thought Holland as she prepared to get back to Pharmacor business.

At the end of the next day's business, Jonas stayed late in his office to catch up on some details, and to review tapes of conversations held in the offices in which he'd had Ike place surveillance equipment weeks before. Daniece Davis' conversations were strictly business, and for the most part very boring. With Holland Matthews however, he had hit the jackpot. As he replayed the conversation between Holland and Jane for the third time, a sinister smile came to his lips as he murmured aloud "it appears the game is on, Miss Matthews."

CHAPTER 23

"Well Ray, I understand that the riverboat cruise committee has elected you chairman. Will you please address the committee and myself, and bring us up to date on what has been accomplished during the past week?"

Ray Titus cleared his throat and rose from his seat to speak. "Thank you Jonas. During the past week, we've made significant strides in all areas. First of all, a paddlewheel steamer named the BUCKEYE BELLE, has been procured for Saturday the 21st of September. It was difficult to arrange due to the relatively short notice, but with a little financial persuasion on the part of Mr. Trina, we are assured of having a beautiful vessel at our disposal. Secondly, I understand that two local groups have been selected to be our musical entertainment for the evening. Mrs. Davis and Miss Matthews tell me that one group plays an assortment of 60's and 70's tunes for us old codgers, while a more contemporary band has been found that should suit the younger crowd. Megan Stewart has assured me that the lushes in marketing... err, I mean her marketing associates have made all of the proper arrangements to insure that adult libations may flow until the cruise ends. Also, I understand we have three bids from local print shops who are eager to get started printing up the invitations as soon as we give them the order. Speaking of invitations, Jonas I believe that you said you were going to have the finished draft of the invitation available for today's meeting. May we take a look at it?"

"Of course Ray. Miss McKinney, would you be so kind as to pass out to everyone their rough drafts of the invitations."
Nancy McKinney did as instructed and soon each of the twelve-committee members had a stapled pair of papers in front of them. The top sheet had a border with alternating camels and date palm trees on it, and the words Mediterranean Breezes emblazoned at the top. The second page had the text of the invitation that read as follows:

An Invitation to an Enchanted Evening

You are cordially invited to attend a gala event on Saturday September 21ˢᵗ. It will feature a riverboat cruise aboard the paddle wheeler Buckeye Belle, with all costs provided. The food, beverages, and musical accompaniment will kindly be donated by the Cleveland Pharmacor staff members. Surely you'll be blown away by the musical entertainment, and you are certainly guaranteed to enjoy the Middle Eastern themed cuisine. Feast upon delicacies such as warm pieces of baklava, or perhaps taboule, or stuffed grape leaves. Alcoholic drinks and softer beverages shall be in abundance, and with advance notice perhaps we will be able to furnish your personal favorite. The captain says this cruise is "to die for", and the scenery at this time of year is breathtaking. Other interests maybe in store for you as well. Gaming tables will be set up below, with shuffleboards on the deck. An assortment of video games will also be available. We think that with the Ohio moon overhead, far and away the most popular activity shall be dancing upon the river. We're sure that all who attend will have a great time. Hope to see you there!!!!!!!!!!!!!!!!!!

"Well people, does it pass inspection?" questioned Jonas

Though some may have had some small reservations, none were willing to bring up any creative deficiencies to the head of the company, who had in fact penned the manuscript, and the invitation was verbally approved. The meeting adjourned shortly thereafter with all members in agreement that the event planning was on the right track. As the committee members were shuffling out of the conference room, Holland felt a touch upon her shoulder. Turning around, she came face to face with Jonas Trina, who had an engaging, almost pleasant look on his face.

"Miss Matthews, I wonder if I could have a word with you in private before you return to your duties?"

"Of Course Mr. Trina, excuse me for just a second. Daniece, could you go on without me and let the department know that I'll be a few minutes."

"Will do Holland," answered Daniece as she made her way out of the room, leaving only Jonas and Holland.

"Miss Matthews, may I call you Holland?"

"By all means Mr. Trina!"

"Very good. Holland, I was wondering if I might impose upon you one additional task regarding the riverboat cruise."

"Certainly Mr. Trina, ask away."

"Well, I was thinking that it might be good to have some type of representation from Cleveland at the cruise in order to help coordinate the entertainment and to accept the accolades that I envision should be forthcoming from such a gala event as the Cincinnati staff is going to enjoy. You strike me as the type of effervescent spirit who might be an ideal candidate to represent us in a good light and to help maximize the benefits this evening hopefully, will secure for the entire corporation."

"What is it you would like me to do there Mr. Trina?"

"First off, I'd like for you not to make the journey alone. You may feel free to invite a boyfriend, or staff member, or both, to accompany you if you so desire. It really should be an enjoyable evening, and should be viewed as a reward to all in attendance. As far as your duties go, simply be yourself; and make yourself available to accept any and all extensions of thanks directed towards the Cleveland plant for all you people have done to make the event a success. If anyone should ask about where the funding for the event came from, simply say that it was from a reserve fund we had for promotional purposes. Last, but certainly not least, enjoy yourself. For all of the hard work that you've put in these past few weeks, you've earned a little R&R. Does this request meet with your approval?"

"Yes, by all means, Mr. Trina. It sounds grand."

"I guess it's agreed then. Please let me know how things went when you return to work the following Monday, if you would."

"Of course Mr. Trina."

"Well Holland, I'd better let you get back to work before the HR department crashes in your absence. Have a pleasant remainder of the day."

"I will. You do the same sir."

As Holland made her way back to her office, she wasn't sure if she felt elation or trepidation, but one thing she was positive she felt was confusion. For all of these months she had thought that Jonas the Almighty had barely known she existed. Now, not only had she had been selected to be part of an elite committee, but had been handpicked to handle a special assignment at his personal request. And what was with that "May I call you Holland stuff?" She certainly hoped that Jonas Trina was not in the early stages of making a move on her. Holland wasn't quite sure how she would be able to diplomatically refuse someone of his stature. Perhaps she could convince him that she was already involved with someone in a more than platonic relationship. As Holland entered the human resource department, her mind was already formulating a plan that would bring her and John Kazek in close proximity to Jonas. Once that was accomplished, she could show him that she was already romantically involved, thereby nipping a potential complication in the bud.

Barely had Holland had time to sit down in her office when she
became aware of a light knocking on the door. At her request, the door
opened, and in waltzed Jane, sporting a tan approximately twenty
shades darker than she'd left town with the week before.

"I was a bit concerned after you left that my request for you to stop by
Sutton Industries might monopolize a large portion of your vacation
time. However, from the looks of that tan, I can see that you were able
to sneak in a bit of time for relaxation," Holland said bemusedly.

"Well, remember that first and foremost I was on vacation. Plus as we
know, all work and no play make Jane a dull girl! But fear not Miss
Matthews, I have completed my out of town assignment in diligent
fashion, and I think you will be most interested in my findings."

"Before you do that, would you mind closing the door all the way?"

"Yes m'am." As Jane completed the task, she turned back to Holland,
and in a conspiratorial manner said "I'm glad you're sitting down
because you're going to be amazed about what I found out for us at
Sutton regarding Jonas' rise to the top."

"Do tell."

"When I first got to Sutton I was kind of given the runaround by a
secretary who treated me like I was sent from above with the expressed
mission of ruining her day. As she was about ready to ask me to leave,
in walks a middle aged woman named Triste who had just been
downsized from Sutton after twenty some years at the place. She'd
come to collect her last paycheck, which the secretary had at her
station. As this Triste woman was leaving, I got an idea and followed
her out the door. After introducing myself, I asked her how long she'd
worked at Sutton. When she said over twenty years, I asked her if she
remembered Jonas. Well, that led to us having lunch together, and she
was a veritable storehouse of info on our man in question. It turns out
that he started out in their engineering department, but at one point was
sent on a secret mission to Afghanistan in order to help get the bugs
out of one of Sutton's weapons systems. He came back as kind of a
hero, but it was all kept pretty hushed up for some reason. She
remembered that when he came back from that mission, he was held in
pretty high esteem within the company.

He got to be president of Sutton a few years later as the result of a
mysterious tragedy. A big explosion in a storage bunker occurred

which killed her direct boss at the time, some guy named Carter, and a few other engineering guys. The company president took the blame under some very suspicious circumstances, and resigned immediately. For some reason, he named Jonas Trina to be his successor. Triste thought that was very strange, because as far as she knew, the president of Sutton couldn't stand Trina. Also the three guys who were killed in the explosion were all from Jonas' department and were potential rivals to his moving up the corporate ladder. One secretary spread some scuttlebutt at the time that Jonas had arranged for the three men to be in the ill-fated storage bunker at the same time, which seemed very odd. However, he had an airtight alibi in that he was in the company of the current C.E.O. at the very moment that the explosions started happening. Anyway, nine months or so after that, the C.E.O. announces that he is resigning for health reasons, and he likewise names Jonas as his successor. He stayed C.E.O. at Sutton for about a dozen years before accepting the C.E.O. position at a medical equipment company prior to joining us. She said that he was a real bastard to work for, and that when he went to a new company, they partied for a week at Sutton. However, she did say that he was effective in getting things done, kind of in the same way that Hitler and Stalin were effective."

"Wow, it looks like highly unusual and deadly circumstances seem to follow him wherever he goes."

"Yes and no. I asked Triste if they had any unusual problems during Jonas' tenure as the C.E.O. at Sutton, and she said not to her memory. Nor was she aware of any major problems with his new company after he left Sutton."

"I guess that what you found out doesn't prove anything conclusive regarding what has taken place here at Pharmacor. On the other hand, there is certainly enough in Jonas Trina's checkered ascent to corporate hierarchy to warrant further study, wouldn't you say Jane?"

"I'd say so. Anything else that I can do for you in regards to our corporate witch hunt or any other matter?"

"As a matter of fact there is something I'm going to do for you as a bit of a perk for your services rendered in Chicago. How would you like to accompany me, and perhaps my friend John, to be part of the riverboat cruise in Cincinnati on September 21st? All you'd basically have to do is eat, drink, and be merry."

"Gee I don't know, it sounds like pretty rough duty to me. But I suppose it's a dirty job that someone's got to do, so count me in! I assume that we're going to spend the night there."

"Naturally, my little Mata Hari! I'll look into getting us rooms at a nice hotel. We can enjoy a leisurely ride home Sunday afternoon, after pigging out at some fabulous brunch spot."

"How did you arrange to go on this little mini vacation anyway?"

"Strangely enough, Jonas asked me if I would attend the affair and accept any thanks that the Cincinnati staff wanted to throw out for our plant's supposedly providing their party, which is actually being paid for by Trina himself. He feels that someone from Cleveland should be there to represent us, and I guess he thought that I was as good as anyone. He suggested that I bring a friend or two, and that's where you and John come in."

"Sounds like fun. I'll look forward to it. Keep me posted."
As Jane sauntered out of the office, Holland picked up the phone and dialed John's work number.

"Kazek here."

"I'm sorry. I'm trying to reach J. Edgar Hoover."

"I'm afraid you're going to have to call very long distance to reach him miss, because his body's at least six feet under and probably in Washington. As for his soul, from what I understand, it's probably located far, far, far below where his remains are now residing. Well Miss Matthews, to what do I owe the pleasure of this call during office hours?"

"Because as luck would have it, I wish to offer you an evening of recreation and entertainment, which even the elusive John Kazek F.B.I. will have difficulty turning down. How would you like to escort two of Cleveland's most eligible bachelorettes on a riverboat cruise upon the Ohio River, all expenses paid?"

"Tell me more, fair damsel."

"You know the riverboat cruise that I've been telling you about for our Cincinnati plant? Well, my suddenly new best bud, Jonas Trina, seems to think that the only way that we can reap the most benefit out the evening is if yours truly is in attendance to accept the heartfelt thanks of our Cincinnati brethren. Or some horse crap like that. Anyway, who cares! I get to go on a riverboat cruise and I'm allowed to take along a few folks of my choosing, and I choose you! And I plan on bringing Jane from work to reward her for some favors she's done for me. It's on Saturday September 21st, and I will not take no for an answer, John Kazek F.B.I. It'll be a really fun time, and we get to stay over at some posh hotel. And, if you play your cards right, who knows where the night might lead? Seriously John, I'd love to have you share the experience if you can get away. What do you think?"

"Sounds great! Especially the part about not just one, but two of Cleveland's most eligible single foxes! Don't worry though Holly-Brit, there's plenty of old John-boy to go around."

"Why is it I just knew that you'd say something like that? Well, be advised John-boy that just because you're escorting us doesn't mean that we intend to act like escorts, if you catch my drift."

"Wonderful, I just love a challenge. Truthfully sweetie, I'm looking forward to sharing a great time down in Cincinnati. Hopefully, all of the bad guys in the world will take a little hiatus so that I don't get called away to duty at the last second."

"We'll just have to arrange to make you incommunicado for a few days. Surely the world can survive if the great superhero John Kazek F.B.I. enjoys a little R&R with his honey for a weekend. Tell your boss that you've been kidnapped by two sex starved supermodels."

"No can do. I used that excuse last week."

"Very funny lover boy. Remind me to polish your family jewels with a well placed high gloss stiletto pump when I see you."

"Sorry, but you know how in demand us playboy jet set F.B.I. hero types are. Unfortunately, I've got to get back to work now. But hey it sounds great. I'll call you later tonight to see if we can arrange a little rendezvous before then. After all, that's still a few weeks away, and I think I'll need a little dose of Holly-Brit long before then."

"You know the number babe. Ciao for now."

"Hello," said Ike, as he answered his cell phone knowing full well who the caller once again was.

"I'm sorry to disturb you, but I'm afraid that vacation time must come to an end."

"That's alright. Things were starting to get a little boring around here anyway. What's up?"

"I need you to do a little favor for me on your way back home. I'd like you to stop off in the Chicago area and pay a visit on an old acquaintance of mine from my old employer. I'll furnish you her current address, description, and what I'd like your visit to accomplish. I'd appreciate it if the visit can be arranged in the next 3-4 days if possible."

"I think I can work that into my schedule."

"Beautiful, Compensation will be arranged as usual. Goodbye."
Later that same evening, Jonas reviewed the taped telephone conversation between Holland and John. He almost felt a tinge of remorse for what he knew lay in their collective future.

CHAPTER 24

"Alright people, we only have a few short weeks left to finalize all of the arrangements for the cruise, so enlighten me as to where we now stand. Daniece, why don't you begin with your department's accomplishments?"

"Well Mr.Trina, last weekend a few of us got together and arranged to listen to both of the bands that we selected for the event. I must say that they sounded pretty darn good in our estimation. I think you'll all be impressed at both their talent and their repertoires. Wouldn't you agree Holland?"

"Absolutely! Both groups looked and sounded fabulous. I'm confident that they will suitable."

"Excellent," said Jonas. "Megan, why don't you go next?"

"We've procured cases of both Glenlivet and Chivas Regal for the scotch crowd, Jack Daniels and Jameson's for the "whiskeyites" and some Old Grandad for the bourbon drinkers sure to be found down in that area. Also there will be plenty of beer and soft drinks. We're finalizing the wine selections today."

"Good. If you need an accomplished palate to inspect the wine selections Megan, I'm prepared to offer my services. Now Miss McKinney, please bring us up to speed on the status of the invitations."

"I spoke to the printer this morning. They assured me that they would be finished with the invitations today, and that they would be working overtime to get them into the pre-addressed envelopes we furnished. They are planning on airmailing them so they should arrive tomorrow morning by 10:00A.M."

"Wonderful Miss McKinney. I knew that I could count on you as always."

"Oh, by the way Mr. Trina, I took the liberty to correct a few grammatical errors which the people at the print shop were kind enough to point out, so the final print...

"NOOOOOOOOO!" screamed a scarlet-faced Jonas as he flew out of his seat enraged at the seemingly innocent words he'd just heard. The other committee members sat dumbfounded with mouths agape at the extreme overreaction on behalf of the C. E.O.

"Miss McKinney, you will go back to your office immediately and make contact with the printer," roared Jonas. "Tell them they are to print the original text as they were sent with absolutely no changes if they expect to be paid for their efforts. When you have gotten a commitment out of them, leave a note on my desk with their name, telephone number and contact person. You may then clear out your desk and begin a search for your next career opportunity. If the information is not accurate, I will see to it that you not only do not receive your last paycheck, but also your severance package will be affected. Please go now. This meeting is officially over people."

With a look of extreme aggravation and disgust, Jonas swept out of the room. As he left, all eyes were averted from his intense glare in order to not risk provoking his anger any further. Only when his retreating footsteps were safely out of earshot did anyone dare speak.

"Remind me not to volunteer as one of his speech writers," quipped one of Megan Stewart's marketing cronies."

"Shut up Henry!" shot back Megan as she watched the devastated Nancy McKinney attempt to make her way out of the room.

"Here Nancy, let me help you with the door," offered Holland as she hastily strode toward the entrance.

"Don't worry Nancy. You'll have something better in a week. And you can damn well bet it will be working for someone who is a helluva lot nicer!' daringly stated Daniece, all the while staring defiantly at Ray Titus, almost daring him to report her insolence back to Jonas. As Holland led Nancy out of the room, those remaining were left to ponder exactly what had just occurred, and why.

"What in the hell just happened here?" asked Megan.

"I'm not sure, but I think we just witnessed an example of why you don't want to challenge or overturn anything that our C.E.O. does or says," offered Ray Titus

"There's more to it than that, but I'm not sure just what." said Daniece "I will say that was the biggest overreaction that I've ever seen in the business world."

"You can say that again. I didn't know that a human being's face could turn that shade of reddish purple," said Henry.

"I don't know about the rest of you, but I think that the safest course of action at this point is to let Jonas cool off. I think that the less said about this the better for the time being," pronounced Daniece.

"That sounds like sage advice to me. Now I suppose the proper thing to do is get back to work so that we don't run the risk of antagonizing Mr. Trina any further," said Ray Titus, and with that the meeting broke up with the shuffle of chairs being replaced and briefcases closing.

Jonas had stormed back into his office and slammed the door. He was upset, but he wasn't sure if he was angrier at Nancy McKinney or himself. He prided himself on anticipating all eventualities, and heading off potential trouble at the pass long before it had a chance to manifest itself. Now he had made a sophomoric oversight by not mentioning to Nancy the fact that he would accept no changes to the invitation prior to her sending it on to the printer's office. That had resulted in the circumstances that brought about his gross overreaction. This now threatened to jeopardize his plans if anyone was clever enough to put two and two together. While he felt reasonably safe that no one would figure things out, his oversight had created an unnecessary risk. Steps would have to be taken to defuse the situation. He would make sure to redouble his future planning efforts so these types of incidents could be avoided.

At this point, Jonas needed a pick-me-up. The incident had upset him terribly and had resulted in his letting his guard down. He needed something to recharge his vitality again, and he had just the thing. Walking to his desk, Jonas opened his top drawer and took out a compact disc. He turned on his oversized plasma television, inserted the disc into the player, and turned off the light.

The screen initially showed a peaceful island many miles away. The island was set low on the horizon as if being viewed from the deck of an approaching ship. Palm trees swayed in the distance. A blinding white light suddenly shattered this tranquil setting. As the light began to fade. a cloud of fiery dust began to boil upward from the bottom of the picture screen. The cloud grew rapidly and seemed almost to defy nature itself in the vehemence. The picture began to shake noticeably, and an appreciable roar filled the room even with the sound turned down. After a short time, the cloud began to structure itself, rising skyward in column-like fashion. The upper portion of the column began to change shape, assuming a mushroom shaped crown. The pace of the cloud's growth now finally began to taper off and the angriness of the cloud slackened as the crown turned whitish and the column stabilized into a medium gray color. This 1950's Bimini Atoll nuclear blast always was one of Jonas' favorites.

The plasma television once again burst into a brilliant white as a picture of the very first atomic blast at Alamagordo, New Mexico, which ushered in the Atomic Age filled the screen. Next was a French explosion in the Pacific, followed by a smuggled copy of the first Chinese test at Lop Nor in 1964. While all of these were impressive, they paled in comparison to the next two that were immense hydrogen bomb blasts from the U.S.S.R. These explosions took place in the early 60's before the signing of the Nuclear Non-Proliferation Treaty, and they seemed to set the very atmosphere itself on fire.

As the immense roiling shaft of the blasts lurched skyward on screen, a peculiar reaction began to take shape within Jonas' person. An offshoot of watching this disc of explosions was that it always produced a Viagra-like effect upon Jonas. The incredible phallic type rise of the pulsing nuclear column, coupled with the mushroom head was certainly reminiscent of male genitalia. The similarity was almost undeniable. However, this was not the reason Jonas enjoyed the movie. Indeed, he usually was totally oblivious to the reaction. It was the immense power depicted on the screen that he craved. Power, the ultimate aphrodisiac! His reaction was merely an unintended by-product and nothing more. Normally, however this time…

The office door opened slowly, and Nancy McKinney tentatively stepped across the darkened threshold. She could see Jonas plainly, silhouetted in front of the light emitted from the plasma set. He was not yet aware of her as his body was turned at an angle away from the door. Her eyes crept downward from the screen to take in an odd protuberance pushing his trouser front outward. Though she tried to ignore the sight, and twice deliberately forced herself to view the screen, each time her gaze returned to Jonas' pants.

Sensing a presence close-by, Jonas suddenly wheeled and silently confronted Nancy with an angry glare. Before he could open up on her, Nancy wisely took the offensive and began to speak.

"I'm sorry for intruding sir, but I knocked lightly several times, and I guess that you didn't hear me. You said that I should come to your office after I straightened things out with the print shop. They are going to change the invitations back to the original format as per your request, and they will have them delivered in plenty of time. I very much wish to apologize for my terrible mistake. It certainly was not my intention to overstep your authority in any way. I wish that there was some way to make it up to you."

Jonas' look softened a tiny bit, as even he was appreciative of the sincerity of the apology. Nancy took this opportunity to make her move. Casting caution to the wind, she bravely (and brazenly) approached Jonas, and in a seductive fashion reached down and began to caress the bulge in Jonas' trousers.

"Even as impressive as those shapes are on the television, this is the mushroom head and shaft that I prefer." As she slowly dropped to her knees and began to unzip his fly, Jonas finally uttered his first words.

"Miss McKinney, I believe that it is possible you have just discovered the ideal position within this organization which best suits your talents."

Three hours later, an e-mail from Jonas Trina went out to all who were in attendance at the meeting. The message detailed an apology to all who witnessed the event, and offered up an explanation for Jonas' unusual behavior. A reaction to an over the counter medication was to blame, nothing more. Miss McKinney had been reinstated with an appreciable raise, and the matter was to be forgotten. All attendees were praised for their diligence to the task at hand, and he would personally handle the invitations with the printer.

Later that same evening, Holland and John were enjoying each other and a sumptuous meal at the Oriental Palace, one of Holland's favorite restaurants. Between bites of savory sweet and sour chicken and spicy Szechuan beef, they had been discussing the day's events. Of particular interest was the blow-up at the cruise meeting.

"Holland, please don't get mad at me, but sometimes I think you have a personal vendetta that you want to carry out against this Trina guy. I mean the guy just lost his cool, reconsidered his actions, admitted his mistake, and set about to make things right. And from what you've told me, I think he has done just that with giving the girl her job back along with a raise."

"I suppose I can see how you would think that, but you weren't there John. You didn't see his face turn purple and his eyes bug out over what appeared to be something relatively minor. No, I think that there is more than meets the eye going on here. I can't put my finger on it just now, and yet I think that his excuse is merely a ruse to cover his tracks."

"But why Holland? I mean what could possibly be so damned important about how an invitation is worded. There aren't any tracks to cover. Don't tell me that you still think he's this evil corporate genius who's running around killing people?"

"Let's just say that I haven't totally eliminated that possibility from consideration as of yet. That's enough of this. And if I'm going to still be able to fit into a size six, I'd better say enough of this Chinese cuisine. I must admit it is soooo good! Yum!! Thank you very much John Kazek F.B.I., for bringing me here. As you know, the best way to a woman's heart is through her stomach, or something like that."

"I believe that is supposed to be a man's heart, but your appreciation for tonight's repast has been duly logged and noted. Now, what say we cap off the evening with a walk along the North Shore? It's a beautiful night and after that meal we should probably get a little exercise to lop off a couple of the ten thousand calories we both just inhaled, don't you think? Maybe we'll be able to look across Lake Erie and see Canada."

"I'm afraid that Canada is a wee bit too far over the horizon to be seen from the shore, my dear. But I agree that a walk along the lake would not only be a good idea from a health perspective, but also from a romantic point of view, don't you think'?"

"Curses! Methinks the lady doth seeest through my ulterior motives."

"Be advised, my knight in tarnished armor, that just because fair maiden doth foresee potential ulterior motives does not necessarily mean that she disagrees with said motives."

"Ah, perchance romance awaits me yet this evening."

"Time will tell Sir Lance-a-Little, time will tell."

Long after this evening, they would contemplate why they had
mutually agreed to consummate their relationship physically on this
particular night. It may have had something to do with the carafe of
plum wine they had shared over dinner. Perhaps the beauty of the
September moon shining off the silvery spume of waves breaking on
the rocky shoreline contributed to the evening's spell. The warmth of
their intertwined fingers, as they held hands while combing the lunar-
lit hard packed sand for shells, may have provided the spark. One thing
both could agree on was that John's tripping over a rock and falling to
the beach set the scene for love. As he landed unceremoniously with a
distinct thud, Holland lowered herself to the sand to offer assistance.
When she inquired as to whether John was all right, he silently
motioned her closer to his lips and whispered:

"Methinks I need the sweet kiss of a fair maiden to nurse me back to
health."

"Fear not O gallant prince, your wish is my command."
That first joining of lips released torrents of pent up passion within
both of them that only seemed to build as they ground their lips and
bodies together on the beach.

"Your castle or mine?" Holland panted huskily as she nibbled John's
earlobe.

"Mine's closer and probably offers a bit more privacy."

"Then let's mount thy steed and make haste my prince, so that we
might mount each other in earnest!"

Together they laughingly made their way back to John's Mustang,
stopping at the passenger door long enough to apply a light but
noticeable sucker bite to each other's neck. The trip to John's
fashionable townhouse was normally a twenty-minute trip from this
lakefront location, but they made the trip in twelve. Upon entering the
house, the pathway from entrance to bedroom was strewn with various
articles of hastily discarded apparel. Holland would fondly recall the
next several hours as the happiest of her life. John proclaimed that he
could now die a totally fulfilled man. Of utmost certainty was that from
this night on, their love, their lives, and their fates would be as
intertwined as their fingers had been on the beach.

The following week Holland and Daniece were seated in Jonas Trina's office going through projections for their department for the next quarter. To Holland, Jonas seemed somewhat distracted and distant compared to his normal demeanor. As the meeting came to an end and the ladies began to get up in preparation of leaving, a commotion arose outside of Jonas' office door.

"I told you that you can't go in lady," screamed Nancy McKinney. A moment later the door flew open, and in the portal stood a smallish middle aged woman who appeared to be of Hispanic descent.

"Rosa, you know better than to come here," admonished Jonas.

"Please Mr. Trina, I had to talk with you one last time," the woman answered.

"Daniece and Holland, I believe we were all finished."

"Yes sir, we'll be leaving now," said Daniece as she and Holland began backpedaling out of the office.

As they left, Jonas closed the door sharply and lowered the shades. The woman's animated voice could be heard imploring Jonas about something. Holland's antennae were perked up as she attempted to ascertain exactly what was going on in the office. Unfortunately, Nancy McKinney was glaring at Holland in an effort to protect her boss's privacy. Holland and Daniece slowly made their way past Nancy's desk as Holland strained her ears to catch an additional word or two as they departed. Out in the hallway Holland turned to Daniece.

"What do you suppose that was all about'?"

"I'm not sure, but if I had to hazard a guess, I would say that it has something to do with Trina's estate and the hired help he employs to run it. I overheard him talking on the phone in the past to someone named Rosa, and I'm pretty sure that the conversation centered on his home and her duties."

"Interesting. Daniece, I think that I'm going to take this opportunity to freshen up in the ladies room. Why don't you go on without me and we'll hook up later on in the day to go over what we discussed with Jonas and the revisions to our quarterly projections."

"O. K. See you later Holly-Brit."

Holland ducked into the ladies room while Daniece proceeded down the hallway back to her department. Checking around, Holland determined that she was alone in the restroom. She cautiously opened the restroom door a crack and glancing down the corridor in both directions, she saw that the hallway was deserted. Good. She could view Jonas' departmental entrance without arousing curiosity. Several minutes later, the door she was observing opened, and out stepped Rosa, who appeared to have been weeping. As she walked slowly past the restroom door, Holland motioned to her to come in and join her. The Hispanic woman was apprehensive, but Holland's insistence and trustworthy countenance won over the woman's confidence. She entered the restroom, and Holland began to speak.

"Please don't be afraid. My name is Holland Matthews, and I was in Jonas Trina's office when you came in there. It appeared as though you were pretty upset when you went into his office, and I was wondering if there was anything that I could do to help?"

"Thank you very much Miss Holland, but I'm afraid that now there is not much that anyone can do to help me."

"You might he surprised. May I ask about your association with Mr. Trina'?"

"Well, until yesterday I was his housekeeper. I had been his housekeeper ever since he moved to Cleveland many months ago. He is a difficult man to work for, but he paid well. That is until he fired me yesterday."

"Why did he let you go?"

"It's a long story."

"With that in mind, why don't we go someplace away from here where we can discuss this freely, and somewhere with a little more elegance than the ladies room?"

"I don't know. We just met and I'm not sure..."

"Look Rosa, that is your name right, Rosa'?"

"Yes"

"Rosa, it seems to me that you could use a friend or two at the moment, and I might be just the person to get you back on your feet. I have a few matters pertaining to Jonas Trina right now that could perhaps put us on the same side regarding him. Anyway, how about if I treat you to something to eat at Lou's bakery across the street? There you can fill me in as to the circumstances of your dismissal. Then I'll see if there is anything we can do to help you. Afterwards I can give you a lift home, or anywhere you would like to go. Alright?"

"Why, are you being so nice to a complete stranger?"

"You can consider it as me doing my good deed for the day. Also I'm curious as to what you might be able to tell me about Jonas' house. I've never been there, but people tell me it's fabulous, and I guess that I'm hoping that you can give me some description of what it's like."

"That I can surely do. That man lives like a king. O.K. you've convinced me that it would be safe to meet with you. You say that Lou's bakery is right across the street?"

"Pretty much. When you go back out the main entrance, turn to your right and go to the end of the block. It's right across the street from there. We can get a booth in back. Don't worry. Jonas never goes in there so we'll he safe from his prying ears. You leave now, and I'll he there in fifteen minutes."

"O.K. Miss Holland. And thank you. I'll see you in fifteen minutes." Rosa made her way down the hallway in the direction of the main entrance. A couple of minutes later, Holland raced back to her department and rushed into Daniece's office where Jenny and Daniece were conversing.

"Sorry to burst in on you like this Daniece, but something's come up, and I've got to take off for a couple of hours. I'll fill you in when I get back.

"That's fine Holland, but don't forget that we've got those quarterly revisions to work on."

"Don't worry. I'll be back in time to finish those."

"If you ask me, I'll bet that I can hazard a guess as to what has just come up that needs Holland's urgent attention. I'll bet it's located just slightly south of Mr. F.B.I.'s pants zipper," playfully added Jenny.

"Actually, miss horny toad, it has nothing to do with him. However, if that was the case, believe me that it would be a significant distance north of where his zipper ends if you catch my drift!" Daniece could merely shake her head as Holland turned to rush out the door, leaving a silent but envious Jenny to chew on her words as she departed.

Five minutes later Holland entered the bakery and peered around the room for Rosa. At first she couldn't find her, but playing a hunch she decided to check out who might be hiding behind an upraised menu in a booth towards the back of the bakery. Advancing on the booth, Holland looked over the top of the menu and was met by a pair of timid chocolate colored eyes.

"Rosa I've found you. For a minute I thought that perhaps you had changed your mind."

"I guess that I'm still a little worried about meeting this close to Mr. Trina's office."

"Don't be, he never comes in here. He's much too arrogant to eat where the commoners would be able to rub elbows with him."

"I'll try to relax."

"Good. Have you ever been here before?"

"No."

"Well, if you like nut rolls, I'd suggest trying Lou's happy cakes. They're fabulous. The strudel is outstanding too. The coffees here are a little on the strong side, but very flavorful also." The waitress came over and took their orders, and Holland got down to business.

"Rosa, I don't mean to pry, but may I ask what you did that warranted Trina's firing you."

"Yesterday in the early evening Mr. Trina mentioned to me that he had lost his favorite pen. It is very expensive because it has a lot of jewels set right in it. He asked me to see if I could find it. Then he went down to his office in the basement. You should see his office. It is a huge room, and it must have cost a few million dollars to make it look the way it does. Anyway, a little while later I found his pen and I went downstairs to bring it to him. His office door locks automatically when it closes as a precaution to protect Mr. Trina's privacy. I went to knock on the door, and I realized that the door was open just a crack. I didn't mean to spy on Mr. Trina, but I peeked into the room and I was amazed by what I saw. He has a big chessboard mounted on the wall with large chess pieces sticking out from it. You can actually play a game of chess on the board. Well, I saw Mr. Trina move three or four pieces, and all of a sudden the chessboard opens up. In the center of the wall that was uncovered by the movement of the board was a wall safe. Mr. Trina put in the combination and opened the safe. I know that I should not have watched, but I couldn't help myself. Also, by the time he had done these things, it was too late to let him know that I was there watching him all of the time. He reached into the safe and pulled out what looked like a gold plated notebook. He opened the notebook and put several sheets of paper in it. Then he closed the notebook and put it back into the safe."

At this point the waitress brought their order which consisted of two cups of coffee, some apple strudel, and four pieces of nut rolls. Everything looked and smelled divine. The women took a short break from the story to sample the tasty offerings.

"So what happened then?" inquired Holland between bites of happy cake.

"All of a sudden I felt two arms grab me from behind. It was Karl the butler. He yelled at me for sneaking around and spying on Mr. Trina. I told him that I wasn't spying on Mr. Trina and that I had just come to give him back his pen. Mr. Trina asked Karl how long I had been standing there. He had no way of knowing, but he said that I might have been there as long as a few minutes. Mr. Trina asked me what I had seen, and I told him nothing. Karl said he thought that I was lying. I started to get afraid, but then the doorbell rang twice, followed by a pause, and then one more ring. That is the signal that my two large cousins have come to pick me up for the evening and take me back to my apartment. Mr. Trina told Karl to answer the door and let them in. When he went upstairs, Mr. Trina said that my services would no longer be needed. He quickly wrote me a check for my wages, plus five hundred more dollars for severance pay I guess, and took me upstairs. He had a strange look on his face as we went through the house to the front entrance. It was very mean looking, but it didn't seem like it was anger. It seemed more like a cruel face. I was very happy to get out of the house and to be in the protection of my cousins."

"With what you just told me, I guess that I'm a little confused as to why you came to Mr. Trina's office to try and get your job back today."

"After I got home, I started thinking. Even though I am a little afraid of what Mr. Trina or Karl might do to me, the pay is very good there. It is almost impossible to find a job in my line of work that will pay me as much as I made at Mr. Trina's."

"But what if it wasn't safe for you to work there?"

"You don't think that he would really try to hurt me do you?"

"Let's just say that I wouldn't put it past him."

"In that case it probably wouldn't be worth it."

"I agree. I've got some friends who might be able to turn you onto some job prospects. In fact, I have a friend who has her own cleaning business. Perhaps she could use some extra help at this time. Why don't I take you home and get your telephone number and I'll have these people call you.

"That would be very kind."

"It would be my pleasure. Here is some money for you to pay the bill and to leave a tip. I'll go get my car and meet you in front in about five minutes.

As Holland pulled her red Ford Taurus in front of the bakery door, one of those unfortunate twists of fate was about to occur. On the next block down from the bakery was a drug store. It was only about 50 yards from the bakery. Jonas Trina emerged from the store's door clutching a package. Glancing to his right he saw a smallish Hispanic woman come out of the bakery door and get into the red Taurus. Had he not seen Rosa at length in his office within the past 90 minutes, his brain probably would not have made the mental connection.

The car pulled quickly away from the curb and accelerated to join the flow of midday downtown traffic. However, the bright blue letters on the white background of the Ohio vanity license plate were still quite visible to Jonas' eyes even as the vehicle changed lanes to make a turn at the next corner. The letters HOLLY BRT rounded the corner and disappeared from view. Jonas thought to himself that he may have underestimated his opponent somewhat in this matching of wits which neither had acknowledged to the other as of yet. Miss Matthews must be given credit for a rook due to her discovery of Triste in Chicago and gaining insight into Jonas' past. Now he would have to at least give her credit for another pawn in her obvious befriending of his former housekeeper. Her move to capture his rook however had already been compromised, and he could see little benefit to her from her latest coup with Rosa. Besides, it was all of little consequence, because on September 21st the match would come to an end with him being declared the only combatant left standing.

Rosa's disloyalty was another matter altogether, which he would have to contemplate and pass judgment upon. Taking into consideration her previous service to him and the fact that he had grown somewhat fond of her, Jonas made a rare decision. He decided to spare her life and forgive her transgressions against him. This made her a member of a very select club. That was the club of those who had crossed Jonas Trina and not been made to pay dearly for it. As Jonas crossed the street to go back to his office, he made a mental note to monitor his office surveillance equipment later this afternoon. It could be interesting.

Holland arrived back at the office 45 minutes after leaving the bakery with Rosa. She quickly made her way into Daniece's office.

"Sorry I had to take off. I'm ready for those quarterly revisions now."

"Good, but before we get into that, Jane came in here looking for you a few minutes ago. She seemed pretty upset about something, but she wouldn't talk about it with me. Why don't you check in with her before we begin and see if you can help?"

Holland made her way to Jane's workstation. As she approached, she could plainly see that Jane had been crying. She compassionately put her arm on Jane's shoulder and suggested that they go into Holland's office where they could have some privacy. Upon closing the office door, Holland gently inquired as to her problem. Between sobs Jane answered;

"Holly-Brit I ca...ca...called my mo..mo..mother in Chicago during lunch. As we were ta..ta..talking she mentioned to me that the newspapers had a story about a woman who had b..b..been burned to a crisp in her own bathroom yesterday. It appeared that sh...sh..she had been taking a bath when her plugged in hairdryer fell into the bathtub. Her name was T...T..Triste Johnson and until recently, she had worked for Sutton Industries in Chicago. The police were speculating that she may have been despondent over losing her job, and they are investigating the m..m..matter as a suicide. Hol...Holland I'm scared. What if Mr. Trina found out about us talking and decided to kill me. Maybe even you too! Oh Holland!!"

"Easy Jane, easy. I'm terribly sorry that this lady that you met has died, but there is no indication that it was a murder. Also, how would Trina find out that you met with her and why would he suspect anything, let alone consider murdering us? That's a pretty drastic leap if you ask me. I'm sure that we have nothing to worry about. Now let's go to the washroom and clean up that sweet little face of yours."

"You're s..s...sure everything will be alright?"

"Of course. Everything will be just fine"

As they left her office and proceeded toward the door to the hallway, Holland tried to keep up a solid exterior for Jane's sake, although she had concerns of her own deep down inside. Once again, strange timing and strange circumstances had resulted in another death related to Jonas Trina or Pharmacor. She remembered a couple of old sayings that her father used to tell her: "If it walks like a duck and it quacks like a duck, then chances are it's a duck. Also, where there is smoke, there's fire." Why does death seem to follow Jonas Trina around like a constant companion? Entering the hallway, the twosome began to make their way to the washroom. A door opened farther down the hall and out strolled Jonas. As he approached the women he glanced at Jane's tear streaked face and asked smugly, "Did we lose something ladies?" Not waiting for a reply he continued down the hallway towards the front door. Holland seethed with rage over the comment. White-hot daggers of hate shot from her eyes at the back of the smug C.E.O. "The son-of-a-bitch had her killed. I just know it! But how! **HOW DID HE FIND OUT?**" As they entered the washroom, Holland felt a cold chill of fear creep up her spine as she realized that they could be the next victims.

Jonas Trina casually continued his stroll towards the front entrance of Pharmacor. While there was a small part of him that desired to turn and gloat at the two women who were no doubt continuing to wallow in their misery, he knew that it would be tempting fate to acknowledge that he could possibly have an inkling of the cause. Besides, it would be so unnecessary. After all, he'd already won this battle.

"Good day Mr.Trina!" said the receptionist to Jonas, as he swept past her on his way out while he whistled a tune from Tannhauser.

"Scratch one rook." Jonas thought to himself as he entered the September sunshine.

Later that evening over dinner, Holland told John about the incident in the hallway. John dismissed Trina's comment as nothing more than a passing observation. To him it appeared to be a perfectly natural thing to say, and that Holland was overreacting. He did suggest that if she were truly concerned, she would be welcome to stay at his townhouse for added protection. She thanked him for the offer and said she would consider it. As the next few days unfolded, there were no suspicious happenings, and slowly Holland began to dismiss her fears as being groundless. Furthermore, it would be almost impossible for Trina to have access to Holland and Jane's plans these past few weeks. Holland eventually found that she was growing more relaxed, and in fact excited as the end of September approached and the riverboat cruise date grew near.

CHAPTER 25

Saturday, September 21st introduced itself with a glorious cloud free sunrise. Condensation on the grass that hinted at a cool evening past would soon disappear as the sun rose in the sky. A single beam of sunlight crept under the window shade and persistently began to tickle Holland's eyelids with radiance as it began to bring her out of deep REM sleep. Like golden fingertips, it sought to gently lift up her eyelashes and start the awakening process. Almost imperceptibly, first one, and then the other eyelash began to flutter ever so slightly. At the same time, her olfactory senses kicked in and subconsciously registered a delicious aroma. A thin line of steam was emanating from the nightstand beside the bed. It was issuing forth from the narrow, delicately curved neck of a silver coffee urn and was floating in Holland's direction. The fragrant scent effectively banished the last vestiges of sleep to the nether regions of her mind, to be revisited many hours from now. Instinctively her hands formed themselves into fists and made their way to her eyes. Lightly rubbing her eyes with the balled up fists removed the majority of the "Pixie Dust" from them. Opening her hands and rubbing the lower palms gently against her eyes completed the task. She suddenly had the sensation of her feet being tickled and they quickly retreated under the covers to escape the assault. Rapid fluttering of her eyelids helped to bring her world into focus.

"It's time to arise, my little mink."

"I see that we're not big on allowing a weary lady to ease into her day, are we Mr. Kazek."

"The day is a-wasting my buxom beauty! In my own defense, I've taken the liberty to brew up a pot of Hazelnut/Caramel/French Vanilla/Cinnamon coffee to help welcome you back to the living. Would you like some poured into this exceedingly gorgeous Cleveland Browns mug, or should we start an intravenous drip?"

"The mug should suffice just fine, my sweet. May I ask where you got that beautiful silver urn?"

"It was given to me by an aunt who thought that it might add a touch of class and elegance to my poor neglected bachelor pad."

"No offense, but I thought as much. Somehow I just couldn't see you going into a nice store and picking something that elegant and classy out for yourself. After all you are a mere male."

231

"Hey wait a minute. I picked you out all by myself didn't I, and you're pretty elegant and classy, right?"

"Touché`."

"Well, it's going on eight o'clock and if we're going to pick up Jane by nine thirty, I'd better jump in the shower while you finish your coffee."

"Mr. Kazek F.B.I. you surprise me. As a taxpaying citizen I'm appalled at your apparent indifference to national policy. And to think, that you are a member of a governmental agency. Tsk! Tsk! Aren't you aware that just as the government encourages carpooling to save gas, so too they encourage shower sharing to save one of our most precious natural resources, good old H2O."

With that being said, Holland put her mug down, arose from the bed, and began to slowly walk towards John. As she did so, she seductively allowed her thin robe to fall from her shoulders to the floor, revealing her full firm breasts and pubic area to John's eager eyes. As she continued forward, she grabbed John's hand and gently led him towards the master bathroom.

"This is one governmental policy that has my full support," said John as he closed the bathroom door."

Tariq Al-Salem's morning was starting off vastly different. His force of sixteen men was diligently working on their assigned tasks. Nine were continuing to prepare the food, a process that had begun in earnest the day before. Four stoves were baking away in the sprawling dilapidated house in the backwoods hill country of Northern Kentucky. Money from Jonas had been used to secure this property that served as their base of operations. Located just thirty miles from Cincinnati, it was close enough from a logistics point of view and yet secluded enough to offer the privacy that they so urgently needed. Two other men were painting the words Moroccan Interlude in Matura Scrip on two white Ford Econoline vans. The other five men were at an abandoned warehouse beside the Cincinnati riverfront where they were pretending to be part of a roofing crew. This crew and their leader, Nishil Najir, would be responsible for preparing a large motorboat for tonight's mission.

All sixteen men had been hand selected, and each had received extensive training both in the Middle East and here in the United States. Most of the men had been in the country for over a year, and they had assimilated themselves into the American culture. Each could speak English fluently, and all were adept at a wide variety of arms and martial arts. Tariq was very proud of his fighting force, and soon America would find out why. Although eventually his group would have made their presence known in the U.S., Jonas Trina had served to be the impetus to move up their timetable significantly. His knowledge of the target, his ability to get the men in close proximity to the target, and his willingness to provide needed funding were all important in the selection process. The Cincinnati riverfront would soon have the dubious honor of being chosen as the jumping off point for Tariq Al-Salem's, "Fist of Rage" jihad force. Soon America would learn what those in many other countries already felt. While a great victory had been achieved with the felling of the Twin Towers a few years ago, the fear effect of that event had by now been diffused. His, "Fist of Rage" group would instill in the American populace the realization that they could be reached even in the heartland of their country. No longer would they be able to go to bed secure in their belief that they were safe behind their oceans and mountains. Death would soon be afoot in the land.

The purpose behind his cadre of men was to act as a guerrilla force in the United States. They would hit targets at their own time and choosing throughout the U.S. and then disband to their prearranged safe houses. They would be widely disbursed, and with very limited knowledge of any of the other's whereabouts. Thus, even if one or two were compromised, they would not be able to jeopardize the group as a whole. Their tactics would be to hit hard, hit fast, and disappear, only to reappear weeks or months later to strike again. The enemy would be made aware of who was responsible for each act, so that there could be no doubt as to who was responsible and for what cause they were fighting. Their victims would be found in big cities and small towns. Killing would come to county fairs and Sunday socials. Malls, political rallies and sporting events would fall victim. All would know that they were not safe in their own communities. Terror in all its heart rending, nerve-shattering forms had come to America.

The noonday sun felt pleasantly warm as it shined down on the blue Mercedes convertible. Ike Steele was coming up on the Columbus, Ohio exit that he knew would take him to the famed horseshoe shaped stadium that was home to the Ohio State Buckeye's football team. For a brief moment he felt an urge to get off I-71 South at this exit. His Penn State Nittainy Lions were playing the Buckeyes this afternoon in Columbus, with the game scheduled to start in fifteen minutes from now at 1:00 P.M. The thought was just a passing fancy, for Ike knew what his duties were for today, and certainly football watching was not among them. He was to check in at the swank Charter House Hotel where he had two rooms reserved under his Trevor Graham alias. These upper floor rooms provided a good view of the Ohio River. One of the rooms would be for Jonas, who would be joining him later that afternoon. Jonas had requested Ike to join him this weekend in Cincinnati to evaluate the performance of their new associates. Additionally, he had picked up some gear that would be necessary to properly view the scheduled event, and some beverages to enjoy before and after the show. Cocktails were scheduled at 6:15. A gourmet in-room meal would arrive at 7:30. Dishes would be cleared at 8:30, and they would prepare for the main event that would occur at 9:00. "Yes, I'm certainly going to enjoy this evening," thought Ike as he approached downtown Columbus, only 90 minutes from his Cincinnati destination.

While Jonas would have preferred the convenience of flying, it ran the risk of an unwanted paper trail, and that was one thing that he wished to avoid this weekend. While there was certainly no law against his being in Cincinnati this weekend, it could lead to questions that might prove dangerous, should his whereabouts this evening become known. Thus it was much more prudent to drive and reduce the risk of discovery. Though Jonas viewed trips of any length to be a tedious bore, at least in his cream-colored Cadillac Escalade he was accomplishing the trek from Cleveland to Cincinnati in style. He glanced at his Rolex timepiece and then at his in dash clock, and was pleased that they were both still correct to the same exact second. Both said 2:04:14 P.M. Jonas hit a button on his control panel and the onboard GPS monitoring system told him that he had two hours and six minutes to his destination at his current speed. That should be perfect, thought Jonas.

He was a bit surprised at how much he was looking forward to seeing Ike again. It had been long before the Social Club fire when last he'd seen him. Though Jonas was essentially a man of limited social needs, he was not a hermit. He always relished a stimulating and thought provoking conversation, and with what was on their plate for this evening, he was sure there would be no dearth of camaraderie to be gleaned from the experience. Jonas depressed the accelerator a bit more and the GPS indicator revised the estimate by four minutes as the Escalade began chewing up the miles with renewed vigor.

"Well it's about time we made it here," sighed Holly-Brit as the trio entered the elevator to be whisked vertically to their tenth floor rooms at the Hyatt.

"And I suppose you think that it's my fault that we're so late," exclaimed Jane.

"If you didn't have to check out every restroom between Cleveland and here we'd have made better time."

"Can I help it if I happen to have the bladder capacity of a small kitten? Besides, wasn't it you who just had to examine every single bauble and trinket at that Cracker Barrel we stopped at for coffee?"

"By that time I knew that we weren't going to have any time to do any serious window shopping in Cincinnati, so I figured that was as close as I was going to get." In reality, Holland knew that she didn't have a leg to stand on regarding their late arrival. The shower with a friend idea had led to an hour-long love making session which neither Holland nor John was in any hurry to finish. This led to their arriving at Jane's at 10:20, instead of between 9:00 and 9:30, as originally planned.

"All right ladies, let's sheath our claws for the moment," offered John. "We still have a little bit of time. My watch says its 3:45 now. What say we go to our respective rooms, unpack and freshen-up? We could meet down in the lobby at 4:15. The hotel receptionist said it's only a twenty minute walk from here to the dock where we'll be boarding the Buckeye Belle. That would give us almost an hour to see the sights if you two will quit barking at each other, O.K.?"

"Oh all right," said the girls together.

It was time for Tariq to make his 4:00 P.M.call and check on the status of Nishil's end of the operation. Tariq and his eleven operatives had arrived at the Buckeye Belle almost an hour ago. They had been busy transferring their prepared delicacies from the vans to the grand ballroom on the lower deck. The crew had been attempting to get as close as possible to view, smell, and hopefully sample some of the exotic cuisine. However, Tariq's men had done a fine job of good naturedly keeping the crew-members at bay during the unloading process. The soft drinks and alcoholic beverages had also been stowed below earlier in the day, so everything from his end was going as planned. More importantly, two containers labeled cooking oil but actually filled with explosives and an attached detonator, had been positioned on the lowest level of the vessel. The crew had been instructed to ignore these and that they were simply reserve supplies.

Al-Salem went up on deck and found himself a secluded spot away from prying ears. He dialed a number into his cell phone. Less than a mile away, Nishil Najir picked up his phone.

"Yes"

"Is all still going well?"

"Yes"

"Is the product stored in their correct containers?"

"Yes and the topping has been applied."

"Good. Have we had any interruptions?"

"None."

"Very well. I shall call again at 6:45."

"Goodbye."

Nishil replaced his cell phone in his pocket and made his way over to one of nine 55-gallon drums that were being loaded onto the fenced-in bed of a large truck in the warehouse. The truck was supposedly to be used for roofing work, but that was merely a ruse. Nishil took a screwdriver and used it to pry open the top of the drum. It appeared to be full of a tar emulsion. Nishil took a nearby wood paint stirrer and dipped it into the tar. As he plunged the stirrer into the emulsion, he noticed that after the initial three or four inches, the stirrer met with less resistance. That was good. That would be where the ammonium nitrate/diesel fuel mixture began that filled up the remainder of the drum. The topping should be sufficient to dissuade any curious patrolmen from examining the drums any further, should the need arise. Perhaps this was an unnecessary precaution, but better safe than sorry. He put the top back on the drum and helped his men roll it up the ramp to the bed of the truck for delivery to the final destination.

"Did you see the look on that costume store owner's face? I think he was afraid that I was going to make off with his oversized clown's feet that I tried on," said Jane as the three-some strolled towards the Cincinnati riverfront

"I don't think he was as afraid of that as much as he was afraid of you stretching them out and making them unusable for anyone else," giggled Holly-Brit.

"Look who's talking Miss 26EEE gunboat girl. I don't think anybody is ever going to think that your hooves got the way they are by undergoing that ancient Chinese custom of tight wrapping to achieve petite feet!"

"Look ladies, we've almost made it to The Belle."

"Oh John, it's beautiful."

The Buckeye Belle was painted bright white and stood three stories high. Her gangplank was festooned with a large banner welcoming the Pharmacor employees. Red white and blue buntings were intermittently draped over the white painted railing, and they fluttered gaily in the light breeze. Thin plumes of smoke streamed almost translucently from the twin smokestacks. The large white paddlewheel stood at rest as it preserved its strength for the arduous effort it would expend on the boat and its guests for the evening cruising up and down the river.

"Jane, it looks like those memos's we sent out must've done some good. It's only 5:25 and there must be at least 250 people in line already."

"That's the good news. The bad news is that there are 250 people between me and the first of about four Long Island iced teas that I have my heart set on."

"Better take it easy on those teas my friend. After all John boy here is a member of the F.B.I. That of course stands for the Federal Bureau of Intoxication. He might just have to put the long arm of the law on you for public drunkenness."

"Speaking of arms, maybe I can persuade one of the crewmen to show me his yardarm or something."

"That sounds to me like a little bit of sexual innuendo," John said with feigned embarrassment.

"Why, would I ever talk suggestively in front of my best friend's beau?" coyly asked Jane as she coquettishly batted her eyelashes in John's direction ala Scarlett O'Hara.

"Watch out John. My horny little friend here is attempting to use her feminine wiles to try to entice you away from me. Well, I'll have you know Miss Queen City Lolita that my friend John is a eunuch, so there!"

"I'm a WHAT?"

First Holland, then Jane, and finally John all burst into uproarious laughter causing half of the assembled line to look upon them amusedly as the trio took their place in the queue.

Captain Stanley Smith was the epitome of what a captain should be. Six feet four inches tall and ramrod straight, the 54-year old stalwart fairly oozed authority. It didn't hurt that he still maintained a thick white mane, and a trimmed salt and pepper beard, which along with his rugged good looks helped accentuate his position. The gleaming white uniform adorned with gold shoulder braids complete with the traditional white captain's cap furthered the role he played in guiding the boat. However, there was no denying that the chief advantage he had in maintaining his firm grip on this or any vessel under his command was pure regal bearing. His stately manner and firm authoritative voice demanded and got respect. It was little wonder that the ship was immaculate as the visitors began to make their way up the gangplank to set foot on the vessel.

"Welcome aboard the Buckeye Belle. Enjoy your cruise!" the captain's voice boomed out again and again to the guests as they began to fill the decks in search of fun and merriment.

Ike Steele looked out the window of his sixteenth floor suite and could see that for the moment, the Ohio River was calm and virtually devoid of traffic directly in front of his perch. He estimated that he was approximately 600 yards from the river's edge, and that the river was perhaps 600 yards wide at this particular stretch. Assuming that the action later tonight took place in the middle of the river, that would be at least 900 yards from his window, which should be sufficient

238

distance to offer protection. Ike noticed a motorboat with a skier in tow making lazy S-curves in the almost deserted river. The bikini-clad skier skipped effortlessly over the boat's wake as she cut through the spume kicked up by the boat. The skier's graceful meanderings at the end of her tether had a calming effect on Ike and his mind began to drift. The prescient knowledge of the future that Ike possessed now allowed him to subconsciously view a different scene. His mind envisioned a dark background with pockets of flaming debris floating upon the water's surface. Police boats and motorboats were racing to the scene with lights blazing and horns blaring. The centerpiece of his vision was... His thoughts were interrupted by a knock on the door of his suite. As he strode to the door, Ike glanced at his watch. It was 6:15 exactly.

"Good evening Isaac. My, my, let me look at you. The face is still basically the same, but I see the trademark dark moustache is no longer. Also, aren't we graying a bit prematurely and since when do you need glasses? All things considered, it's a significant change. I suppose it might serve to confuse those who may be on the lookout for the old Ike Steele, or whoever you're parading around as these days."

"Hell Jonas, my own mother wouldn't recognize me. Won't you come in?"

"Why thank you. I see that we've got an excellent view of the river here. Where's the Buckeye Belle?"

"As near as I can figure, she must be around that bend in the river just west of here."

"Very well. Do we have the night vision goggles?"

"They're in that box on the bed."

"Lastly I believe our festivities for the night called for cocktails at 6:15 and here I am without a drink in my hand and my timepiece says 6:20."

"Would you prefer Glenlivet, Stoli, or Crown Royal?" asked Ike laughingly as he filled a glass with ice.

"Glenlivet on the rocks with a splash of water would be just fine."

One of the myriad duties of being a riverboat captain is being a jovial host when called upon to do so. The time was 6:45 and Captain Smith strode to a podium in the grand ballroom and picked up a microphone that awaited him there.

"Ladies and gentlemen, may I please have your attention!" The booming voice worked the command effect over the audience and a hush quickly ensued throughout the room. "Has everyone found where the bars are located yet?"

A resounding cheer went up from the multitude with Jane's voice being heard the loudest and longest."

"Very good. I've been asked to speak on behalf of the fine folks at Pharmacor South here in Cincinnati. They would like to express their appreciation to their wonderful corporate brethren in Cleveland whose generosity has made this festive occasion possible. I understand that there is a Holland Matthews in the room. Holland, would you please raise your hand. Ah, there you are. Miss Matthews won't you please come up here and accept a token of esteem from the Pharmacor South staff?"

On her way to the podium, Holland endured some good-natured back patting and inadvertent jostling as she made her way through the crowd. She was carrying a small bag with her as she approached the stand. Finally she stood side by side with Capt. Smith.

"Holland, won't you please accept this beautiful plaque for the people at Pharmacor Cleveland?"

"Thank you Captain Smith. And thank you Pharmacor South for your expression of gratitude. I don't know how many of you have had a chance to read the plaque, so here is what it says: "Thank you to our Cleveland brethren, whose generosity has made this riverboat cruise-day truly a memorable one in the illustrious history of our company. May your days be filled with nothing but prosperity and sunshine, and we look forward to doing our part to achieve our mutual goals and visions for the future."

Your Corporate Friends at Pharmacor

South

Tears began to well in Holland's eyes as she lifted the plaque up high amidst a thunderous applause.

"I'll see that this beautiful expression of our combined vision for the future finds a place of honor in our corporate offices in Cleveland. I've been instructed by our C.E.O., Jonas Trina, to also present someone here with this." Reaching into the bag, Holland took out a dark rich looking walnut case. "Is Hank Robinson here?"

The tall middle-aged plant manager of Pharmacor South made his way jovially through the crowd, amidst much backslapping, to join Holland. She addressed the assemblage again. "Hank, I've been asked to give this to you to commemorate this evening."

A puzzled Hank took the case and opened it as he smiled to the audience. Inside the case was a gold pocket watch. Hank stepped up to the microphone and began to read the inscription. "It simply says; "Bon Voyage Hank." I sure hope that this isn't some kind of a hint to retire, is it Holland?"

Holland answered laughingly, "I don't think so Hank. It's just a token of appreciation for a job well done, I'm sure. Now by the delicious aromas wafting around the room I can tell that it is time to eat, so I'll do the proper thing and get the heck out of your way. Enjoy your evening everybody!" With that Holland left the podium, and after enduring ten minutes of congratulatory well wishing, she was finally able to find her way back to John.

"Well Holly-Brit, I see that you've finally had your fifteen minutes of fame. How'd it feel?"

"Great, but it would feel a whole lot better if I could dig into some of that delicious Middle Eastern cuisine that I've been dying for the past twenty minutes. I hope that it isn't all gone by the time we get to it."

"Not to worry my pretty pomegranate. From what I understand, Arabic people are renowned for providing outrageous feasts and large portions when they entertain. My guess is that if they were told that the guest count was 300, they probably made enough of everything to feed 400."

"Well that's a bit of a relief, but as they say, the proof is in the pudding, or would that be the taboule? Anyway, let's get in line before we both starve to death amidst all this plenty. By the way, have you seen Jane lately?"

"The last time I saw her was about ten minutes ago. She was blowing on the whistle that was draped around some crewmate's neck, and she didn't appear to be entirely sober. However, she was still standing, so I suppose she couldn't have downed her four Long Island teas as of yet."

"Don't be too sure about that. I just hope that she doesn't get to be too much of a handful for us as the evening goes on."

"I'll second that, because all that I want a handful of tonight is you Holly-Brit."

With that having been said, John slipped his hand around the back of Holland's backless evening gown and gently pinched a tight fold of skin near the bottom of her spine. Holland gave John's hand a light squeeze and they took their place in one of the food lines.

Al-Salem was making his way back towards the grand ballroom. His watch showed that it was now 7:07, and he could tell from the commotion that the buffet style meal had already commenced. He had intended on being back in the ballroom with his men by the time the meal began, however his latest call to Nishil had taken more time than he had intended. As he approached the entrance to the room, he was almost bowled over by a large uniformed man making his exit.

"Excuse me my good man, but aren't you the head chef?" inquired Captain Smith.

"Yes I am Captain."

"Don't you think that your place would be with your staff at the serving tables?"

"Yes, that is right. I apologize for my tardiness. There were some pressing last minute details which had to be taken care of."

"All is in order now?"

"Yes, everything is under control."

"Good. Then I shall not delay you any further from attending your post. I must admit that I envy all those who are able to enjoy this feast, and who are not pulled away by the call of duty."

"Captain, I shall have one of my men bring some platefuls of food up to the bridge for you and your men to sample."

"Excellent! Carry on my good man."

Al-Salem watched the captain stride purposefully away. He begrudgingly had to admit a feeling of respect for the man. From the polished brass, to the immaculately scrubbed deck, to the spotless glasses and utensils aboard the boat, Tariq could tell that the captain was a man of dignity and discipline, much as himself. As he entered the grand ballroom and took in the scene, Tariq experienced a brief moment of regret for what he knew the future held for both the riverboat and its guests. He took in the gleaming chandelier casting its brilliance upon the revelers as they gaily went about their partying. Everyone seemed to be having a wonderful time. He almost began to pity the boat, its captain, and these people for what he knew their collective fate to be. Sounds of merriment and the abundance of delicacies helped to snap him out of his momentary lapse of purpose. "The Great Satan laughs and gorges itself, while my people live in squalor and destitution. After tonight, all of that changes," thought Al-Salem as he made his way to a table where a steamship round of beef was being carved. Grabbing a sharp long bladed Granton Slicer carving knife out of the hands of one of his stewards, he commenced to slice long thin strips of rare beef from the round.

"Out of my way you pig butcher, and let a master show you the correct way to carve this beast so that we may give these people a proper sendoff."

Nishil nervously glanced around in the fading light as he took stock of the scene surrounding him at the river's edge. The men were lashing the last of the nine 55 gallon drums to the railing of a large motorboat they had secured to a pier. Five of the drums had blocks of Semtech explosives affixed to them. One of these blocks had a detonator stuck into it that was connected to an electronic receiver. Now was the critical time. If any police came and investigated the area now, they would almost certainly have to kill them, which would inevitably lead to aborting the mission and attempting to evade capture via previously planned avenues of escape. To distract last minute complications, he had one of his men prepared to serve as a decoy and take any snooping police on a high-speed wild goose chase. The rest of the men would take the boat into the river and choose the next best available target if it came to that. However, hopefully there would be no complications and everything would proceed as planned. That would result in a glorious victory for Allah and their cause, and would strike wide spread fear into the hearts of their enemies.

"How is your shrimp and lobster Isaac?"

"C'est tres magnifique! And how is your beef Wellington?"

"Superb. You say that the main event should be occurring directly in front of our window at 9:00. How can you be so sure of the time?"

"I made a few calls to the parent company of the Buckeye Belle and asked a few questions regarding the captain. The man's name is Stanley Smith, and he is a real stickler for discipline and punctuality. If the plan calls for the boat to cruise in front of our position at 9:00, which it does, then you can make book on it doing so according to the ship's agent with whom I spoke."

"Very good. Now please pass me some more of that excellent merlot."

True to his schedule, at 7:30 Captain Smith ordered a 180-degree turn that would put the riverboat on an easterly heading. This would take the boat back to Cincinnati. The cruise plan called for the boat to leave dock at 6:15 (which it had) and travel westward at 6 knots for 75 minutes. Then the boat would make a u-turn and head back eastward 2 ½ hours at 6 knots. Following a second u-turn the boat would arrive back at the dock in another 75 minutes. Allowing 15 minutes total to accomplish the u-turns would bring the vessel to the dock at 11:30 P.M. Announcements for departing the boat would begin immediately upon docking. At 11:45 the lights would be turned on and off to expedite the guests to depart. At midnight the ship's whistle would sound, which would be followed by a polite but insistent message indicating that all should depart immediately. At 12:10 most of the crew would begin leaving, and at 12:15 the vessel would be secured for the evening. It was a schedule that Captain Smith had established and had accomplished hundreds of times without ever having an incident that he and his crew could not handle. Tonight would be disastrously different.

At 8:05 P.M. Roger Madak's phone began to jangle. The phone rang four times before Roger broke away from his furious typing and put the receiver to his ear.

"Madak here, it's your call and you'd better be quick about it," he said arrogantly.

"Is this Roger Madak the newsman for Channel 6 news?" said a voice with a heavy Middle Eastern accent

"Well it ain't the son-of-a-bitchin tooth fairy pal and I'm extremely busy, so I'll give you three seconds to say something important buddy, otherwise I'm gone, do you understand?"

"This call will terminate when, and only when I say so Mr. Madak, and I hope that YOU understand. Now then, I represent an organization known as "The Fist of Rage," Perhaps you have heard of us?

"Not really."

"Soon you shall. This evening we have chosen your insignificant city to make our presence known to America in a very big way. Do you have access to a helicopter Mr. Madak?"

"Hey pal, this isn't funny." Just who the hell are...

"It was not meant to be funny Mr. Madak. If you have access to a helicopter you will want to fly over the Ohio River area near what you people refer to as the I-71 bridge. Our show will commence at 9:00 P.M. It will not last long Mr. Madak. I have been told that you are a very ambitious person. Is that true?"
Suddenly a staffer burst into the newsroom occupied by Madak and several other Channel 6 personnel as they worked diligently to prepare the evening news stories.

"Hey listen up everyone. A big blast has just leveled part of an apartment building on the near East side. If we don't want to miss the story we'd better get hopping before the other channels scoop us!"

"Look pal it's been fun chatting with you but we have a bona fide story here to cover."

"Yes I know. We arranged the apartment building explosion as a diversion. Mr. Madak you can send a television van and crew to cover that story. If you would like to make true television history and put yourself on the national news for the next several days, you will take a helicopter to the Ohio River as I have told you. Have a pleasant evening Mr.Madak."

Roger Madak hung up the phone and looked around to see several sets of eyes peering intently at him for direction. He made his decision. "You heard the man, let's get a van rolling to that apartment building people. Put Kate Davidson on that van. She's always good on emergency stories. Joni, get a tape made of that last call that came into my phone and alert the police. I think they're going to be interested in it. Also call Bart Johnson at headquarters and tell him I've taken the helicopter to cover a lead. Keep your fingers crossed people. Tonight we may be the biggest, baddest boys on the news. Coleman, grab a camera. You're coming with me. Akers, page our flyboy Bartow and tell him he's got fifteen minutes to meet us at the chopper pad. Ten minutes would be better. Let's move it people!"

Nishil Najir put his cell phone in his pocket. He could hear fire engines and police sirens racing towards the east side of Cincinnati. They would be heading to the apartment blast he had heard about during his call to Roger Madak. It was a smart piece of planning to set off that blast to divert attention from their position at this time. The apartment had been rented by one of their men for the past few weeks. Rigging the gas stove to spew natural gas into the unit had been child's play. "That should keep the enforcement agencies busy until it is too late," thought Nishil.

Holland and John were helping Jane attempt to climb the stairs leading to the deck from the grand ballroom. Her obvious inebriation was complicating their efforts.

"So Jane, what happened to the budding romance that John told me you had going with one of the crew?"

"Who knowsh! One minutsh we're makin out pretties good, an the ness minutsh the yittle dweeb is hishtory."

"Listen to you Jane. You're so drunk I can hardly understand you. You're slurring your words something terrible," said Holland.

"Shpeaking of terrible, it looks like my plansh to get laid in the Queen City fells tru. Wait, thas it! Tha dweeb probly WAS a queen or sumthin'. I knowsh, I'll bet he was a eunuch like your ole John boy here."

As John continued to help Jane up the stairs, Holland felt herself being gently restrained from following by a matronly blue haired lady who had been following them. As Holland opened her mouth to protest, the elderly woman spoke first.

"Don't worry sweetie. Just because your man doesn't have all of the necessary equipment to play the game doesn't mean that you can't enjoy a rich rewarding life together. My Harvey's no longer a ball of fire in the sack either, but we share other joys and interests together that make our lives worthwhile. His having a nice income hasn't hurt either. Your John, does he make a good living?"

Trying hard not to laugh, Holland played along and said that he did. She then thanked the matron for her solid advice, and promised to keep it in mind. Instead of attempting to catch up with John and Jane, Holland chose to go back to the ballroom to scrounge up a cup of hot black coffee for Jane. As she entered the room, she noticed a station set up for espresso that should be just what the doctor ordered to help Jane's condition. Glancing around however, she was unable to locate any of the Moroccan Interlude staff to pour her a cup. Taking matters into her own hands, Holland secured a cup and saucer and made off with a steaming cup of the thick rich liquid.

Making her way topside, Holland eventually found John and Jane. John was watching over Jane like a mother hen as Jane proceeded to snore excessively from her horizontal upturned position on a cot. John had removed Jane's shoes at her request just before she passed out.

"Well doctor John, how's the patient doing?"

"She's sleeping like one hope's a baby never sleeps, but at least she is inhaling and immobile. Assuming that she doesn't swallow her nose with all this snoring, I think she'll be all right. What happened to you?"

"I was abducted by a well meaning grandmother type who wanted to impart to me some of the finer points of relationships. I'll have to tell you all about it sometime. After I broke free from Granny, I thought that I could do Jane some good if I got her a cup of coffee. I'd have been back sooner, except that I couldn't locate any of the Arabic guys to get me a cup."

"I can tell you why you couldn't find any of them. They all went overboard about five minutes ago. A Z boat sidled up to the riverboat, and they all made their getaway. I was busy with Jane, so I didn't get a chance to ask them what was going on. Another guy talked to them briefly and I was able to ask him what they said. He told me that they had another obligation that they had to attend, and that the captain had given them permission to leave right after dinner without cleaning up or anything. That struck me as kind of odd."

"Me too. Not to mention that it's going to piss off a lot of people when they go to get drink refills or a quick bite. It's only 8:40, so there's still almost three hours of the cruise left to go. Oh well, I guess we'll all just have to rough it. Why don't we try out our sea legs and hit the dance floor. I like the song the band's playing."

"And tear myself away from Sleeping Beauty here? I suppose if I must."

Tariq Al-Salem spoke into his cell phone as the escape craft bounced along the Ohio River throwing spray into the faces of him and his men. "You may ring the bell. I repeat you may ring the bell."

"Acknowledged. The bell will be rung at 9:00. Repeat, the bell will be rung at 9:00." Nishil picked up a flashlight and flashed it on and off twice in the direction of their large idling motorboat that was straining at it's leash. The Buckeye Belle had passed their position several minutes ago on its return trip upriver. Two scuba-clad men seated in the boat were ready, willing, and eager to take up the chase. One of the men in the boat returned the flashlight signal with two quick flashes. The mooring rope was cast off and quickly the craft leaped from the dock and gave chase to the brightly lit paddlewheel splashing noisily in the distance.

Roger Madak was normally irritated by a helicopter flight. The incessant noise drove him crazy. This time he barely noticed it, so intent was he upon finding the story he spiritedly sought.

"Coleman, you see anything yet? How about you Bartow? Anything on your side?"

"Nothing here."

"Hell its 8:51, and that supposed "Raging Fist", or "Fist of Rage" or whatever he called himself guy said that something big was gonna happen at 9:00. I sure don't see anything happening around here. Let's head east towards that paddlewheel party boat. At least we can take some footage of that and maybe the girls in arts and life or the entertainment department can find some use for it. Wait, what's that shadow running with no lights? About a half mile in back of the paddle wheeler. Shine your lights on it flyboy and see if there's anything interesting happening aboard."

"There you go Roger. Can you make anything special out about it?"

"No, how about you Coleman?"

"Not really, except I wonder why he has all of those drums fastened to the railings. I've done a decent amount of boating in my time, and I've never seen anyone with a reason to attach a bunch of what looks to be 55 gallon drums to their boat."

"Aw who knows, with all of the eccentrics and weirdos running around nowadays, anything goes. Try shining your lights on the riverbank to see if we pick up any activity. If not, then pan your lights back on that motorboat in a few minutes. It does strike me as kind of unusual that an unlit boat would be cruising out on the river after dark. Besides, beggars can't be choosers, and there sure ain't nothing else going on out here." As the boat closed to within two hundred yards of the Buckeye Belle, the scuba-clad men aboard rigged the boat to maintain its course and prepared to jump overboard, secure in their minds that the boat's current heading would soon intercept the Buckeye Belle. As they were abandoning the craft, the helicopter once again illuminated it with the searchlight.

"Boy that doesn't make any sense. The motorboat is still going all out, and it doesn't look like anybody's steering the damn thing. On its current course, it's just a matter of a few minutes before it runs smack dab into that paddle wheeler. I'd swear I saw two scuba-divers jump overboard right when you shined the light on the boat. Did you catch that Coleman?"

"Not really, but I do agree that nobody's steering that puppy now, and it certainly will intercept the paddle wheeler before too long."

"With these night vision goggles on, you sure can make out the individual figures and items. I saw those two scuba divers jump more clearly than if I'd been seeing it in broad daylight."

"You can say that again Jonas. They turn night into day for real. It won't be long now. I estimate that they've only got another two hundred yards to go before the shit hits the fan."

"Yes Ike, tonight will be a night that Cincinnati, Pharmacor, and in fact all of America will remember for a long time, and we had front row seats to the show. I only wish that we could go out on the balcony to experience the full effect."

"That's a risk not worth taking my friend. I'm not sure if the glass will hold at this distance or not, but better safe than sorry. In fact we'll have to move quickly to see the start, and then run for the bathroom or hide under the bed until the effect passes. In fact I'd better go wrap up the Cristal now to make sure it survives for our celebratory toast."

Holland gazed up at the hauntingly beautiful late September moon as it bathed the river with its milky rays. She could make out the Big and Little Dippers, and Orion the Hunter in the cloudless night sky. Wrapped in the strong arms of her love as they glided around the deck accompanied by a Righteous Brother's tune from the 60's, she felt dreamy and complete. Rarely had she known such a sense of peace and inner bliss. She said a silent prayer of thanks for such a perfect time in her life.

"A penny for your thoughts, lover boy," Holland cooed into John's ear.

"You probably don't want to know right now."

"Oh try me."

"If I do it'll probably spoil your mood."

"I think you've already accomplished that Mr. Romantic. Go ahead now."

"I'm sorry, but I'm starting to get concerned with something."

"What is it?"

"Here, I'll show you." John swung Holland around so that she was facing the starboard rear quarter of the Belle. "Do you see that motorboat out there?"

"Yes."

"It's been following us for several minutes now. That helicopter overhead shined its light on the boat a few minutes ago when the boat was still a decent distance away. Now it's only about 150 yards away, and it looks like it's on a collision course with us. Do you notice anything else funny about the boat?"

"No, should I?"

"There is nobody at the controls."

"That's odd."

"Also I've been trying to get a handle on what those drums could be for which appear to be lashed to the railings. I'm not sure what's going on here, but it's got my senses tingling."
John closed his eyes briefly in order to focus his thoughts on the puzzle at hand. A thought popped into his head. "U.S.S. Cole, U.S.S. Cole, U.S.S. Cole, **U.S.S. Cole!!** Grabbing Holland by both arms, John jumped into action.

"Holland, take off your shoes and run to the far side of the boat towards the middle. Find three life rings from the railing and bring them with you. I'll go grab Jane and meet you there as quick as I can."

"But John..."

"GO! NOW!"

As Holland began to kick off her shoes, John raced towards the cot where Jane lay dead to the world. Scooping her up on the run, John maneuvered around a kissing couple that broke their embrace just long enough to view the madman rushing by with the woman in his arms. As John arrived at the railing with a sputtering Jane, he was met almost simultaneously by his now three-ringed girl friend. Looking back in the direction of the paddle wheelers starboard quarter, he could see that barely 90 yards now separated the pursuing craft from the festively lit Buckeye Belle. Grabbing a ring from Holland, John plunged it over Jane's head, eliciting squawks from their incoherent cohort. Without a word, John unceremoniously heaved the now screaming Jane over the railing and into the murky darkness below. Clutching a life ring Holland screamed out "John Kazek, you'd better have a damn good reason for what you are..." Holland suddenly found herself flying over the railing, likewise propelled by John's strong arms. Kicking off his shoes, John raced several yards toward the rear of the boat. As he did so he passed a dozen stunned onlookers who had taken in the entire scene. Ignoring their cries and protestations, John mounted the railing and without hesitation plunged into the cold Ohio River, carrying the last life ring with him. Racing towards the rear of the boat had brought him into fairly close proximity with Jane. Following her cries for help, John quickly swam to her side. Grabbing Jane across her chest, he kicked with all of his might to get them both out of harm's way as the paddle wheel thundered by, pushing the Belle down the river with the motorboat closing in rapidly.

"Holland can you hear me?" yelled John at the top of his lungs.

"I'm over here to your right, you insane son-of-a-bitch. Do you know what you've just done? This isn't funny, you.."

"Listen, I know this all seems crazy, but you're going to have to trust me on this. In about sixty seconds or so there is going to be a tremendous explosion. When that happens, let go of your life ring, take a deep breath, and swim as far down as you can as fast as you can. Do it as if your life depends on it, because it does. I'll do the same with Jane and me over here. Good luck Holland Brittainy Matthews! I love you, I always will."

"And I love you John Kazek F.B.I., but you'd better not be joking with me on this or I'll kill you."

"I pray that we live through these next few minutes so that you get the opportunity."

As the motorboat closed to within twenty yards, the helicopter was trailing the boat by some one hundred yards. The chopper's occupants had already witnessed John, Holland, and Jane taking the plunge, which caused them concern and still more confusion. It was at this point that Roger Madak came to the same conclusion that John had come to over a minute before.

"Bartow, turn this chopper around, and get us out of here now! Coleman, keep the camera focused on that boat for as long as you can. Bartow, move this bird FAST! Unless I miss my guess, we're about to have the wildest ride of our lives!"

Nishil Najir peered intently through his binoculars as he attempted to ascertain the two boat's proximity to one another. Not that it really mattered, for surely another ten yards would not make any difference. However, he wished to prolong the tension of the moment in order to experience every precious and delicious second. Finally the chase boat pulled even with the riverboat, to the consternation of many who stood onboard the Buckeye Belle, curiously awaiting the end result of their ill-fated coupling. Nishil smiled as he pressed a button on a transmitter that he held, and the results were almost instantaneous.

A nanosecond after the depressing of the transmitter's button, the generated electronic signal was picked up by a receiver aboard the motorboat. This receiver was attached to a detonator, which was imbedded in a block of Semtech plastic explosive, which in turn was attached to one of the 55-gallon drums of ammonium nitrate/diesel fuel mixture. An electronic pulse went out from the receiver that was more than sufficient to trigger the explosive power of the detonator. In turn this set off the violently powerful plastic explosive that melted the steel drum and set ablaze its confined combustible mixture. The resultant blast ignited the eight other drums and four other blocks of plastic explosives onboard the motorboat in the twinkling of an eye. The superheated conglomeration spread out in a fury in all directions as it sought to escape that which had started the rush to oblivion.

Mere wood, metal, flesh, bone, and sinew were never meant to encounter such a force as this. All proved to be unequal to the task before them. As the hot breath of hell transferred it's might in the direction of the Buckeye Belle, the windows and bulkheads shattered. Planks, rivets, shards of glass, white hot metal, thousands of nails, liquefied paint, and scores of other boat components were accompanied by temperatures in the thousands of degrees which raced from one side of the boat to the other. Bodies disintegrated before the onslaught to join in the unholy amalgam. Many people simply melted from the superheated air as it rushed by, leaving only tooth fragments and skeletal remains. The others were torn, ripped, and shredded to pieces by the force, heat, and shrapnel of the blast. For those aboard the Buckeye Belle, there would be no escape. There could be no escape. To insure the complete destruction of the Buckeye Belle the transmitter had also set off the explosives hidden in the two fake containers of cooking oil which resulted in huge holes being blown in the bottom of the boat.

At the moment of the blast, The Ranger helicopter had reached an altitude of 700 feet, and had managed to cross over land 315 yards from the site of the blast. It was not far enough. The power and heat of the explosion quickly caught up with the fleeing helicopter. Though Bartow fought valiantly to keep the Ranger airborne, the forces arrayed against him were simply too powerful. The blast wave flipped the helicopter over and over as it literally somersaulted out of control. The propeller hit the ground first with a shattering ear splitting sound. Next came the crunch of the fuselage as it crumpled into a tangled mass of glass, metal, and humanity. Finally the rotor blade hit the ground, spinning off crazily before digging itself a place to rest. The video camera was flung out of the fuselage upon impact. Its contents would be salvaged, and within hours would provide America with the cause of the disaster and the chilling final moments of three brave, but ill-fated newsmen. As desired, "Fist of Rage" would have their triumphal moment once again immortalized on film.

"Holy shit, will you look at the size of that fireball, and it's still spreading!"

"Jonas! Run for the bathroom and close the door, I don't think the windows will be able to stand up to the blast."

Jonas sprinted the short distance from the window to the bathroom and slammed the door closed. He had just slid to the floor and joined Ike there when the shock wave from the blast arrived at their windows. The entire room shook for a good ten seconds. The windows rattled and bowed inward, but in the end they held up remarkably well to the beating they had taken. Only a couple of cracks were visible after the wave had passed. Sixty seconds after closing the door, Jonas and Ike came out from the bathroom and stared both at the windows, and at the nightmarish scene on the river below. Flaming floating debris dotted the surface of the river in a broad almost elliptically shaped pattern. There was absolutely no trace remaining of the motorboat. As for the Buckeye Belle, all that remained of the once proud and beautiful vessel was a pile of burning flotsam. The huge paddlewheel had broken into two large pieces, both of which were blazing furiously near what used to be the stern of the boat. The smokestacks, which had been blasted into the water, looked like oversized charred logs working their way down the river to meet their end at some distant lumber mill. The vessel itself resembled a Viking funeral pyre as its flaming hull floated slowly towards an unknown destination. Nevermore would the Buckeye Belle or the captain have a schedule to keep! At least not in this life!

"Well Ike, in your professional opinion, how would you rate the performance of our associates this evening?"

Gazing out the window, Ike was admiring the eerie shadows being cast upon the rivers' debris by the light of the Belle's flaming remains. Occasionally he thought he could almost make out a head and some arms moving amidst the wreckage, but he knew that was impossible. Finally he answered Jonas.

"Pretty damn thorough. There's absolutely no way anyone could have lived through that. I'd say that they've proven that they know their craft. I'm all for our mutual cooperation in future ventures."

"I agree my friend. I'd say that this calls for a celebration. I think that now is a good time to open that bottle of Cristal. I'll grab two glasses if you'll get the bottle."

"With pleasure," said Ike as he passed in front of the window and took another glance at the flame strewn river below.

CHAPTER 26

As the motorboat exploded, Holland didn't wait around to admire the scene. Gulping down an entire respiratory system full of air, she plunged her head into the water and began to kick for the bottom with all of her might. The Belle's continued progress down the river after Holland had been thrown from the boat placed her about 110 yards from the stern of the paddle wheeler when the blast occurred. Initially she was swimming in cold, dark, murky water as she breast-stroked for the bottom. Unlike a normal dive however, this time the farther down she swam, the warmer and lighter the water became as the hellish hurricane approached. As she reached what she estimated as 12 feet, the water became extremely warm, almost as if she were in her shower at home. The water took on a reddish orange hue and was accompanied by a terrifying noise. The tremendous force of an underwater wave suddenly struck Holland. The wave drove her deeper as it catapulted her over and over several times before it moved past to disrupt the river beyond her.

Regaining her control, Holland realized that she could not hold her breath much longer. To make matters worse, the underwater buffeting she had endured now left her disoriented. She began to panic as she tried to determine which way was up in the once again murky darkness. She got an idea and forced herself to be perfectly still for a couple of seconds. Remembering that her body would tend to float towards the surface, Holland concentrated to ascertain which direction her body was being pulled. Feeling a subtle tugging on her feet, she flipped 180 degrees and began stroking harder and faster than she thought possible. Her oxygen reserves were gone and her throat and lungs felt as if they themselves were on fire. She dared to open her eyes, and gained a glimmer of hope by dim light above her. Three more hard fast strokes would take her to the limits of her endurance, and then she would have to open her mouth and take a deep gulp. Time would tell if that gulp would contain life giving air or death dealing river water.

As she completed the third stroke, her lungs could endure no more. She involuntarily opened her mouth and tasted water as she gulped a huge lungful of whatever fate had in store for her. Fortunately the water she tasted was only the spume from her having broken the surface of the river with her last desperate stroke. The remainder of her taken breath contained air. Due to the surroundings on the surface, it was without a doubt not the freshest air she'd ever breathed. However at this second, to Holland her gasps were filled with the sweet nectar of life itself.

Holland had swum to within ten yards of where John and Jane were treading water when the explosion occurred. Thus their experience should have been very much the same as Holland's. Unfortunately it was not. Due to Jane's inebriated state, she was not fully grasping the gravity of the situation as John desperately pleaded with her to focus on his instructions before time ran out. When the motorboat blew up, John screamed at Jane to take a deep breath. After taking a huge breath of his own, John prepared to dive towards the bottom. Glancing at Jane, he saw her mesmerized by the huge fireball that was churning their way at an unbelievably fast rate. Grabbing her by the shoulders he screamed at her; "TAKE A DEEP BREATH, AND DIVE DAMN YOU!" As she did so, he again inhaled mightily and plunged his head underwater also. John stroked like a madman in his attempt to put as much greenish river water between himself and the open gates of hell whose fiery wind would be upon them any second. Above him and to his left he could detect the committed but much feebler efforts of Jane, who appeared to have finally understood the urgency of the situation. As the water grew lighter and warmer, John fought with himself over whether or not he should swim back towards the surface to assist Jane. Rightfully deciding that he could accomplish little by doing so, he continued his downward momentum. When the brunt of the blast's effects hit, John was protected by 16 feet of the Ohio River. Jane was barely covered by 6. Those ten additional feet would prove to be crucial.

When the underwater wave hit, John tucked himself in a ball to minimize the wave's effects, and to maximize his body's protection. As the wave passed, he found his way to the surface with less difficulty than Holland had experienced. As he broke the surface, John began peering in all directions for any sign of Jane. The light given off by all of the flaming wreckage provided enough illumination to foster some hope that John might be able to see Jane if she in fact had regained the surface herself. Yelling her name in all directions, John suddenly became aware of an answering cry. It was Holland who was in the process of swimming the fifteen yards that now separated them. John's heart leaped with joy and he began a furious dogpaddle to help Holland close the gap.

As they came together, Holland threw her arms around John and kissed him as hard as she could. John attempted to return the kiss as best he could. Unfortunately, with the combined weights of their two bodies, coupled with Holland inadvertently blocking his arms from stroking, John's feet simply were unable to support the joyful reunion any longer. The river closed over the slowly sinking couple as they ground their lips together. Breaking apart and sputtering to the surface, a new thought entered Holland's mind.

"Where's Jane?"

"I was trying to find her when I heard you calling to me. We were separated during our dive. I pray to God that she was able to get deep enough to escape the blast's heat and violence, but I'm not sure if she did or not."

"Shh John, I think I hear something."

Over the crackling of the fires, the sloshing of the floating smokestacks, and water caressing the shoreline, Holland could hear a low moaning sound. Straining her eyes to gaze into the darker area away from the floating fires, she thought she saw a shadow bobbing up and down on the water's surface twenty yards away. She began to swim towards the shadow, followed closely by John. As she approached the floating shadow, she heard the moan again, this time much clearer. As Holland got to within 10 feet of the shadow, she could tell that it was a human being. She prayed that it was Jane. Just before she got to them, the person let out an agonized wail. This stopped Holland and John dead in the water. They were unsure if they should touch the person who was in obvious pain. Taking a chance Holland yelled out. "Jane is that you?"

"Yes." a mournful feeble voice responded.

"Are you hurt badly?"

"I'm badly burned," she cried. "Even the water feels hot to me."

"Hang in there, I'll send John to find something that we can use as a raft to support you with until help arrives."

As John swam off in search of the proper piece of floating debris, Holland swam to Jane's side.
"I know that you're in a lot of pain honey. Try to focus your mind on something else."

"Ooohh." Jane moaned.

"I'm sure that it won't be long before help arrives."

Five minutes later John reappeared at their sides bearing four charred but serviceable life rings that he had found bobbing unattended atop the gentle waves. They put two of them under Jane's torso with her elbows resting in their holes. The other two they positioned beneath her legs to help distribute her weight properly. Although the positioning of the rings caused Jane great pain, she realized that it was for the better and endured the process with as little wailing as possible.

They had been able to hear sirens for some time now, but the sounds were all coming from various areas of the city that would do them little good at the moment. Suddenly Holland thought she heard a faint siren from a new direction. Looking westward down the river, she could make out two lights spaced widely apart, proceeding rapidly in their direction.

"John, I think those are police patrol rescue boats coming towards us, what do you think?" As she said that one of the approaching boats let out a long blast from the siren.

"I know that's what they are baby, I can tell by the sound of the sirens."

"Do you hear that Jane? We're going to be rescued!"

"Ooohh" was all she could manage.

The patrol boats easily plucked John and Holland from the water within five minutes after their arrival. Jane's severely burned status required special handling, but after thirty minutes Jane was aboard and was being helped. Her condition required immediate hospitalization. Holland chose to stay with Jane and go with her to the hospital. John and Holland both agreed that it might be a benefit to the police if John were to stay on the scene and tell them what he knew about the attack. John transferred to another police boat while the one bearing the women went careening down the river to get Jane to the nearest hospital. By this time there were five police patrol vessels on the scene. They would soon be joined by at least a dozen private boats whose owners insisted on doing what they could to assist in rescue operations. Due to the size of the tragedy, the patrol boats were grateful for the assistance. Searchlights crisscrossed the river slowly as the efforts to locate survivors swung into high gear. Throughout the night the search would continue, eventually having over 40 boats lending assistance. Unfortunately no other survivors would be found.

Two hours after they had begun to search for survivors, the patrol boat with John aboard decided to leave the search to the other boats. This would allow them to get John to headquarters where his eyewitness account of the attack could be taken and added to any other information that may have surfaced from other sources. Although he was physically and emotionally drained, he was still anxious to do all he could to help. John agreed to accompany the police and give his statement at headquarters.

When they arrived, John asked which hospital Holland and Jane had been taken to. He was informed that they were in the burn unit at Mercy General in downtown Cincinnati. Grateful that he had discerned their whereabouts, John got down to the task at hand and began to tell the police all he knew about the attack. He talked about the Buckeye Belle's chartering by Pharmacor, and how many people were aboard. He described the motorboat, and told them about the members of Moroccan Interlude. He told of their abandoning the Buckeye Belle thirty minutes before the attack. Lastly he described the ferocity of the blast and his opinion on what would be required to produce such an explosion. John's testimony coupled with the taped call made to Roger Madak at the Channel 6 news department provided convincing evidence that what many in the country feared had actually come to pass. The United States now had an active Middle Eastern terrorist cell operating within its own borders.

Al-Salem and his men had also been extremely busy these past several hours. Two of his men had been dropped off at the Greyhound bus terminal to get rides to their assigned safe houses in Detroit. Six others went to the airport, where they had previously parked their cars in order to be inconspicuous. They had split up from there, with each going to a predetermined safe house in a variety of Midwestern cities. They would be contacted as needed in the next few weeks.

The remaining three men including Al-Salem himself, returned to their base in the hills of Northern Kentucky. They sank the vans in a large pond on the property and prepared the house and outbuildings for destruction by setting time delayed fuses. The fuses would go off in six hours. By that time Mohammed Al-Salem and his men would have effectively dispersed, well on their way to blending in with the general populace to start another day. The three men bid each other farewell and got into two separate vehicles for their journeys. Five hours from now Al-Salem would be amongst trusted allies in a house on Toledo Ohio's East side. The other two men would resume their cover as graduate students at Ohio State University where they had an apartment off campus. None of their professors or fellow students would have any clue as to their extracurricular activities this weekend.

Nishil Najir's men would follow basically the same format of escape. After the two scuba clad boat drivers had made their way back to the warehouse on the waterfront, they quickly changed and got into a car for their trip to a safe house in Pittsburgh. The other two would head North along with Nishil to join the throngs of Arab Americans in Cleveland as they would begin to scout out their next planned attack site. "America has only begun to pay," thought Nishil as he put his van in gear and prepared to head for the highway.

While Jonas would've preferred to stay in Cincinnati during the weekend, he knew that he must return home to field the myriad phone calls that he was sure the explosion would engender. Also, this would provide a credible alibi as to his whereabouts should the need ever arise. He sincerely doubted that he had been recognized in that virtually no one had seen him arrive in Cincinnati. He made sure that few if any had seen him leave. The biggest concern he had was being pulled over for a traffic violation, so he dutifully observed the speed limit on his way home. Arriving back at his Hunting Valley home near 3:00 A.M., he was certainly tired, but he also felt a bit of elation for the vast number of his sworn enemies he had disposed of this evening. He felt a sense of retribution and looked forward to spending time in the coming days to adding their names to the golden notebook stored in his wall safe. Making his way up to the master bedroom, Jonas set his alarm for 8:45. He looked forward to seeing the morning news which no doubt would be featuring the attack.

Daniece Davis poured herself a cup of java freshly made from her coffee maker. She tightened the cloth belt around her robe and opened the front door to retrieve her Sunday edition of the local newspaper lying on the front lawn of her stylish condominium. As she did so, in scampered Mittens, her male gray and white feline with white paws. Mittens wove a furry figure eight between Daniece's ankles as he rubbed up against her doing one of those endearing things that cats do.

Unfortunately she almost tripped over him, eliciting a curse that was delivered with sufficient verbal venom to send the cat scurrying behind the couch. Having gathered up the thick Sunday paper, Daniece went inside and walked to the living room. After setting the paper on the couch, she pulled out a tray table to set up as her base of operations for breakfast. Within minutes the small table was filled with coffee, a fruit cup, and a thick cinnamon raisin bagel slathered with strawberry cream cheese. Settling down on the plush sofa, she reached for the remote.

While waiting for the picture, Daniece took a bite of her bagel and sorted through the paper for her favorite sections, which were the Metro and Entertainment sections. As the television came into focus, the screen showed a body of water with floating debris and rescue boats. Daniece turned up the sound and took a sip of her coffee. The announcer's voice came on stating... "And for those of you just joining us, this is the scene from the Ohio River in Cincinnati. What you see behind me is all that remains of the Buckeye Belle paddle wheeler which was apparently attacked last night..." Daniece involuntarily began to choke as the coffee went down her windpipe due to her sudden gasp at the news she'd just heard. Regaining her breath, she lunged for the remote. Turning up the volume she strained to hear every syllable. The announcer continued;

"The search for survivors has been called off and the focus now is on the recovery stage. Unfortunately for the most part, due to the enormous size of the blast that destroyed the boat, only body fragments have been recovered at this time. As we said at the beginning of the broadcast, only three people are known to have survived this wicked attack. A group calling itself "The Fist of Rage" has claimed credit for the blast that demolished the Buckeye Belle and law enforcement agencies are taking the claim very seriously. The F.B.I. has been called into the investigation and..." She turned the television set off, and through a veil of tears set the remote on the tray table.

Daniece arose from the sofa. As she went into the kitchen to get her purse, she realized that she was perspiring and felt light headed. She pulled her cell phone out of her purse, and with trembling fingers dialed Holland's cell phone number. After the seventh ring a recorded voice asked if she wished to leave a message. Frantically Daniece dialed Jane's cell number and got the same response. Tears began to stream from her eyes as she tried to remember if Holland or Jane had mentioned which hotel they would be staying at this weekend. Finally it came to her and she called directory information for the Cincinnati Hyatt Inn. Connecting to the Hyatt she rang their room but got no response. The front desk could offer no assistance beyond the fact that neither of the women had checked out as of yet. Desperately Daniece called the Cincinnati Police Department. On the 26th ring her call was answered by a frazzled dispatcher who informed Daniece that no information was being given out at this time pending notification of next of kin. In fact they were still trying to compile a list of those who had been scheduled to be aboard the Buckeye Belle for the cruise. Frustrated, angry, and worried beyond belief, Daniece resigned herself to the fact that she would just have to wait for final confirmation of their fate. If only she had continued watching her television.

Jonas Trina awoke a bit groggy from lack of sleep, and the effect of the previous night's imbibing. However, he soon was in an ebullient frame of mind, much like a child who awakes on Christmas morning in anticipation of presents. Karl the butler brought up some coffee, juice, a muffin, eggs benedict with Hollandaise sauce, and the morning paper to Jonas' sleeping chamber. Knowing his master preferred to take breakfast in solitude, Karl retired to another room down the hall. Turning on the sixty inch television from the remote at his bedside, Jonas began to view the very same broadcast that Daniece had seen. He smiled as the river scene came into focus with the cameraman panning over the nearby waterfront. He was particularly pleased with the commentator's assertion that only body fragments were being found for the most part. He cheered inwardly as he heard that only recovery efforts were now being conducted. "And that, Miss Matthews is how the game is played. I will lay down your king because the match is over," Jonas thought smugly to himself. Suddenly Jonas' senses were piqued as he heard the newsman utter the word survivors and he looked off camera as if in anticipation of someone approaching to be introduced to the viewing audience. Jonas hoisted his juice glass and continued to view the screen with curiosity. His eyes did a double take as Holland Matthews and a man he was unfamiliar with were brought before the camera.

"DAMN YOU, DAMN YOU, DAMN YOU!" screamed Jonas as he hurled his juice glass against the door of his walk in closet. Next he upset the tray of coffee and food, sending prepared projectiles flying in all directions. After turning off the television, Jonas flung the remote at a bureau against the wall. Livid and disgusted, he stormed out of the master bedroom much to the consternation of Karl, who had come to see what all of the commotion was about. Karl could merely shake his head as he began the task of cleaning up after the master. Ten minutes later, the first of the day's forty seven news reporter calls commenced ringing. Jonas was as cool, calm, and composed with the last as he was with the first. And of course he had nothing but congratulatory praise for Holland, John, Jane and their stroke of good fortune at having survived.

By 10:00 A.M. John and Holland had given their statements to the police and the F.B.I., and had been featured on three different television stations. Additionally John had spent the night helping to conduct the search for survivors while Holland stayed with Jane at the hospital. Neither had been to bed in over 27 hours. Also, they had taken a call from the governor of Ohio who praised their courage and who vowed to use all of the tools of his office to bring the terrorist cowards to justice for the terrible tragedy they had visited upon the state. It finally dawned on someone in authority that the twosome was exhausted and they were driven back to the Hyatt with instructions that they were not to be disturbed before 6:00 P.M. The management at the Hyatt refused the government offer to pay their bill, and told Holland and John they could stay as long as they desired, free of charge. The weary couple went to their respective rooms to keep up appearances. Holland called Daniece and let her know that they were all right. Daniece let out a whoop that Holland was sure they could hear in Columbus. She also informed Daniece that they would be staying an extra couple of days at the request of the authorities. Daniece said that was understandable and she looked forward to giving them all a big hug when they returned. Holland told her about Jane's terrible burns. Daniece promised to pray for her and said that she would spread the word amongst their friends at Pharmacor. As Holland hung up the phone, her head hit the pillow on her bed and she slept straight through until 6:00 P.M.

The F.B.I. and local law enforcement agencies combined forces and conducted the most thorough investigation in Ohio's history. By the end of the week they knew the type and amount of the explosives used. They had discovered the riverfront warehouse and made a complete sweep of it from top to bottom. The explosions at the Kentucky farmhouse had alerted them to the group's base of operations for the Cincinnati attack. Wheel tracks led them to the pond on the farm's property, and the vans were brought to the surface. Little of any real use was discovered in them. They had a good idea of the number of men in the group. They even had several sets of fingerprints that they were attempting to match up with known terrorists. What they didn't have was the current whereabouts of a single one of the terrorists, nor did they have a clue as to where they may strike again.

Jonas Trina had come under suspicion at the start of the investigation. He had recommended the Morroccan Interlude and the authorities were interested in why and how this decision had been made. Jonas was naturally very helpful, and he told them of the bakery where he had been given the suggestion that he use them as his caterer. Of course now the bakery was closed, and the owners had disappeared without a trace just in the past week. He told them that a gentleman who went by the name Tariq owned the bakery and also had the catering business on the side. After stopping at the bakery one evening to sample the cuisine suggested for the cruise, Jonas had decided to utilize their services. That was all he knew of them. The alibi checked out and Jonas was dropped from the list of suspects.

Holland returned to work on Thursday morning. When she walked in to the Human Resource department, all of the employees stood up and gave her a round of applause. Daniece came out of her office followed closely by Jenny and Ernesto. They each took turns giving her hugs and telling Holland how brave she was and how much they missed her. For Holland, unfortunately the wounds were still too fresh and too deep. While she appreciated the support, she told everyone that it would be best if they instead remembered those who had given their lives and she asked for all to pray for the speedy recovery of Jane who was still in bad shape.

All Pharmacor employees worldwide were given Monday September 23rd off, and all were encouraged to attend the mass funeral service which would be held the following Sunday at a park outside of Cincinnati. Over 18,000 people showed up for the funeral service, including the President of the United States, along with the Governor and Senators of Ohio. Most of the Cleveland and Cincinnati Pharmacor employees were in attendance. Both Jonas and Holland presented eulogies in addition to the aforementioned dignitaries and religious leaders. Jonas' tribute to the fallen employees was especially moving because he was able to name several of the individuals who had lost their lives. It wasn't too difficult for him to recall them since during the week he had entered each one of the 304 fatalities in the golden notebook in his estate's wall safe. In honor of the tragedy, state flags in Ohio were lowered to half-mast for a week.

A curious footnote to the event was to be found within the first three weeks after the horror had taken place. The strike that had closed the Cincinnati plant for five weeks earlier in the summer had allowed replacement workers to get a decent knowledge of how the plant was run. Immediately after the funeral, these replacements were contacted by phone and offered positions at Pharmacor South at wages higher than most were making elsewhere. The majority accepted the jobs, and within two and a half weeks, the plant was operational again. This was good, because due once again to American empathy, incoming orders were 300% higher than the previous year. Business had never been better. Neither had Jonas Trina's bonuses.

CHAPTER 27

The week following the funeral service, Holland was like a zombie at work. While she was able to perform most of her duties, her mind was never really on her work. She'd simply been through too much, too recently, to devote herself to duty. For some, work and/or a hobby is the perfect cure to help alleviate the mental anguish one would experience following an ordeal such as Holland had endured. Such was not the case with Holland Matthews. She found that she couldn't confide her true feelings to anyone. Not even John. The only time she felt worthwhile was on the weekend when she would drive the 500 mile round trip to be with Jane at Mercy General Hospital in Cincinnati to support her in her own hour of need. Associates at work tried everything. They empathized. They sympathized. They joked. They cried. Nothing seemed capable of helping her ease the inner torment that was consuming her. At one point Holland and John had been requested to stand alongside Jonas Trina to do a photo shoot for a major magazine story. Being forced to smile while in close proximity to Jonas was the hardest thing she had ever done in her life. She wanted to jump out of her skin and yet she had to appear happy, well adjusted, and in control.

Two weeks after the tragedy, Holland requested and got a leave of absence from her job in order to work through her feelings. Confiding to Daniece, she said that if she didn't get away, Holland felt that she might literally lose her mind. A couple of therapists were recommended, and she promised to consider them. Once out the door, she dismissed them from her mind. Holland knew what she needed, but there was no one she could discuss the problem with in Cleveland. She called John right after leaving work and told him about her leave of absence. He asked her if there was anything that he could do for her, but she told him no. This was something that she would have to work out for herself. She told him that she still loved him, but she had to get away for a while to sort out her feelings. Holland said that she was going to get a room in Cincinnati for a few days to be close to Jane. After that she would call and let him know how her own inner therapy was progressing and in which direction she might feel a need in her life to proceed towards. John said he understood and that he would always be there for her, no matter what. The conversation ended with a couple of melancholy "I love-you's," and the connection was broken.

At home Holland packed a few articles into a couple of small pieces of luggage, and threw them into the back seat of her Taurus. Pulling out of her driveway, she couldn't help feeling that she had never experienced this degree of separation and loneliness before. But she knew that wasn't the real problem. The real problem was gnawing at her from the inside, though she couldn't let it out. It was a secret that she so desperately wanted to shout to the world, but knew that she dare not. Maybe when she got to Cincinnati she would feel different. Time would tell. She remembered someone once said that the truth shall set you free. God, how she longed for both the truth and escape from the thoughts that tormented her! She continued to drive. And she began to pray.

"Fetch it Daisy, fetch the Frisbee," yelled Nishil Najir as the plastic discus shaped object dipped and soared in the wind coming off of Lake Erie. Daisy, a full-grown Golden Retriever took off like a shot in pursuit of the round disc. With a leap, Daisy caught the Frisbee in midair 35 yards from the launch point, and triumphantly brought it almost all the way back to Nishil. Three feet short of her master, Daisy sat down; daring him to try and catch her if he wanted the Frisbee back. When he gave a quick lunge in her direction, Daisy proved too quick as she and her plastic prize eluded capture. Nishil snuck up on her and lunged again, but Daisy once again made off with the orange Frisbee ensconced firmly between her teeth. She almost looked like she was laughing at him.

Someone who definitely was laughing at the dog's antics was patrolwoman Michele Steward, one of the guards at the Rock and Roll Hall of Fame in Cleveland. Nishil glanced in her direction as he pretended to be concentrating solely on Daisy. He was pleased that the patrolwoman appeared to have taken the bait. With a stern command, Nishil was able to get Daisy to relinquish her treasure to him. Nishil drew back his arm and let the Frisbee fly "accidentally' towards where the guard was standing. In a masterful stroke of canine agility, Daisy once again plucked the spinning disc out of the air and fell to the ground just feet from where patrolwoman Steward was manning her post. On a playful urge, Michele dropped her guard and approached the retriever.

"Daisy, may I have the Frisbee?" asked Michelle.

Daisy trotted towards her and stopped just short, daring this newfound playmate to test her skills against her own canine cleverness. Slowly inching closer, Michelle took off her hat revealing long golden tresses that tumbled down past her shoulders. She pretended to toss her cap to the left of Daisy. The dog was distracted just long enough for Michelle to swoop in and grab the orange reward for her efforts. Daisy shot a surprised look at Michelle and immediately began playfully jumping around the officer in an attempt to reclaim the prize that had been so deceitfully taken from her.

"Bravo, bravo!" shouted Nishil as he closed in on the dueling duet. "See Daisy, you're not so smart after all are you?"

"I have to admit that I cheated a little," offered Michelle in Daisy's defense, as she held the Frisbee high to keep the dog from getting it back too easily.

"No need to downplay your victory, officer. Daisy doesn't get beat often, so it's good to see her get a taste of defeat every now and then. I didn't realize how big the Rock Hall of Fame was until I got up close. This place is huge."

The ruse to use Daisy to lower the guard's normally wary and observant nature worked. Within half an hour of kibbutzing with Michele like they were long lost cousins, Nishil had obtained significant amounts of valuable information. He skillfully had extracted from her details on manpower, shift changes, size and composition of the Hall, and the expected size of the security force and weaponry expected to be on hand for the upcoming November 17th induction ceremonies. As Daisy and Nishil bid farewell to their new friend, Nishil carefully counted his steps back to the street in front of the Hall. That would give him the approximate distance from the street to the building. That information coupled with the composition info would be very helpful to their planning. Nishil waved a final farewell to the officer as Daisy joyously bounded at his heels. "Sucker broad." mumbled Nishil under his breath.

There was a knock on the door of Jonas' office. "Come in," he said brusquely.

In walked Ray Titus.
"Jonas, we appear to have a problem with the Rock and Roll Hall of Fame gathering."

"What's the problem?'

"Since the September 21st disaster, employee morale has hit rock bottom. The scuttlebutt around the office is that very few people are showing any interest in attending the induction ceremonies."

"Well Mr. Titus, just what exactly does the title of Sales Manager behind your name denote? Doesn't that theoretically mean that you supposedly have a shred of salesmanship ability in you? I want you to go out to the staff and let them know the importance of being in attendance. We've spent big bucks to get tickets for the event and to get our name attached to this ceremony. I'll not see it all go up in flames just because a bunch of babies suddenly don't want to go. I especially expect the fifty and older crowd to be in full attendance. Hell, two of the groups being inducted are from their era. They owe the musicians their attendance for all of the listening enjoyment those singers gave to them back when they were in puberty. I don't care how you do it, but attendance is mandatory, do you understand?"

"Yes sir."

"Good. Now go make it happen, and I don't expect to hear any more unpleasantness in connection with this great upcoming event.

Jane was emitting an almost constant low guttural moan during the procedure. The process of removing peelings of dead skin from burn patients was excruciatingly painful. That coupled with the fact that she had been hospitalized for almost three weeks with no end in sight was sheer torture to a young lady who had been cut down in her prime due to a cruel twist of fate. Fortunately for Jane, she had covered her face with her hands when the fireball scorched over her. Her lovely face had virtually no damage whatsoever. However the rest of her body was a mass of second and third degree burns. When she had been admitted to Mercy General's burn unit, she had resembled a boiled lobster. Her tanned skin had been almost maroon colored by the heat of the blast. If only she had been able to get deeper in the water. Two days after the procedure, Holland was permitted to make her daily visit. With the risk of infection being a very real danger to someone in Jane's condition, Holland made sure that she was well scrubbed and in her sanitized hospital blue gown, as she entered Jane's burn unit room.

"Hey kiddo, how we feeling today?" asked Holland in a cheerful demeanor.

"Like a half eaten piece of beef jerky, all dried up and worthless and ready to be thrown away."

"Now, I'll have none of that. You are not dried up and worthless, and I resent you saying something like that about my good friend Jane."

"It's the truth."
Holland approached the bed and looked Jane right square in the eyes as she said;

"Jane, I know what a blow this has been to you. I won't deny that you've experienced something that I wouldn't wish on my worst enemy. I also know that you have a long tough fight ahead of you to get your health back, not to mention the mental and emotional scars something like this can leave. But I also know that you are a fighter. And I know that a lot of people care about you very deeply and who even now are hoping and praying for your speedy and complete recovery. Plus, let's not forget the fact of all of the money that I've spent on room and board in Cincinnati these past several days means that you owe me. You certainly don't think that I'm going to allow you to quit on me until I get paid in full do you?"

A thin smile crossed Jane's lips as she pondered Holland's pep talk. "Why you sneaky little bitch, Holland Brittainy Matthews. I'll have you know that one of the nurses let me in on a little secret that you are staying back at the Hyatt, and they have graciously allowed you free room and board for your stay, so there! I ain't gonna reimburse you squat. Just wait until I get back on my feet so that I can kick your skinny little butt up around your ears where it belongs! Now I thought you were going to bring up some crossword puzzles for us to conquer. Or was that just another one of your bald faced lies?"

"That's the spirit! You'd better watch how you talk to me though, or I'll sic my big bad eunuch boyfriend on you."

"Fair enough. Now, bring on the mind games."

Holland laid out the crossword puzzle book on Jane's bed, and the girls took turns finding key words as they talked about everything under the sun except for Jane's physical problems. They passed a carefree hour delighting in each other's company. Slowly however, Holland's mood began to lose its spark, and now it was Jane's turn to come to the rescue.

"I would say a penny for your thoughts, but knowing what a money hungry bitch you are Holland, I'll say fifty bucks for your thoughts."

"Oh nothing."

"Don't oh-nothing me! You're the one who helped snap me out of my funk, now the least you can do is to let me return the favor."

"It's kind of complicated."

"What, you're afraid that I have a hot date that I'm going to miss if I let you spend time spilling your guts to me? C'mon sister, out with it."

"Well, don't get me wrong, because the real reason that I came down to Cincinnati was and is, to see and support you Jane. But I have to admit that something else helped me to make the decision to leave Cleveland for a while. It's something that I've been afraid to talk with anyone else about."

"You can tell me Holly-Brit. I promise that it never leaves this room, cross my heart and hope to die, blow a boat up in my eye!"

Smiling now, Holland picked up where she had left off;

"As you know, for the longest time I've been under the impression that Jonas Trina has been behind the incredible run of bad luck that has plagued Pharmacor. People have been dying left and right and it all started when he came to town. Well every time something bad happens, I bring up how it benefits Jonas, and everybody says that I'm crazy. They say that I'm paranoid and that I should stop thinking like that before I get in big trouble with Jonas and Pharmacor. I can't help it. To me it just makes sense that he's involved up to his arrogant beady little eyeballs. Unfortunately, there's always a fantastically good excuse for the deaths that have occurred, and all suspicion is directed away from Jonas Trina.

With the riverboat cruise attack, once again hundreds die, and no one suspects Trina. Even though it was his idea to have the cruise, his money really that financed the cruise, and his idea to get the caterers that just so happened to be the bad guys to blow up the cruise. And yet if I bring this up to anyone, they'll really think I'm crazy after "Fist of Rage" has taken credit for the attack. Maybe I really am crazy and I'm carrying a personal vendetta too far because I just don't like the guy. At least that's what John thinks. But there's even more to it than that."

"Go on Holly-Brit."

"I used to be happy-go-lucky without a care in the world. At least a lot of the time I was like that."

"I agree. So what are you getting at?"

"Over the past several months I've become a new person, and it's someone who scares me."

"You've been through a lot."

"Regardless, I've changed my whole outlook on life. I'm not trying to, but these past few months have kind of morphed me into a hateful human being."

"Oh I wouldn't say that."

"You're not inside my head. And it all centers around one person. Jonas Trina. Jane I truly do despise him because in my heart of hearts, I'm just so sure that he is behind all of these deaths, and no one seems interested in pursuing him as a suspect. I honestly think that I could find the will to kill the man if I was given the chance."

"Holland you don't really mean that."

"Oh yes I do! Especially if I had definite proof that he was behind these killings."

"And just how do you propose to get definite proof that he was involved in any of the deaths?"

"That's just it, I don't know. But I'll bet if I could get a peek inside a certain wall safe in his office at his estate, I'd find some interesting items with which to begin the hunt."

"And I suppose that Jonas will invite you over for tea and give you the keys to his office and combination to the safe to make that happen, right?"

"Probably not."

"That's right, so we'll have to put our thinking caps on to come up with a better plan on how to get in there."

"Jane, you said we'll have to... does that mean that you agree that he's behind all of these evil happenings?"

"Excuse me, but didn't I go to Chicago to check up on his past, and aren't I the one lying here like an overdone French fry. If he had anything to do with the Buckeye Belle, or any of the earlier tragedies, you can bet that I want to do anything I can to help bring the bastard to justice. I certainly have the time these days to do a little planning and figuring. But right now, this is a little more than I can handle emotionally, so can we just get back to our crossword puzzles for the time being?"

"O.K. my B.F.F.. Thanks for letting me vent. I was beginning to think that I'd lose my mind if I had to keep everything bottled up inside me much longer."

"Glad to be of service."
Holland and Jane went back to crossword puzzles and played for another half hour.

"Holland, can you think of a ten letter word which you R.S.V.P. to?"

"Give me a second... yeah, I think it fits. Try the word invitation."

"Perfect, it fits. Thanks."
Suddenly, a blank expression came over Jane's face. The look was quickly replaced by one of keen interest, almost as if she had solved a puzzle of her own.

"Holland could you bring me my purse."

"Jane, you really don't have to pay me for figuring out that last word." laughed Holland.

"I might have figured out a puzzle that is far more important."
Holland gave Jane her purse, and she went rummaging through it, looking in a particular nook for a particular piece of paper the way only a purse's owner knows just exactly where to look. Triumphantly, Jane held aloft a folded up piece of paper.

"Great Jane, you found a folded up piece of paper, congratulations."

"Here, you open it Holly-Brit and tell me what you see."

"I see the invitation to the Buckeye Belle cruise. With what you've been through, why would you keep that?"

"Maybe for a morbid keepsake, but we may be glad I did."

"Why?"

"Do you see anything else on the paper?"

"Not really, should I?"

"Remember when you told me how pissed off Jonas got when he found out that Nancy McKinney was arranging to have changes made to the invitation?"

"Yeah, so...?"

"And he was so insistent that the invitations had to be exactly as he had written them with absolutely no changes?"

"Go on."

"Unless I miss my guess, I'll bet that if you and I really examine this little piece of paper, we can figure out the reason why he was so pissed."

"All right I'm game, but I don't see where this will lead us."

"I'm not sure either, but you never know."
With that the two sleuths began a new word game in earnest as they examined the words Jonas Trina had "penned" many weeks ago which turned out to be a prelude to disaster:

An Invitation to an Enchanted Evening

You are cordially invited to attend a gala event on Saturday September 21ˢᵗ. It will feature a riverboat cruise aboard the paddle wheeler Buckeye Belle, with all costs provided. The food, beverages, and musical accompaniment will kindly be donated by the Cleveland Pharmacor staff members. Surely you'll be blown away by the musical entertainment, and you are certainly guaranteed to enjoy the Middle Eastern themed cuisine. Feast upon delicacies such as warm pieces of baklava, or perhaps taboule, or stuffed grape leaves. Alcoholic drinks and softer beverages shall be in abundance, and with advance notice perhaps we will be able to furnish your personal favorite. The captain says this cruise is "to die for", and the scenery at this time of year is breathtaking. Other interests maybe in store for you as well. Gaming tables will be set up below, with shuffleboards on the deck. An assortment of video games will also be available. We think that with the Ohio moon overhead, far and away the most popular activity shall be dancing upon the river. We're sure that all who attend will have a great time. Hope to see you there!!!!!!!!!!!!!!!!!!

They had busied themselves for twenty minutes carefully examining the invitation's text when Jane let out a gasp

"Oh dear Father in heaven, Holly-Brit, look at this."

"What is it?"

"Look here."

Jane took her finger and slowly traced a grouping of words whose meaning could leave no doubt as to their intent. She peered over at Holland when she was finished. Holland's face was reddened with a look of pure unadulterated hatred.

"Hand me the phone Jane." commanded Holland
Jane did as ordered, and Holland dialed a number she knew by heart. On the third ring the call was answered on the other end with a quick "Hello."

"John, it's me Holland. I need you to drive to Cincinnati tonight. I'll be in Jane's room at Mercy General."

"Darling, you know I love you, but can I ask as to why I'm to come on such short notice after you told everyone that you had to get away?"

"Because John I'm going to show you something that is going to turn some worlds upside down!"

A loud buzzer went off at the Trina estate indicating that someone was at the front gate, 400 yards distant from the mansion Jonas was standing in as he answered the buzzer.
"Yes."

"It's the lawn service. May we be let in?"

"I'll open the main gate. Proceed up the drive and bear to your left when the drive splits. You may park by the rear entrance and I'll let you in through the garage."

"Very well."

The gate swung open, and the lawn service truck drove onto the grounds. The driver and his partner wound their way through rows of overhanging maple trees for the first three hundred yards, which gave way to neatly trimmed hedges as the mansion drew nearer. The truck pulled around the rear of the estate that the driver quickly calculated as being between 10,000-12,000 square feet in size. A large overhead door opened up at the rear of the grand edifice, revealing an eight car heated and carpeted garage. The men parked the truck and entered into the garage. As soon as they did, the overhead door began the slow descent ushering the men towards a lighted doorway adjoining the garage to the main building. As they made their way towards the door, the men couldn't help but be impressed by the array of vehicles they passed. In addition to Jonas' Ferrari Moderne and his Viper, representative models from Jaguar, Infiniti, Cadillac, BMW, and Porche lined the walls of the oversized room. The showpiece was a beautiful gold toned Rolls Royce that looked like it had never seen the light of day as it shimmered in the dim garage light. As the men approached the man door, it opened and Jonas Trina himself was there to let the two service men into the residence.

"Gentlemen, I trust that you had no difficulty in finding my home."

"None, whatsoever."

"Good, then if you will follow me down the hallway, we'll get down to business."

The three men strolled down a long marble hallway on what they guessed to be the lowest floor of the estate. They passed an ominous looking full size knight in shining armor just before they went around a corner. The knight was on a three-foot tall pedestal, and it was brandishing a mace over the head as if prepared to strike a fatal blow upon some long ago enemy of the realm. Faux torches lit the way giving off the appearance of an underground passageway in ancient times, which was precisely the effect the owner of the estate wished his guests to have as they traversed this floor.

"The knight who we just passed is from medieval England, and it dates from the thirteenth century, or so I've been told. The spiked mace weighs almost ten pounds, and as you can imagine it would cause quite a headache to the recipient of one of its swung blows. I'll now take you to my office. As they reached the huge office door, Jonas punched in the door's combination on the keypad, and the heavy wooden door swung open, revealing the splendor to the new arrivals. As the service men entered, Jonas closed the door behind them and briefly allowed them to take in the grandeur of his downstairs sanctuary.

"As you gentlemen may have noticed, there is a bit of a theme to my office. I've always been interested in medieval European history, and when my means reached a certain level that allowed me to indulge myself, I took advantage to create that which you see here. My own little bit of Camelot, if you will."

"And the chessboard, is that also a touch of Camelot?" asked the service driver.

"No, that is here merely so that I may stay in touch with a favorite pastime of mine. Do either of you play?"
Both men answered negatively.

"I find chess to be very challenging. It allows me to stay sharp and focused, and it keeps me aware of the ever present need to always keep looking numerous steps ahead. That enables me to anticipate and shape the future to that of my own choosing. It also allows me to indulge in the spirit of competition. As you can see by the pieces that have been taken off the board I am in the middle of an interesting match at this time which I must say I am enjoying immensely. My opponent is proving themselves to be a far worthier competitor than I imagined. Ah, but I digress. Won't you have a seat while I get us a libation? I believe that Perrier was your previous drink of choice was it not?"

Both men answered positively. Jonas brought over the drinks. As the men accepted the Perrier's, Jonas poured himself a snifter of brandy.

"By the way, we may now speak freely. This room is virtually soundproof. I wanted to maintain appearances in case a member of my household staff might have been able to overhear us. I must admit Mr. Al-Salem, that your previous outfit as head chef was a trifle more becoming than your lawn service uniforms."

"I agree Mr. Trina. However we decided that the chef outfit might look a bit out of place for our current vocation. Isn't that right Nishil?"

"Absolutely."

"Gentlemen, may I offer up a toast for your outstanding work on the waterfront in Cincinnati. Here's to a long and successful partnership to achieve all of our desired goals."

The three men joined their cups together in celebratory fashion. As they pulled away and drank freely, Jonas motioned them to once again take their seats so that they might get down to work.

"Tell me Tariq, how are the final preparations coming for our next venture?"

"We are ahead of schedule. In fact our men will be making what you Americans refer to as a dry run this week on all three phases of the operation. Of course, you are fully aware of two of the three phases, but you know little of the third."

"That is correct. All that I know of the third is the location. I thought that was an excellent suggestion that you made whereby none of us know the entire plan except for you. That way in case we are compromised, we will not be able to give away the entire plan."

"Unfortunately, due to the nature of our work, there are always those parties who are eager to learn what we are up to next. As we have learned throughout the world, our enemies are not averse to using very persuasive means to extract information in order to foil our plans. However our operatives cannot reveal that which they do not know. Hence, the purpose behind our secrecy, even from ourselves. In fact Mr. Trina, you are the only other person within our organization who is aware of more than one phase. Outside of this room, my men believe that their part of the mission is in fact the only part."

"I feel honored Mr. Al-Salem, that you trust me to the degree that would allow you to reveal more to myself than to even your most trusted associates."

"You have earned the trust through your support for our cause, and the achievements which you have made within your own organization. Let us proceed."

"Indeed. On the train phase planning, we have been successful in convincing an employee of the commuter train company to help our people board the train with their weapons and equipment intact. The amount of money it took to turn the employee was a mere pittance compared to the havoc his treachery will wreak upon his countrymen. We have allocated four of our men to accomplish this phase, which should be sufficient. After the train's driver has been eliminated, the men will herd the commuters into the trailing cars. They will lock the speed controls so that the train continues to speed up on the trip to downtown Cleveland where it should cause a nasty pile up under the Terminal Tower. The escape plan calls for our men to clear the train just after locking down the controls while the train is just beginning to accelerate. They will keep the passengers from attempting to slow the train down by setting fire to the lead car where the driver's controls are located. Everything should be accomplished within a matter of 3 or 4 minutes. Any passengers who try to interfere will be shot."

"Excellent! That sounds like that should work. Now what is the timing of the train crash?"

"It will occur around 6:45 P.M. on November 17th."

"Perfect. That should bring the emergency units, police, and fire departments running to that location for our next surprise at 7:30."

"Yes it most certainly will."

"I don't feel that we have to go over any of the plans for that operation at this time. As I told you previously by e-mail, we've been planning our own operation for Phase Two for quite awhile now, so that has been effectively put to bed. The men who volunteered for this assignment are all prepared to accept their glorious fate, should it come to that. They very much look forward to their rewards in the afterlife. I expect that many virgins will be on hand when their time comes to welcome these heroes of the jihad. I envy them their mission. The vans have been procured and are being stored in a warehouse outside of the city. Sufficient quantities of both ammonium nitrate and diesel fuel have been accumulated over a long period of time to utilize in our efforts. Our idea to establish lawn service companies in order to buy fertilizer in bulk without raising suspicions has reaped enormous benefits. Those chemicals, when coupled with diesel oil and Semtech, should be more than enough to demolish the structure. As for the third part of the evening's events, that shall remain a secret to you for the reasons previously stated. I can assure you that it also will dramatically alter the Cleveland area. It should make a pretty picture for Monday morning's newspapers. I hope that they can take an aerial view of the entire city so that the true scope of our evening's efforts can be fully appreciated. Now Mr. Trina, Nishil and I would like to discuss taking you up on your offer to use your boat to both view the event, and to affect our escape to Canada across Lake Erie."

"I'll have the thirty-five footer at your disposal on the 17th. Barring any really inclement weather, I'm sure it will suit your needs."

"Outstanding Jonas. We'll look forward to watching the late season fireworks display as it balloons over the shoreline on that night. It should be quite a sight."

"It certainly should. Well gentlemen, unless there are any more urgent matters I believe that wraps things up. I'll show you out the way you came in, and I look forward with great anticipation to the Rock and Roll Hall of Fame induction ceremonies on November 17th. It should be a real blast."

"Hi Holly-Brit. Can a weary bedraggled traveler come into the room?"

"Of course, oh weary traveler, but try to be quiet. Jane fell asleep about twenty minutes ago, and she needs her rest in order to be strong for whatever procedures they'll have her undergo tomorrow. John, you can't believe how good it is to see you."

"Likewise, ma cherie. Are you feeling any better than when you left?"

"Tremendously so! Jane has been a real source of strength and inspiration for me at a time when I came down to try and be that for her. I guess that we just feed off each other to the mutual advantage of both. Ultimately though, the way that I feel is going to be determined in large part by yourself and others when I get back to Cleveland."

"O.K., now you've lost me a little bit."

"I know Mr. Kazek. How about if we go to the cafeteria and get a cup of coffee and I'll bring you up to speed on some things?"

"That would be great. I'd hate to think that I drove 240 miles for a prank phone call."

"Trust me John. The only pranks that have been played concerning us have not been played by me, and these pranks which I'm going to show you are a hell of a lot deadlier than anything that I could ever dream up. I'll advise the nurse that we're going to get a cup of coffee, so she can tell Jane in case she wakes up. C'mon lover boy, I've got to fill you in so that you can appreciate the female intuition for the amazing gift it truly is."

The sole member of the hospital staff assigned to cleaning up the cafeteria at this late hour was sweeping under a table not far from where Holland and John sat. One thing you could usually depend on at a hospital was cleanliness, even if the food was not always four-star caliber.

"Thank goodness the cafeteria was still open. That sandwich really hit the spot. I can't believe how hungry I was. Now that I think about it though, it has been almost nine hours since I'd had something to eat. You on the other hand hardly ate anything. Are you feeling all right Holly-Brit?"

"I'm fine. I'm just making sure to watch my weight so that I don't run the risk of losing my loving little eunuch boyfriend to a more nubile lass than myself."

"Fat chance of that happening. Well, we've eaten and drunk enough coffee to float a battleship. Don't you think that it's time for the mystery that I drove from Cleveland to Cincinnati to find out is revealed?"

"I suppose so. Although I have to admit I'm a little tentative about showing you, because I'm afraid of your reaction."

"My reaction?"

"Yes. I fear that if you don't react the way that I hope you do, our relationship could be in serious trouble. Not to mention that my psyche could be in serious trouble."

"You're not kidding are you?"

"Not at all."

"Well I'll try to put my compassionate hat on and be as understanding as I can possibly be."

"No John, that's not what I want."

"Well what is it that you do want?"

"I just want you to be yourself and to give me your true feelings and thoughts about what I show you."

"I'll always show you those, but now Holland, I have to admit that I'm getting more confused by the minute. How about if you just let me see what it is you brought me down here to see, and trust that I'll make the right call."

"All right then, I'll cross my fingers and give it a shot. Here we go. As you know I've had the suspicion all along that Jonas Trina has been somehow either behind all of the deaths at Pharmacor, or at least had some ties to them."

"Well yes, but honey we've been over all of that before."

"Just hear me out John, O.K.?"

"All right," John said as he took a deep breath and tried hard not to roll his eyes.

"I've never dismissed Jonas as being innocent in all of these terrible occurrences which keep plaguing Pharmacor. Yes, even though there was always a plausible explanation for each tragedy, somehow I always felt that Jonas was involved to some extent. That included the Buckeye Belle disaster."

"Oh Holland, "Fist of Rage" has already claimed..."

"Quiet John, I'm not finished yet. As I was saying, that included the Buckeye Belle murders. I knew however that if I brought up my suspicions once again with no proof, I'd be made a laughingstock and probably ridiculed to no end. I couldn't let that happen. And yet I had no proof, nor any real hope of getting any proof against Trina. That's why I had to get away. I had to either reconcile myself to the fact that Jonas Trina was either; A. innocent (which I couldn't believe) B.guilty (but I couldn't prove it) or C.guilty (and I was somehow able to at least provide some type of proof). Well, as I stand here before you, I'm going to show you something that I pray to God convinces you that you don't think I'm crazy, and that perhaps I've been onto something all along. Speaking of praying, I prayed all the way from home to here that God might shed some light on the murders, and Jane and I believe he has. We hope you agree."

"I hope so too Holland, but I have to admit, this had better be good."

With that, Holland took out the invitation and laid it on the table in front of John. As she finished unfolding the paper, she grabbed John's hand and asked him to put out his index finger. As he did so, she proceeded to move his hand on the sheet in such a manner as to point out the vile deadly phrase which Jonas Trina had incorporated into the text of the invitation to reveal his true intentions for the ill fated people aboard the Buckeye Belle. Holland retraced her steps with John's finger so that there could be no doubts about the wording. As she finished the second time, she gently raised John's chin to look up into her moist pleading eyes.

Her eyes were met with a look of such utter hatred and disgust that Holland's first thought was to bolt from the room. But then John spoke.

"That murderous son-of-a-bitching bastard! I'll see that he dies a thousand deaths for every person killed on the Buckeye Belle. I'll have the F.B.I. make him wish he'd never been born. That no good evil mother..."

In his rage, John had neglected to focus on Holland's reaction to his vehement outburst. As he looked into her eyes, he saw shock and a kind of fearful amazement brought on by his fury. He regained his senses and stood up to hold his trembling Holland in his arms.

"Oh Holly-Brit, I'm so so sorry. I'm so sorry that I've scared you now, but I'm even sorrier to have ever doubted you. You've been right all along, and we've all been making your life miserable by doubting you. That clever bastard had everyone fooled except you. But don't worry; now we'll get him. Can you ever forgive me for not believing you?"

Looking up at John with a tear-streaked face, Holland was too overwrought with emotion to speak. She gamely tried to smile through the tears as she slowly nodded her head to offer John absolution of his sin. Holland squeezed John tightly as she tried to bring her emotions under control. Finally she was able to speak.

"John, we can't go to the F.B.I. yet. Or the police. Or to any of the authorities."

"Why not Holland? I realize that this in and of itself doesn't offer total proof but it's a good enough start that we could start trailing him and nail the clever bastard when he..."

"That's just it John. Jonas Trina IS a clever bastard. He's a chess fanatic from what I've learned. That means that he's always planning many steps ahead in his affairs. I'm sure that Jonas has several contingency plans to thwart the authorities if they come knocking. Also I'm sure that he's aware of the possibility that he might be followed and he's probably always on the lookout to avoid compromising himself. No, the only way to catch him is to outsmart him. We have to beat him at his own game. It has to be done utilizing the element of surprise. In fact Jane and I think we might have a way to get the goods on Trina. I'd like to share it with you now, get your input, and see what you think of our nefarious little plan."

"Lay it on me babe, I'm all ears. If your plan isn't feasible, then we'll just stay here until we devise a better one, because this is one S.O.B. who has got to be brought down."

CHAPTER 28

Holland returned to work the following week, revitalized from her time away, and with a renewed sense of purpose, which was noticeable to all the well wishers who welcomed her back. On her third day, she went to Jonas' office and requested an audience with him for a few minutes. Nancy McKinney took the request into Jonas Trina.

"Mr. Trina, Holland Matthews would like a word with you if possible. She says that it will only take a couple of minutes, and it might be of a personal benefit to you sir."

"That I very much doubt Miss McKinney, but you may show her in with the proviso that she take no more than five minutes, because I'm quite busy today."

"You may go in now Miss Matthews," said Nancy in a snooty manner.

Holland swept by Nancy without acknowledging her affected air and opened the door to Trina's office.

"Well Miss Matthews, to what do I owe this unexpected and undesired interruption to my exceedingly busy day?"

Ignoring the rude comments, which were not altogether unexpected, Holland jumped right into the reason she had come, and for which she would not be deterred.

"Mr. Trina, I was actually wondering if I might be of some service to you on a personal basis."

"Why Miss Matthews, I didn't know you cared.""

"Actually, I was referring to the housekeeper situation at your estate. I understand that since that Rosa woman was dismissed, you have gone through three housekeepers in a matter of a month. I also heard that you were currently without a person in that position."

"You seem to be quite well informed. May I ask where all of this information comes from?"

"Oh I just happen to overhear things from time to time. However, that really is not important. What is important is finding a qualified housekeeper who will diligently perform her duties while being trustworthy and reliable. I know of such a person who has her own business, and who would welcome an additional client at this point in time. She has excellent references, and has been in the cleaning business for over ten years. She is a cousin of mine who has lost a couple of her better clients recently due to relocation. I spoke with her last night and she said she would gladly entertain the possibility of showing you the quality of her cleaning service. It sure would beat breaking in a new person every other week or so, don't you think?"

Jonas paused warily to contemplate the offer and to deduce what ulterior motive could possibly be behind such a seemingly benign and useful suggestion. It was true. He was perturbed by the poor quality of the housekeepers sent to his estate. His butler Karl, and some of the other staff, were beginning to grow weary and impatient by the parade of domestic losers that continued to shuffle in and out of the position. Deciding that no real harm could come from giving a real businesswoman a shot, Jonas began to consider giving into the suggestion. After all, the cousin must be a good housekeeper, because surely Holland knew there were nasty repercussions that could entail if, in fact, she was not all that she was purported to be.

"All right Miss Matthews, I will take you up on your hopefully magnanimous offer and grant your cousin the housekeeper an interview with my butler Karl tomorrow evening. I'll have Miss McKinney provide you with directions to my estate. I, of course, shall not be involved personally with so mundane a task as selecting the hired help. However, Karl has my utmost confidence, and if he sees fit to give her the position, she may start immediately."

"Great. I'll get the directions and contact my cousin."

"Of course. You may go now Miss Matthews. By the way, I applaud your initiative in recognizing where a problem exists, and taking steps to rectify it. That is a trait that can take a person far in this world. I hope that this works out for all parties concerned. Oh, and Miss Matthews, I'm glad to see that your leave of absence appears to have been beneficial."

"Thank you sir."

As Holland left his office, she couldn't help but think that she shared Trina's wish that all parties would benefit by this arrangement. Little did Trina realize that for Holland, those parties included herself along with the police, the F.B.I., and family members of hundreds of executed Pharmacor employees and retired persons.

The four Arabic men stood on the rapid transit train platform in long coats that did not appear out of the ordinary on a cool fall night. They casually spoke amongst themselves as they worked their way towards the farthest section of the platform, thereby offering them the best chance to sit in the lead car with the train operator. Under each of their coats was a stick. Each stick was approximately the length of the weapons that they would be carrying onto the train with them in 2 ½ short weeks. The small crowd sharing the platform with the foursome paid them little heed as the majority of them simply minded their own business. Soon a "clickety-clacking" sound alerted everyone that a train was approaching. As the silver train pulled abreast of the platform and braked to a stop, the doors slid open. A handful of people disembarked from each transit car, only to be replaced by new passengers, akin to a carnival ride. The four Arabic men got on the lead car and grabbed onto the overhead bar to secure their balance for the ride to the next station up the line. As the train began to pull away from the stop, one of the men began a practiced conversation centering on the mythical wedding of a relative that supposedly was going to be taking place soon. This would dissuade fellow riders from eavesdropping due to the private nature of the subject. As they talked, the men looked around observantly as they conducted their reconnaissance to prepare them for the real thing.

In the car with them were a group of teenagers who were excitedly jabbering away about who among their eighth grade peers had the hots for whom. A young mother had her hands full keeping her twin five year olds in check. Several commuters had their heads buried in a magazine or newspaper to pass the time. A small number of people simply stared out the windows of the transit into the dark as the train traversed the barren railway on the swift paced journey to the next station. Not a single person appeared to give the quartet as much as a glance during the five minute commute to the next stop. While the riders changed with each station, one thing remained constant. No one was concerned in the least with four Arabic men in long coats riding the train alongside them. That contrasted sharply with the commuter rides these men had taken in other parts of the world. They envisioned that lackadaisical aspect of the American psyche would change dramatically in the next month. The four men would make the same trip three more times over the next two weeks with no complications whatsoever. By November 17th phase one would be ready.

"Hey buddy, hold up there a minute," yelled the security guard to the driver of a white van with the name Damascus Drywall stenciled on the side.

The driver, Mustafa Zayed, came to a stop as the portly balding security guard slowly made his way over to the van that had just entered the underground parking facilities of the Terminal Tower in Cleveland. Mustafa prepared to give the guard his most engaging smile as he had been trained to do in these situations.

"Yes officer, is there a problem?"

"It's just a routine security check for vans and trucks entering the area. What do you have in the back?"

"My partner and I have drywall tools for our business."

"Mind if I have a look inside?"

"Not at all, be my guest."

The guard opened the rear door of the Dodge Ram 2500 van and perused the van's contents. He saw buckets of drywall compound, taping knives, drywall tape, drywall hammers, tape rules, and drywall taping guns, among a hodgepodge of other paraphernalia necessary to the average drywall installer.

"You look pretty damn legit to me. My watch says its 6:15 P.M. Isn't that a little late in the day to be starting a drywall job?"

"Not really, not where office buildings are concerned. We often work Saturday nights and on Sundays in order to minimize office disruptions during regular hours. However, tonight we're here to give an estimate to a gentleman at a law firm in the building who is talking about renovating their offices."

"Yeah, I think that I heard something about that awhile back."

"If this is like most of the jobs with law offices that I've done, I'm sure that I'll have to come back several times over the next month before we get the contract. I imagine I'll be seeing quite a bit of you officer, uhh...

"Zitko. Les Zitko. If you show up around this time at night you'll see plenty of me buddy. I work the late shift from 3:00 P.M. until 11:00 P.M."

"Very good officer Zitko. I'd better be going now so that we're not too late for our appointment. See you around." Zayed and his partner drove under the massive tower complex and parked near a support beam.

"Mustafa, it appears that you have made a new friend," said the partner.

"Yes, and a very valuable friend indeed. We will become such good friends over the next two weeks that by the 17th of November, I'll be able to come into this garage with a tank and my new friend Les Zitko would not question it." Four times over the next two weeks Mustafa found a reason to park at the Terminal parking garage, and each time he greeted guard Zitko with a gracious smile, and a few pleasantries. The stage was now set. By November 17th Phase Two would be ready.

Akmed Allan drove his truck slowly through the downtown Cleveland streets as if he were looking for a particular address. His truck was one which people see on the streets of America's cities numerous times every week. The logo emblazoned on both sides of the truck and also on the back was a staple of the American way of life, almost as much as baseball, hot dogs, and apple pie. Few would question the legitimacy of such a vehicle on a downtown street virtually at anytime of the day or night. That was part of the relevance to the planning of Phase Three. Akmed and his brother Abu cruised the city streets to familiarize themselves with the area, and to gauge the wariness of the populace, both civilian and authoritative. They elicited no response from the fools they passed by whatsoever. They must have gone by at least half a dozen patrol cars who didn't bat an eye in their direction, either today or the other two times they had traversed this area. The other two trucks that were part of the operation had reported similar disinterest. For the fourth time in a week, Akmed drove his truck past the Rock and Roll Hall of Fame and took in the surrounding area. His concern was in getting as near as possible to the actual structure when the proper time came. All of his and his brother's focus was squarely

on doing whatever was necessary to complete the mission. They thought nothing of escape. Akmed and Abu were realists. There might be no escape from this operation. Both men long ago had made their peace with their maker, and in fact looked forward to fulfilling the glorious destiny which fate had now lain at their feet. It was only a matter of time now before that fate would be tested.
For although an escape plan was in place, death was a very real possibility and this they accepted.

Over the next two weeks Akmed, Abu, and their counterparts in the other two trucks made their final "dry runs" past the target area with no complications. They all reported that the attack had an excellent chance of success, and that the mission should proceed as planned. By November 17th Phase Three would be ready.

Holland and her cousin Deena Peterson sat on a sectional arrangement in Deena's beautiful ranch style home on a secluded bluff overlooking the Cleveland Metropark. The October scenery was breathtaking in the afternoon sun, as the slanted rays reflected off multi-hued leaves of the various deciduous trees native to Northeast Ohio. A couple of large orange leaf filled pumpkin garbage bags flashed their black gape-toothed smile at Holland as she looked out the back door. An ever-growing carpet of red, gold, orange, yellow, brown, and purple fallen leaves covered the valley floor. An occasional light breeze would rustle the leaves of the big maple, oak, and elm trees, releasing a new legion of pigmented paratroopers to ride the wind currents down to their final resting place. The warmth of the sun was resisting the inherent coolness soon to be taking the proper place on a mid autumn Ohio day. However, you could only stall Mother Nature's timetable for so long before the season caught up and the temperatures began the rightful downward trend predicated by the calendar.

"The trees seem to be holding onto their leaves longer this year," said Holland as she admired the view out of the sliding glass door that led to an expansive leaf covered deck.

"That's because we really haven't had any appreciable rain or windstorms since the leaves began to change colors," offered Deena.

"That's probably it. It's nice to be able to appreciate the changing colors a while longer this year for whatever reason. Shall we go over the plan one more time before we head over to Trina's place to meet with the butler, or do you think you've got it down well enough?"

"I don't think that's necessary. I'm pretty sure that I understand what I've got to do. I just hope that the timing works out in our favor."

"Deena, are you sure that you want to go through with this? As I told you, this is certainly not without risk, especially if we get caught with our fingers in the cookie jar, so to speak. I'm convinced that Trina has done away with many people, and I'm sure there is nothing which he is not capable of doing to those who cross him."

"That's exactly why I've got to help you by seeing this through. Look Holland, we've been through some scary scenarios before when we were growing up and it's always turned out all right. Remember when we were girl scouts hiking in the park and those bees attacked us?" We got away by being smart and jumping in the lake before they could sting us. And that time when that pit bull came after us, but you grabbed that tree branch and held him at bay until help arrived. We're a good team, you and I, and we'll see this through to a successful conclusion just like all the other times. I'd hate to think that this Trina puke would get away with everything because I didn't help catch him when I had the chance."

"Oh thank you Deena. You don't know how much it means to have you by my side in this. But I do want you to realize how dangerous this could become."

"Hell little lady, I eat danger for breakfast. Let's ride!" said Deena in her best imitation of an old wild-west type hero. The twosome put their arms around each other's shoulders and headed for the front door.

The autumn sun was setting as they got off the highway. They headed east on a state route with two lanes in each direction. The lanes would soon narrow to one lane as they approached the exclusive Hunting Valley community. The quaintness of the narrow road belied the affluence of the local residents who preferred the traffic limiting, one lane roadway which discouraged many from taking this route. It also virtually eliminated the truck traffic which was desirous to the community's prestigious inhabitants.

"Do you have the video recorder well concealed in your purse?" asked Holland.

"Yes, and for the third time, yes it is fully charged, and yes it has a brand new cassette in it."

"Good. Do you have the hook attached to the strap of the video recorder?"

"Sure do."

"O.K. I hate to be such a mother hen, but once I go into my act inside, you're only going to have maybe a minute to accomplish everything, so preparation is critical."

"I understand Holland, believe me I do.

"All right then. His house should be coming up shortly, so let's put our game faces on."

"Gotcha coach."

Holland found the address and pulled into the driveway. They announced themselves at the gate, and the gate swung open to allow their entrance. Arriving at the house, Deena was struck by the sheer size and grandeur of the structure.

"The guy may be a puke, but you gotta admit that he sure knows how to live."

"Yeah, crime always does pay well, until you're caught. Let's ring the bell, and commence to start catching the slime ball."

"Right behind you Holland."

Almost a full minute after the bell had been rung, the door opened and a tall, dour, stern faced man ushered them inside.

"I am Karl, Mr. Trina's personal butler. Which of you ladies is Deena Peterson?"

"That would be me," Deena answered cheerily as she attempted to brighten the butler's rather stuffy disposition.

"I've arranged to have some tea and coffee prepared in the kitchen. Perhaps you would like a cup while I look over your references."

"Why yes, that would be lovely."

"I was unaware that you would be escorted by Miss uh..."

"Matthews. Holland Matthews. Pleasure to meet you Karl. I've heard so much about you from Mr. Trina."

"Of course. You ladies may seat yourselves at the table. I have the coffee and tea services on the counter. There are also cream, sugar, and lemon slices for your pleasure. I'll return in a few minutes."

"Thank you very much," said both women.

As Karl left the room, Deena turned to Holland and whispered; "Our boy Karl needs to lighten up a little don't you think?"

"Are we sure that Karl is his real name? It seems to me that Igor would be a bit more appropriate. Of course I suppose that having to play the part of the butler for jolly old Jonas could tend to sap the exuberance for life out of anyone. Let's have some tea."

Fifteen minutes later Karl reentered the kitchen. Though it was left unsaid, all three people in the room knew that Karl had been busy checking on Deena's references. They were assured that the references had been acceptable when Karl offered them a tour of the estate. It took almost an hour to tour the ground level and upper floor. Karl showed off the gleaming gold handles on the fixtures of all five full bathrooms as he interspersed the tour with his own expectations of Deena's future duties. Soon, hopefully, it would be her job to make the handles gleam.

A highlight of the tour was the visit to the master bedroom. The king sized four-poster bed with the attached canopy was immense. Even knowing whose body usually resided between its sheets didn't dim Holland's desire to at least give the mattress a test sit to determine its plush-ness for herself. Karl looked on disapprovingly as Holland and Deena bounced on opposite corners of the bed.

"I would very much appreciate it if you would refrain from ruffling the covers. Miss Peterson, your duties, should it come to that, will of course include making the bed each day in just the manner as you saw it. I'll now show you the master bath."

The master bath was immense with a marble floor, oversized bathtub with water jets, shower, and combination steam room and sauna; in addition to the commode stall. The marble vanity stretched for 18 feet with three deep bowls complete once again with gold handles. Two operating sun lights were overhead to allow for a nighttime view of the stars as one relaxed in the tub after a long hard day. Deena could only imagine the work it would require to keep this place ship shape.

Finally the time came that both of the women had been waiting for. The trip down to Jonas' underground sanctuary. Karl led them down the steps, and instead of taking the direct route, he took them on a journey down a side hallway that led in from the garage. This allowed him to point out the knight in shining armor that Jonas had recently shown off to his guests. The ladies expressed their due admiration for such a fine piece as they made their way to Jonas' office.

Karl instructed Deena and Holland to step away while he entered the numbers on the office keypad that would permit the door to open. Only Jonas and Karl had the code to open the door, and that was the way it would remain. As the door swung open, the trio slowly entered the vast room. Deena let out an audible gasp as she attempted to take in the sheer opulence that surrounded them. The bejeweled chess pieces, the Camelot tapestry, the two knights, the long necked trumpets, etc., were simply awe-inspiring. Deena soon regained her senses, and began to go into her act, as she and Holland had practiced.

"Karl, that tapestry on the wall over there is so beautiful, could you please tell me about it?"

For the first time since they arrived Karl showed a tiny spark of personality as he commenced to discuss the tapestry and some of the other key aspects of the room. The more he talked, the more Deena questioned. This had the desired effect of Karl losing sight of Holland as she slipped from the room. Holland surreptitiously made her way down the hallway in the direction of the knight with the spiked ball they had previously passed. She reached into her purse and took out a plastic bag that she had brought along for just this purpose. Releasing the contents of the bag on the floor, she immediately let out an ear splitting scream, followed by two more screams of similar shock and decibel value. The screams had the desired effect, as Karl came tearing out of the office to see what had prompted them. As he bolted from the room, Deena sprung into action.

She opened the purse that she had slung over her shoulder for the entire tour, and took out a small mini cam video recorder. Racing over to one of the knights, she slid open the metal headpiece and inserted the mini cam. She used the hook to attach the video camera to a portion of the helmet so that it was secure and so that it was the proper height for her purposes. Now she turned the camera on, and after a soft initial whirring sound, it was virtually inaudible. She slid the metal headpiece back to the original location, and peered inside. She could see the camera lens looking back at her through one of the eyeholes, and it was focused squarely on the chessboard upon the wall. She couldn't believe her luck to have accomplished the deed on the first try. At the same time, Karl had located the source of all the commotion. Holland was standing by the knight on a pedestal, in the hallway with a look of fear in her eyes.

"Miss Matthews, are you all right?" asked the butler as he approached her.

"Look there, on the floor by the pedestal."

Karl did as instructed, and he saw a fierce looking but utterly harmless big hairy wolf spider that Holland had smuggled into the mansion. "You mean to tell me that this is what all of the screaming was about?"

"Of course! Just look at that ferocious thing. I'm scared to death of spiders. Please kill it Karl, please!"

By now the spider had crept into a crevice between the pedestal base and the wall. Karl took off one of his shoes and attempted to smash the eight-legged intruder, but he couldn't get at it. He tried to wedge his shoe into the spider's temporary refuge, but it was too big. Holland cheered inwardly for the spider's cunning, because it was accomplishing the purpose beyond her wildest expectations. It was buying Deena time to fulfill her mission.

"I'll fix you, you hairy little bastard." exclaimed Karl as he went down the hallway and opened a small closet door. He came back with a long handled broom, which he brushed into the crevice. With one brisk stroke, the furry arachnid was expelled from the hiding place and now lay exposed in the middle of the marble floor. Retrieving the shoe that he had removed before, Karl brought the leather footwear down on the spider three times to insure the hairy creature's demise.

"Oh thank you Karl. You're so brave. Boy was that thing big."

"That's quite all right. Now why don't you tell me why you were wandering around the hallway in the first place?"

"I'm just fascinated by genuine medieval relics, and also I wanted to take another look at these fake torches which you have lining the walls. I'm thinking of doing something to the exterior of my house, and I think this might look kind of neat.

"Oh really." exclaimed Karl with a jaundiced expression. "I believe that we'd best get back to the office. Now, what do you suppose became of Miss Peterson?"
As they reentered the office, Deena was meekly hiding in one of the corners.

"Miss Peterson! If you are going to be employed in the Trina household, there are certain rules that must be adhered to. Rule number one is you are never, I repeat, NEVER to be in Mr. Trina's private office alone. Either Mr. Trina or I must always be present when you are in this room for whatever reason. Is that understood?"

"Yes, Karl."

"Good. Why didn't you come with me when I left to investigate the screaming?"

"I was afraid."
"You were afraid of what?"

"I didn't know. But from the way Holland was screaming, I figured it must be something pretty bad, and I didn't want any part of it."

"Miss Matthews, please tell her what all of the screaming was about."

"It was a spider. A really big hairy creepy one."

"That explains it. Holland's been scared to death of them ever since we were kids. I've seen her take on pit bulls fearlessly, and handle swarms of bees no problem, but something about her and spiders..."

"You are not afraid of spiders are you Miss Peterson."

"Spiders, me afraid?" No way. I kill them all the time around my house."

"Very good." said Karl as he cast a condescending eye in Holland's direction.
With the spider episode a thing of the past, the perfunctory tour began to wind down. Within ten minutes the threesome stood back upstairs in the foyer as Deena and Holland prepared to take their leave of the estate.

"Thank you very much for the tour of the home Karl. This is truly a magnificent house. I'd be honored to have it entrusted to my professional care, and I'd vow to do my utmost in keeping it clean," said Deena earnestly.

"I would expect no less from you or anyone. Well, normally I would take a few days before making my decision in such matters. However, due to the fact that you were highly recommended by your references, you seem capable enough, but mainly because I've grown weary of doing the housekeeping here these past several days, I'm prepared to offer you the position. When would you be able to start?"

"I see no reason to delay. I can start tomorrow if that would be all right with you."

"That would be acceptable."

"Would it be O.K. if I got here around 9:00 A.M.?"

"That would be fine. You will be coming alone won't you." he asked as he glanced briefly toward Holland.

"Of course."

"Very well, we shall see you tomorrow at nine. Have a pleasant evening ladies."
With that Karl opened the door and ushered the women out. As they were walking to the car Holland turned to Deena and asked;

"Were you able to plant the recorder?"

"With all the time you and your little hairy buddy gave me, I could've planted the back forty. Everything went great. The camera is lined up with an eye socket in one of the knight's helmets, and it is focusing directly on the chessboard like you wanted."

"Great. Now all we need is for Jonas to do his part in the matter, and we can get ready for part two of "Mission Improbable.""

"I guess we'll just have to keep our fingers crossed."

"That we will." said Holland as she grabbed hold of Deena's hand and gave it a squeeze just before they got to the car.

Shortly after Deena and Holland left, Jonas arrived back at the manor. Telling Karl to make him a sandwich and a salad, Jonas fixed himself a drink. As Karl prepared the meal, he filled his master in on the day's events, including the hiring of Holland's cousin to fill the housekeeper position. Jonas' reaction to the news was difficult to judge. It was basically a we'll-wait-and-see response. Karl brought the meal on a tray over to where Jonas was having his drink. Jonas excused his butler, citing a desire for privacy, and prepared to retire for the evening to his sanctuary in the basement.

It had been awhile since he'd had the opportunity to sit quietly and reflect upon his accomplishments since he'd taken over the reins at Pharmacor. He knew he should be pleased with all he had overseen up to this point, but he knew that he was nowhere near satisfied. Long ago pledges and promises made still needed to be kept. Yes there was still much to do. And yet the mind and body required rejuvenation. The body wearied. The spirit waned. A little pick-me-up was sometimes necessary. Tonight Jonas would once again find the needed boost in his wall safe. It was hidden right behind his golden notebook.

Making his way downstairs, Jonas came to the office door. Inputting the code upon the keypad obtained the desired result, and the heavy oaken door swung open. As Jonas entered the room, he had an uneasy feeling. Something seemed amiss. It was almost as if a sixth sense was warning him of danger. He slowly looked around the room, but he could detect nothing out of the ordinary. Still his internal alarm did not disconnect. Jonas had experienced these feelings before, and he knew not to summarily dismiss them, so he examined the room in even greater detail a second time. Once again, he came up empty. Now he began to relax and he decided to simply chalk it up as a case of nerves. After all, wasn't he down here looking to get his batteries recharged? Surely these feelings were a part of that. In a little while, all would be made right again.

Jonas made his way to the chessboard, and with a few practiced moves once again got the board to reveal its guarded secret. Spinning the dial of the wall safe to the correct coordinates resulted in the opening of the heavy steel door as it always did. Jonas moved the golden notebook out of the way, and reached into the far recesses of the safe. He withdrew his arm, and in his hand was a bottle. It was a very unremarkable bottle by all indications, and yet by its mere touch, Jonas could feel energy coursing through his body. As he brought the bottle in front of his face, a transformation of sorts took place. The aloofness, arrogance, and egotism that characterized Jonas daily countenance softened considerably. That which replaced those hard feelings was almost childlike in contrast. A solitary tear fell from one of his eyes as he brought the bottle briefly to his lips and delicately kissed it. Jonas thought to himself how ridiculous he would look to the outside world had there been a camera present to capture these innermost feelings. He put the bottle to his forehead and held it there, almost as if he were melding his mind with the bottle's spirit by doing so. Slowly he withdrew the bottle from his aura and replaced it back into the wall safe. Now he took out the golden notebook. As he leafed through the pages, the old hard look came rushing back. The more he read, the more sinister his appearance became. As he closed the book and replaced it in the wall safe, Jonas stared directly at the knight that held the video recorder. The nasty and arrogant visage captured for posterity by the mini cam attested to the fact that the real Jonas Trina was back.

The next day Deena Peterson reported for duty at 9:00 P. M. as promised. Most of the day was spent in eye opening fashion as Karl showed her the ropes detailing what was expected in each room. Deena was used to her customer's nuances and eccentricities, having been in her line of work for a decade. However, she was not prepared for the insane degree of perfection that Karl was attempting to get her to commit to in each and every room. In order to keep from having to hire two helpers to comply with the time necessary to meet all of the demands now being placed upon her, Deena began to assert herself. She began to view each new room as a battleground to be negotiated over. Slowly the tide began to turn in her favor as she kept to her guns and pointed out what was reasonable to expect, and what was above and beyond expectations. As they negotiated, they cleaned. As they cleaned, they negotiated. All of which was a mere prelude to the grand finale of the day that was once again, Jonas' office.

Karl punched the code into the keypad and the massive door swung open. Deena entered, armed with dust cloths, a spray bottle, a telescoping handled device for dusting elevated areas, and her trusty sweeper. She had been careful not to empty the sweeper throughout the day in order to justify the move she was about to make. Having plugged the sweeper into a wall socket, Deena hit the power button. The sweeper electronically screeched to life, and Deena began to perform the push-pull sweeper waltz known the world over. Shortly after commencing, she reached over to the vacuum and turned it off. As it powered down, Karl shot a quizzical look in her direction.

"Bag's full. I'll have to empty it."

Without waiting for permission or direction, Deena released the dirt holding receptacle from the appliance, and began to carry the dust-laden bag toward some garbage bags she had brought with her for that purpose. As she approached the knight that held her video recorder, Deena deliberately lost her footing. The contents of the bag spewed out in all directions, with a liberal amount being focused on the knight's helmet and armor. A pronounced shriek issued from Karl.

"You clumsy fool! Now look what you've done. You will stay until this entire mess has been cleaned up."

Deena pretended to be truly embarrassed and repentant as she commenced to clean up every speck of dust. She was especially thorough with the knight, even lifting the helmet to make certain that all of the dust was vacuumed from every nook and cranny within. Forty-five minutes later the room was free of all vestiges of the woman made dust storm that had been visited upon it. As Deena left for the evening, she took with her all of her cleaning supplies (which Karl dutifully checked for pilfered items just to make sure.) Included in the articles that went into the trunk of Deena's car that late afternoon was a black dust filled garbage bag with a small video recorder in an airtight bag right in the middle of the gray powdery mixture.

Tuesday, November 5th, dawned cool and crisp with an overcast sky, light rain, and a steady breeze blowing out of the north. An occasional v-wing of Canadian geese could be seen hurrying south, as these trusted harbingers of the next season were crossing Ohio towards warmer southerly climes. Daniece Davis shook off her umbrella before closing it as she approached the entrance to Pharmacor. The breeze helped push her into the lobby where the receptionist mentioned for the seventh time that morning that today was a fine day for ducks. A brief nod verified Daniece's agreement with that statement, as she pushed through the double doors on the first leg of her daily trek to her office. The time was approaching 10:00 A.M. and Daniece was in a hurry. She'd had a dental appointment that morning which delayed her arrival. She hated to be late, but it was impossible to get a weekend appointment with her dentist. She had put off a checkup for almost 15 months. That was nine months too long in her book, thus she had acquiesced and agreed to a midweek exam.

Upon entering her department, she noticed that her arrival was barely acknowledged. That was a good sign. That meant that everyone was busy with work and taking care of business. That also meant that few would notice her late arrival, thus getting less ribbing that she would have to tolerate. Approaching her office in the rear of the department, she saw a handwritten note on the door. Holland was requesting a meeting today in Daniece's own office, if that was at all possible. Her first inclination was to veto the proposed meeting due to her late arrival and the need to play catch-up. However, on second thought, Daniece had worked extra hard the previous week in anticipation of her dental appointment. Therefore, she really didn't have a tremendous backlog of urgencies that had to be addressed immediately. She knew Holland well enough to know that if she had requested a meeting, she probably had a very good reason behind the request. In that frame of mind, she contacted Holland and said that a 2:00 P.M. meeting would be good, if it was brief. Holland said that was fine. She also mentioned that she had a couple of surprises for Daniece, but she wouldn't elaborate. Daniece hung up the phone and jumped into her tasks with both feet. Working straight through lunch, she lost track of time. A knock on the door interrupted her enough to glance at the clock on her desk. The digital timepiece showed 1:58 P.M. as Daniece told the person at the door to enter.

The door opened, and in rolled the front half of a wheelchair with what almost appeared to be a mummy seated in it. Before the wheelchair could turn into her office, initially all Daniece could see was the legs. Gauze bandages encased the lower half of the wheelchair's rider. As the chair rounded the corner and passed through the doorway, Daniece slowly let her eyes move up the bandaged trunk of the person seated in the chair. She was almost afraid to gaze at the face, and yet she knew she must. Elevating her eyes a couple of degrees, Daniece at last looked into the eyes of the chair's occupant. There sat a glowing, smiling Jane, being pushed by Holland, serving as the chair's driver. Behind them both was Jane's boyfriend John.

"Remember me?" asked Jane ebulliently as she took in Daniece's astonished reaction to her unexpected presence.

"Remember you, REMEMBER YOU? Hell child, there hasn't been a day since September 21st that I haven't had you in my thoughts and in my prayers. Holland Matthews, you wheel that poor lady over here by my desk and let me get a good look at her. Damn it's good to see you girl."

"Believe me, it's good to be seen," gushed Jane.

"We were going to tell you, but then we changed our minds and figured we'd surprise you Daniece. Did we?" asked Holland.

"You know better than to ask that question Holly-Brit. How long are you in town for Jane, before you have to go back to Cinci?"

"That's just it. Mercy General in Cincinnati arranged to have me transferred to Charity hospital here in Cleveland. They thought that I was well enough to be transferred, and they felt that it would speed up my recovery and bolster my morale if I was closer to home, so here I am."

"Well that's marvelous. I'd give you a great big bear hug, but somehow, I don't think that would help your recovery any at this point in time."

"If you were to give me a big hug with the condition of my skin underneath these bandages, you might see the first woman to go into orbit without the assistance of a missile launch. I do appreciate the sentiment though Daniece, and right back at you. Now how about if we close the door, and show Daniece what we really came to show her. O.K. guys?"

"We're ready if you're ready," exclaimed John.

"Oh my, where are my manners John. I've been so busy fawning over Jane that I totally failed to even acknowledge you were here. It's good to see you again. I assume that you are keeping Holly-Brit in line."

"As much as can be expected Daniece. It's good to see you also. Now we've all got something to show you that we think you will find very interesting." With that Holland opened her purse, and laid a copy of the Buckeye Belle invitation on Daniece's desk. As Daniece studied the document in her desk, Holland began to speak.

"Daniece, several months ago after the Social Club fire, I confided in you regarding my thoughts that Jonas Trina might have had a hand in the tragedy. You, rightfully so I might add, cautioned me about entertaining such thoughts. You cited the fact that I could put myself in jeopardy if I were to make my feelings known to others. I knew that you were only looking out for my best interests, and I tried to follow your advice. Unfortunately, my feelings were too strong to ignore.

Then when the Buckeye Belle disaster came, I once again had the same feelings. Although logic dictated that the terrorist group was really at the center of the murders, as they announced to the world, I just couldn't shake the idea that our C.E.O. had somehow been involved."

"Holland Matthews, do you know what you are driving at?" cautioned Daniece.

"Hear her out if you would please Daniece," requested Jane.

"I had to take that leave of absence, because my true feelings in this matter were literally driving me crazy. I knew it defied logic, but I still couldn't deny my inner self. I drove to Cincinnati, because at the time I felt that Jane might be the only person in the world to whom I could make my true suspicions known. As Jane and I were working on some crossword puzzles Jane, bless her soul, got the idea to review Jonas Trina's invitation. We thought we'd see if we could determine what had aggravated him so much when he found out that there were going to be changes made to his original wording. Jane happened to have a copy of the invitation and we set to work. Lo and behold after awhile Jane stumbled across some very incriminating text in the invitation. I showed it to John, and he agrees that it is no mere coincidence. Now we'd like to bring you into the loop and see what you think. We'd also like to see what your thoughts are as to the direction we take from here."
With that Holland grabbed Daniece's hand. As she had done with John's index finger in the hospital, so too did she trace the incriminating phrase with Daniece. She repeated the procedure so that Daniece also would have no doubt as to what she had just read.

"Great God in heaven, the man is a murderer," blurted out Daniece without taking time to reflect on the true impact of her statement.

"Oh, thank goodness you do agree with us," said Jane.

"After what you just showed me, there can be no doubt that he was definitely involved. The man went ballistic when he found out that the wording on his invitation was going to be changed. It was the most glaring overreaction that I've ever seen in my life. Now it makes perfect sense. The slick son-of-a-bitch was just toying with all of us. He figured that we were too stupid to ever figure out his hidden meaning. I assume that you've gone to the police with this."

"Absolutely not," exclaimed Holland. "We all think that Trina is too clever to allow him to be trapped merely because we've discovered his hidden message. We're sure that he has a couple of contingency plans to weasel out of any blame for what has been occurring around here. Certainly the evidence leads one to look in other directions on each tragedy that has taken place at Pharmacor under his watch. Also, we're not sure how or even if the "Fist of Rage" group suddenly figures into all of this. But I'll bet you my bottom dollar that Jonas has been involved up to his eyeballs in all of the disasters which have befallen us in the past year or so."

"So, how do you people propose to go about catching him?" asked Daniece.
"By playing his game better than even he plays," said John matter-of-factly.

"Holly-Brit, tell Daniece where we stand as of right now."

"We've been able to place my cousin Deena in Trina's mansion as the current housekeeper. On the initial interview for the job, I went with her. I knew from talking with the previous housekeeper that Jonas has a wall safe hidden in his downstairs office. It is my guess that the safe contains valuable information that could tie our C.E.O. to many of the recent deaths at Pharmacor. Deena and I devised a plan to hopefully give us a chance to take a look at the safe's contents. We secretly planted a video recorder in the office that focused on how to gain access to the safe. Deena was able to retrieve the camera, and with some technical help from John's friends at the F.B.I., we have been able not only to figure out how to get to the hidden safe, but we also have the combination. What we don't have as of yet is the code needed to enter the office itself, or a workable plan on how to get one of us into the office alone in order to effectively make off with the contents of the safe. We wanted to bring you into the loop, not only because you are a trusted friend of all of us, but also because I'd need you to cover for me if I have to disappear from work occasionally in order to give us a chance to gain access to the safe. Right now we're leaning towards a plan of distracting the butler by double-teaming him. That is what we did in order to plant the camera in the office. However, first we need the code. Well, what do you think?"

"My first thought is that you people are crazy. You're talking about criminal deeds here. Not only are you stealing. You're stealing from a powerful man who, by your own admission may have killed hundreds of people. If he gets an inkling of what you're up to, what do you think of your chances for enjoying a rich full long life? Who is going to protect you in the case of an emergency?"

"I'll be within a quarter mile of the Trina estate whenever Holland would venture there with Deena." said John.

"That's all well and good, but it might take you ten minutes to actually get onto the grounds and into the house. A lot can happen in ten minutes, my friend. I suggest that we all give this more time and see if we can come up with a foolproof plan to catch this murderer in his tracks. I'm on your side in that he must be brought to justice for what he apparently has already done. Now it's a matter of how. You asked for my input. Now you have it. Any comments?"

"I for one think that Daniece makes some valid points" said Jane. "We sometimes tend to forget exactly how much peril we may be in if Jonas gets wise to us. If we are going to err, then let's do it on the side of caution. We've all seen what he is capable of, and I don't know what I'd do if anything happened to one of us because we made our move before we were ready."

"I agree." spoke John. "Especially considering that for the most part it is going to be Deena and Holland at risk here, I'd like to see as safe a plan as possible."

"All right then. Why don't we all put our thinking caps on over the next week and let's see what we come up with?" Daniece said authoritatively. "Now I suppose that some of us had better get back to work before we find ourselves out on the street looking in, which would make it that much tougher to keep an eye on our boy Jonas. Let's reconvene back here in my office in one week and make definitive battle plans then. It was great seeing you Jane. I'll make a point to stop in and see you at Charity hospital now that you're back in town."

"I'll look forward to it Daniece."

With that the meeting broke up. Holland and John took Jane back to the hospital as Daniece got back to work. Unbeknownst to any of them, opportunity was about to come knocking.

The following day Jonas stayed late at the office, telling Nancy McKinney that he had some reports to go over. The real reason was to review tapes from Holland and Daniece's offices once again. He started with Holland's because that was generally the one that bore the most fruit. This time however, there was nothing out of the ordinary regarding the conversations of the past several days. That was certainly not true of Daniece Davis' office conversations. As Jonas listened to the bombshells dropping between the foursome in Daniece's office the previous afternoon, his face contorted into a purplish rage-filled mask of indescribable anger. So that was the real purpose behind the new housekeeper. Score one knight for getting her cousin into the house, and one bishop for the video camera photos. Suddenly he was in trouble. Serious trouble! And it was all because of that bitch Matthews and her scorched friend. Why couldn't Matthews and her two friends have the common decency to die on the Buckeye Belle? Then Jonas could devote all of his energy and intellect to the upcoming attacks. However, deep down, Jonas knew that the real cause of his troubles at this moment lay in the fact that he had underestimated his opponent. He never expected anyone to catch on to the hidden message in his riverboat invitation. He knew he had to think of something clever and quick in order to diffuse the situation. He listened to the tape several times as he attempted to plot his strategy. Suddenly an idea struck him. It was a thought so deliciously devious that Jonas began to chuckle without realizing it. He began to laugh louder and louder. So loud in fact that the noise was picked up by a young security guard who happened to be passing by. A polite knock on the door brought Jonas back to his senses.

"Yes."

"Uh...sir is there anything wrong in there Mr. Trina."

"There is nothing wrong in here son. Absolutely nothing at all." smirked Jonas. As the security guard left the vicinity, Jonas picked up his phone and dialed a number that he knew by heart. The call was answered on the third ring.

"Hello."

"Good evening Ike. I hope that I didn't disturb you. The reason for my call is that I'd like to invite you to a dinner party at my estate on Friday, the 15th of this month."

"Wonderful. Are there any formal dress requirements?"

"For my other guests, no. For you however, if it is not too much trouble, I'd like you to wear a butler's uniform for the party. You'll have some duties that will fall into your area of expertise. I'll send you an e-mail outlining your responsibilities. I think you'll find the party most entertaining."

"What type of party is it?"

"For the majority of those in attendance, it will be a dinner party with a surprise. A very big surprise."

"Very well, I'll look forward to it."

Daniece Davis poked her head into Holland's office the next morning as she was passing by. "Holly-Britt, have you read your e-mails this morning?

"Not yet, why do you ask?"

"Because our illustrious leader Jonas has requested that you and I meet in his office at 10:00. There was nothing further to the message, so I haven't a clue as to what it may be about. If you're nice, maybe I'll let you walk with me to his office."

"I guess it's a date. See you at 9:50."

At 9:55, the duet arrived at Jonas Trina's office where they were shown into the room by Nancy McKinney who asked them to please be seated. Jonas had stepped out for a minute, but he would be joining them momentarily. As the women took their seats in front of Jonas' huge desk, Holland spoke first;

"So, what do you suppose we've done wrong now?"

"As far as I'm aware, business wise we've done nothing wrong. On some other fronts well..."

"Good morning ladies. It truly is a beautiful morning isn't it?" said Jonas as he swept past the twosome and took his seat in the plush velvet covered chair on the owner's side of the desk. "The sun is out, the birds are chirping, and the weatherman says we may hit 61 degrees today. Very pleasant weather indeed! May I have some type of refreshment brought in for either one of you ladies?"

Both Daniece and Holland declined the gracious offer. Even if they were dying of thirst, it was doubtful that either of the women could have recovered from their shock at Jonas' jubilant mood sufficiently enough to drink anything.

"Well then, I suppose that I should let you know why I requested your presence here today. It is nothing of a negative nature I assure you. The third quarter figures have been released, and we are well ahead of projections in all areas. Your human resource department is humming along significantly ahead of budget, for which I owe both of you a great deal of thanks. That is why I've asked you here. I would like to reward you both for your service this year, and I'd like to do something especially nice for you Holland. My butler Karl is quite pleased with the performance of our new housekeeper. He says that she is the best we have had in a long time, and I have you to thank for that. When things go smoothly around my house, it makes every aspect of life more pleasant. Don't you agree?

I guess that I'll just cut to the chase now. It would please me a great deal if both of you and your significant others would be my guests for a dinner next Friday, November 15th at my estate. I would also like to extend an invitation to that poor young lady in your department who was so terribly burned in the recent Buckeye Belle disaster. I understand that she has returned to Cleveland. By the way Holland, I've already had Karl invite your cousin Deena to the party, and she has accepted the offer. Oh I almost forgot. I plan on giving you all the afternoon off that day, and I'll arrange to have a limousine pick all of you up and drop you off after the affair. Now, may we expect to see both of you and your dates there on the 15th?"

"I can't speak for Holland, but my husband Walter and I would be honored to be there"

"You may count me and my boyfriend John in as well. It sounds delightful. Thank you very much for the invitation Mr. Trina."

"Excellent ladies. I'll see that the meal and refreshments are all first class, and I look forward as well to a very pleasant evening. Unless there are any pending urgencies of which I am unaware, then you may both resume your regular duties. Thank you both, and have a wonderful day."

As Daniece and Holland walked down the hallway to the HR department, they looked at each other, and simultaneously stated:

"Beware of Greeks bearing gifts."

The surprise of them both uttering the same phrase at the same time sent them into a giggling fit that lasted ten seconds. Holland recovered first.

"So what do you suppose Jonas the fox has up his sly little sleeve?"

"I don't know Holly-Brit, but this is certainly one way to gain entrance to the castle. Now if we can just get the code to the office, we may be able to get a look-see into that wall safe of his."

"You know Daniece, believe it or not, that had actually slipped my mind. Of course, this represents a great opportunity for us to get a shot at seeing what secrets he has hidden within that million-dollar office. We still need that code to the office door."

"Maybe we'll get a break. Perhaps we can sneak a peek when they give us the nickel tour of the estate that I assume they'll do at the party. Time will tell."

Later that day Jonas sent off an e-mail to Tariq Al-Salem stating that he would be incommunicado for the evening of November 15th. He expressed his regrets, but something of an urgent nature had come up which required his full attention that night. He did not expect any problems or delays to be associated with the "problem", and he looked forward to a fruitful November 17th.

One of the definitions of the word kismet is fate or destiny. Surely kismet played a part in her fortunes, thought Deena Peterson on Friday the day after the dinner invitations were extended. As per usual she had followed Karl downstairs to Jonas' office. This time though, an unusual event occurred that would have significant repercussions. As Karl approached the office door, his cell phone began to ring. As he answered the phone, it appeared that he became distracted. Where he normally guarded his inputting of the code numbers as if the entire world's well being depended upon it, this time he was lax in his execution. He dwelled over each number as he talked, and he failed to conceal the keypad from view with his body as he had always done before. Regardless of the reasons, the end result was that Deena got a clear unobstructed view of the code that she quickly and accurately committed to memory. Excusing herself to go get something out of her car, Deena dialed Holland's work number.

"Holland I got it."

"Who is this?"

"Holland, it's me Deena. I got it, I got the code to Trina's office."

"You're kidding. That's fantastic. Can you give it to me right now?"

"Yeah, but then I've got to go. Karl's waiting for me. Here goes: 0691513. Bye."

Holland could hardly contain her excitement as she raced to Daniece's office. Bursting in, she interrupted a phone conversation with a wildly gesturing hand signal. Daniece put the caller on hold.

"Just what is so damn important that you burst into my office and start doing the Macarena, or whatever that hand gyration was supposed to be."

"Deena got the code."

"She what?"

"She got the code to Jonas' office."

"Shh, someone might hear you. That's great news. Let's get the team together in my office on Monday to make plans."

"Will do."

Jonas' private cell phone number rang as he had expected it would. "Yes."

"It's me, Karl."

"Well Karl, did the fish take the bait."

"Almost certainly. She is out making a call from her car right now. I assume that it is to alert her cronies about the code numbers."

"Are you absolutely sure she got them."

"I couldn't have made it any clearer for her unless I had a chalkboard. From her reaction, I'd have to say yes, she definitely got the correct numbers. Having me text you to call at just the right time was a stroke of genius. She certainly figures that I was distracted"

"Very good Karl."

"May I ask why you suddenly wish to let others know the code to your beautiful office?"

"Let's just say Karl, I intend to use this to set a trap in order to catch some weasels."

Ike Steele changed out of his golf shoes and began to lace up his street shoes after playing nine holes at Rustic Woodlands Saturday morning, November 9th. He was satisfied with his score of 40, especially considering the limited number of rounds he was able to play these days, and the fact that he'd three putted a green. As his clubs lay beside his car, a Jeep Cherokee pulled up beside him and took the parking space right next to his car. The driver got out, and they exchanged pleasantries. The driver of the Jeep popped his trunk, and took out his clubs that he laid right beside Ike's. The golf bags looked identical, even down to the brown towels affixed to them to wipe dirt from the clubs. As the new arrival put on his golf shoes, Ike picked up the Jeep driver's clubs, and put them into his own trunk, slamming the lid shut in the process. That bag was noticeably heavier than his. It should be. It had a metallic silver canister full of a substance called Sarbrun in it.

"Hit 'em long and straight and make all the putts." Ike cheerfully wished upon the new golfer as he closed his car door and started the vehicle's engine.

"Good luck yourself," wished the man as he slung Ike's bag over his shoulder and set off for the clubhouse.

Akmed and Abu Allan strolled past the Rock and Roll Hall of Fame for one final inspection prior to the main event only days from now. They were pleased to see workers in the process of building a large stage and temporary bleachers on the concrete courtyard in front of the Hall. They strolled up to one of the workers and asked for what purpose the stage was being constructed. They were told that it was for a concert to be staged by the group being inducted into the Hall on Sunday. The worker mentioned they were expecting upwards of 10,000 people to be on hand for the concert and induction ceremony. Thanking the worker for the information, the brothers went on their way.

"I wonder if they will have the good sense in their preparations to bring 10,000 body bags," Akmed said quietly.

"Doubtful, very doubtful," answered Abu.

"Mr. Zayed, twice in one week! And on a Thursday night no less. To what does the Terminal Tower owe this pleasure?" asked Les Zitko as the familiar white van of Damascus Drywall pulled into the underground parking area beneath the massive Tower building.

"We got the contract, and I wanted to stop and drop off a few items since we were in the area. Would you like to check the van?"

"No need of that Mustafa. I think I've got a pretty good idea of what you've got in the back of your van from my previous checks."

"Suit yourself Les. Oh, by the way, we'll be showing up Sunday night around 6:15 or so, probably with two vans. We're going to be starting in earnest and working through the night."

"Whatever floats your boat."
Mustafa turned to his partner as he drove to a secluded area of the lot and parked the van.

"If he liked what he saw of our supplies the past few times, he's going to get a real kick out of what we bring Sunday night." Both men chuckled as they walked toward the Tower's entrance.

"Give it some more gas Tariq, and let's see what this thing can really do."

Obligingly, Tariq Al-Salem pushed the throttle of the 35 foot boat slightly forward and the twin 454 horsepower Mercruiser engines responded, pushing the craft harder and faster into the four foot waves as they headed farther out on Lake Erie. Spray kicked up by the boat shot over the railing. The spray gleamed in the chilly night air as it was caught in the reflection of the vessel's running lights. The bottom of the boat repeatedly slapped the water's surface as the vessel rose up and then plunged down on the waves.

"We must take it a little easy Nishil. I would hate to damage our good friend Jonas' toy needlessly. We should only take chances when they are required. Also, there is no sense in attracting undue attention. We will be duly recognized come Sunday night."

Tariq pulled back on the throttle, and the boat began to slow. He put the craft into a wide turn and slowed down even more. Standing up as he clutched the steering wheel, Tariq estimated they were about 1 1/2 miles from shore. As he looked back at the Cleveland beachfront, the rear of the Rock and Roll Hall of Fame was plainly visible. Wild colored neon lights blazed all around the structure as it proudly pronounced the presence to one and all. It was quite a sight. This would be a perfect spot to take in the view of Sunday night's festivities.

"Remember what this looks like Nishil my friend. Soon it will be no more."

CHAPTER 29

"Damn Walter, you know you clean up pretty well," Daniece chided to her husband of ten years.

"Same to you Mrs. Davis. You know, you're looking so good that I'm half tempted to just give that limo driver a twenty when he shows up, and send him on his merry way. That way I can peel you like a grape and do the wild thing with you for about three hours."

"Walter Davis, you mind your manners. Now just how would the host of tonight's dinner party feel about that? Besides remember we've got some work to do while we're there."

"Oh yeah, that's right. I still don't know why you don't take me up on my suggestion to just let me beat the snot out of this Trina guy and whoever else I have to, and then we call the cops."

"Because Sugar Ray Davis, we don't have enough evidence quite yet to prove our suspicions. But if tonight works out the way we hope, we'll have enough on this scumbag by the end of the evening to turn him into some prison's lifetime bitch. Did you hear something?"

"It looks like the limo just pulled up out front."

"I guess we'd better get a move on then."

Three minutes later Daniece was bowing slightly as she thrust her head into the stretch limousine's side door.

"Well good evening everybody. Walter, get that 39 year old carcass of yours in this fine ride right now so that I can introduce you."
Five seconds later a handsome mustached face with twinkling brown eyes and a mischievous grin poked itself inside the limousine.

"Going my way?" kidded Walter as he eased himself inside the limousine door.

"You sit that cute little tail of yours down beside me Mr. Davis, so we can get going. Holland, I believe that you've met my husband Walter."

"Yes. Nice to see you again Walter."

"Likewise."

"Walter, this is Holland's boyfriend John. The pretty half mummy to John's right is our dear friend and co-worker Jane. She is the brave young lady I told you about who was injured on the cruise. And last but certainly not least is Jane's cousin, Deena Peterson."

"A pleasure to meet all of you. Now Jane, if Daniece gets out of line ribbing you like I just heard..."

"Don't worry Walter. I've already told both her and Holland that when I get better, payback is going to be a bitch."

"Good for you young lady."

The driver got on the highway for a short time and then got off long before Holland knew he should if he was going directly to Jonas Trina's estate. The driver proceeded down a main road for a couple of miles. Next he turned into an apartment complex that looked vaguely familiar to Holland.

"Excuse me driver, but where are we going. This is not the way to the Trina house."

"That is correct miss. I have one more person to pick up."

"And who would that be if I may ask?"

"See for yourself, here she comes."
The door opened, and in the entrance appeared a meek looking Hispanic face. Holland had a look of incredulity on her face as recognition suddenly set in upon her.

"Rosa, Rosa how good to see you. Come in please. Everyone, this is Jonas Trina's former housekeeper Rosa Sanchez."
After the introductions were finished, Holland once again turned to Rosa.
"So tell me Rosa, do you have any idea why Jonas invited you this evening? I mean no offense. but the last time that you and I saw each

other, I was under the impression that your association with the Trina household was at an end."

"So did I miss Holland, but Mr. Trina called me personally a couple of days ago and apologized. He said that the butler needed an assistant, and if I would come back he would give me a $100 a week raise and two weeks paid vacation. I just couldn't turn that down. Then he mentioned you people were having a party and requested that I be there as my first official duty of being back, even though I don't have to do anything tonight. I thought that was kind of strange, but it sounded good to me. So here I am."

"You're right Rosa, that does sound rather strange, but hey, the more the merrier."

Forty-five minutes later the limousine was pulling up to the front of the Trina mansion. The group got out and headed towards the elegant front door.

"So this is how the other half lives," exclaimed Walter.

Daniece quickly corrected him. "Try the other one half of one thousandth of one percent sweetie. I think you'd be closer to the truth. Let's knock on the door and get this party started."

As they did so, a tall silver haired butler with striking blue eyes and agreeable manner answered the door. He was certainly an improvement over Karl The Dour.

"Good evening everyone! Please come in! You may put your wraps in the hall closet to the right," said the butler as he greeted the guests. As the new arrivals proceeded to hang up their coats, the host himself came amicably down the long hallway towards the foyer to extend his personal greetings to his invited guests.

"Welcome, welcome everyone. How good of you all to come. I see that you have all stowed your coats. Excellent! Has everyone met Isaac? He will be our butler for this evening. Isaac is taking the place of Karl, my usual butler, who was given the day off today. Let's all proceed to the great room if you would. There are a couple of service bars set up for anyone who is so inclined to fix themselves a cocktail. You'll also find plenty of hors d'oeuvres to please your palates. Won't you follow me please?"

"You don't have to tell me twice," exclaimed Walter.

"I'll second that," said Deena

As the party got under way in the great room, the women gathered around Jonas.

"This is a magnificent home in a terrific location. How did you ever find such a property?" asked Daniece

"When I agreed to take over the position of C.E.O. at Pharmacor and relocate to Cleveland from my home in Chicago, I enlisted the services of a professional group who specialize in matching affluent clients to their preferred choice of housing. I met with them one afternoon in Chicago and gave them my particular requirements. Additionally, I gave them a list of unfavorable aspects to be avoided at all costs, and they took it from there. They really were very good I must say. I only had to spend one day house-hunting in this market in order to make a decision. We looked at three properties, each of which was admirably suited to my tastes, and I chose this one. Certainly either of the others would have been most acceptable, but this one afforded me a bit more privacy and I liked the oversized garage and lower floor better. But enough about me. Now I would like to propose a toast to the lucky trio of Holland, her boyfriend John, and our co-worker Jane, who cheated death in the recent Buckeye Belle tragedy."

Jane almost choked on her drink at this suggestion as she nervously glanced at Holland and John for direction in handling this tactless situation. Likewise, John shot a quick look at Holland searching for guidance. Holland desperately but graciously took the ball and ran with it in order to continue the ruse they had planned for the night. Raising her glass she addressed the intimate group.

"I'll drink to that. But I'd also like to propose that we drink to that AFTER we observe a moment of silence to commemorate the three hundred some people who were not as fortunate as the three of us."

"An excellent suggestion," agreed Jonas.
Quickly the room went silent, with heads bowed, bodies still, and eyes unmoving. After a full minute had passed, Holland issued a reverent "Thank you" to the group. She clasped hands briefly with John and Jane in a shared moment of remembrance. Next Holland raised her glass and casting off the somber mood that had threatened to derail the festivities she praised:

"And here's to the fastest thinking boyfriend in the world, and the bravest best friend a girl like me could ever ask for! Without both of these two, I doubt that I would be here tonight. I thank you John for saving my life. And thank you Jane for saving my spirit. I love you guys!" Someone shouted "Hear, Hear, and the entire group applauded.

Shortly after this celebration, a brief period of silence ensued, which was broken by a question from Deena to Jonas.

"It seems like we're missing a few people this evening from the usual crew."

"Quite true Miss Peterson. I gave the entire staff the night off as a gift. Isaac and I will be acting as your servers this evening. It's a bit of a tradition passed down to me from my mother that a good host personally serves one's guests," Jonas lied.

"That is an admirable tradition," offered Rosa.

"Yes my mother taught me well," Jonas lied again. "May I get anyone another drink?"

As Jonas was entertaining in the great room, Ike had taken the opportunity to slip out the front door and approach the limousine driver who was waiting patiently outside as he had been instructed and paid to do.

"Nice night for mid November isn't it?"

"I suppose," answered the driver between puffs on a cigarette.

"Care for a drink?"

"Can't, I'm driving. Against the rules you know."

"Oh yes, of course. If you could drink, what would be your preference?"

"I'm pretty much a straight whisky and beer man as most of my buddies can attest."

Ike mentally gave himself a pat on the back for guessing correctly as he reached into his pocket and pulled out a flask. He handed it to the driver and said;

"Well if that's the case, then let me propose a toast. In this flask here is almost a pint of Canadian Club. Drink up."

"Hey pal are you hard of hearing, I just told you I'm not allowed to drink."

Ike grabbed the man by the throat and poked him in the sternum with a handgun he had produced from his coat pocket.

"I'm changing the rules pal. Now drink up, and I mean all of it. And you'd better make damn sure you swallow!"

"All right, all right, just don't shoot."

It took a couple of minutes for the driver to choke down the fiery liquid, but finally he had drained the entire flask.

"Good boy. Now turn around."

With Ike still holding the gun, the driver did as instructed. Ike pulled out a hypodermic syringe from his coat, plunged it into the man's neck and depressed the plunger. The driver almost immediately went limp in his arms. Ike put the man into the driver's seat of the limo. "Sleep well pal," he said as he headed back inside the house.

Jonas saw Ike as he passed in front of the great room doorway on his way to the kitchen. Jonas shot him an inquisitive look, and Ike answered with a slight smile and a subtle nod. He then proceeded to make his way in the direction of the kitchen to finalize last minute dinner requirements.

"Ladies and gentlemen, I would like to suggest that you freshen your drinks if you so desire. I'm going to join Isaac in the kitchen for a few last minute preparations to the feast that we have planned for all of you tonight. We should be eating in ten minutes, so if everyone would soon take a seat in the dining room off the main hallway, we'll be able to commence. By the way, just in case you haven't determined tonight's meal by the delicious aroma, I'll give you a hint. We'll have on hand an exquisite chardonnay and chablis to go with tonight's repast."

The guests did as recommended, and one by one made their way into the dining room. The room had two entrances, each with its own sliding door. It featured a beautiful large chandelier that was situated over a huge cherry table. There was enough room for at least twenty to be seated comfortably at the table, although there were only settings for nine required tonight. At one end of the table were numerous warming chafing dishes and a wicker basket. A couple of ice filled pewter buckets held the wine bottles. The two men took the lead in checking under the lids to get a sneak peek at the dishes.

"I found some corn with red things in it here, what did you find in your dish Walter?"

"Well John, mine looks to be buttered Brussel sprouts."

"For your information Mr.Kazek, those red things happen to be pimentos, and it sounds delicious," corrected Holland.

"I see lots of rolls in this big wicker basket," offered Nadine.

"Here's one. It's cinnamon applesauce with a big chili pepper in it. That's interesting. I'd have never thought to do that." said Jane

"Get a load of this. There must be fifteen pounds of mashed potatoes in this one. You can sure smell the garlic in it. Also it appears to have a bunch of other spices..."

The lights dimmed appreciably, which had the effect of making everyone look towards the doorway. There was Jonas with his left hand on the dimmer switch, an engaging smile upon his face, and a ten inch diameter pumpkin pie in his right hand.

"I see that we've discovered the side dishes to this evening's meal. Oh those extra spices in the mashed potatoes are chopped garlic, salt, dill weed, lemon pepper, and chives. I'll go out on a limb and say that once you try these, it will be difficult to go back to plain mashed potatoes again. There is gravy in a couple of the serving dishes. Now if everyone will please take your seat, I'll have Isaac bring in the main course." As everyone sat down, Jonas turned the lights down even lower.

"You may come in Isaac."

With a flair for the dramatic, the butler strode through the portal with a flaming 22-pound turkey. Cognac poured over the turkey and then lit had accomplished the flame. The blazing bird was replete with apple/cranberry/giblet stuffing. A mandarin orange and grape garnish enhanced the elegant dish on the silver platter. A round of applause in appreciation for the grand entrance swept the room. The fire was extinguished with a puff. As the lights rose in the room again, the platter was placed at the head of the table for the host to perform the carving.

"Seeing as the date of the dinner was so close to Thanksgiving, Isaac and I figured that no one would object to getting a bit of an early start on the holiday. Could I interest anyone in a slice of turkey?" With all answering enthusiastically, the meal began in earnest.

The tinkling of crystal goblets interspersed with the clinking of silver forks and knives upon fine china served as an unspoken compliment to the chef. Serving dishes were being whirled about the table as the diners responded to various requests for one dish or another. Laughter and convivial conversation completed the scene as the dinner began to take on the appearance of a festive family gathering. As the meal was proceeding in full swing, Holland excused herself to visit the washroom. Barely anyone seemed to notice as the conversations continued unabated.

"Mr. Trina, everything is just fabulous! And those potatoes are to die for!" gushed Daniece. "I'll have to get the recipe."

"And the wine is as good as advertised," giggled Jane

"I'm glad that the meal is satisfactory. You have Isaac to thank. He deserves all of the credit." As Isaac accepted the kudos, Jonas began to speak again.

"Oh Isaac, I just remembered, we're forgetting the big surprise which we have in store for everyone. Please wait right here while Isaac and I go upstairs to fetch something that we are sure will knock all of you off your feet."
John, Daniece, and Jane all went into a panic as Jonas and Isaac made towards the nearest door.

"Uh, Mr. Trina couldn't you just wait a couple of minutes for Holland to return. I'm sure that she'd like to be in on the unveiling of your big surprise," said John in an attempt to keep them from leaving the room.

"Yeah, she'd probably feel disappointed if we all got to see whatever it is before she did," valiantly offered Jane.

"Oh nonsense. We'll make sure that we don't totally unveil it until she gets back. Please everyone, continue eating and enjoying yourselves, and Isaac and I will be back shortly." Jonas closed the door as they left the room.

"All right, let's not panic. They said they were going upstairs. Holland is downstairs. There's a very good chance that neither of them will run into each other, even when Holland is making her way back upstairs." said John.

"What is everybody talking about?" asked Rosa.

"You'd never believe it if we... Does anyone hear a hissing sound?" asked Daniece with a tinge of alarm in her voice.

Suddenly Walter's face slumped onto the table, followed in quick succesion by Deena and Rosa as those nearest to the quietly hissing nozzle mounted on a high shelf quickly succumbed to the effects of the unknown agent spewing from it.

"Gas," gasped John as he shot from his chair and attempted to bolt from the room. He was struck down mere feet from the nearest door. Seconds later everyone was unconscious and laying in various positions of disarray around the room. Thirty seconds later the nozzle stopped hissing. Shortly thereafter, a gas-masked Isaac opened the doors to let the room air out.

After leaving the dining room, Holland had faked a trip to the restroom. She lingered just inside the bathroom door for about a half-minute in order to insure that she was not being followed. Verifying that she was not, she swiftly made for the stairway leading to the downstairs level and Jonas' office. Hurrying across the marble floor, Holland came to the office door and the coded keypad. Pulling out a slip of paper from her pocket, she glanced at the numbers written on it and began to enter them onto the keypad, 0-6-9-1-5-1-3. As she entered the final number in the sequence, the heavy oaken door began to silently swing open. She scurried in and closed the door as quickly as possible.

Making her way to the chessboard, Holland noticed that several pieces were missing from both sides. She prayed that the necessary pieces required to reveal the wall safe were still intact. Looking at the right side of the board as she stood before it, the three critical pieces seemed to still be in place. Referring to her notes on the piece of paper she had pulled out earlier, Holland set to work. She first moved the pawn on the bottom right side two spaces forward, and one space up and secured it into position. Next she took a knight on the upper right and moved it one square forward and two squares toward the bottom of the board. Lastly she took the queen and positioned it forward six squares from the original starting position. As she clicked the queen in place, the king on the left side of the board fell down, and an audible electronic sound began to issue from the chessboard. Suddenly the board began to divide into four equal pieces, with each piece retreating from the center of the board like the four arrows on a computer keyboard. The wall safe came into view. Holland looked briefly at her watch. It had been almost four minutes since she had left the dining room.

"So far so good," she mumbled under her breath. Now she once again referred to her notes as she approached the combination dial on the safe. Putting her hand on the dial she twisted the dial two complete turns to the right before entering the numbers: 39 right, 24 left, 36 right. With a slight pull, the safe's door opened up. Holland wanted to let out a scream of joy, but had the presence of mind to simply continue with her mission. As she looked into the safe, Holland's joy turned briefly to confusion and then to consternation. The vault appeared to be empty. She reached into the dark inner recesses of the safe, and her hand touched something. She clutched the item in her hand and brought it out into the light for examination. It was an old brown medicine bottle similar to those seen years ago at drugstores. From the faded writing on the prescription affixed to the bottle, Holland could barely make out the words. She could read the customer's name as Kurt Stevens, and the date of September 23, 1969 was still legible, but the actual prescription itself could not be deciphered. As she put the bottle back into the safe, she prepared to close the vault's door.

"AHEM," said a loud voice behind her. Holland visibly jumped as the voice had startled her.

"Looking for this my dear?"

Holland blushed deeply as she turned to face her accuser. There by the door were Jonas and the butler Isaac. Jonas held a thick golden notebook in his left hand and a .357 handgun in his right. Holland knew that she had been caught red handed, and that no possible explanation would suffice, so she stayed silent.

"Miss Matthews, since you happen to be standing by the chessboard, I wonder if I could impose on you for a couple of favors. First close the safe door. Then, return the three pieces you moved back to their original places."

Holland did as instructed, and the king stood upright. Immediately following that, the board began to come back together to the original position, thus covering the wall safe.

"Now, if you would be kind enough to remove the bottom rook from the right side of the board as well as the two center most pawns. You may place them on the floor for now. Bravo for you, you earned those for the clever way you left the dining room and were able to get into my safe in under five minutes. I'd have thought on your initial attempt, it would take you longer. Now if you would please remove the remaining bishop from the left side and two more pawns. Those unfortunately you lost about five minutes ago. Thank you for your cooperation."

Holland, though embarrassed and terrified, was able to build up her courage enough to respond to Jonas immediately after doing as instructed.

"Can I ask why you just had me take those pieces off the board just now?"

"Certainly. A very logical question I should think, don't you agree Isaac."

Ike nodded his approval as Jonas continued;

"Those are the pieces which your side and my side have lost this evening in our ongoing match. They were lost due to very calculated and strategic moves made by both of the participants in the match. I must admit that you have been a most worthy opponent. I'm almost going to hate seeing our match come to an end because I have enjoyed it so. You will of course notice that your left side of the board is missing slightly more pieces than my side. That is to be expected due to my superior knowledge and experience in playing this game. However, give yourself a pat on the back because whether by cunning, intelligence, or just plain dumb luck, you have accomplished much. I was particularly impressed with the way you were able to smuggle the video recorder into my very office, get the pictures, and get the recorder out again. Very ingenious. It's a shame you'll soon be leaving us because I could use someone with your talents on my staff."

"Since when did you and I have a chess match going on?"

"We've been matching wits for months now as I'm sure you are aware. Though formal "hostilities" were never declared, I think that we both were cognizant of the battle. I simply decided to utilize the board as a way of keeping score between us.

"Aren't you forgetting something?"

"Such as? Oh yes, you are absolutely right. I also need you to remove your queen from the chessboard, because as we are all aware, I have now captured you."

Holland did as instructed and then she spoke again.
"That was not what I was referring to that you had forgotten."

"What then?"

"There are six people upstairs at this moment that are going to miss me if I don't return to the gathering."

"Oh I've been remiss in telling you about them. Won't you please fill Miss Matthews in with the details Isaac?"

"We filled the room with a gas known as Sarbrun shortly after you left the room. Your friends are all sleeping like babies at the moment. They'll continue to be that way for four or five hours, at which time the agent will dissipate in their bodies leaving only a slight headache in it's wake. That is if they had lived long enough to experience the headache. Unfortunately, they and the limo driver are going to be involved in a terrible accident that will result in their untimely deaths. A real pity."

"May I ask how you found out about our plan."

"There I must admit that I played a bit unfair." With that Jonas walked over to his desk and pulled out a tape recorder. He hit the play button. Holland's voice was recognizable on the tape, as were Jane's, John's, and Daniece's.

"You bugged Daniece's office?"

"Not only her office. but yours as well I'm afraid."

"Then you've known all along..."

"That's right, I've been aware of your conspiratorial treachery right from the very start. I even knew of your friend's visit to Sutton Industries in Chicago."

"Then it was you who killed that Triste... you evil conniving piece of..."

"Temper, temper young lady. If you don't watch your tongue, I may have to reconsider doing something for you that I plan on doing. By the way, that was Isaac's handiwork with Triste Johnson."

"Just exactly how many people have you killed?"

"I assume that you are only interested in Pharmacor related deaths. To tell you the truth, I've lost track myself. Why don't we have a look?"

With that Jonas opened the golden notebook and began to turn through the pages. He flipped through many pages rapidly before slowing down and taking on a concentrating visage.

"Let's see. We have the Buckeye Belle, and the Social Club fire, the Macklin retirement party..."

"I figured it was you behind the social club fire, but the retirement party?"

"Yes it took us a while to get our hands on just the right virus to pull off that party favor, but it was well worth the wait. Then of course we had Mercurio Enterprises..."

"Mercurio Enterprises? You had something to do with that!"

"Miss Matthews, you underestimate your opponents! Isaac and I had everything to do with that. We just wanted to keep it our little secret. That is until now. Please let me get back to my counting. Thomas Schultz, Triste Johnson, forty-six other retirees early on, which I believe you learned of through Donsky and Associates. I would say that considering everything, we're right around seven hundred so far. Present company excluded naturally. Of course when you and your friends pass away later this evening it will add another eight to the count, including the limo driver."

"You sick twisted bastard."

"Flattery will get you nowhere my dear. Believe it or not, that seven hundred figure pales in comparison to what that figure will be by the end of Sunday. However, since you will not be around to take in the spectacle, I shall not go into that right now.

"But why? Why must there be all of this killing? Surely the amount of money that you stand to make on the retirees benefits decreasing doesn't justify the mass murders."

"Of course not. That has merely been an amusing and beneficial sideline to all that has taken place. The real reason has roots much deeper than money. In fact, the bottle that you held in your hand has much more to do with the corporate genocide, if you will, than the dollars. The answer to that and basically to everything that I've done in my life is contained in this golden notebook. It makes for an interesting read. You are probably wondering why I've told you all of this, and I have to say that I'm not sure myself.

I suppose that part of it is to honor your valiant attempts to thwart my plans. Part of it is admittedly ego driven. Everybody likes to be recognized when they have performed brilliantly. Of course due to the nature of our activities these past several months, we really couldn't let too many people on to what we were up to. Your surprise at our Mercurio and Macklin involvement validates our brilliance. Since you will not be in a position to reveal any of which I've divulged to you, I now feel safe in bringing you "into the loop." I'm afraid my dear, that unlike the old Batman episodes that were popular when I was a child, this time the good guy or gal does not escape after the villain's secrets have been exposed. However, before we depart company for both this evening and forever my dear, we would like to present you with a little token of our esteem. Isaac, won't you please give Miss Matthews the package which we brought for her?"

Isaac approached Holland and handed her a gift-wrapped package. Though Holland seethed at all that was taking place, she accepted the offering and began to open it in the fervent hope that she might be able to somehow utilize the package's contents as a weapon. As she ripped the ornate package wrapping and bow off, an exquisite stained walnut case came into view. She opened the case and discovered two gold watches. One had the words, "To Holland Matthews" engraved on the front. Opening the watch she found additional print on the inside. It read, "In admiration of your efforts. Sincerely, Jonas Trina." The second watch had a plain golden exterior. When Holland opened this watch, there was only one word present. In bold underlined engraving was the word **CHECKMATE!**

"Is this some kind of sick joke Trina?"

"On the contrary my dear, this is a very real expression of my feelings behind the effort which you put into foiling my plans. You were truly a worthwhile opponent. I must admit however that this gift does serve a dual purpose. You see, tomorrow when the authorities are investigating the horrible accident which you and your friends are involved in, they'll discover this token of my esteem which should help to further preclude my having anything to do with your ill fated demise. There is also an additional meaning behind the gold watch's significance, which is rooted in my past, but I shall not go into that. I'll of course have to remove the "checkmate" watch from your body prior to your ill-fated limo ride."

Holland took the gold watches and threw them at Jonas' head. The flight of each watch was intercepted by Isaac, who caught each in a leather-gloved hand, which he had seemingly donned in the past minute for just such an occurrence. Ike handed both watches to Jonas.

"See Isaac, didn't I tell you that she would throw them at me? Isn't it a great gift to always know what your opponent is going to do even before they do? My chess upbringing is to thank for the insight it has taught me over the years. I would heartily recommend chess as being a requirement for all children to learn as they are growing up. Unfortunately time grows short if we are going to finish all that is on our plate for this evening. Speaking of which, we now have a real treat in store for you. Isaac is quite an accomplished ladies man, and he has been admiring you from afar for some time now. I told him that we'd have a little time for romance before we place all of our guests in the limo for their final drive. I believe that we have about an hour before we have to wrap up our party for good. That will give you two lovebirds an opportunity to get to know each other a bit better. You'll be able to sample Isaac's charms and relate him to your F.B.I. boyfriend's lovemaking abilities for comparison purposes. This way we figure you'll be able to depart this world with a smile on your face. It's the least we could do since you've been such good sport. Oh and don't worry about the formality of laying down your king to signify your defeat in our match. I'll take care of that for you. I'll also make sure to have the gold watch with the checkmate inscription on it placed in your coffin. It will be something of a final joke that only Ike and I will know of the significance."

Jonas walked confidently toward Holland, and as he brandished the handgun in her face, he forcibly shoved the gold watch which praised her into her pants pocket. Sheer terror gripped Holland as the meaning of Jonas' words struck home. The leer on the butler's face confirmed her fears.

"Now Miss Matthews, in order to be sporting about this I've decided to give you a fifteen second head start on Isaac. Of course with those somewhat high-heeled shoes that you have on, he'll have absolutely no trouble catching you at all. I'd strongly suggest that you remove them before you begin running."

In a panic, Holland began to do as suggested. Then she heard Jonas' voice again.

"Fourteen...thirteen... twelve."

Kicking off the shoes, Holland broke for the doorway, blowing past the now laughing twosome who let her pass. As her stocking feet flew over the office threshold, Holland lost her footing on the slippery marble floor. Her feet went horizontal as she flew up in the air, only to fall back upon the hard marble with a thud. Her elbow and forehead immediately began to throb and bruise from the impact.

"Oh, do try to be more careful when running on the slippery surface. Eight... seven."

Picking herself up in desperation, Holland took off, taking small measured steps to avoid a repeat of her fall. She decided on attempting to make her way out through the garage, thus she went for the long hallway with the faux torches. She had made scant progress down the hall when she heard a loud "Zero" in the distance. Glancing ever so briefly over her shoulder, she saw Isaac shoot out the door in hot pursuit. He was taking long strides and didn't seem to have any difficulty in running on the slippery marble. The thought that he must have good rubber soled shoes somehow seeped past the panic in Holland's mind. She lengthened her stride a bit to accelerate somewhat, but she could tell by the rapidly approaching sounds of her tormentor, that this contest of speed could have but one conclusion. As she reached a sharp turn in the hallway, Holland could hear the lustful panting of her pursuer over her own labored breaths.

In despair, Holland attempted to cut the corner close as she entered the sharp turn. Her stocking feet betrayed her, and she once again went airborne. Bravely opening her eyes in mid-flight, Holland saw that she was headed for a collision with the pedestal upon which the mace-holding medieval knight stood. Shielding her face with her arms, she flew feet first into both the top of the pedestal and the feet of the armored knight. The knight began to topple off the perch, and Holland assumed a fetal position, covering her head as best she could for protection from the ensuing crash. As the knight fell, the heavy armored suit, without benefit of the pedestal's support, pulled the spiked mace loose from the wall. The menacing mace swung in a wide momentum-gathering arc as it plunged towards the floor. The heavy metallic cacophony of the armored suit impacting the marble was accompanied by a loud sickening thud. As the reverberating sounds lessened, Holland steeled herself in order to summon up the courage to meet Isaac with as much defiance as she could muster.

Bravely she opened her eyes. Holland was dumbstruck by the scene in front of her. She stared uncomprehendingly at the now prone butler lying on the blood-spattered floor. Half of the man's skull was crushed in and grayish matter could be seen oozing out amidst the matted hair of the bloody scalp. The unseeing blue eyes gazed straight ahead, registering nothing. The bloody mace that lay a few feet from the dead man's head told the tale of his final moments. As the knight began to fall, the butler had rounded the corner unaware of what was happening. He literally "never knew what hit him," as the mace completed its fall by smashing in the upper left side of Ike's cranium, crushing it like the proverbial melon. Sickened by the sight, but relieved by her reprieve, Holland began to rise to her feet.

"NOOOOO!!!!" screamed a voice in a primal rage. There stood Jonas, gun in hand, viewing the unmoving corpse of his long time friend and ally. His contorted face took on a purplish hue, and the hand holding the gun began to visibly shake.

"You, YOU! YOU BITCH! YOU'VE KILLED HIM!"

"I didn't mean to, it was an accident," stammered Holland.

"MY ONE TRUE FRIEND IN THE WORLD, AND NOW HE"S GONE! WHAT AM I TO DO! What am I to do now?"

For a second, Holland almost felt a tiny bit of remorse for what had taken place these past few moments. Jonas had taken on the persona of a beaten, hopeless man/boy who was truly alone in the world. All of those thoughts disappeared with Jonas' next words.

"I know what I'll do. First we must avenge his death. Come with me you disgusting vermin. We'll retire to my office where you will meet your maker properly."

Pointing the gun menacingly in her direction, Jonas herded Holland back towards the office which had been the scene of so much already. As the twosome entered the office, Jonas ordered Holland to face the wall and get on her knees. He also ordered her to not turn around. She quickly did as instructed.

"I'm going to do for you something which you did not do for my friend Isaac. I'm going to give you a minute to say your last prayers as you prepare to meet your maker. Then I'm going to shoot and kill you."

With those words, Jonas withdrew behind Holland towards his desk. As she kneeled, Holland could hear Jonas rummaging through his desk. She knew that she should be taking full advantage of this precious time to do exactly what Jonas had suggested and say her prayers. Something inside of her however, was fighting that idea as it sought determinedly to find some way out of her predicament. As her mind valiantly searched for a shred of an escape plan, she continued to notice Jonas' noise at his desk.

She also became aware of a teak plaque on the wall staring her in the face. At first the plaque seemed to be just a weird composite of scrolling. Drawing upon a long ago course that she had taken for two years in high school, Holland suddenly realized that what she was staring at was Latin words engraved in the teak. She was able to decipher them well enough to understand their meaning. "Never give a sucker an even break." How typical of him she thought as she heard Jonas step away from the desk and begin to move in her direction.

"I certainly hope that you have utilized your last moments wisely Miss Matthews."

As the approaching footsteps drew nearer, it suddenly dawned on Holland that Jonas had no intention of shooting her at all. He could have shot her in the hallway. In fact he could have shot her any number of times. "Never give a sucker an even break". "Never give a sucker an even break." The words echoed in her head as she tried to make sense of the situation as she continued to kneel.

"Miss Matthews, I'm afraid your time is up. Three... two..."

Holland made a lightning fast move and flattened her body out while at the same time rolling to her right. As she did so Jonas' hand came plunging down, striking air where it had expected to meet the resistance offered by Holland's shoulder, which had occupied that space a quarter of a second before. In his hand was a syringe instead of a gun. The force of his errant strike caused Jonas to lose his balance, and as he did so, he tripped over Holland. As he fell Jonas instinctively dropped the syringe in order to free his hand to assist in breaking his fall. The syringe fell directly on Holland's stomach as Jonas continued his tumble. Seizing the opportunity, Holland grabbed the syringe and without hesitation plunged it into Jonas' arm. As she did so, she immediately depressed the plunger as far down as it would go. Realizing what had just taken place, a look of outrage and shock came over Jonas' face. The look was quickly replaced by one of fatigue as Jonas passed out within seconds of the injection.

Holland stared at Jonas for a full thirty seconds to make sure that he was indeed unconscious. Verifying that, she tried to get up to her feet. As she began to rise, Holland's knees began to shake. The shaking spread and soon she was trembling all over. As she sat back down on the floor, the shaking subsided. Holland gave herself a quick check for injuries. Except for the bruises on her elbow and forehead, she was unhurt, so that wasn't what was causing the shaking. Suddenly it hit her and she started to laugh. The laugh grew until it was loud and raucous. As quickly as it began, the laughter died and was replaced by crying just as intense as the laughter had been. Her body was wracked by uncontrollable sobs as she realized what had brought on the shaking. I'M ALIVE! All that has happened, and I'm still alive! She couldn't believe her good fortune. She had cheated death twice in the past few minutes and had brought down those who had meant to harm her. Her body was simply reacting to all of the fear and adrenaline that had been coursing through her the last fifteen minutes during her life and death struggles.

Holland sat quietly for a few minutes as she attempted to calm down and regain control. Trying once again to stand, the shaking was still somewhat evident, but much less than before. Slowly Holland made her way to a phone on Jonas' desk. She tapped in three numbers and after one ring the phone was answered by a professional sounding female voice.

"You've reached 9-1-1 emergency response. What is the nature of your emergency?"

"Lady I hope you are sitting down because I've got a hell of tale to tell you. My name is Holland Matthews and I'd like to report one death at the Jonas Trina estate at the address appearing on your screen. Also here are several people who are unconscious due to the effects of some type of gas. Furthermore there are two people here who were directly responsible for the deaths so far of seven hundred people and are plotting the deaths of many more." This news was met with a pronounced silence for several seconds. Finally the voice at the other end responded.

"Excuse me, but could you repeat what you just said."

"I know it sounds crazy, but once your people arrive I'll show them proof that seven hundred people have been murdered because of the efforts of two people here. Also I may have information of a huge calamity that is to take place Sunday. Please believe me and get the police here quickly. This is not a joke or prank. They'll see when they get here. I'll have to see if I can figure out how to open the gate to let the emergency units in, so I'd better go now. Please hurry."

Holland found Jonas' gun and put it in her pocket just in case he should wake up. Next, she picked up the golden notebook that she found lying on his desk. She rechecked Jonas to make sure that he was still out and then she left the office, closing the door on her way out. She got an idea and went to the hallway closet she had seen Karl get a broom out of several weeks before. Finding a coil of rope in the closet, she took it back to the office door. She tied a knot around the office door handle and then took the rope down the hallway to another door and secured the rope around that handle as well. Therefore if Jonas awoke and tried to get out, he would be unable to leave his office.

After a five-minute search upstairs, Holland located the controls to the front gate, and opened them. Finally she was able to pay some attention to her friends. Holding her breath, she gingerly entered one of the doors leading to the dining room. She could see the unmoving bodies lying in various positions around the room. There was no sign of a struggle and no blood was evident, so perhaps Jonas had been telling the truth about the gas. She prayed that all of her friends would indeed wake up a few hours from now with only bad headaches to show for their ordeal. Time would tell. With nothing more that she could do, Holland opened the front door and prepared to listen for the emergency vehicles to arrive. As she waited, she grabbed a chair and sat in the lighted foyer leafing through the golden notebook. She was amazed at the bloodlust orgy that she found within. Knowing her time was limited she concentrated on the parts of the book concerning Pharmacor in order to substantiate her story. Also, at the very end of the book were many pages that appeared to be reserved. They all had the date 11/17 on them. Sunday's date.

Thinking she heard sirens, Holland went out on the porch and looked towards the entrance to the estate. She could see the lights of a small caravan of vehicles wending their way through the trees and up the winding drive leading to the house. As the vehicles pulled up in front of the house, Holland came to greet them. The lead police car stopped and out stepped an officer.

"I'm officer Don Thorpe. Are you the woman who placed the emergency call?"

"Yes, my name is Holland Matthews."

"Is anyone armed or dangerous inside that we have to worry about?"

"Not at this time, however that's not to say that..."

"Well Miss Matthews, I hope for your sake that at least some of what you said to the dispatcher is true, because there are very stiff penalties for faking an emergency. To be perfectly honest with you that story you told our dispatcher..."

"Officer, could you and a few of your people please follow me. Oh, and I don't know if it's still necessary or not, but if you people have gas masks, it might not be a bad idea to put them on before you go into the dining room. It's been airing out for awhile, but I'm not sure if that's sufficient time or not."

"All right, we'll continue to play this straight for the time being. Men, come with me inside. It doesn't appear to be a particularly dangerous situation, but as always, be on the alert. Tell the emergency rescue guys to stay put for now while we secure the house. All right lady, how do we get to the dining room?"

"Just follow the main hallway straight ahead, and the dining room is on your left. Also downstairs you'll find the dead man in the hallway, and the mastermind behind all of the 700 deaths which I alluded to is unconscious and locked up in his office. You'll see ropes tied to the door."

"Sure lady, whatever you say. All right, let's move in."

Five minutes later officer Thorpe and another policeman came running out.

"You emergency people, we need you inside on the double. I've got six unconscious people in the dining room, and another one downstairs. Also we've got a stiff in the downstairs hallway." Holland rolled her eyes as it was finally beginning to dawn on the police that she was telling the truth.

"Lady, do you happen to know anything about the gas they used?"

"I think they said something about Sorbonne, or something like that."

"How about Sarbrun?"

"That's it, Sarbrun."

"Very effective, but non-lethal. They should wake up in a few hours if that's the stuff. In the mean time we're not going to take any chances."

A policeman who had checked out the limousine parked in the driveway interrupted their conversation;

"Hey Don, we've got another sleeping beauty over here. This one smells like it's more than just gas of some type. He smells like 100 proof something or other. Kind of unusual for a limo driver on duty if you ask me.

"I doubt that the driver was responsible for that either," quietly suggested Holland.

Thirty minutes later the emergency crews had a full load, with the six-gassed victims from the dining room occupying all of the space in their vehicles. By now, the unconscious Jonas had also been brought upstairs to await his departure. Holland pulled Officer Thorpe aside.

"Officer, this man is responsible for all of the tragic deaths which have occurred at Pharmacor this year."

"Hey isn't that the company that had the big Social Club fire awhile back?"

"Yes, and he is the one who orchestrated the whole affair, in addition to many other disasters, which killed hundreds of people."

"How do you know all of this?" Officer Thorpe asked skeptically

"Because he told me right before they tried to rape and kill me, and also because it is written in his golden diary over on the porch."

"You don't say," Thorpe said, his voice dripping with sarcasm.

"I DO say! And I'd also like to say officer, that I am getting pretty damn tired of this condescending, questioning attitude which I for some reason am being forced to endure..."

"Now listen here, Miss Matthews..."

"No YOU listen. Whether you choose to believe it or not, that man on the stretcher over there has tried to have me killed several times. He has also pulled the strings that have resulted in seven hundred deaths so far, and has a plot working that will kill thousands more, according to what he said tonight. My F.B.I. boyfriend, who is one of the gas victims in the emergency vehicles, and myself have been attempting to get evidence on this man for sometime now to prove his culpability in these murders. Have I lied to about what I said you would find in the house?"

"Well, no."

"And I'm not lying to you now. This man should be public enemy Number One, and according to what I read in his diary, he has now joined forces with terrorists and is using them to help him with his killing spree. They combined to blow up the Buckeye Belle riverboat down in Cincinnati in September, and they are working on something even bigger right now."

"He had something to do with the Buckeye Belle?"

"Damn it, he masterminded the whole thing, and now he's got these terrorists doing his killing for him. It's all in that book over there if you don't care to believe me! The important thing is that we've somehow got to find out what Trina and his friends are up to Sunday."

"If what you say is true..."

"IT IS TRUE!! READ THE DAMN BOOK!!"

Officer Thorpe looked at Holland with amazement. He was taken aback by the incredible passion and conviction in her voice and in her very being. Composing herself, Holland started up again.

"Look officer, I'm sorry for my outburst just now, but I've seen what this man is capable of. When he brags that the seven hundred dead so far pales in comparison to what the figure will be after this weekend, I know that he is not just blowing smoke. Unfortunately neither I nor the notebook can furnish any details as to what his plans are for Sunday."

"All right Miss Matthews..."

"Holland."

"All right Holland, you've convinced me. I'll get in touch with my chief and see what he thinks."

"No offense, but I believe that we should be getting in touch with the F.B.I. also, and perhaps even the Homeland Security people. With the strong possibility that terrorists are involved in something close by, I'm sure that they would want to be part of this."

"Well I don't know if this warrants..."

"Officer, just how much of a career do you think you would have left if thousands of people are killed in Cleveland, and the press finds out that you had knowledge that it might happen and did nothing about it?"

"O.K. I'll make some calls. But first I still have to call my chief to get the ball rolling. Chain-of-command and all that. I'll let him know the seriousness of the situation, and see if we can get some F.B.I. boys down here."

"That's a start."

"Here's another. Hey you guys near that guy on the stretcher over there. I want you to cuff him for now. It appears he is a very dangerous man. Also, before those rescue vehicles leave, I want to you remove this lady's boyfriend. He's an F.B.I. agent and I'd like to have him onsite for questioning when he wakes up. You can replace him with the limo driver. Let's go men. It looks like we've got a long night ahead of us."

CHAPTER 30

Three hours later there were half a dozen police cars and an additional seven or eight F.B.I. vehicles in the large drive in front of the house. The agents were concentrating their search on Jonas' office in hopes of finding information relating to the threat which Holland by now had related to six different law enforcement officials. Jonas was still unconscious despite repeated efforts to awaken him. John Kazek was beginning to wake up from the Sarbrun induced four-hour nap he'd taken. As he lay on a sofa in the living room of Trina's estate, John began yawning and rubbing his forehead. He slowly opened his eyes to find Holland, a couple of guys in suits that he didn't know, and his direct supervisor, Pete Burkett, all staring at him. John chose to focus his eyes on Holland as he spoke.

"Did anybody get the license of whatever it was that hit me to give me this headache?"

"We did even better than that honey, but I'd better let you wake up a bit more before I tell you about it," answered Holland.

"What happened to the party, and why is my boss here? No offense Pete, but I wasn't aware of you being on the guest list."

"No offense taken John. You've had quite a night. But not quite as interesting as your friend Holland has had. Is your head feeling any better?"

"Compared to what?"

"I've heard that Sarbrun tends to leave one with a bit of a migraine type after effect."

"Sarbrun. Is that what hit me?"

"That appears to be the case. John, I'd like to introduce you to a few gentlemen. This is special agent in charge Rich Madsen and agent

Jeremiah Schillace. They're with the Joint Terrorism Task Force. I'd like to be able to give you time to recuperate from your gassing, but I'm afraid that we're a little under the gun at the moment. What I need you to do is to relate what you know of Jonas Trina's activities to these two men. Holland Matthews has given us background information on this man, as well as supplied us with a very incriminating notebook detailing his activities. We'd like you to corroborate this evidence with your testimony before we take the next step."

"Gladly gentlemen. I'll do anything to help put that slime ball behind bars where he belongs."

For the next twenty minutes John spoke, authenticating Holland's depiction of Trina, and validating why they were at Trina's estate this evening. At the end Holland filled him in on what had taken place while the rest of the guests had been unconscious. John visibly shuddered as he realized how close he had come to losing his Holly-Brit. He reached for Holland and pulled her close to kiss her. Holland stopped him.

"I'm sorry John, but I'm not through. Before Jonas tried to have me killed, he said that seven hundred dead pales in comparison to how many will be dead by the end of November 17th."

It was now special agent Madsen's turn to speak;

"John, in your professional opinion, do you think that Jonas Trina has combined forces with terrorists, and are they capable of pulling off a large terrorist act even bigger than what they purportedly did in Cincinnati?"

"Without a doubt, sir. There is absolutely no question in my mind."

With that, Madsen turned to agent Schillace.

"Have the prisoner Trina brought to the kitchen table, and make sure he is still cuffed. Then do whatever is necessary to wake the bastard up. If that means electric shock, then so be it. We've got to get that man talking and soon." With that Madsen put on his coat and headed for the door."

"Hey, where are you going Rich?" asked Pete Burkett

"Just out to my car to get something."

"Brass knuckles I hope," said Pete only half kidding.

"No, something a bit more subtle, sodium pentathol."
As the special agent in charge walked out the door, Holland looked at Pete inquisitively.

"Truth serum," Pete said as he slowly nodded his head thoughtfully.

Some people are not very good subjects when it comes to giving up information when under the influence of truth serum. Jonas Trina was not one of these. He sang like a parakeet under the sodium pentathol's persuasive spell. It may have been due to the fact that he was just coming out from one drug induced sleep when he was immediately put under, thus not giving his mind a chance to fight against it. Or it may have had to do with the expert questioning of Madsen and agent Schillace, who seemed to have a knack for this type of work. Regardless of the reason, after two hours of questioning Madsen deemed that they had all of the information that they were going to get. Bleary eyed but triumphal, the two F.B.I. men strode from the kitchen into the living room where several people were gathered. Madsen saw the two people he was most interested in, and approached them with his hand extended.

"Holland and John, The United States Government and the people of Cleveland, Ohio owe you both a tremendous debt of gratitude. Thanks to your efforts, we now know of a huge terrorist threat before it has taken place. Jonas and his friends have plans to be very bad boys this weekend. Let's all pray to God that we can stop them in time."

After shaking both of their hands, Madsen, Schillace, and Burkett all left the living room. As they walked down the hallway, Burkett turned to Madsen and said;

"May I assume that what transpired here, for the record, never took place?"

"That's affirmative."

"Boy if the A.C.L.U. ever got wind of this they'd have a field day."

"And if I gave two shits about playing by their rules we'd definitely have about ten thousand corpses lying on the streets of Cleveland Sunday night. I think I'll be able to sleep all right with the decision I made to use the methods that I chose to use. Excuse me, but now I've got to go wake up some people in Washington. Nothing I like better than to piss off the President bright and early on a Saturday morning.

****

It had thus far been a slow night at the Strategic Information and Operation Center. Paul Pulig stifled a yawn as he got out of his chair to get his third cup of coffee. As he poured the coffee, Pulig noticed the time as being 3:17A.M. "Great" he thought sarcastically. Still over three and a half hours to go before his shift ended. Being the duty agent on counterterrorism assigned to the graveyard shift at the Center, Paul knew that he actually should be grateful for a quiet night. That meant that America could have a relatively peaceful night's sleep. However, it made the hours drag interminably sometimes.

Paul's mind began to wander as it skipped ahead with anticipation to the end of the month. His vacation was planned for the week right after Thanksgiving. Sun and fun in Aruba, here we come. Eight glorious days and seven exotic nights with his latest conquest Tiffany, an airline stewardess who had agreed to his offer to spend the time exploring new erotic pleasures in paradise. Only a few short days until... The priority telephone's jangling interrupted a fantasy that was just beginning to unfold in the inner recesses of Paul's libido.

"Operation Center, duty agent Pulig speaking."

"Pulig did you say?"

"Yes sir, Pulig. Who am I speaking to and how may I assist you."

"Agent Pulig, this is special agent Rich Madsen. I'm calling from the Cleveland Ohio area, and I hope that you are well rested, because I'm about to tremendously complicate your life."

For the next fifteen minutes special agent Madsen laid out all of the details regarding the impending threat to Cleveland, along with his opinion that this was a 100 percent bona fide situation that required immediate and urgent action at the highest levels. The duty agent agreed. As Pulig busied himself in-putting an urgent report to be passed up the chain of command, he called the counter-terrorism center in Washington. By 3:55A.M. Eastern Standard Time special agent Madsen was explaining the situation to the Director of counter-terrorism. By 5:05A.M., an intra-agency call with high ranking members of the Homeland Security Council had begun. At 6:03 A.M., a meeting of the National Security Council was deemed necessary.

President Lawrence W. Ambrose was awakened at 6:17A.M. and almost immediately began to be briefed on the situation. The threat was real and imminent. The outlook was desperate. Action must be taken. The wheels of Washington were turning. Death was on the doorstep.

Secretary of Defense Warren Komar glanced at his watch from the backseat of a large black government limousine as he continued to be briefed by one of his staff members on his ride into the National Security Council meeting. It was 6:49 A.M.

"...and also Mr. Secretary, the estimates are for casualties exceeding the ten thousand mark, the majority of which would be expected to be terminal."

"I see," answered the Secretary of Defense. "And how reliable in your estimation is the threat level and the casualty estimates."

"Mr. Secretary, this information came up through the chain of command with an absolute Most Urgent Priority assigned to it. I trust the people who have compiled this information implicitly. Naturally, I have my people turning over every stone possible to verify everything, but from all indications, we are dealing with the same people who were responsible for the bombing of the Buckeye Belle riverboat. This time we have inside information on their next target and the timetable, as I stated before, is tomorrow."

"All right, that will be all for now. Of course you will keep me abreast of anything else that you view as critical. Oh and Henry. Thanks for the good work."

"You're welcome Mr. Secretary." Twelve minutes later the limousine pulled up to The White House where the National Security Council meeting was to take place.

"Ladies and gentlemen, I believe that we have a quorum, so let's call the meeting to order."

The statement was directed to a large gathering of the highest-ranking military and civilian figures in the U.S. Government. As Secretary Komar looked around the situation room, he couldn't help but be a bit awestruck at the talent level of the assembled entourage. Four-star generals, admirals, various secretaries of cabinets, the vice president and other high-ranking officials were in attendance. The President was due shortly. Secretary Komar began again.

"Director Kish, I understand that one of your people was responsible for discovering the plot and getting the ball rolling so to speak. Could you please fill all of us in on what we know at this time?" Director of the Federal Bureau of Investigation, Jordan Kish strode to the podium. As all eyes were on the F.B.I. director walking to the front of the room, a door to the rear of the room quietly opened and closed. The director began his review of pertinent facts.

"Thank you Mr. Secretary. Around midnight past, one of my special agents in charge was made aware of a possible serious threat upon the security of this country. Through the use of truth serum on a subject in capture, a tangible plot against the citizens of Ohio was uncovered. The C.E.O. of a major U.S. company confessed to being involved with probable "Fist of Rage" operatives in helping to plan attacks in Cleveland. All of you have probably heard of the extraordinary amount of bad luck which has been plaguing Pharmacor Company this year. Well it is their C.E.O., Jonas Trina, from whom the plot was extracted. A diary implicating Trina and others in the Buckeye Belle disaster that befell his company was found at his estate. In addition, he appears to have been involved in other Pharmacor tragedies that have taken place recently. It appears that Mr. Trina may have been working behind the scenes to bring about the downfall of the very company whose care he had been entrusted with. By the way, this information was also verified by one of our own agents in Cleveland who has been quietly following Mr. Trina's activities for some time.

The threat itself is of a three-pronged nature. A small group of terrorists plan on derailing a passenger train under the Terminal Tower building around 6:45 P.M. Two vans filled with a diesel fuel – ammonium nitrate mixture and plastic explosives are to be detonated at 7:30 P.M. in the parking garage underneath the Terminal Tower by a second group of operatives. This presumably would result in the destruction and collapse of the Tower, killing as many rescue workers, police, and firemen as possible. Also, this would have the desired effect of drawing away security forces from their main objective. That is to be an attack by additional "Fist of Rage" terrorists on the Rock and Roll Hall of Fame in Cleveland, which is holding a concert and induction ceremonies tonight." Our agents on the scene estimate casualty figures in excess of ten thousand dead with several additional thousands injured in the three attacks." An audible murmur swept the large room at the revealing of those figures.

"Excuse me director, but could you enlighten us as to the connection between this C.E.O. and the terrorists? Also what motive is behind this man apparently killing off his own employees?" All eyes turned to the back of the room where the question had been raised. There stood

President Ambrose who had come in as the Director had made his way to the podium.

"Gladly Mr. President. After conducting a background investigation on Jonas Trina, we discovered that he was part of a small undercover group that was sent to Afghanistan during the early stages of the Russian-Afghan war in 1980. Their mission appears to have been connected with the shoulder fired missiles we were supplying to the Afghan mujahideen. Sutton Industries, Trina's employer at the time, was the manufacturer of the missile systems. The group's mission, as I understand it, was to discover and correct problems that were plaguing the missile systems in the hands of the Afghanis. The problems were solved, and Trina came back to the States as an undercover kind of hero. It is presumed that he made friends and connections with future Middle Eastern heavyweights while in Afghanistan, and that he has maintained his connections with them through the years, as he rose to become a captain of industry. Under the circumstances, it is not beyond the realm of possibility that he might be viewed in Afghanistan as a hero due to his service to them during the Russian war. Thus it would be a natural that they would be willing to join forces with him in serving both of their purposes to bring terror to his company here in the states. As for why he has chosen to kill hundreds of those working for him, we're still looking into that. We think that it might have something to do with revenge. We do know that according to one of his employees on the scene when he was taken into custody, upwards of three hundred Pharmacor employees were expected to be on hand for tomorrow night's induction ceremonies."

"Very good Director. Now can you please bring us up to speed on what is being done to counter this threat, and what additional steps in your estimation need to be taken to negate these acts of terrorism."

"For the answers to those questions, I'd like to defer to the head of Homeland Security, Harold Varholich. Harold, if you would please." With that Harold Varholich took his place at the podium.

"Ladies and gentlemen. Since early this morning, in fact since VERY early this morning, we have had interagency discussions going on, centered around those exact questions. We have come to the conclusion that this is a huge threat against the people of the United States. At the same time this is a huge opportunity for the people of the United States. This is an opportunity to show "Fist of Rage" and the rest of those who look to terrorize America that we do not, and will not, stand idly by when others attempt to harm us. We have determined that there are two distinct roads that can be followed to meet today's threat. One is the easy, safe, and prudent call. The other is the gutsy, chance taking possibility of a devastating failure call which could leave us open to every second guessing human being on the planet." Varholich let his words sink into each one of those in attendance before he began again. "Our interagency members believe the second course of action is the correct one. Here are the reasons why:

First of all let me say that we feel that it is entirely within our means to effectively eliminate tomorrow's threat from taking place. This could be done by raising the threat level to the red or highest level in Cleveland, alerting the public that we know of an imminent threat. We would then reveal that threat and shut down those activities and sites that are threatened, thereby eliminating the attractiveness of the proposed targets to our enemy. We feel that such actions would cause the terrorists to cancel their plans for the time being and wait for a better opportunity. This would certainly ensure that lives that were at risk would no longer be threatened. Furthermore it would buy us time to continue tracking down the "Fist of Rage" operatives within our borders. This is the easy, safe, and prudent call.

Unfortunately, this call also has some very bad resultant effects. This serves to drive the terrorists underground. Who knows where they will strike next? I'd like to say that we are hot on their heels, and that it is only a short matter of time before we catch them. However, we have very few clues as to who they are at the moment. We have no names or aliases. We have no fingerprints that we have been able to match with a known terror suspect. We have little reason to believe that we will apprehend them before, during, or after their next attack. Perhaps not even the ones after that. These people are the cream of the crop, and are very good at what they do, which is to stay low and cover up their tracks when they hit. And as we found out with the Buckeye Belle, when they hit, they have the ability to hit damn hard.

So while we can make the people of Cleveland Ohio safe tonight, we run the very real risk of opening other targets in the country to the threats of these very same people in the future. Furthermore, without having the advance notice that we have here, chances are we will be ill prepared to meet the force that they will be able to bring to their next party. That is especially true if they hit at a soft target, like a county fair or high school football game.

On the other hand, we do have very credible intelligence for their targets in Cleveland. We have the location of each of the three attacks. We have the time and the station where they will board the commuter train to cause the derailment. We not only have the time and location of the Terminal Tower bombings, we actually have the license plates of the vans that are to be used in the bombings. Because of these elements, I feel very strongly that we can thwart these two aspects of the plot. Thus we can stop these threats and eliminate many terrorists in the process. Unfortunately, concerning the main threat, the attack on the Rock and Roll Hall of Fame, we have very little to go on. We know the location and the approximate time, but we don't know any of the specifics of the threat, nor the force of the enemy. Just because they used a bomb on the Buckeye Belle and are planning to use them on the Terminal Tower does not mean that will be their modus operandi in an attack on the Hall of Fame. All we could get out of the truth serum subject was that they expected virtually 100% deaths at the Rock and Roll Hall of Fame attack. He appears to have been kept out of the operations loop on the planning of that mission.

With the foreknowledge we have, a strong undercover security contingent can be put in place to safeguard the induction ceremony and weed out the terrorists before they can strike. We are at this moment mobilizing agents from all over the country to converge on Cleveland ASAP to join in the proposed manhunt to stop the terrorists in their tracks. This plan is not without risk. Let me make that perfectly clear. I am NOT standing here in front of you and guaranteeing a 100% success rate in eliminating casualties if the second proposal is adopted. They may somehow get around even the best security net we can throw up and still cause massive casualties. I cannot and will not say differently. However, we feel very strongly that this offers us the best chance at catching the terrorists that we may ever have. Ladies and gentlemen, and especially you Mr. President, this is our evaluation of the current crisis and how to deal with it most effectively. The choice is now in your hands."

With that, Harold Varholich left the podium, as a growing undercurrent of discussion was heard throughout the room. For the next hour, discussion on the proposed alternative action plans was bandied about the room. Alternative suggestions were brought up, discussed, and dismissed. Sides were drawn. Heated arguments flared up. Political and military careers were put on the line. In the end, it all came down to that which everyone in the room knew it would from the outset. Regardless of all the conjecture, pros and cons, risks and rewards, all of the discussion was mere food for thought for one individual and one individual alone. The final decision would come down to the word of the President of the United States. That decision would certainly be influenced by what had taken place within this National Security Council meeting the past few hours, but the decision would come down to the word of the man who occupied the Oval office. The responsibility to make the ultimate decision was his and his alone. This ultimate gut wrenching decision that he knew could be consigning thousands of his countrymen to an early grave if he chose wrongly.

President Ambrose thanked the council members, and asked them to stay seated while he took a brief walk around the hallway corridors to make his decision. As he left the room, President Ambrose had the feeling that the weight of the entire world lay directly on his shoulders. Certainly he had made difficult decisions before. Several of the choices he had made were responsible for the betterment of one group of society in the country against the arguments of others. He had been forced in external matters to send young people off to die on foreign shores to protect fledgling democracies, and to preserve the freedoms and liberties enjoyed by his countrymen and women. Always he had done what his heart and mind told him was right. Down deep he truly was a good and moral man. But what to do in a situation like this? He was indeed caught between the devil and the deep blue sea at this point in time. Caught between a rock and a hard place. Damned if you do, and damned if you don't, and twenty other clichés symbolizing his plight at the moment. However he looked at it, a decision had to be made. It had to be made soon, and it had to be made by him alone.

As he traversed the halls, the President's mind thought back in time. He thought of others in his rarified position and the decisions that they had made. He envisioned John F. Kennedy agonizing over the Cuban Missile crisis when the whole world stood on the brink of nuclear holocaust. He could feel Franklin Delano Roosevelt's pain in the making of numerous wartime decisions that he knew would determine the fate of millions in wartime and postwar Europe and Asia. He could even draw from the anguish of Abraham Lincoln as he fought with every shred of his being to preserve a tenuous union that many thought was not worth saving, and millions sought to tear asunder. Ultimately however, the decision that he made was drawn from the example of a man in a similar position, though located on the other side of the pond as they say in England.

The time was during the early days of World War II, the place was 10 Downing St., in London England, and the man was Sir Winston Churchill. During the Battle of Britain, the battle between the German Luftwaffe and the British Royal Air Force squadrons, German bombers were exacting a terrible toll upon the citizenry of the cities of Great Britain. Thousands were killed and injured, and millions more were terrified by the nightly raids of marauding Luftwaffe bombers raining death from their bomb bay doors. Then a miracle of sorts took place that would have a tremendous effect on Great Britain's ability to fight the war. British encription teams located at an ultra secret location in

Bletchley Park had cracked part of the German secret code that they used to communicate with their far-flung troops. Now the British would know of the German's plans as soon as their own commanders learned of them. As Churchill was to learn, it could be a double-edged sword that sometimes would have soul searing consequences. Such was the case of Coventry, England in November of 1940.

Though the British still had a long way to go before they would be able to read a large percentage of German code words, they were able to understand enough of a particular message to know with utmost certainty that on the night of November 14th, 1940, a massive German air assault was to target the industrial city of Coventry, England. Churchill could have given the word to evacuate the city, thereby saving hundreds if not thousands of lives. However if the city were evacuated, the Germans would know that their codes had been cracked, and thus would have changed codes, which would've had disastrous results for Allied intelligence. Therefore, Churchill made the heart wrenching decision that no warning was to be given the people of Coventry of the impending attack. On the evening of November 14th, despite the best efforts of the British R.A.F., German bombers succeeded in dropping 150,000 firebombs, 500 tons of high explosives, and 130 parachute mines on the doomed city. The ensuing firestorm destroyed 60,000 of the 75,000 buildings in the city and officially killed 568, although that figure is thought to be quite low. The devastation was so great that both the Germans and British made up a new word "Coventrate" which meant to totally destroy a city. That was the horrible cost of his decision that could be measured.

The benefit which couldn't be measured lay in the fact that through the remainder of the war, Allied high command had access to the innermost secrets of much of the Axis war plans before they struck. The number of lives saved within the Allied troops was incalculable. It has been estimated that having the code and keeping that knowledge secret shortened the war by over a year, so literally it can be argued that the number of lives saved was in the millions. That of course was little solace to those in Coventry who'd lost so much. Whoever coined the phrase "It's lonely at the top" had no way of knowing just exactly how right they were.

President Ambrose knew that others had stood in his shoes before, and now he knew what must be done. With his jaw set determinedly, he strode purposefully through the doors at the rear of the conference room and approached the podium. He slowly peered across the room making individual eye contact with virtually every member of the august body assembled before him without saying a word. Finally he turned towards Homeland Security chief Varholich and said;

"Harold, assemble the forces necessary. We're going to stop these terrorists. We're going to stop them right here and right now. America has come too far from tyranny to start backsliding within our own borders. Our people will not be forced to cower in fear from terrorists who mean to destroy our way of life, which is envied by all who value freedom around the world."

The stirring words brought an unabashed round of applause from the council members.

"Ladies and Gentlemen, this is my decision and my decision alone, lest something go astray. I thank all of you for your candor and your support. I'll also thank all of you for any prayers that you can send to our men and women who will be going into harm's way. That is all."

As the council began to leave the room, the President stood at the entrance and shook each individual's hand. As Harold Varholich stood in front of the President, they shook hands and then the President leaned over to whisper in Varholich's ear.

"Let's make damned sure we catch the bastards Harold."

Harold Varholich's people had been working on plans to catch the terrorists since the initial report had been received three hours before. Several ideas had been tossed out and summarily rejected for one weakness or another. The assembled staff members of the interagency Homeland Security Council already had contingency plans drawn up for scores of terrorist scenarios. Most of what was being discussed today had to do with logistics and detailed minutiae as opposed to attempting to create a counterterrorist plan out of thin air under the pressure of an actual threat. However, that did not mean that there were not still loose ends to consider and additional action plans to implement in order to insure the greatest possible chance of a successful conclusion to the horrific threat that had been laid on their doorstep. The accumulated wisdom of these discussions was presented to Harold Varholich as he telephoned the group immediately after being given the green light by the President to keep the threat secret. Susan Farrell, serving as Homeland Security Council liaison in his absence, answered the call.

"Hello Susan. The President has made the decision to keep the threat quiet, and to stop the S.O.B.'s here and now, as we had hoped he would. Now the heat is on us to perform and eliminate the bad guys before they strike. How have you folks been making out?" Do we have all of the I's dotted and the T's crossed?"

"We have several recommendations which we feel should be used as addendums to the counterterrorist action plan that most closely identifies with the current situation." A slight cough followed these words. The cough seemed more of an attempt to stifle a laugh than an actual cough. Harold called Susan on this.

"I apologize if I'm misconstruing something here Susan, but I don't find anything the least bit humorous about what we are facing today."

"Please forgive me sir, but I couldn't help but cough regarding one of our plans which we know is a bit unorthodox, but that we strongly feel should be implemented. We'll apprise you of it when you get here, along with the other more conventional aspects that we've put together." Raising a quizzical eyebrow Harold answered:

"I'll look forward to reviewing your recommendations upon my arrival. I should be there within the next ten minutes."

Thirty minutes later special agent Madsen answered his phone.

"Special agent Madsen, this is Director Kish. How are you and your people holding up this morning?"

"Bright eyed and bushy tailed sir," he lied. How may I help you?"

"I have some urgent recommendations that I would like to have implemented at the earliest possible time."

"I'll see that your wishes are carried out immediately sir."

"Very good, here they are..."

Fifteen minutes later Special agent Madsen gathered his personnel together.

"Ladies and gentlemen, we've been given the go ahead to engage and eliminate the terrorists here in Cleveland. That means that we are now the front line when it comes to fighting terrorism in this country. I do wish to point out to all of you that the cavalry is on the way. Literally hundreds of agents from all over the country will be converging on

Cleveland over the next several hours to help us defeat the imminent threat that I alluded to all of you earlier. I also want to tell you that these are some very dangerous people we're dealing with here. All of our lives and the lives of thousands of Greater Clevelanders are dependent upon us. Let's all buck up and give a good accounting O.K?

Now then, we need to get the prisoner on a gurney and to get him into an ambulance ASAP! According to the Director, whether he knows it or not, Jonas Trina just had a heart attack and is to be taken to Hillsdale Hospital. Let's make sure that we strap him down nice and tight at all times. This is one very special prisoner we have here. In fact, he's so special that within the hour his "heart attack" will be broadcast on all local radio stations and television channels. This will explain why he hasn't been in touch with his terrorist buddies last night or this morning. Speaking of which, make sure to be on your guard just in case any of his friends show up. We'll lock up here and move the party to our downtown Cleveland office after we drop the prisoner off at Hillsdale, where a security force is already gathering for his arrival. We'll fill you and our new arrivals in on the rest of the plan later at headquarters. All right let's get a move on."

Holland and John were outside as Trina's hospital-type gurney approached. As he was being wheeled past, she looked directly down into the face of Jonas, who was tightly bound to the gurney's rails with duct taped wrists and ankles. His eyes were red-hot pools of molten hatred, glaring at her with the intensity only a rage filled mind could produce. This was a look meant to intimidate and cow Holland's spirit. Jonas had used this ploy successfully many times over the years, forcing opponents to bow to his will. Holland silently returned the glare, matching Jonas' intensity with her own as she refused to allow him to gain the upper hand in this undeclared battle of mental toughness. Jonas sought to try a different tact instead.

"My dear, you are aware are you not, that this is not the last that you have heard of me or my friends. I'm a very powerful man with many friends and resources. Certainly disloyalty such as yours demands retribution, and retribution there shall be."

John took two quick steps towards Trina, but Holland grabbed his wrist and implored him with a look to let her handle the situation. John relented, and Holland began to speak.

"Retribution, RETRIBUTION!! After all that you have done to so many, you DARE to speak to me of retribution!"

Holland turned to walk away, visibly shaking with emotion. She had taken four steps when she thought better of it. Wheeling around, Holland walked purposefully back to the gurney where a smug Jonas Trina sneered up at her.

"You want to talk retribution? Then you shall have it! This is for my poor friend Jane, and Triste Johnson in Chicago, and Thomas Schultz in R&D, and seven hundred other victims of your evil treachery, and last but not least of all for me. Yeah this is also for all of the terrible things which you've done or tried to do to ME!!!'"

With that Holland stepped in front of Jonas and spat voluminously in his face. The two agents wheeling the gurney had all they could do to keep the gurney upright as the livid C.E.O. flailed his body and arms furiously against his restraints in a vain attempt to extricate himself. After half a minute, realizing that his attempts were futile, Jonas quit trying to break his bonds. He let out a string of vile expletives in his frustration. Holland met his venom with a determined rage of her own, born out of a righteous sense of justice for all those who had been victimized by this villainous unremorseful excuse for a human being.

"Be thankful Trina, that you can't break your bindings, because the way that I feel I'd tear out your throat with my fingernails and shove it down the resultant hole into your soul-less chest cavity where most people have a heart! Oh, by the way you bastard, while we're on the subject, I just thought of a little bit more retribution for you."

Looking back towards the front door, Holland saw where the F.B.I. agents were preparing to lock the door and secure the crime scene. She yelled to them to hold on for a minute. When they asked why, Holland turned defiantly to look into Jonas' spittle covered face. Her laughing eyes tauntingly mocked his hate filled orbs. Reaching under the gurney, Holland retrieved a roll of duct tape hanging there, which had been used to bind Jonas. Tearing off a strip, Holland reached into Jonas pocket and pulled out the gold watch she knew was there. She opened it and gleefully displayed the watch with the word **CHECKMATE** in front of Jonas' face. Closing the watch, Holland affixed it tightly to the sticky side of the duct tape and forcibly pressed the watch to Jonas' lips as she wound the long strip of tape over his mouth and behind his head twice for good measure.

"Don't close that door yet. I've got to go downstairs and lay down this loser's king!" She turned and triumphantly began to walk away from the gurney, ignoring the muffled screams and violent bucking of the hospital cart left in her wake.

CHAPTER 31

As the National Security Council was gathering for discussion hundreds of miles to the East, Tariq Al-Salem was beginning his day in a solemn and reverent way at a safe house in the Greater Cleveland area, which he had shared with Nishil Najir the past two days. He spread out his prayer rug on the floor and, facing to the East, he knelt down upon it. Bowing deeply he began his morning prayers. As he concluded his sacred morning ritual, Nishil entered the room. Acknowledging the solemnity of the ritual, and the necessity to mirror Tariq's prayerful beginning on this of all days, Nishil too laid out his prayer rug. Twenty minutes later the two men began to go through a checklist of requirements. As they were discussing the necessities, Al-Salem suddenly rose to his feet and made his way to a computer in the corner.

"Tariq my friend, why do you stop our discussion in midstream and turn on the computer?"

"My apologies Nishil, but it occurred to me that I still have not been contacted by Jonas. I left him two e-mails yesterday evening asking him to contact me, and as of this morning, I have heard nothing. That is not like him. This worries me immensely. Certainly he has not forgotten the importance of our plans, so I am concerned that perhaps something has happened to keep him from getting back to me. Although he is not critical to the actual carrying out of any of the missions, he was expected to play a part in tomorrow's plans. If he has somehow been compromised and forced to tell what he knows, we are in grave danger."

"Tariq, do not worry yourself. I'm sure that there is a good explanation for his not contacting you. He'll probably get in touch with you any minute now. Besides as you said, he is not critical to the success of any particular phase of the operation, and in fact he knows very little of the most crucial phase of all."

"While technically that may be true Nishil, he still knows enough to let the authorities in on what we will be targeting."

Nishil contemplated the implications as he absent-mindedly turned on the television. As the picture came into focus, the face of Jonas Trina appeared in the corner of the screen above a male commentator.

"TURN UP THE SOUND!!" screamed Tariq.

"...attack early this morning. He has been taken to a local hospital in serious condition. This is yet another disaster to strike the ill-fated Pharmacor Corporation which has experienced so much tragedy these past months. Once again Jonas Trina, the C.E.O. of Pharmacor has suffered a heart attack."

Turning off the set, Nishil looked at Tariq.

"I guess that explains why we haven't heard from him." said Nishil.

"If it's true."

"If it's true? What do you mean by that?"

"Let's just say that I don't like the timing of this."

"But as we just agreed, he is not critical to the operation from this point forward."

"That is correct. He is not necessary to help us succeed. On the other hand, he could be used as the key to help us fail. Let's alert the rest of the men to this development. Then let us continue with our plans with even greater diligence than previously planned."

Mustafa Zayed turned off his cell phone and put it back in his pants pocket. It was too bad about the man having a heart attack. The American had been a big help to their cause, according to Tariq Al-Salem. But now that couldn't be helped. He closed the top on another five gallon bucket of ammonium nitrate/diesel fuel mixture. It had been covered with standard drywall-topping compound known in the industry as "mud". Five more buckets would give them a total of 88. This was almost the same amount of the mixture that had been used in the attack on the Buckeye Belle. This time however, the amount of plastic explosive would be ten times greater. Semtech had been stuffed between the inner and outer walls of each of two large white Dodge Ram 3500 vans to be used by Mustafa and his men. The plan called for each of the vans to be parked next to a support column in the garage under the Terminal Tower parking lot in downtown Cleveland. They would be exploded at 7:30 P.M. tomorrow evening. This should be quite a surprise to the rescue workers who by then will have come to help with the devastation caused by the planned train derailment at the Terminal Tower station.

The amount of explosive material to be used would be more than enough to blow away the column next to each van and do extensive structural damage to many other columns which were the underpinnings of the great building. The Terminal Tower had graced the Cleveland skyline since the 1930's. At the time it was completed, it was the tallest building between New York and Chicago. If all went according to plan, Monday morning November 18th, would see a drastically revised Cleveland skyline. Mustafa hoisted the five gallon bucket and put it in one of the Damascus Drywall vans alongside the others.

As he began to fill yet another empty five gallon bucket with the deadly mix, a sordid version of an old bar song he had overheard years ago popped into his head. He started to hum the tune as best he remembered it, and filled in the new sadistically twisted lyrics:

"Eighty eight buckets of death in the van.
Eighty eight buckets of death.
If one of those buckets goes home to Iran
Eighty seven buckets of death in the van."

Rich Madsen glanced at the wall clock that showed the time as being 3:05 P.M. It was time to get the meeting started and bring this large assemblage to order. His task was daunting, and time was running preciously short. Fortunately, his was one of three such meetings that were taking place at this very moment in the F.B.I. headquarters building. He would not be responsible for stopping all three phases of the terrorist's plan that had been laid out before them by Jonas Trina. His assignment called for the group of agents before him to stop the planned bombing of the Terminal Tower. Rich was dog tired, having been up now for thirty three straight hours. He took a deep breath and called the meeting to order. The murmuring of the ninety agents in the room ebbed as he barked out the command for quiet.

"Agents, we don't have the luxury of much time. Nor do we have the luxury of screwing up. At 7:30 tomorrow night, terrorists are planning on detonating explosive material piled into two large Dodge vans that will be parked under the Terminal Tower building. If we don't stop these vans from being blown up, a lot of good people are going to die. That death toll will include each of us in this room if this plan is not followed, so listen up and take your assignment to heart. Do I make myself clear? Good. We will now divide you into your action teams and give you your assigned responsibilities. And remember, you are the best of the best. There is no group in the world that is better trained, equipped, or prepared to handle an assignment such as you are about to undertake. So ladies and gentlemen, take my word for it, you can handle anything that comes your way." With the pep talk finished, Madsen and Schillace broke the group into their individual units and began assigning tasks.

Eight of the agents in the room were experts in ordinance. They would be responsible for disarming the bombs after the bad guys were eliminated. Others in the room would be handling the super sensitive listening equipment that would be in place to listen into the van and pick up the terrorists conversation. Some were chosen because they were fluent in several Middle Eastern dialects. Many of the rest were sharpshooters who would be positioned under the Terminal Tower to offer multiple shooting angles. It was made very clear to the marksmen that under no circumstance were they to shoot if either of the vans were in their line of fire. It would do no good to eliminate the terrorists, and yet blow the vans up with a bullet that went through the skin of a van, thus doing the terrorists job for them. By 4:45, almost everyone in the room had been given their assignments. Agent Schillace went to the front of the room and began to speak;

"Everyone should by now have an assignment, with the exception of you six ladies against the wall. Don't worry, we haven't forgotten about you. By the way, you may have noticed that we asked all of you to dress in civilian garb. That is because we don't want you to stick out like sore thumbs and advertise our presence to the "Fist of Rage" boys. All right, marksmen go down the hallway to the first door on the right. Agent Martin will dispense to you high-powered rifles with silencers, scopes, and appropriate ammunition. Those of you assigned to disarming the bombs, please go down the hall to your left to the second door. In there another one of our agents will see that you get all of the equipment that you will need. Surveillance people stay here. All that you need will be in two vans that will be put in place under the Tower. I need everyone back in this room by 5:15. We will be boarding vans that will take us over to the Terminal Tower, A van will leave every ten minutes with a group of agents in each van. Your purpose is to examine the parking area under the Tower. You are to determine where you would park vans for the best chance of toppling the Tower. Additionally, you are to determine where to put scaffolding that would afford marksmen shooting platforms with the best angles to eliminate terrorists leaving the vans.

It is important that you act like civilians and not trained professionals as you do this, in order to not arouse the suspicions of any terrorist operatives that just might be monitoring the area. Talk good-naturedly and kid around with each other as you go about your assignment. I don't want any group to spend more than five minutes evaluating the area, otherwise we risk becoming a little too conspicuous. After five minutes, look for the stairway up into the terminal area. You will see an agent holding a sign with the words "Madsen Tour" on it. Follow him and he will show you where to go from there. We will have several agents with "Madsen Tour" signs who will direct you as to where to proceed next. This will eventually take you out of the Terminal Tower and onto a bus that will bring you right back here so that we can discuss and evaluate your findings. Is this all clear? Any questions? Very well then. Next, as I mentioned before, we have a special assignment for you six ladies against the wall. Please come with me to special agent Madsen's office, where he will talk to you about your role in all of this."

The ladies were ushered into Madsen's office, and the door was closed. Rich Madsen greeted them, and then he sat down on the edge of his desk, with his eyes moving from one female agent to another. He had a pensive look on his face as he began to speak;

"I want to thank all of you for being here today. Lord knows it's a hell of a way to ruin a weekend, but I guess we all have our lots in life. Ladies, we have a problem. Hopefully it's not an insurmountable problem, but it is a problem nonetheless. On the intelligence side, here is what we know. We know that two vans filled with explosives are going to be coming to the Terminal Tower to be blown up. There will be two men in each van. The two drivers will leave the vans and make their way out of the area. A man will be left in each van when the driver gets out. We don't know at this time if these men will get out of their vans before they attempt to blow them up or not. If they are true suicide bombers who hope to spend eternity, starting this weekend, in the celestial arms of numerous heavenly virgins, we are all in big trouble. We're banking on them planning on vacating the vans and getting a safe distance away before detonating them with a remote signal. From what we know of this group, each of these men has been hand picked and extensively trained with the idea that they will constitute a jihad force within the U.S. to strike repeatedly and spread terror throughout the land. Because of that concept of repeat attacks, we feel confident that they will try to escape prior to setting off the fireworks. With the sound equipment in place under the Terminal, we hope to know more of their plans as the situation develops, so that we will be able to adapt accordingly.

I've told you all this, because I want you to know exactly how precarious our situation is, and what the risks are that we will be facing. If these men get out of the van, it will be the responsibility of our positioned sharpshooters to bring them down. Your mission centers on the drivers. We can't eliminate them with bullets due to their partners remaining hidden in the explosive laden vans. We know that the drivers will also have the means to detonate the vans, presumably with a remote device carried on their person. We need to take the drivers out of the equation silently. They need to be eliminated in such a way that they don't have a chance to press the remote detonators they'll be carrying. That is where you brave ladies come in. We'll present the plan now, and at the end I'll ask for three volunteers.

The average Arabic male is a very macho fellow. He likes to think of himself as capable in most situations, and generally quite virile and attractive to the fairer sex. We hope to use this to our advantage. As you ladies may or may not have noticed, you are all quite attractive and, how do you say, well endowed. It was by design that you six were selected for this delicate but crucial part of the mission. We hope that your attractiveness can be utilized to distract the terrorists from their intentions long enough to bring our plan to fruition. Here is what we propose..."

As Rich Madsen was preparing his group to thwart the plans for the Terminal Tower, so too were his F.B.I. counterparts preparing their people to stop the threats posed for the Rapid Transit commuter train, and the attack on the Rock and Roll Hall of Fame. The limited amount of knowledge that they had to work with made the Hall of Fame attack infinitely harder to prepare for, in that the attack could come from anywhere, and take on any form. An elite counterterrorism force was flown in to handle the assignment. Regardless of what Rich Madsen was telling his agents at exactly the same time, this group was the best of the best. The one hundred fifty members of this elite force were handpicked from the special forces of each branch of the military. Their training and situational preparedness was superior to virtually any group in the world. In addition to being in peak physical condition, and masters of all types of weaponry and hand-to-hand combat techniques, each individual in the unit had participated in hundreds of hours of classroom study. There were few situations that could be utilized by an enemy that they had not trained for, and which they were not equipped to deal with. Four hundred extra F.B.I. agents had been brought in to help, plus another six hundred local police and scores of bomb sniffing dogs to provide surveillance support. And yet with all of the cards that they were able to bring to the table, there was one key ingredient missing which the terrorists had on their side that could negate all of the intelligence and firepower arrayed before them. That was the element of surprise.

"Fist of Rage" knew when and how they were going to strike. That advantage was huge. Unless the counterterrorist force got a break, all they could do was to be super vigilant and hope they found the bad guys before they were able to strike. If the terrorists struck first, chances were very good that thousands would die and they might even be able to eliminate a good part of the counterterrorism forces in the initial blow. Every law enforcement person in the country had by now seen what these people could accomplish. One had to presume that these terrorists had the ability to bring massive power with them on any mission. Getting in the first punch might eliminate the ability to retaliate. Even if retaliation was a possibility, the casualties accomplished by the strike might make elimination of the terrorists seem like too little, too late.

As the head of the elite one hundred fifty man force, Assistant Director Joseph Habanek had been granted the unenviable task of stopping "Fist of Rage's" attack on the Rock and Roll Hall of Fame. Joseph was a supremely confident and competent individual befitting his position. He had the ability likewise to inspire confidence in his troops. Various group leaders under him were sorely testing that ability at this moment. They were aware of the intelligence limitations they were operating under, and the degree of danger to which each person was going to be exposed. Recognizing the challenge laying before them, several group leaders had expressed a desire to reevaluate the decision to stop the terrorists here and now, with so much and so many at risk. Joseph decided that a "shot in the arm" might do some good before sending his troops off to confront the implacable foe. With that in mind, he called all of the leaders into a small room at the F.B.I. headquarters.

"Listen up everyone. I'm not going to stand before you and belittle the risks that we are up against. They are real, and they are significant. Believe me, I know what's at stake here. I also know that the concerns that we are wrestling with are the very same concerns that those higher up the chain of command had to consider before deciding upon our present course of action. Our job is not to make or question policy. Our job is to execute policy. And execute policy is exactly what we are here to do.

In order to successfully execute the policy passed down to us, we have brought in the largest concentration of counterterrorist manpower that has ever been assembled in this country. The best and the brightest will be guarding the streets tomorrow, led by their best and brightest which I am fortunate to have in this room with me now. I am totally confident that before this mission is finished, "Fist of Rage" will have been stopped. Either that or they will have decided not to make an attempt. I sincerely hope that they do not choose the latter, because they haven't a snowball's chance in hell against the talent that we will set against them.

Now people, I want you all to go out and communicate this same message to those who've been assigned to you. Remind them of their abilities and their training. Remind them of their duty. Remind them to be diligent and vigilant. Remind them to observe and question everything. Lastly, remind them who we are as a people and what we stand for. That is all. Good luck and God Bless."

As the leaders were filing out of the room, Joseph Habanek shook their hands as he continued to radiate an aura of confidence and presumed success. As the last group leaders took their leave, Joseph raised his eyes upward as he offered his own prayer for some divine intervention on their side. Deep down he knew that at best it was probably a one-in-four chance that they could stop the evil from taking place. Still, he knew that the current course of action was the right course. After all, if they couldn't stop them with the force he now commanded, what chance did Anytown USA have against these subhuman bastards if they chose to strike there? He turned off the lights, and went to join his forces.

The next fourteen hours were intense, but uneventful as the evaluations and decisions were made, and men and material were moved into place. The constant dread was that all of the assembled security forces were being observed by the watchful eyes of "Fist of Rage" operatives who would report the increased activity back to their superiors and abort their mission. For although the counter-terrorist teams were doing their abject best to disguise their objectives, it would be difficult not to spook a trained observer. The fact that something extraordinary was taking place under the Terminal Tower, at the Rapid Transit station, and at the Rock and Roll Hall of Fame was almost impossible to hide. Fortunately, the terrorists themselves were thinking along the same lines. They too didn't want to risk being too conspicuous in having taken too keen an interest in their intended targets. Thus the decision was made that all preparations were ready, and it would be best not to take any unnecessary chances by being seen in the vicinity of tomorrow night's targets. Therefore all security precautions proceeded as planned into the early morning hours, as the "Fist of Rage" forces rested in anticipation of their calamitous and historic mission Sunday evening.

At 7:00A.M. Sunday morning all of the counter-terrorist teams were ordered to stand down and were taken to their various hotels in order to get some rest. They would reassemble at their individual team's rendezvous points at 1:30P.M. local time to eat and begin preparations for tonight's assignments. The importance of the mission and degree of inherent danger made sleep all but impossible for most, but merely laying down with eye's closed refreshed most of the participants. That and a nervous excitement had all at a high level of readiness in anticipation of the challenges that lay ahead.

CHAPTER 32

A ten-year old Subaru pulled into the virtually deserted and dimly lit Triskett Road parking lot to the Rapid Transit commuter train. As four Arabic men in long dark coats got out of the car, a light breeze blew a discarded hamburger wrapper under a minivan, startling a cat hiding there. As the cat scurried out from its hiding place and scampered across the lot, one of the men reached into his coat pocket. In a blur, a hand withdrew from the pocket and whipped a thin object underhand at tremendous speed in the feline's direction. A brief whitish flash was evident as light glinted off the knife's blade. The cat let out a high-pitched cry of surprise, pain, and fear. Then the animal expired. The man retrieved his knife and wiped the blade with a tissue that he placed in his pocket. Not a word was exchanged by any of the four grim faced men as they made their way towards the silver three-story terminal where they would catch the train. Two chatting couples in their early thirties with department store shopping bags in their grasp exited the terminal building as the men entered.

Entering through the doors at the lowest level of the terminal, they came to a glass window where the train passes were usually purchased. However a sign in the window indicated that no one was on duty and the fare would be collected on the train itself. Apparently it was not expected to be a busy night on the Transit. That was even better for their plans. The men passed through the turnstile and got on an escalator leading up towards a walkway that they would take to get to the train platform. As the Arabic foursome leisurely rode their way upward, six well built jock types complete with gym bags fresh from some pick-up game or workout made their way down the stairs beside the escalator. Three of these men seemed to be kidding the other three about something. Neither group made eye contact with the other as they passed.

Reaching the top of the escalator, the men turned to their left and went through a set of double doors into the walkway. It was glass enclosed and approximately 75 feet long. As the men got halfway across the narrow passage, a face appeared around a corner at the end of the walkway in the direction they were heading.

"This is the F.B.I. Throw down your weapons, take off your jackets, and put your hands in the air!" The men halted and stood frozen, caught completely off guard by this sudden unanticipated turn of events.

"I repeat. Throw down your weapons and put your hands in the air. You are outnumbered and surrounded." Several gun barrels protruding around the wall's corner backed up the claim.

Two of the men began to do as instructed, moving slowly so that their intentions would not accidentally be misinterpreted. Unfortunately for them, the other two chose a different course of action. It may have had to do with their training, or their upbringing, or their reasoning may have had to do with religious zeal and the desire to leave this life fighting for the cause in hopes of a pleasurable afterlife. Regardless of why, their decision would determine the fate of all four in the ensuing seconds.

Figuring that his two partners with upraised arms would buy him some empathy from his foes, the knife-wielding terrorist attempted to repeat the previous success he'd had outside with the cat. He slowly put his hand in his pocket, and then with a lightning move withdrew it launching his blade with deadly accuracy. His new foe however was far superior to a cat in his ability to anticipate his opponent's moves. The F.B.I. agent had begun to move back to the protection offered by the wall's corner when the Arab put his hand in his pocket. The knife was accurately aimed according to where the agent had been a split second before. As the clattering sound of steel upon tile could now confirm, the agent was no longer in the same place.

While the knife attack had been unsuccessful, it had served to drive the agents to seek cover momentarily and that allowed the terrorists a couple of seconds to draw their weapons. With the die now having been cast, all four men threw caution to the wind and began firing their Tek-9's in a blistering assault. For a brief moment they held the upper hand in the battle. Firing continuously, they began to backtrack towards the double doors they had come through to enter the walkway. Bullets shattered glass and chipped tile, sending shrapnel ricocheting in all directions. Two F.B.I. agents hiding around the corner were slightly wounded by deflected bullet fragments. One of the terrorists actually smiled as he slapped another clip into his weapon and prepared to resume firing. The doors to his rear bursting open wiped the smile off his face.

In the doorway stood the six jocks they had passed on the stairway. These F.B.I. agent/jocks now laid down a hail of fire of their own as the terrorists turned to meet this new enemy. Suddenly the transparent walls on the side of the walkway erupted in shards of flying glass as the two couples the terrorists had passed while entering the terminal joined in the fray firing their weapons from below. The combined withering fire cut the terrorists to pieces. In half a minute the battle was over. Four blood-splattered bodies lay motionless on the walkway floor surrounded by spent casings and their own now useless armaments. An eerie silence replaced the din of gunfire. The head agent who had originally given the terrorists the option to lay down their weapons and live, made his way toward the bodies from the far side of the walkway. As he kicked over each individual body checking for signs of life, he stoically reached for his radio. As his call was answered, he stooped to pick up an object.

"All aboard," he said into the mouthpiece while closing the blade of the knife meant for his forehead back into the handle.

Mustafa Zayed looked at his watch once again. The time was now 7:04. Exactly two minutes since he had last checked. The train derailment was to have taken place almost twenty minutes ago. He prepared to implement the contingency plan. If the train attackers were delayed, but still in control of their situation, they knew that they should've alerted Zayed by now. Since he had heard nothing, he must go on the assumption that they had been compromised, and therefore his team should fulfill their part of the overall plan according to schedule. While it would have been nice to have additional infidels under the Terminal Tower when Zayed's men brought it down, it was not critical to their mission. Mustafa knocked on the panel of the Dodge van that separated the cab from the storage area in the rear. A fellow conspirator answered his knock.

"I am leaving now. It appears that the train wreck will not happen. Give us five minutes. Remember, if you do not hear any fighting in that time, you may leave the van and come after us to the designated spot where we will detonate the vans. If you hear fighting of any kind, you have your orders. I know that we can depend on you to do your duty, right Aziz?"

"That is correct Mustafa. Allah Akbar!"

"Allah Akbar," replied Zayed as he opened the door to the van and stepped out.

As he did so, another van door fifty yards away opened and out came Zayed's fellow driver who had been watching Mustafa's van for his cue. Both vans were parked directly beside load bearing support columns, with additional columns nearby. As the two men walked toward each other, Mustafa kept a vigilant eye out for signs that something was amiss. He noticed some scaffolding set up in two different sections of the under ground lot, but that did not concern him. A couple of telephone company vans were also noticeable in the lot, but they too did not seem terribly out of place. He saw a few people making their way towards the lower entrance to the building, while a few others appeared to be heading to their cars. Mustafa and the other driver came together.

"Well my friend, this is it. Do you have any word on the train men, because I've heard nothing?"

"I've heard nothing also. We must assume that something has gone wrong. However, we have our assignment, and that we shall now complete. Let us go."

The two men began to walk in the direction of the underground entrance some sixty yards away. As they did so, Rich Madsen, who was in one of the telephone vans, spoke softly into his headset.

"All right ladies, its show time."

Three attractive women suddenly emerged from the underground entrance, and proceeded to weave their way in the general direction of the two middle eastern males. The women chattered incessantly between themselves as they strolled together, their arms around each other's shoulders. Their walk, talk, and basic demeanor gave off the distinct impression that they had been thoroughly enjoying drinks at some downtown tavern. As the women came closer, a sense of alarm surged through Mustafa. Although the women didn't seem dangerous, their approach was unusual in the very least. He tightened his grip on the transmitter in his pocket as the women came closer. If necessary, he knew that his sense of duty would overcome any thoughts of self-preservation. While he would prefer to live and carry on other missions, he was fully prepared to press the button on his transmitter and bring the entire building crashing down with him under it if that was how the next few minutes dictated that things should end. As the women drew near, they stopped in unison as if for the first time they suddenly had become aware of the presence of someone other than themselves. A statuesque blonde in the middle fixed her gaze on the men as she began to speak loudly to one of the other women:

"Look Laurie, aren't those two men over there just like the one's we were talking about?"

"Yum yum! It sure does appear to be the case. I wonder if these two could be as hot as my other Arab lovers have been. Let's see."
As the women got to within a mere few feet of the men, Laurie spoke again:

"Hey Ali Baba, my girlfriend and I have a little disagreement going on that we were wondering if you could settle. Whose do you think are nicer, hers or mine?"

Mustafa's irritation at being referred to as a mythical Arabian Night's character was quickly forgotten as he and his partner were visually confronted with two beautiful women whose tops were pulled up, bare breasts exposed for their viewing pleasure. Dumbfounded, the two men silently ogled the vision before them.

"Well boys, surely you can't make a decision on sight alone." said Lynn the blonde. "Why don't you come on over here and get a grip on things if you know what I mean."

The total absurdity of the situation had accomplished the purpose of catching the men off guard. While both men subconsciously continued to keep one hand on the transmitters in their pockets, their ardor to complete the mission was waning in the face of this newfound distraction. Like obedient puppies, both men reached out their free hands to sample the sensory pleasures they would derive from fondling Lynn and Laurie's firm full breasts. The cold air quickly hardened the four exposed pink nipples adding to the delight being experienced by the two would be terrorists.

"You know guys, these babies travel in pairs, and you guys only seem to be giving it a half hearted effort. Why don't you use both hands and really find out whose are best?"

With that the speaker Laurie turned her back on Mustafa's partner and gently pulled his hand out of his pocket placing it on her right breast to accompany his other hand which was now centered on the areola and nipple of her left breast. As he did so, she reached behind and began rubbing his groin seductively through his trousers. His pleasured moans told of his enjoyment. Throwing caution to the wind, Mustafa positioned himself in back of Lynn and began to emulate what he was witnessing the other twosome enjoying, as both of his hands cupped and squeezed Lynn's beautiful breasts. Lynn dutifully reached behind to fondle Mustafa's manhood. At the suggestion of Laurie, the men closed their eyes to concentrate on the pursuit at hand in order to determine any subtle variations that might be critical in deciding upon the winner.

It was at this time that the third member of the women's group, a local girl from Ohio named Lisa silently made her way in back of Mustafa's partner. Pulling a wooden handled scratch awl from her sleeve, she placed her left hand over his mouth and with her right hand deftly plunged the awl hilt deep into his temple. The body immediately went limp, and Lisa caught it as it slumped to the ground.

Though the kill had been accomplished as quietly as possible, it still produced enough noise to draw Mustafa's attention. Looking over his shoulder as he continued to caress Lynn's ample charms, Mustafa took stock of Lisa laying his partner down gently on the asphalt parking lot. Alarmed, he broke out of his sex induced state, and reached for his pocket. Laurie lunged at Mustafa and grabbed his wrist to keep him from completing his move. As they grappled for control, Lynn turned to lend a hand to Laurie's efforts. She clamped onto the hand Mustafa was attempting to plunge into his pocket. Though by himself, Mustafa was stronger than either of the women, together the two trained agents were able to fight him to a draw with neither side gaining the upper hand.

With leopard like quickness honed from hundreds of hours of martial arts training, Laurie shot her right leg in back of Mustafa's left. Sweeping her leg back towards herself and kicking slightly upward succeeded in bringing her adversary tumbling down face upward. As Mustafa's head hit the asphalt, both women jumped down on top of him to keep him subdued. They were now able to pin his arms down with their full weight. Mustafa knew his time was running short as Lisa dropped to her knees by his side and raised the awl to strike. In desperation Mustafa opened his mouth to let out a warning cry to his compatriots. Sensing what was about to happen, Laurie reacted with the only countermeasure at her disposal. As Mustafa raised his head to scream, his mouth was suddenly stuffed with a plump breast that effectively muffled his warning cry. It also stifled the last sounds that he would make a second later as Lisa thrust the awl twice into his black haired cranium. The body made one final spasmodic jerk and then relaxed. Reaching into the terrorist's pockets, the agents removed the transmitters found there and took out their batteries. The women quickly pulled the bodies behind two nearby vehicles, and ran for the protection of a large pickup truck where they repositioned their apparel.

Rich Madsen had witnessed the fight from his van. As the women dragged the bodies away, he alerted his shooters to hold their positions and to be subtle about it. He didn't want to spook the terrorists when they came out of the vans. He also reminded everyone to shoot only if the vans were not in their line of fire. Having done all he could, Rich said a silent prayer of thanks that the mission had gone well so far. The drivers had been subdued, and because of the surveillance equipment picking up Mustafa and Aziz's conversation, he knew that the other men would be getting out of the vans shortly. Though they weren't out of the woods yet, his people were off to a good start. He said a final prayer for expert marksmanship and hunkered down to await the next developments.

The door on one of the Damascus Drywall vans slowly began to open, and a body began to extricate itself through the rear of the van. This was no small feat in that the van was completely filled with buckets of the deadly mixture. Finally the man was able to wriggle free, and just at the same time the door on the second van began to open. As the second man emerged, the first terrorist made his way over to join up with him. The two men had a brief discussion, and then began to make their way towards the underground entrance to the Terminal Tower. Madsen could see that both men were warily looking around as they walked. He prayed they wouldn't discover their dead comrades before his men could take them out. Surprisingly, only one of the two men had his hand in his pocket.

The two men were approaching the vehicle that the women had hidden the dead bodies behind. Madsen subconsciously began twitching his trigger finger in hopes that any second supremely accurate shots would ring out and end this deadly drama successfully. He peered towards the scaffolding and saw two rifle muzzles extending over the edge. As Madsen's brain screamed "Fire", he saw twin puffs of smoke emit from the muzzles. Glancing quickly back at the terrorists, Rich saw the arm of one man rising up towards his head when the entire side of his skull exploded in a reddish gray mist. The right arm of the second man was racing towards his pocket when the hand suddenly detached itself from the wrist and went flying against a parked Chrysler 300, leaving a red smear on the white door. As Madsen refocused his attention to the man again, a dark red hole appeared in the center of his forehead, with the force of the shot knocking him violently backwards with the rear of his head smacking hard onto the concrete. "Cease Fire" Madsen screamed into his headset, and no more shots rang out. He was certain the terrorists could not have survived the head shots. and Madsen didn't want to risk the vans being hit by a ricochet. He knew his troops had been exceedingly successful so far, and he didn't want to press their luck any further than necessary. Agents, with guns drawn, swarmed to the bodies, and the transmitters were taken away. Though the immediate threat was now eliminated, the danger persisted. It was now time for the bomb squads to make their appearance.

As all non-critical personnel were removed from the Terminal Tower area, the bomb squad members hurried in to accomplish their task. There was little conversation from these grim and resolute men as they approached the vans. Splitting into two teams, the men set to work. First, two men carefully examined the exterior of each van for any booby traps which may have been rigged to be tripped. After a minute's perusal, the men were confident that no devices were in place. With painstaking deliberation, the rear door of each van was opened. A slight ticking noise could be heard within each van's interior. The team leaders wormed their way through the maze of buckets inside each van, carefully checking for booby traps as they inched their way towards the source of the ticking. Arriving at the ticking time bombs they discovered in both cases, relatively unsophisticated explosive timing devices set to go off at 7:30. This left them about five minutes to work.

Marcus Oberlin examined the many wires that were attached to the detonator. He examined each wire with cool professionalism. Marcus, the son of a professor of Natural History at Grambling, had been with the F.B.I. for six years. In that time he had worked his way up the ladder, exhibiting an uncanny ability to keep his cool under pressure. His father had instilled in him the value of maintaining one's composure when pressed. This trait would be severely tested over the next few minutes.

As he double and triple checked the device, his mind recounted his training and previous successes. In his line of work, one's abilities are apparent by the simple fact of one's continued existence. Marcus made his determination and pulled a small pair of wire cutters out of a roll-up pouch he had brought with him. Looking back at the van door where the other members of his team stood with obvious concern etched upon their faces, Marcus set them at ease with a smile and a wink. Focusing his attention back on the subject at hand, Marcus separated a green wire from the assortment of colored wires running from the device. With an artistic flourish, he smartly snipped the wire in half with his wire cutters and gave a quick smile and thumbs up to his teammates. The concern on their faces was quickly replaced by smiles as they realized the significance of Marcus' gesture. They cleared a path for Marcus as he began to wiggle his way out of the cramped van.

Stretching his legs, he looked over towards the other van where he expected his counterpart Travis Jameson to emerge triumphant after defeating the ticking detonator within that vehicle. Though it was difficult to ascertain for sure from the distance that separated the vehicles, Marcus thought that he detected a sense of panic from the team members gathered around the other van. Trotting quickly over to the other vehicle, Marcus prepared to offer his assistance, which he was sure would be unnecessary. The look on the face of one of the team members peering earnestly into the back of the van said otherwise. Marcus rushed to the back of the van and as the others made way for him, he gazed apprehensively inside. There he could see Travis kneeling before the explosive device. His body was unmoving, frozen in fear.

It is difficult to say what internal qualities and abilities allow one man to overcome something that totally overwhelms another when placed in identical pressure situations. Both Travis and Marcus had received the same training, and both had reached the same level of expertise. Travis in fact had the edge in experience and rank, having been with the bureau for two years longer. Both men had exhibited superior professionalism in their ability to negate virtually any explosive challenge they had encountered up to this point in their respective careers. Both men easily had in their repertoire the acumen and knowledge to disarm the rather unsophisticated devices put before them this day. Yet here knelt Travis Jameson, paralyzed by the detonator before him with sweat streaming off his head and a "deer in the headlights" glaze on his eyes. Marcus sought to break the defeatist spell that his peer was, for some inexplicable reason, now under.

"Focus Travis focus!" implored Marcus.

The only visible response seemed to be a further tightening of the death grip that Travis already had on a pair of cutting pliers that he was squeezing in his right hand.

"Remember your training!" screamed Marcus, to no avail. He knew that precious seconds were ticking away. Time was now of the essence.

"Travis, get the hell out of there, I'll take over!" Those words seemed to at least sink in a little as the beginnings of a look of recognition began to appear on Jameson's face. Marcus knew he needed to expedite the process as rapidly as possible.

"MOVE DAMN IT, MOVE!!! I MEAN NOW JAMESON!!!" The spell was broken, and Jameson began to half crawl, half wiggle his way out of the tight space. As he backed out of the van, a large wet spot in the crotch of his work suit told of the degree of self-control that Jameson had relinquished. Trembling and ashamed Travis exited the van. Keeping his eyes down, he sought to shield his face from the scared and disappointed team members he passed as he slinked away from the van to cower behind a nearby minivan.

Marcus quickly made his way to the detonator and looked at the timing mechanism attached to it. A digital green light indicated twenty three seconds remaining. Twenty three lousy stinking seconds until his life would come to an end. Marcus was good at what he did, but no one was that good. There was no human being on earth who could evaluate the device before him and make a 100 percent guaranteed decision on which wire to cut in only twenty three seconds. His life, and the lives of so many others now lay in his making a lucky guess. This evaluative analysis had eaten up three of the seconds. Here is how the remaining twenty seconds would be spent.

Seconds 20-13: In order to satisfy the professional within himself that dictated he must try, a futile effort was made to attempt to make some sense out of the myriad wires that lay before him.

Seconds 12-10: Marcus conjured up a fervent unspoken wish that Travis Jameson be eternally damned for putting all of the squad members in this predicament. This had the unintended, but welcome effect of bringing the concept of a divine Being into their corner to help them in their time of need.

Seconds 9-5: Intense prayer that God answer their call for help, and intercede on their behalf, imparting Marcus with knowledge of which wire to choose.

Second 4: Grab black wire .

Second 3: Snip black wire

Second 2: See timer still counting down

373

Second 1: Look at terrified team members gathered around van's back door and mouth the word's "I'm sorry."

The timer's green illuminated display now blinked to 0:00. The van's interior was bathed in an otherworldly bright white light created by the initial explosion. Those human beings near the van were immediately incinerated into nothingness. The explosive forces at work engendered by the accumulated wicked material in the van precluded that anything or anyone could actually withstand such power. Not even a small piece of bone fragment would be recovered of any human being within seventy five yards of this catastrophic event. The blast had the additional effect of engulfing the other van which added its explosive might to the event also. The force of the explosion spread in a circular pattern, hungrily devouring everything in the path. Flaming remnants of vehicles and humanity spearheaded the blast's arrival as it advanced in an ever-expanding ring of death and destruction. Those unfortunate enough to have been within a quarter mile radius of the blast site had virtually no chance at survival. Many others, hundreds of feet beyond this distance, succumbed to shrapnel visited upon them in almost volcanic fashion.

The prime target of each of the vans also fell prey to the force of the blasts. Each van had been parked beside a concrete jacketed steel pillar that provided the foundational support for the leviathan building. The pillars closest to each van were virtually sheared off by the explosions, and additional pillars had their strength drastically weakened by damage caused as the blast wave hit them. Without the full complement of structural supports continuing to act in unison as they had for almost eight decades, the building could no longer remain upright.

People occupying the upper floors of the 714-foot building initially only noticed a slight shudder as the Tower's underpinnings began to fail one by one. As each of the remaining pillars began to be subjected to intolerably increasing stresses, they had little choice but to give way. With each destroyed pillar came additional stress loads to be placed upon those that were left. The giant building now began to lean precipitously as the Terminal Tower entered its death throes. Windows shattered by the score, showering the onlookers on Public Square with an additional menace. The trademark flagpole at the building's top swayed drunkenly at an angle never before witnessed by generations of Clevelanders.

As the few remaining pillars continued to crumble, the Tower's end became inevitable. Savvy onlookers took note of the direction that the building was leaning towards, and raced pell-mell away at a ninety-degree angle as quickly as their feet or vehicles would take them. Some of these would probably survive. Other's were simply too awestruck by the sight of the falling building to effect escape. The Terminal Tower's angle of descent had now reached a point where the upper floors began to break off from the main body of the Tower and commenced to plummet earthward. A terrified mother with two small toddlers stood directly under this falling mass. There could be only one horrible way for their fate to end. The mother covered the children with her body in a pitiable and pathetic attempt to shield her precious ones from the certain doom hurtling towards them. Onlookers in other buildings surrounding the square screamed at the horror taking place before their very eyes.

Marcus Oberlin blinked hard and shook his head violently to snap out of the terrible vision that his mind had created. As the timer had hit zero, his conscious brain had snapped, being unable to deal with the horrendous realities of his having chosen the wrong wire to cut. His subconscious had conjured up the ensuing scene based upon the expectations it envisioned taking place. Incredibly, he was alive. ALIVE! Beyond all probabilities, he and his team members now cheering at him from the van's rear entrance were still alive. There had been no explosion. Beyond all reason the blast had not occurred. While he didn't know exactly why it hadn't taken place, Marcus did know that with the tremendous amount of explosive material surrounding him, they were all still at great risk. He signaled everyone to evacuate the immediate area, while he looked to determine the reason why they were all still among the living. It didn't take long to discover the answer.

When the terrorists had been assembling the bomb, they had run wires from the detonator to the timer. However, unbeknownst to them, a sharp piece of metal protruding from the van's wall had neatly sliced through the wire prior to its being hooked up to the timer. The severed wire was hidden from sight by one of the buckets in the van. Regardless of which wire Marcus had cut, there would have been no explosion. As Marcus prepared to extricate himself from the van, he suddenly realized just exactly how parched his lips, mouth, and throat had become. Fear will do that to a man. As he got out of the vehicle, Marcus Oberlin knelt down and kissed the rear bumper of the van. Next he looked skyward, and pointed his finger to the heavens in acknowledgement of the part that he was sure had been played in the event by The Almighty. Finally he turned in the direction of his team members who were a good distance away and gave a two thumbs-up signal. As he walked towards them, he began to be aware of a noticeable shaking in his knees. "That's good," he thought. I'm not too arrogant of my abilities or too stupid to know when to be scared. At least not yet.

The perspiration on Rich Madsen's upper lip and forehead belied the cool temperature of the mid November night as he picked up his cell phone and quickly punched in some numbers. Near the Rock and Roll Hall of Fame, Joseph Habanek's phone began to jingle.

"Hegan can catch another one tomorrow."

Habanek breathed a huge sigh of relief into his phone as he responded with a brief understated "well done," for the news which he had just been given. The Hegan message referred to Jim Hegan, a Cleveland Indian baseball player in the 1930's, who caught a ball dropped from the top of the Terminal Tower over six decades earlier. The message signaled that Madsen's people had been successful.

"Two down, and one to go" thought Habanek as he dialed Director Kish's number to report the good news progress thus far.

"The Tower should've been struck by now," said Nishil as his head bobbed up and down in the cabin of Jonas Trina's 35-foot luxury cabin cruiser floating 1.5 miles offshore from the Rock Hall of Fame. "We should have heard from the men taking over the Rapid Transit train long ago. I do not like it one bit. Something is terribly wrong."

"I fear that you are correct my friend. We have heard nothing. However, I just heard from two of the three trucks prepared to make the key assault, and they report no indication of any danger or complications at this time. While it would've been nice to divert the authorities attention away from our main objective, I'm confident that we can still strike the most important blow at our enemy and achieve a glorious victory," answered Tariq Al-Salem.

"I do not share your confidence. I'm afraid that the infidels have somehow learned of our plans and have been able to counter them."

"That very well may be true. Perhaps the American Trina had a change of heart at the last moment and spilled his guts, or perhaps he had it tortured out of him. Either way, we must assume that it was because of him that the first two pieces of the plan have apparently failed. Let us not forget though that he knew virtually nothing about the last and most important part of the plan. This was precisely the reason for not including him on the planning of the last phase. And it is why I now choose to go ahead with the attack."

"But Tariq, we must call it off, it is much too risky."

"I am in charge of this operation and I say that we continue as planned. Even if our men have been captured, the Americans do not have time to get them to talk and jeopardize our chances of success. Furthermore, regardless of whether they somehow know of our plan, it would be almost impossible to stop us now."

Tariq reached over to a transmitter and as he picked it up, he spoke into the mouthpiece

"Commence Purple Haze. I repeat. Commence Purple Haze. Allahu Akbar!"

Akmed and Abu Allan turned their beer truck onto E. 9th street from Carnegie Avenue and began to head north slowly in the congested traffic. The Bartlestein Beer truck they were driving was a perfectly disguised vehicle for what they had in mind. Bartlestein Beer was one of the sponsors of tonight's Rock and Roll Hall of Fame event, and it was natural to see one of their trucks in close proximity to the Hall. By the time anyone got wise to the danger, it would be too late. The truck continued to proceed slowly down the street, crawling along with the rest of the traffic headed for either the Hall of Fame or one of the showplaces in the theater district.

John Kazek was at his post on E. 9th street, vigilantly surveying the area as part of the F.B.I.'s attempt to thwart the expected attack. Initially the F.B.I. was not going to allow John to be part of this effort, deeming that he had done more than his share already. However, John was so insistent that he be included, and allowed to see this operation through to the end, that the F.B.I. relented. He was assigned a spot well away from the Hall of Fame, in an effort to minimize his chances of being injured. Though he protested the obvious attempt to safeguard him, good soldier that he was, John obeyed his superiors and took up his assigned post.

John's thoughts wandered even as he attempted to keep them fully on the task at hand. While he knew that he must do his best to remain vigilant, he was having a difficult time concentrating. His focus kept returning to his deep concern for Holland's safety. Going against all thoughts of reason, personal safety, and even her love for him, Holland had insisted on taking her place at the Rock Hall of Fame ceremonies this evening. She knew that she was putting herself in harm's way. She knew all about the risks. They'd had a heated argument over the matter. John insisted that it was sheer lunacy for her to deliberately choose to put herself in danger knowing the very real possibility of an attack. Holland argued that it was her duty to attend, along with the hundreds of other Pharmacor employees who would be in attendance, not having the foreknowledge that she possessed. She didn't think it was right for her to be off hiding, knowing full well that most of her close friends and associates would be there. Holland was sure that she could never live with herself if she stayed away due to having inside knowledge while all of her co-workers were killed. Furthermore, wasn't it true that John and the rest of his peers were deliberately putting themselves in jeopardy? Hadn't John been offered an opportunity to take a well-deserved night off, and yet he too chose to be where the action was expected. Were their decisions really any different?

Though Holland pointed out that she was being protected by John and the rest of the F.B.I, still John did not buy it. When the time came for him to take his post, he tried to gamely accept her decision, but he'd had a tough time parting company. He was deadly afraid that this was the last time that either would ever see the other. His eyes filled with tears as he held her close one last time and kissed her deeply. Holland returned the kiss, tear for tear, fear for fear, and love for love. As they slowly pulled apart, Holland pulled a "reverse Bogart" on John. With a forced smile and tear filled wink she somewhat playfully borrowed Bogey's famous line from Casablanca as she said;

"Here's lookin' at you kid."

An involuntary smile came to John's lips. Holland followed this with an imploringly simple

"Please protect me John." John nodded solemnly and swore that he'd do his best as he closed the door and went off to duty.

A beer truck proceeded down the opposite side of the street, followed closely by a small car filled with what appeared to be college students. John noticed a college bumper sticker on the car, and a certain boisterous nature of the car's occupants. These two vehicles ground to a halt as traffic in their direction came to a standstill. Suddenly the passenger doors of the car flew open and out popped two young men. John's initial thought was that these two men would race around the car and exchange places in a time honored harmless show he'd seen young people perform numerous times in his life. However, the two men instead raced to the beer truck directly ahead of them and pulled up one of the side panels. They pulled out two small "pony" kegs of beer and ran as best they could back to their car with their ill-gotten booty. As the car's doors closed, the vehicle made a quick U-turn, and hastily took off in the direction from which it had originally come. The driver of the truck poked his head out of his now rolled down window, screaming at the beer thieves to no avail. The truck driver appeared to be of Middle Eastern descent.

John, though he made no attempt to apprehend or pursue the beer crooks in any manner, did take an interest in their getaway. In their haste, they chose to ignore the rules of the road, and ran two red lights. They safely made it through the first with no problem, but they were not so fortunate at the second. The smallish car and the stolen cargo were T-boned by a pickup truck. While the crash was significant, it was by no means of sufficient force to create what took place next. The car blew up in a huge fireball and went airborne, flying over eighty feet through the air directly through some second story windows of a downtown office building. The pickup truck was blown backwards, completing three full somersaults before finally coming to rest on the roof. Both vehicles were charred remnants of their former selves, as were their occupants. The buildings on all four street corners sustained considerable damage and hundreds of windows were shattered in the blast. Thanks to incendiary material that had been implanted within the kegs in addition to the explosive mixture, dozens of small fires had now begun to burn in the vicinity of the crash site. This was obviously no ordinary car crash.

John's attention instantly flashed back in the direction of the beer truck. As he commenced a trot across the street, traffic began to move and the truck began to resume the forward motion northward. It was headed towards the Rock and Roll Hall of Fame and the thousands of fans who were unknowingly in dire peril. John now broke into a sprint in an effort to flag down the beer truck. Fortunately for him, the traffic was such that the truck could not proceed above 10 miles per hour at this point, and John was able to close the gap. As he gained on the truck, the Bartlestein logo caught his attention. In a final burst of speed that surprised even him, John pulled parallel with the truck and as he jumped on the footboard, he grabbed onto the side mirror for support. Peering intently through the driver's window he could make out two faces. Even in the semidarkness, with only the luminescence of building and streetlights, John could see two Middle Eastern men who appeared to be very agitated. The passenger was simply glaring at John, while the driver had a cell phone in hand and was just about to begin a conversation.

John pulled out his F.B.I. badge and as he plastered it against the driver's window, he screamed at the driver to stop the truck. The driver ignored John and began to speak excitedly into his phone. As he did so, the other man made an ominous movement to retrieve something from under his seat. John repeated his command to stop the truck, and he brought his face to the driver's windshield so that the driver could not possibly ignore him or mistake his intentions.

A bright flash erupted from the passenger's side of the truck cab. The windshield exploded in a shower of glass fragments. The sound partially deafened John, and he could feel dampness and pain on the left side of his face and his left ear. Instinctively John jerked his head back and thus the next bullet only caught the very tip of his nose instead of the complete side of his face, which is where the shooter had aimed. John's reflex move had achieved another desirable effect in that now the driver's head shielded his own from further target practice. While still hanging onto the side view mirror with his left hand, John reached into his holster with his right hand. Whipping his service revolver out in practiced fashion, he concocted a desperate plan. John fired a round through the driver's window, and into the driver's temple just as he was bringing a machine pistol up from the truck cab's console. The driver's head slumped onto the steering wheel. As the driver's head went forward, John loosed several rounds into the shocked face and upper torso of the passenger. At such close range, the sight and sounds of John's slugs were almost too gruesome to bear.

There was no time for self-congratulations as the large truck began to pick up speed and to veer alarmingly as the dead driver slid off the steering wheel, falling partially onto the console separating the cab's seats. The truck was now preparing to jump the curb and run straight into the side of an office building. The collision might be sufficient to set off the rest of the truck's fiery cargo. As the huge vehicle jumped the curb, John lunged halfway through the driver's shattered window. Seeing that the driver's right leg was still in close proximity to the brake pedal, John grabbed the man's ankle. With all of his might, John jammed the foot as hard as he could onto the brake pedal and held it there. Even from his awkward position John could sense that the truck was slowing down rapidly. Before the truck could come to a complete controlled halt, it smashed into the side of the building. Fortunately since it was now traveling under five m.p.h., the impact was insufficient to dislodge its cargo's fury. John reached up and turned off the key.

Climbing into the cab, John took stock of the situation and mentally began to prioritize the steps that now should be taken. First and foremost he must ascertain exactly who and what he was dealing with. Reaching into the pockets of the driver, John pulled out a small transmitter. The meaning behind this discovery seemed all too clear. The pockets of the deceased passenger produced a similar transmitter. After first removing the batteries, he smashed the devices to pieces with his gun butt, rendering them inoperable. Now, for the first time, John became aware that a small crowd had gathered and was taking in his every move. John jumped down from the cab and pulled out his F.B.I. badge.

"This is an F.B.I. matter. Everyone please step back."

As the crowd began to do as instructed, a couple of patrol cars screeched to a halt at the scene. Not knowing exactly what the situation was, the officers hastily got out of their vehicles, pulled out their weapons, and took cover behind the doors of their squad cars. With his eyes focused squarely on John, one of the patrolmen began to shout out commands.

"Put the gun down and lay face down on the ground, NOW!

"I'm an F.B.I. agent," responded John.

"I repeat, put the gun down and lay on the ground. Don't make me have to shoot."

A thought flashed through John's head of how ironic it would be to be shot by police after all he had endured at the hands of the bad guys. He slowly, V-E-R-Y S-L-OW-L-Y, put his weapon down so that there could be no mistaking of his intentions. Taking two steps away from the gun, he slowly dropped to his knees and lay face on the ground. Two officers rushed to take control of the supposed prisoner.

"If one of you will reach into my right front pants pocket, you'll find my F.B.I. badge. I'm here with the full knowledge and cooperation of Director Habanek and special agent Madsen."

John's professional demeanor and naming of two high ranking F.B.I. figures known by the patrolmen to be in Cleveland at this moment persuaded the officers to give their collar the benefit of doubt. Doing as instructed, one of the officers pulled out the I.D. badge from John's pocket. This he gave to the other officer who appeared to be the higher-ranking officer on the scene. He glanced briefly at the badge before he began to speak.

"O.K. pal, it seems by your badge that you are one of the feds. What's up with the mess with both you and the truck?"

"I was just getting to that when you pulled up. Unless I miss my guess, this truck is filled with an immense amount of explosives designed to make a very big hole in the Cleveland landscape. There are two Mid Eastern types in the cab. I subdued them after witnessing some college kids making off with pony kegs of beer from the side of the truck. The thieves put the beer in their own vehicle and tried to make their getaway. As they did so, they were broadsided by a pickup truck. The collision produced a tremendous explosion and resulted in the damage and fires that you can see in back of you. It was my conclusion that the explosion was the result of what was contained in the kegs. With that thought, I pursued the beer truck and was able to climb aboard. After identifying myself to the driver, I was shot at twice by his partner. I returned fire and was able to eliminate the shooter and driver while bringing the truck to a halt."

"It sounds to me like you've had a pretty exciting last ten minutes or so. Why don't you step into the squad car and let's see if we can get you patched up a bit while we check out the truck."

"No time for that. I've got to make sure of what we're dealing with, and then I've got to send the info up the chain of command."

With that, John headed back in the direction of the truck. The patrolmen followed his lead. Opening the driver's door, he pointed to the two dead men. They could be left alone for the moment. Next he headed for the side of the panel truck with two of the officers following at his heels. As he slowly lifted the panel door, John became aware of a faint regular sound. Asking to borrow a flashlight hanging off the belt of one of the officers. John directed the light's beam toward the sound's source. He could make out a clock with wires running from it to an ominous looking device. He played the beam off the clock's face and looked at his own watch. With great concern etched upon his face, John took out a two-way radio that each agent had been issued for this mission. Seconds later a voice responded at the other end.

"Base here."

"I need to speak to Assistant director Habanek"

Seconds later a new voice came over the radio.

"Habanek here."

"Sir, this is agent John Kazek. I'm at the corner of E.9th St. and Superior. I've apprehended a Bartlestein beer truck that had two Middle Eastern males in it. I killed them both in self-defense. I have reason to believe that the truck is filled with powerful explosives along the lines of those that destroyed the Buckeye Belle riverboat. The truck has what appears to be a detonator attached to a clock that is counting down as we speak. The explosion seems to be set to go off thirty-two minutes from now at 8:30 P.M. Can we get some people here in that time to defuse it?"

"Agent Kazek what makes you so sure that this truck is filled with explosives?"

"I witnessed some college types steal two small kegs from the truck, and while making their getaway the thieves' vehicle got broadsided. At that point it exploded in an immensely destructive blast. Plus the ticking time bomb and the effort the beer truck's occupants put up to keep me from stopping them. It all adds up sir."

"Sounds like it to me too. We'll get someone up there pronto to defuse the bomb. Clear the area as best you can and, by the way, good work agent Kazek." As assistant director Habanek disconnected from the call, he turned to his communications specialist and began issuing commands.

"Get a broadcast message out to all agents immediately to be on the lookout for Bartlestein beer trucks. If they spot one, have them notify me immediately. Get in touch with the bomb squad units and have them proceed with the utmost urgency to E. 9th and Superior to defuse a device. Contact Burke Lakefront airport and have them get our chopper in the air. Also make sure the C-130 will be ready to deploy if necessary. It looks like we've got a hell of an interesting next half hour ahead of us."

Holland glanced over her shoulder for the umpteenth time in the last five minutes.

"What's the matter Miss Fidgety, got ants in your pants?" inquired Jenny, who was seated to Holland's right in the Pharmacor section of the Rock Hall of Fame temporary bleachers.

"Why don't you stay off her case tonight Jenny, O.K.?" suggested Daniece, who was seated on the other side of Holland. Daniece knew that something was going on, but due to the fact that Holland had not divulged any of what she knew to anyone, Daniece had no inkling of what might be troubling her friend.

The duly chastised Jenny silently consoled herself with a sip of Bartlestein beer from a plastic cup with the brewery's logo on it. The moment was lightened considerably in the next few seconds as a figure strode to a microphone in the center of the distant outdoor stage.

"Ladies and gentlemen, let's give it up for tonight's main event. Cleveland's very own Rock Hall of Fame inductee... AMERICA'S SONG!!!!

A spontaneous earsplitting cheer went up from the assembled audience as a phalanx of lights opened up spotlighting the seven-member group onstage as they went into their first few chords. The cheering was replaced by rhythmic clapping as the multitude recognized the hypnotic beat of the group's opening song "Safe Haven Home." The band, "America's Song", had sprung up in the aftermath of the Vietnam War. They had sought, through their uplifting lyrics and harmonic melodies, to help heal the country's wounds and return America to a kinder and gentler day. Though it ultimately proved to be somewhat of a lost cause to accomplish, many fans throughout the land were both appreciative of the group's efforts and good intentions, as well as the quality of their music. Their induction into the Hall of Fame tonight was truly well deserved and overdue. Due to the band's Cleveland roots, the Rock induction committee had granted a waiver of sorts and allowed a ceremony to be held in Cleveland in addition to another ceremony that would be held next month in New York. Close to nine thousand Clevelanders had turned out this evening to show their appreciation for the opportunity to cheer one of their own.

Holland took yet another look around, nervously scanning the crowd, for what she did not know. Perhaps it would have been better had she not come this evening. And yet that was not an option. It was her duty to be here tonight. While she felt tremendously apprehensive and useless, she knew that she would've felt ten times worse had she stayed away.

A group of older revelers in the Pharmacor section were celebrating with unbridled enthusiasm. Holland recognized several of them as having been recent retirees from the company. That fact was verified by a large banner two of them waved about which read:

"Great Show! Thanks for the tickets, Jonas!"

A pang of remorse swept over Holland as she finished reading the banner. "If they only knew," she thought to herself. Within minutes they, and the entire assembled multitude may be dead, killed by some unknown means delivered by numerous unknown assassins. She tried to comfort herself with the fact that if the murderers were successful, at least it would be the last hurrah of Jonas Trina. That was little solace when compared to the possible elimination of thousands of her fellow countrymen and women. The burden of keeping the secret of what she knew to herself was almost beyond belief. How did people in power do it and still be able to live with themselves? A heavy hand pushed on her shoulder from directly behind her. She turned abruptly with a disconcerting look upon her face to see who was semi-accosting her.

"Hey boss lady, lighten up! It looks like you've seen a ghost or something. Why don't you pound down some of this Bartlestein brew and try to enjoy yourself."

Ernesto, her Puerto Rican friend and co-worker, slid a large plastic cup in her direction to back up his friendly gesture. Holland took the offering and slugged down a large gulp to ease her nerves.

"Thanks Ernesto. I needed that."

"No prob, my pleasure. Hey why don't you leave whatever it is that's bothering you at the office and forget about it, at least for the evening?"

"I'm afraid it's not quite that simple."

"Suit yourself, but you're gonna miss out on a pretty good concert if you don't start paying attention. I'm sure that whatever's buggin' you ain't a matter of life or death."
Holland took another swig and quickly gave the cup back to Ernesto as she turned away to hide the tears that she felt beginning to form.

Two minutes after the initial message was sent out, Joseph Habanek was handed a receiver by one of his communications people.

"Habanek here."

"Sir, this is agent Liddy calling from just west of Cleveland, in a suburb called Lakewood. I'm trailing a Bartlestein beer truck right now. It doesn't appear to be doing anything out of the ordinary at this time."

"Agent Liddy, in what direction are you headed at this moment?"

"We're headed east, towards downtown Cleveland. If we stay on this heading, we'll be getting on the West Shoreway in a few minutes. Once we get on the Shoreway, it's about a ten minute trip to downtown Cleveland."

"Agent Liddy, I need you to see if you can get a look in the cab of that truck and give me a description of the driver."

"Will do."

Sixty seconds later agent Liddy's voice was heard again.

"Sir I have a male of Middle Eastern appearance driving. There is a rider accompanying him who appears to be of the same ethnic makeup."

"Agent Liddy are you familiar with the Greater Cleveland area?"

"Yes sir. Born and raised here."

"Good. Is the area you are in now heavily populated?"

"Very much so."

"How about the area bordering the Shoreway, is that heavily populated also?"

"No sir it is not. Sir, there is a short tunnel coming up in a few minutes if that might be of interest."

"Good, we'll make our play there. Continue to trail the truck for now agent. We'll get back-up units to you immediately. Let us know the second you get on the Shoreway. That's all."

"Yes sir."

Habanek issued commands to get other units to the shore way entrance ASAP.
No sooner had that been accomplished, that another urgent call came in.

"Director Habanek this is agent Hughes calling from just East of Cleveland. I'm on Route 2 approaching Willoughby. I've been following a Bartlestein beer truck for the last couple of miles."

"Agent Hughes, are you headed towards Cleveland at this moment?"

"Yes."

"Agent Hughes, I need you to take a look in the cab of the beer truck and tell me if you can make out what the driver looks like."

Within a minute the answer came back.

"Sir, I've got a Middle Eastern male driving with a rider who appears to be the same."

"Very good Hughes. Can you tell how long it would take you to reach downtown Cleveland at your present speed and heading?"

"Approximately twenty minutes sir."

"And can you tell me if the area abutting the shore way is heavily populated between Willoughby and downtown Cleveland?"

"We've got wall to wall people on both North and South sides of the Shoreway until you are almost to Burke Lakefront airport just short of downtown."

"Thank you agent Hughes. Keep in contact with the truck, and we'll keep you posted."

Habanek's mind was going a mile a minute as he wrestled with what courses of action should be taken. Time was pitifully short, and the decisions were painstakingly crucial. His calls must be right if disaster was to be averted. Joseph looked at a large map of the Cleveland area spread out before him. The relative positions of the three known beer trucks were plotted. It appeared that the enemy had planned a pincer movement with forces converging on the Hall of Fame from three points of the compass. Certainly the main focus was protection of the crowd gathered at the Rock Hall of Fame at all cost. Habanek's next goal was to keep collateral casualties to a minimum. This was going to be very tricky with a foe hell bent on probable suicide attacks with vast explosive power at their fingertips. THINK, JOSEPH, THINK! As the radio crackled to life again, a plan began to formulate itself in Habanek's mind based on the information available to him at this time.

"This is agent Liddy. We are about to get on the west Shoreway heading east towards Cleveland."

"Agent Liddy, stay with the truck. Within seconds a couple of patrol cars should be joining you. When they get there I want all three vehicles to attempt to get the truck to pull over. Take extreme caution. We have every reason to believe that these people are heavily armed and may fire at you. If that happens, drop back immediately and do not, I repeat DO NOT return fire. That message will go out to all units. We cannot take a chance on hitting their vehicle with bullets until the time is right. Understood?"

"Yes sir. Sir, I see the patrol cars approaching at high speed from my rear now."

"Good, both you and they know what to do. Keep us posted."

As that call ended, another was initiated.

"Get the helicopter gunship on the line and have him proceed towards the West Shoreway. Also have the pilot and copilot of the C-130 transport at Burke alerted to be ready to take off ASAP."

Now Habanek turned his attention towards the threat advancing from the east.

"Attention task force agents close to the Rock Hall of Fame. This is Assistant Director Habanek. I need you to commandeer three of the busses and their drivers waiting there. Time is of the essence. Let us know when you have secured the vehicles. Attention SWAT units. I need two SWAT trucks to get to the Eddy Rd. exit off the East Shoreway. Within five minutes, the tasks had been accomplished. Habanek now gave them their assignment.

We need to have the busses proceed immediately down the East Shoreway. When you get to the Eddy Rd. exit, get off and prepare to get back on the Shoreway heading west. We'll let you know when to get back on, and what to do at that point."

"This is Agent Liddy coming down the West Shoreway. We attempted to get the truck to slow down and pull over, and we were greeted by automatic weapons fire from the truck. We're shadowing the truck for now. Our present position puts us about 1 ½ miles from Edgewater Park."

"Very good. We've closed off the West Shoreway, so things should be clear behind you. All units on the West Shoreway may stand down now. We'll take it from here."

The crowd at the Rock Hall of Fame was jamming to the music of "America's Song" when they were jolted by a blast of air from a low flying helicopter streaking through the night sky directly over them on a western heading.

"There goes some yahoo flyboy in a hell of a hurry to do something." said Daniece to Holland.

"Probably just some rich jerk showing off," chipped in Jenny.

Holland apprehensively followed the flight of the black chopper as long as she could before it vanished around the Cleveland Browns stadium on a path down the West Shoreway."

"Habanek to Nightbird."

"Nightbird here."

"Are you in position?"

"I'm about one mile east of the tunnel which you spoke of."

"Good, don't get any closer. We have no clear idea of the blast radius we're about to be dealing with here. Just to be on the safe side, be prepared to high tail it out of there as soon as you let your sparrows fly. Your orders are to fire upon the truck as soon as you see it coming out of the tunnel. Then get the hell out of there."

"Roger."

"The target should be approaching any minute."

Meanwhile the truck's driver was looking for some guidance of his own.

"Tariq, they know who we are, and I assume they will attempt to stop us. Shall we continue?"

"Fools! It doesn't matter if they know or do not know. You are only a couple minutes from your target. They dare not and cannot stop you now. Soon you will claim a glorious victory for the cause and you will have earned your way into eternal Paradise."

"It shall be done as you say."

"See how our forces are being compromised," said Nishil.

"You shall have proof of our divine victory my friend, within minutes when the blast lights up the sky," countered Tariq Al-Salem.

"However we will not achieve the full effect if only one truck detonates instead of combining the effects of all three simultaneously as we had planned."

"That is true, but it will still make for a very effective kill. We probably had more firepower than we needed anyway. Also, do not forget that we have unit three rolling in from the east. Perhaps it may still prove possible to get two of the three trucks to release their fury onsite. Unfortunately, after the brief communication with unit one before they went off the air, we must conclude that they are lost for good."

"Let us hope for the best."

"This is agent Hughes on the East Shoreway. We have just passed the E. 140th St. exit, and should soon be coming up on the Eddy Rd. exit."

"Thank you agent Hughes. Busses, get back on the Shoreway now, heading west. When you get on, I want you to spread across the width of the Shoreway, three abreast so that the beer truck which will be approaching from your rear cannot get by you. Then I want you to slow down to about twenty miles per hour so that the beer truck will be right behind you and moving slowly. We'll let you know what to do after that. Good luck men."

As soon as that call ended, Habanek made his next call to Burke Lakefront Airport, detailing their part of the plan. It centered on the capabilities of a C-130 Hercules transport plane which was on standby there.

"Is Hercules ready to go?

"As ready as he'll ever be."

"Good. We're only going to have a few precious moments to pull this off, so we've got to be ready to take off at a moment's notice."

"You deliver the package sir, and we'll get it airborne for you."

The beer truck approaching from the west was now within sight of the short overpass

"The pursuit has dropped back. They have stopped attempting to get us to pull over. It won't be long now. We are entering a short tunnel. Soon after that, the target will be in sight. A glorious victory will soon be ours. I can see the end of the tunnel just ahead. We are now… WHAT IS THAT!!! AIEEEE!!!!"

A tremendous sound resounded through Tariq Al-Salem's receiver, forcing him to fling it across the cabin of the boat. Tariq and Nishil simultaneously grabbed binoculars and rushed on deck to see firsthand what was happening onshore. They were met with an unreal spectacle taking shape in front of them as the night was transformed into day. A brilliant orange/yellow/red/and white dumbbell shaped fireball was expanding magnificently just to the west of downtown Cleveland. A tremendous boom reached the deck of the cabin cruiser eleven seconds after the initial explosion. Even at this range, the sound was jolting. The blast continued to expand, and both Tariq and Nishil continued to view the effects through their binoculars. Secondary fires were already beginning to dot the darkness as the incendiary mixture took hold on flammable surfaces far from the blast site.

Thirty seconds after the initial explosion the fireball began to subside. What it left in its wake was complete and utter devastation. A thousand yards of the road way had been transformed into viscous bubbling tar. The tunnel had been split upright as if a volcano had erupted underneath it. The trees lining the Shoreway had been set ablaze as they were being blown over. Hundreds of them lay burning furiously in the flaming grass. The metal fence that ran along the perimeter of the trees was torn and twisted. Another item that was conspicuous by its absence was the people. There were no people near where the blast had occurred.

Habanek's choice of location to initiate the blast had been fortuitous. Also having blocked off both ends of the Shoreway from the approaching truck had worked tremendously to keep the casualties down. The only people killed in the blast other than the terrorists themselves were two carloads of teenagers who had swerved around a police blockade laughing riotously as they raised their middle fingers to the furiously waving cops. Many unfortunates who were at Edgewater Park were seriously burned, but all would pull through.

The force of the blast had rocked the nearby neighborhood. Hundreds of residents came flying out their front doors to see what had caused the house-shaking explosion. They were met with an unbelievable sight! Incendiary material raining down from the explosion had set porches and roofs ablaze throughout the area. Shop owners grabbed garden hoses to attempt to battle the fires in order to preserve their livelihoods. Cries of alarm were heard everywhere.

It didn't take long for the terrorists to realize that something had gone wrong. The explosion had occurred much too far away from the Hall of Fame to have had any effect upon the people gathered there, except perhaps for some shattered eardrums. While the blast was certainly stupendous, the damage appeared to be minimal. Nishil could make out numerous houses and light industrial types of buildings that were ablaze, and there were quite a few vessels at the Edgewater Yacht Club that were burning furiously. However, it seemed from what they could see, the bulk of the blast's fury had been channeled up and down the virtually deserted highway. This was due in part to the explosion probably having taken place within the tunnel itself, which would've produced a funnel type effect to the blast's power. The roiling elongated flaming dumbbell had almost stopped expanding. Nishil subconsciously estimated that it encompassed almost a mile from one end to the other.

Tariq shifted his sight from the blast towards the downtown area, and as he did so, he was able to make out a fleeing helicopter shape silhouetted against one of the office buildings. That supplied the answer to the mystery behind the premature explosion. He raced back into the cabin and picked up the radio transmitter.

"Unit three. Come in unit three.

"This is unit three."
"Unit two has just been destroyed by a helicopter. Be on the watch for helicopters, and try to stay close to other vehicles for protection if you spot one. Also, figure that you have probably been discovered already. You are our last hope, unit three. We are depending on you to carry out your mission to the best of your abilities regardless of the consequences to your personal safety. Is that understood?"

"Understood."

"Very good. May Allah be with you."

"We will leave our radio transmitting so that you may hear exactly what happens from here on."

The temporary stands had stopped shaking at the Rock Hall of Fame. The crowd was virtually silent, as both they and the band had been awed into submission by the sight and sound of the blast that had occurred about 1 1/2 miles away. The tremendous din of the explosion had now passed, but the ringing in the ears persisted, as did the confusion over exactly what had just happened. A bright orange red glow lit up the western sky. Though the Cleveland Browns stadium and some other large buildings obscured the scene, it was not hard to tell that large fires were burning near the West Shoreway. These had to have been caused by the explosion that rocked the Hall of Fame. Ernesto broke the bewildered silence amongst the Pharmacor contingent.

"Wow man, these "America's Song" dudes sure know how to put on a blow out party."

"I'm sure that had nothing to do with the show my friend," observed Daniece.

"What do think happened Holland?"

"Maybe a gas tanker-truck collision or a chemical storage tank explosion. I'm sure that we don't have to concern ourselves with it," she lied.

"Listening to all those sirens, it sounds like every fire truck from here to Ashtabula is coming to fight the fires," contributed Jenny. "From the looks of that glow, it must be one hell of a blaze. Can you imagine if that had happened right here at the Hall of Fame? We'd all be crispy critters now."

Holland visibly cringed as Jenny had just verbalized the exact thoughts that had been running through her head. She suddenly had a terrible fear for John's safety. If he was anywhere near that blast, he wouldn't have had a prayer of surviving. She began to shake noticeably. Ernesto wrapped his big arms around her to help warm away what he thought was a case of the chills.

"Come to think of it, it is getting a bit cool here. Maybe I'll grab some marshmallows and see if I can get myself a seat a little closer to the fire."

His attempt at humor fell short, though Holland did appreciate the warmth of his arms that were having a calming effect on the case of nerves that had temporarily overcome her. As her shaking began to subside, a voice came over the loud speaker. It was the lead singer of the band.

"We hope you all appreciated the fireworks show which we just staged for you fine people. Next time we'll have the guys doing the fireworks try to space the explosions a little farther apart instead of just one big boom. What say we get back to the music and do what we came here for? Would anyone out there like to hear "Call of the Heartland?" A resounding cheer went up from the crowd as the bass guitarist played the first few notes from the group's 1976 bestseller. Soon the band had everyone in the crowd singing and swaying along with them once again. All except Holland Brittainy Matthews.

The explosive laden beer truck was now bearing down on the slow moving busses as it passed the Eddy Rd. exit.

"Tariq, we have not detected any helicopters as of yet, however we have three slow moving busses blocking our path just ahead."

"How fast are they going?" asked Tariq

"They are slowing us down to 20 miles per hour."

Tariq glanced at his watch that read 8:15. "You are within four miles of your target, and you still have fifteen minutes before the set time unless you choose to move up the timetable from your own transmitter. You can just follow behind the busses. They will also provide you with cover from any helicopters."

"The busses are slowing down even more. We are now only going 10 miles per hour. At this rate we will not arrive at the target in time."

Nishil broke in "It's a trap! Get around them any way you can, and get to the target quickly before they can spring the rest of their trap!"

The truck driver swung his vehicle to the left shoulder of the road and began to speed up. This move was countered by the busses as all three veered in unison to keep the truck from passing on the shoulder. Next the truck swerved across the highway and attempted to get by on the right. Once again, the attempt was stymied by the quick reactions of the bus drivers.

"To hell with the infidels, we'll blast our way through." With that, both terrorists pulled out their automatic weapons and began to pepper the busses ahead with a withering fire. The staccato sounds of the weapons and the noise from the shattering windows and punctured metal were plainly audible over the radio as Tariq and Nishil took in the battle. The windshields of all three busses disintegrated under the barrage, and the middle bus driver took a round to the shoulder. Had it not been for the quick reaction of the task force agent riding along who took the wheel, the truck would have been able to break through. Even though the agents on board each bus were armed, they could not fire back for fear of setting off the truck's contents. The busses could only withstand this punishment a few seconds longer before they would be blown away.

The efforts of the terrorists to blow through the busses had distracted them from noticing the black vans approaching from behind. The lead step van pulled even with the beer truck, whose attention was devoted to the busses in front of them. The passenger door of the step van slid open a crack, and the muzzle of a rifle poked through. The terrorist driver sensed something happening to his left and glanced over, just in time to see the initial muzzle flash which would spell his own doom. The first of six rounds expended from the marksman's weapon caught him flush in the forehead, and took off a large portion of his scalp. Round two entered and exited the center of his mouth. Round three missed the mark, shattering the truck's windshield. Round four passed just over the driver's now slumping head, and entered the left cheek of the truck's terrorist passenger. Round five struck slightly higher, completely obliterating the side of the man's head. Round six tore out the man's windpipe, depositing much of it through the window onto the road surface.

"This is unit one. The beer truck has been compromised. Busses, you are clear to commence braking operations."

With that the bus drivers lifted their heads for the first time since the battle had begun and took stock of the truck's position. Although the firefight had indeed been furious, it had taken place at slow motion, with none of the combatants ever hitting 20 miles per hour. Now even though both terrorists were dead and their vehicle was operating on its own, it was still centered on the roadway, moving relatively slowly. The middle bus was directly in front of the beer truck. The F.B.I. agent now manning the wheel began to apply the brakes gently allowing the truck to ease toward him. The truck was slowly picking up speed as there was no longer anyone alive capable of putting on the brakes in the vehicle. The truck came on relentlessly and slammed into the back of the crawling bus. There was a severe crunch as metal ground into metal. The bus-driving agent now applied full brakes in an effort to bring both vehicles to a complete stop. The weight and momentum of the truck was too much for the bus to overcome as the tangled tandem inexorably screeched onward. Another of the bus drivers gunned his bus to take the lead. As he pulled in front of the agent's bus, he applied his brakes as both bus and truck continued slowly charging forward. The three vehicles now slammed together. As they did so, the lead bus driver applied his brakes fully to add to the stopping power of the other bus. Between them they were able to bring the slow moving mass of metal to a halt.

Now the van pulled up alongside and several team members jumped out. They raced to the beer truck and after a quick check for booby traps, threw up the side of the truck's panel doors. As the rest of the team examined the truck's content's, the team leader grabbed a radio.

"This is team one to base. We have the East Shoreway beer truck in our possession. What are your orders?"

A big cheer went up from those at the base upon hearing the news.

"This is Assistant Director Habanek. Great work men. Did you examine the truck's cargo and find a timing device?"

"Yes we did. It is set for 8:30."

"Are any of the men there trained in disarming bombs?"
A quick check revealed a negative response. Joseph Habanek's watch showed the time now as 8:21.

"Listen up team, here's what we are going to do. You should be only a mile or so away from Burke Lakefront airport. Are you familiar with it?"

"Yes sir."

"I want you to take that truck there as quickly as you can. We may not have time for you to get off an exit and work your way around to enter the airport runway properly. Unless there is something that absolutely positively prevents you from doing so, I want you to crash through the airport fence and drive to the back of the big C-130 transport plane that will be awaiting your arrival. Drive up the plane's ramp into the underbelly of the plane that will then lift off immediately. Good luck men. We have less than nine minutes, so go quickly. May God go with you."

The team members unceremoniously dumped the dead terrorists on the side of the road, and the two senior men present were chosen to man the truck on its short but perilous mission. They jumped in the truck and quickly wheeled it around the busses, heading west towards the airport. The airport tower was visible just up ahead on their right. The driver examined the side of the road. While they would have to negotiate a sizeable curb, there was no creek, or concrete wall, or any other major obstacle that would keep them from plowing through the fence. As they sped towards the airport, the waiting C-130 came into sight perched at the far end of the runway. Having reached the start of the airport fence, the driver strained his eyes looking for a particularly flat area of the terrain ahead with which to exit the shore way and do his "fence busting." He wanted to jar the content's of the truck as little as possible, not knowing exactly how much the cargo could take before it turned them into a gigantic Roman candle. One hundred feet ahead the ground looked dead level. With a quickly muttered prayer, the driver swung the truck's wheel hard to the right and jumped the curb. With a jarring thud, the truck hit the ground off the pavement and careened towards the fence directly ahead of them. There was a tremendous crash as the charging Bartlestein beast blew through the reinforced ten foot high metal fence much as an enraged bull might do to its split rail cousin.

The time was now 8:25. The C-130 was another 600 yards up ahead. This was going to be damn close. The truck got onto a runway that led towards where the C-130 was preparing to get airborne. As the truck approached, the giant dark shape of the transport started to move. It began to pick up speed slowly as it continued to lumber down its own runway gaining needed momentum to accomplish liftoff within the time constraints which had now been forced upon the winged warrior.

The truck reached the runway bearing the slow moving transport, and he executed a hard right turn onto the intersecting concrete ribbon. The driver gunned the engine for all it was worth, and began to close on the C-130 from the rear. The plane's speed had now reached 30 miles per hour and it was increasing. The truck driver swore at the plane's pilot under his breath. "Why is the son-of-a-bitch making this so damn impossible for me to catch him and get on board? The greenish glow from his digital watch flashing the time of 8:26 supplied the answer. He glanced at his speedometer. He was doing 65 m.p.h. and had nearly caught up with the transport that was now approaching 50. The trucks lead tires hit the ramp hard as he shot up the bouncing metallic incline doing over 70 miles per hour. Two men in the cavernous under belly of the plane jumped aside as the truck barreled over the top of the ramp and into the plane's midsection. Responding to furious yells and hand signals, the truck driver braked hard to a halt with the rear of the truck just beyond the top of the ramp.

The plane's engines were screaming as they strained with all of their might to reach liftoff velocity. The sound of the planes tires clacking off the concrete of the runway added to the din already reverberating around the cavernous interior. Slowly, almost imperceptibly the Hercules began to leave the ground and rise into the sky. At the most they had ninety seconds before the truck would have to be dropped. The pilot would've liked to have the luxury of going straight and dropping his cargo. Unfortunately there was a large ore carrier plying the cold dark waters of Lake Erie up ahead. Executing a left turn as rapidly as the giant bird allowed, the pilot scanned the waters for a secluded area as devoid of nautical traffic as he could find. He could hear a ticking clock blaring in his mind as he sought to get as far away from the shoreline as possible, while not dropping the immensely destructive cargo on the deck of some unsuspecting boat or ship. A rather large dark area of the water appeared ahead which he chose as a last resort. He would've liked to reconnoiter the area before dumping tons of explosive material, but there was no longer any time.

The pilot barked the command "NOW" throughout the intercom system. The truck shot backwards toward the ramp. At the last possible second, the driver jumped clear, and the Bartlestein beer truck plunged for the black water one thousand feet below. As the truck plummeted to its watery landing, the pilot noticed that he could just barely make out a cabin cruiser sitting dead in the water with no running lights whatsoever. The truck would land within 100 yards from them. He felt a pang of remorse for the boat's occupants knowing that he had just effectively executed them. "The damn idiots shoulda had their lights on," he thought to himself as he attempted to will the plane to speed up and put as much airspace as possible between them and the truck in these next sixty seven seconds.

Tariq Al Salem and Nishil Najir had come on deck not knowing exactly how the last fifteen minutes had ended. A bullet fragment from one of the rounds had damaged the beer truck's radio, so they had been left incommunicado ever since. All that remained was a slim hope that somehow their men had been able to overcome their attackers and proceed on to the target. As 8:30 drew near, they chose to go above and gaze at the Hall of Fame in the distance, praying for a magnificent grand finale to fulfill their mission. As they clambered on deck, they were somewhat taken aback by an immense plane flying directly towards them with its underside cargo bay door open. Silhouetted against the backdrop of the plane's interior lights, they could make out the fact that the plane had dropped something large that was going to hit the water not far from where they were now floating. Nishil grabbed a night scope and peered intently at the falling object. To his horror just before the object hit the water, he could make out the Bartlestein beer logo on the body. His last words on earth was the plea; "Allah be merciful."

"America's Song" liked to wrap up their concerts with their own rendition of "America the Beautiful." As they were belting out the final words of the last stanza "from sea to shining sea", an intense light lit up the water offshore directly beyond the stage upon which the band was playing. The crowd's applause tripled to show the appreciation for the dramatic climax to the band's concert. The audience misinterpreted the explosion as having been staged for their benefit in order to bring the curtain down on the performance in the same manner that a final rapid firing off of scores of rockets often signals the close of fireworks festivities. As the band continued to bow and wave in acceptance of the kudos being lauded upon them, some in the crowd began to grow apprehensive. While the initial effect of the "lightshow" was dramatically surprising, the immense growth of the blast coupled with the fact that it didn't seem to be abating began to alarm many concertgoers. As the blast furnace wave of fire of the angry explosion drew shoreward, and the tremendous roar from the blast swept over the Hall of Fame, a small panic began to set in amongst the more squeamish in the audience. Fortunately, before the panic could turn into a wholesale stampede, the explosion began to subside, having covered over a third of the distance from its inception point to the shore. As the fireball died out, the crowd started to head for their cars.

"Great concert, but I believe they went a little overboard with the little nuclear bomb blast at the end, don't you think?" mumbled Jenny as the group started to make their way home.

"I liked it," chimed Ernesto. "I think that it was meant to tie in with the band's Vietnam War background.

"You know, I wonder if the other explosion was also meant to be let off in the lake, and something happened to explode it prematurely," questioned Daniece.

Holland merely shrugged her shoulders, and looking up to the sky, silently offered her thanks to all who'd had a hand in staving off the horrendous tragedy that she alone amongst the audience knew had just been averted.

Though the hundreds of agents continued to keep a watchful eye over the city for the next several hours, the general feeling among the authorities was that the threat had been quelled. Thirty minutes after the concert ended, The President's personal priority phone rang in the Oval office where he'd been keeping a vigil.

"Mr. President, this is Harold Varholich. I've just received news from our men in Cleveland. Though there were some explosions, and we didn't get off un-bloodied, the casualties appear to have been exceedingly minimal."

"Do you have any specifics at this time Harold?"

"Reports are that a car explosion took place in downtown Cleveland, apparently killing less than ten people and damaging some office buildings. An immense blast occurred on what is known locally as the West Shoreway, a highway leading into downtown Cleveland. The exact death toll and damage estimates are inconclusive at this time. Fortunately, the Shoreway had been shut down by our people. To keep casualties to a minimum, it was necessary to have one of our helicopters blow up one of the trucks on a lightly populated section of highway.

Their plan apparently was to drive three explosive laden beer trucks from different directions, all to converge on the Rock and Roll Hall of Fame simultaneously. Had they accomplished their task, there would've been nothing standing for perhaps a mile radius of the blast site. Fortunately, their forces were never allowed to meet, and we were able to pick them off one at a time. Details are still coming in as to how we uncovered their modus operandi. My understanding is that the helicopter blew up one of the trucks as a last resort a little over a mile from the Rock and Roll Hall of Fame. Another truck was effectively dumped into Lake Erie, where it exploded dramatically but harmlessly. The third truck's cargo was overcome by one of our agents in downtown Cleveland. Its cargo was quickly defused. I should mention also that the Terminal Tower and Rapid Transit threats were eliminated with no fatalities amongst our forces. All-in-all, I'd say our people put up one hell of a showing."

"This is wonderful news. The city of Cleveland, and indeed this great nation of ours, owe your people a tremendous amount of thanks. And of course let's not forget to thank God Almighty for divine intercession on our behalf. In your estimation, has this terrorist organization been eliminated?"

"It may be a bit premature to answer that question definitively Mr. President, but all indications show that if we haven't totally eliminated them, we've certainly hurt them badly. By our count we know of fifteen terrorists confirmed dead, and the one we have in custody, the C.E.O., was "persuaded" to divulge information concerning the masterminds of the operation who were supposedly in a boat offshore. Their exact whereabouts as of right now are unconfirmed. We'll keep you posted on new developments as we learn of them."

"Once again Harold, we offer our thanks to you and your people for bringing this affair to, what appears to be, a successful conclusion."

"I'll express your appreciation to the troops sir. Mr. President, with all due respect, there are a few other people that should be thanked, without whose guts and persistence this threat would never have become known until it was too late. It's been made aware to me throughout the day that a huge part was played by a member of the Pharmacor company, one Holland Matthews, and her boyfriend John Kazek, who happens to be one of our F.B.I. agents in Cleveland. They were responsible for uncovering the plot and alerting the authorities. It is my understanding that surprisingly, it was Holland, not John, who was primarily responsible for discovering the plot and convincing local enforcement agents of the urgency of the situation. She seems to have been the one to get the ball rolling, and it appears that she had to be damn persistent in order to get people to believe her. I think that something special should be done to show her our thanks."

"Thank you for pointing that out to me Harold. I heartily concur that we should not ignore the contributions made by this young lady. I'll take the matter under advisement with my staff and see if we can't come up with some special way to thank Miss Matthews."

Holland had parked her car at the distant F.B.I. building. She'd deliberately walked the twenty blocks or so to the Rock and Roll Hall of Fame in order to burn off some anxiety. The trek back loomed as more daunting, and she was grateful when Daniece offered to drive her back to her car. As Holland thanked Daniece for the ride and opened the door to get out, Daniece spoke;

"Holly-Brit, there's something you weren't telling us tonight, wasn't there?"

"Why would you say that?"

"You were distracted all night long. You were hardly yourself. What is it Holland? You can tell me."

"I wish I could tell you Daniece, but I just wasn't feeling myself. Maybe I'm still trying to get over the jitters from our close call last night at Jonas' dinner party."

"That was something wasn't it? But we got him didn't we! I hope that son-of-a-bitch rots in some federal prison the rest of his life for what he tried to do to all of us at the party. I thought of staying home from the concert tonight, but I decided that it might do me good to go and not dwell on what might have happened last night."

"Yeah, I know what you mean."

"Well, take care hon and I'll see you at work Monday, minus one big, dangerous, pain-in-the-ass C.E.O."

"I'll second that."

As Daniece pulled away, Holland made her way into the semi darkness and entered the F.B.I. parking garage. She longed to call John, but she knew that she didn't dare. There was a very real possibility that he was still on assignment, tracking more terrorists. He of course would have his cell phone turned off. Another possibility, which Holland dare not think about, was that he had been caught in one of the explosions she'd heard tonight. She prayed as she walked that John was still safe. She didn't know what she'd do if she ever lost him.

Holland made it to her red Taurus and put the key into the lock. As she opened the door, she turned to look around out of force of habit in keeping aware of her surroundings. "Kind of silly in an F.B.I. parking garage," she thought to herself. However, she suddenly didn't think so as a tall figure emerged from the shadow of a nearby pillar and slowly began to walk in her direction. Panicked by the stranger's surprise appearance, Holland hurried to open the car's door when she heard a familiar voice call out, "Here's lookin' at you kid."

As panic gave way to recognition, Holland turned to face the approaching figure. The person now entered the dim light and Holland could make out some bandages on his face.
"Something tells me this could be the renewal of a beautiful relationship, Holly-Brit Matthews," said the nicest voice she could imagine. Holland left her keys hanging in the door and ran the twenty feet to be swept up into the strong arms of John as he sauntered towards her.

"John, you're alive my precious, you're alive! But you're hurt. What happened darling?"

"One of the terrorists decided to use his weapon to nibble me apart piece by piece. Unfortunately for him, I decided to take big bites out of him with my service pistol. Don't worry sweetie, he didn't rearrange too much of my mug, so in a few weeks I should be back to my same old gruesome self."

"Try gorgeous self babe, it fits better. John, do you think we're safe now?"

"The scuttlebutt is that we've eliminated all three of their primary threats. Their plan appears to have been to have three beer trucks explode at the Rock and Roll Hall of Fame in unison. Fortunately, we learned of their plan in a roundabout way, and we were able to track them down and stop them before they could reach the Hall. The big explosion on the West Shoreway was caused by a helicopter firing rockets to detonate one of the trucks. That spot was chosen as a last resort because it was relatively secluded compared to anywhere else on the west side.

Regardless of whether we're totally safe or not, I know that we're all a hell of a lot safer than we would have been if a very bright, brave, and determined lady I know hadn't followed through on her instincts. I apologize again for having doubted you Holland. Of course I should've known better than to doubt the brains of someone who was smart enough to pick me as their boyfriend."

"I see that the terrorist's bullets didn't quite accomplish a necessary task," said Holland through a wide happy grin. "Let's get you home where I can nurse you back to health and perhaps remove some of the excess ham that your previous statement indicates that you still have hanging around, Mr. Chauvinist Piggie."

CHAPTER 33

Eventually the bloodhounds in the press corps learned of the decision-making process that resulted in stopping the terrorists plot. The president's political opponent's had a field day berating his use of ten thousand Clevelanders as bait to draw out the terrorists. Furthermore, the A.C.L.U. went ballistic when Jonas Trina's high priced attorney screamed in outrage that his client had been subjected to sodium pentothal without any regard to proper legal procedure. They also had serious doubts that the terrorists in the Terminal Tower battle had been given a chance to surrender prior to being attacked. The cry for the President's resignation resounded throughout the land. Demands for articles of impeachment to be initiated against him were bandied about in the halls of Congress.

To defuse the situation and to explain fully his actions on the recent threat, President Ambrose did as his predecessors had so often done when faced with difficult national concerns. He took his cause directly to the people. On Wednesday evening, the day before Thanksgiving, President Ambrose went on national television to plead his case to the entire country. Seated in a rocking chair in front of a lit fireplace with a sweater tied around his shoulders, and his pet beagle Foster at his feet, the President epitomized the very essence of hearth and home. That theme would be replayed millions of times across America tomorrow on Thanksgiving Day. The President began his talk with a simple, oft spoken, yet time-tested opening line.

"My fellow Americans. In the past week we have seen great challenges to this experiment in freedom that we call "The United States of America." Foreign nationals endeavored to wreak tremendous havoc, destruction, and loss of life upon one of our key Mid-western cities, that being Cleveland, Ohio. Regrettably, it appears as though their cause may have been furthered with the help of one of this country's corporate giants. That matter will be resolved in a court of law. What is known is the following: On the evening of Sunday November 17th, between seventeen and twenty trained Middle Eastern terrorists attempted to carry out a coordinated attack upon Cleveland. Their plan was to blow up a passenger train under the Terminal Tower. When emergency personnel arrived in force to help with rescue operations, the terrorists planned to detonate massive explosions within vans situated under the Terminal Tower building's foundation to effectively topple the building onto both rescuers, the train's injured and dying, and bystanders alike. It appears that as horrific a scenario as this would be, it was merely a prelude to what they had planned as their prime target. While these terrible events were being carried out, three beer trucks loaded not with beer, but with explosive and incendiary material, would make their way to the Rock and Roll Hall of Fame. When they arrived, they were to simultaneously detonate their cargoes. My advisers tell me that the resultant blast would have killed every living creature within an approximate one-mile radius. There were almost ten thousand spectators attending an induction ceremony at The Hall of Fame at this time. I mention all of this to show you the type of hate-filled human debris we are dealing with here.

Our national security advisers first learned of this plot at 4:00 A.M.on the morning preceding the attack. They immediately began marshalling their forces to intercept the terrorists if that was the strategy to be employed. Two schools of thought were debated during the early morning hours that day within the National Security Council. We could notify Cleveland of the imminent threats and shut down the city and/or the specific threat sites. This would have been relatively easy and safe to accomplish. Unfortunately, this would have had the undesirable effect of driving the terrorists underground. They would have resurfaced somewhere else to strike, almost certainly with no advance warning, upon a defenseless populace to spew their venom and death.

It can be argued that had we driven these vermin underground, it would've given us more time to find out who they were. Perhaps we might get a lead that would result in our apprehending them without taking such a huge risk. However, the possibilities of us catching them before they could strike again were viewed as extremely remote. These were the same terrorists who blew up the Buckeye Belle riverboat in Cincinnati in late September. Seven weeks of intensive investigative analysis of that crime had resulted in virtually no clues, so it was probable that their next target would be struck without warning.

Because we had specific information on the sites and timetable of the Cleveland attacks, it was deemed that our best chance of catching and stopping these cowards was here and now in Cleveland. While we realized that this meant exposing thousands to a certain degree of risk, we sought to minimize the element of risk from the equation as best we could. This was accomplished through the use of hundreds of highly trained and skilled F.B.I. and elite counter terrorist forces being flown into Cleveland en masse to both protect the populace, and eliminate the threat. Additionally, key air units were activated to help in the city's defense. Further measures were taken within the local police departments to ensure that we would provide overwhelming cover and surveillance.

As you all know by now, the strategy was successful in that the train, Terminal Tower, and Rock Hall were unscathed. Furthermore, this highly trained batch of terrorists, representing the best that our adversaries had to offer, has been both defeated and eliminated, thereby making our streets that much safer for the foreseeable future.

The decision to utilize this particular strategy did not come easily, nor was the responsibility for the results taken lightly. This was without a doubt the hardest decision that I have ever in my life been forced to make. I pray that neither myself, nor my successors, will ever be forced to make such a choice again. However, I feel that the decision that was made was the correct one, and I would do it again and again if faced with the same alternatives.

I'd like to speak now concerning the possible abrogation of rights afforded to the American currently being held in custody for his connection to this matter. It is my understanding that the American Civil Liberties Union has filed a lawsuit on behalf of the accused. They claim that the person in custody was injected with sodium pentothal in order to obtain information and/or a confession. This supposedly was done as he was being held prisoner by the F.B.I. Allow me to say this about that. I did not authorize the use of truth serum, nor was it made known to me that a subject was under arrest and the use of sodium pentothal to gain information was being considered. I was not present, and have no direct knowledge of exactly what did or did not take place in regards to the prisoner's rights in this matter. That being said, I would like to state my views of such conduct for the record here and now.

If a representative of any law enforcement agency in this country is ever in the future confronted with the same circumstances that we had this past week, I would hope that they would utilize all methodologies at their disposal to obtain critical, indeed life saving information. If in fact that was how we first learned of the terrorist plot, then I believe that the people responsible for obtaining that information should be decorated with the highest award this country has to offer. I realize that this viewpoint and candor rankles many of you out there watching this at the moment. I'm afraid that cannot be helped. I would like to think that if a terrorist was about to explode a nuclear bomb in downtown New York City and we had personnel trying to obtain information on how to keep the infernal thing from going off, they would not waste a hundredth of a second worrying about whether the methods they were using to extract information were acceptable to one and all or not. And I, in my position as President, would do everything in my power to protect such people from ever having to defend such a righteous use of tactics.

The same thought process applies as to whether or not the terrorists under the Terminal Tower were given a chance to surrender. Our law enforcement people had indisputable evidence of what the terrorist's plans for the destruction of the Tower would involve. Each terrorist would have a transmitter in their pocket that could detonate the tremendous explosive power in the vans with one simple push of a button. A transmitter was indeed found on each of the terrorist's bodies after the battle ended. There was no opportunity to give those men any warning with the certainty that they would explode the vans immediately if their mission was threatened in any way. Thank God that most of us in this country, I believe, recognize this fact.

Also be thankful that we had good people on the scene that had the wisdom and the resolve to bring this mission to a successful conclusion. They, without a doubt saved the Terminal Tower from crashing down, and saved untold hundreds if not thousands of lives in the process. Perhaps those who feel differently would like to visit each of the agent's families who were at the scene and explain to them how a terrorist's rights are much more important than the life of their family member who is trying to do their sworn duty of protecting this country.

This is not to say that we should let loose the constitutional safeguards and turn this country into a police state with authorities conducting pistol whippings on every corner. However I do believe that there are certain circumstances whereby the good of all outweighs the arguable rights of terrorists. This past week in Cleveland, Ohio, I believe that we had such circumstances. If America finds my views on this subject abhorrent, or if you feel that I made the wrong decision in how I chose to defend this country last Sunday, I suggest that you contact your congressman and let them know your feelings.

Ladies and gentlemen I now bid you a good, safe, and blessed evening. May you and your loved ones enjoy a joyous and peaceful holiday! Good night."

Immediately the pundits representing the entire political spectrum began dissecting the president's talk on all forums of the national media. His supporters praised his straightforward honesty and courage. They also stressed the fact that the threat had indeed been eliminated with a relatively small death toll, considering the enormity of the risk. His detractors attempted to beat home the message that America had a foolhardy person running the show. A person willing to take unnecessary gambles with the lives of his countrymen and women in order to grandstand. In the process they painted him as one who is ready, willing, and able to set aside constitutional protections at the proverbial "drop of a hat" if he alone deems it desirable.

As both sides wrangled vehemently back and forth, the American populace went to work. The vast majority didn't need to be spun a version of what they had just heard. They'd seen the president's talk with their own eyes. They'd observed the concern etched upon the man's face. They'd witnessed how deeply President Lawrence Ambrose took his responsibilities. And they'd been imbued with the overwhelming sense of honesty the man exuded, which was one of the key attributes responsible for elevating him to the loftiest position in the land in the first place.

Minutes after the president's speech had ended, phone lines across America were overloaded as millions of "his fellow Americans" sought to make their views known. Phones in congressional offices went unanswered as minimal evening staffs of aides attempted unsuccessfully to keep up with the onslaught of thousands of calls. In Washington D.C., faxes by the score inundated representatives with incoming messages. Hundreds of e-mails each second crisscrossed the electronic cyberspace of the country's geographic borders. In time, thousands of additional e-mails from outside the country would be sent from all points of the globe, responding to the president's actions and views.

While there were some dissenters, the messages that came in supported the president by a 20 to 1 margin. Typical of the president's supporter's responses was this e-mail sent to one of his most vocal opponents by one of their constituents.

Dear Congressman,

This evening our family watched the president discuss his reasons for the actions that he took in order to defend Cleveland, and in fact the rest of the country at the same time. We have spent the last ninety minutes discussing the speech and whether he was right or wrong. We acknowledge the fact that a great risk was taken and that thousands of lives were put in jeopardy. However, there were even greater risks in forcing the terrorists underground. Certainly if hundreds of trained F.B.I. agents who knew of the plot in advance had difficulty corralling the terrorists, what chance would a hand full of local cops at some high school football game across America have? What about a shopping mall, or other so-called soft target?

These terrorists, through the simple facts that they were already here, well trained and well armed, were not going to be prevented from killing people and breaking things. That was a foregone conclusion. The president wanted to dictate the time and place where the confrontation would take place once the opportunity was presented. In this way only could overwhelming force be brought to bear on the terrorists in order to foil their plans We are in agreement with his decisions. We would take an exceedingly dim view of anyone in office that would use power and influence to attempt to have this great man removed from office, and we would vote accordingly.

Sincerely,

Vincente Mediate and family

P.S. There are six registered voters in my immediate family. Next week I'm going to be attending a family reunion of approximately two hundred fifty Mediates most of whom are over eighteen. I bowl in a league of eighty voters and I'm a member of the local Rotary and Lions club. I'm also quite active on the internet as you can see. I can guarantee that I will make this matter a point of discussion at each and every opportunity. Pick your battles carefully Congressman.

With the tremendous support received across the country following his speech, there was little the president's opponents could do except attempt to retreat and save face as best they could. Impeachment talk disappeared overnight, and though editorials and talk shows would continue to weigh the pro's and con's of the entire terrorist affair handling for weeks, President Ambrose's star, though somewhat tarnished, would continue to shine over Washington D.C. and the United States for the remainder of his term.

CHAPTER 34

A light snow was gently falling on the city's sidewalks, helping to accentuate the feeling that Christmas was right around the corner, and indeed it was on this early December day. The Cleveland storefronts and restaurants were dressed in their holiday finery welcoming in the season. Reindeer and bells were hanging from the streetlights and festive wreaths and oversized candles were in evidence throughout the city's center. With sprayed on snow and multi-colored lights, windows everywhere heralded the approach of Christmas. The small group made their way out of the Pharmacor headquarters to take their place amongst the midtown lunch crowd strolling down the street.

"It sure is a neat time of year," said Jane as her wheelchair blazed twin trails through the fresh fallen snow.

"You can say that again," agreed Daniece.

"Everyone seems so full of life and invigorated as you look at them hustling and bustling about," added Holland.

"I don't know. Sometimes I find this time of year to be too overwhelming, what with all the shopping and the demands placed on you, I kind of get stressed out," countered Jenny.

"Party pooper," retorted Ernesto as the group waited to cross the street.

"Hey, speaking of full of life, I wonder how many of these people we're passing on the street owe their lives to our girl Holly-Brit here," said John proudly as he squeezed her hand, eliciting a blush from his beloved.

"All of us here," suggested Daniece.

"I'll second that," added Ernesto.

"I'll add my thanks to that too," offered Jane. "I'd also like to thank Holland for all she did to help remove that puke Trina from our lives. That man was the devil incarnate."

"You know, he was even worse than I imagined. When I was reading his golden notebook as I waited for help to arrive at his house, I was amazed at the total insensitivity he had to others. Do you know who his first victims were?" asked Holland. The group, all except John, responded with a "No" in unison.

"His own parents. He waited until both his parents got sloshed, which happened on a fairly regular basis I guess. Then he shot his mother and father, and made it look like a murder suicide."

"I guess this guy was a real sweetheart right from the very beginning," said Daniece.

"Stop walking for a second and I'll fill you in on the details," began John. "I was contacted last week by some of the F.B.I. agents in charge of the follow up investigation into Jonas Trina's life and motives. From their efforts, here is what they've pieced together from interviewing townspeople where he grew up, and those he worked with over the years. The majority of the evidence comes from the golden notebook that Jonas Trina had been compiling himself. This chronicled from start to finish all of his dastardly deeds over the years, usually providing the reasons behind his actions in the process.

He grew up as an unloved loner. Even his parents despised him, probably because they despised themselves. His only real friend appears to have been a teacher, some guy named Stevens, who after befriending him got him involved in chess. They were very close for three years. The teacher died unexpectedly because of some bogus asthma medication he got. Jonas Trina was devastated by his death. He vowed in his heart as a teenager to make the pharmaceutical company that he felt was responsible pay for killing his one and only friend. Being a master of chess, his mind worked many steps ahead when plotting his moves. He calculated that by killing his hated parents, the townspeople would take pity on him and better his life, which is exactly what happened. He got help getting a scholarship to Purdue, and when he graduated, he ruthlessly set out to make his mark in the world.

He effectively stepped on anyone who got in his way on his rise to the top. According to his notebook, he eliminated all of his key rivals either through death, extortion, or intimidation. He became C.E.O. of Sutton Industries, a major defense company at a young age. Most would be elated at that. To Jonas Trina, however, that was merely a steppingstone to his ultimate goal. He felt confident that if he gained a reputation in the business world as a shrewd tough administrator who made his company mega profitable, he'd get other opportunities. When a chance to enter the medical field presented itself, he jumped at it, and became C.E.O. of a health care company. This was another step in his ultimate plan.

Finally when the chief executive position opened up at Pharmacor, his lifelong goal came into his reach. The bottle of bad asthma medication taken by his mentor about thirty five years ago came from Pharmacor's Cleveland plant. Now he was in position to have access to the individual or individuals he'd vowed revenge upon. He reasoned that someone who worked at the plant thirty five years ago was responsible for his teacher's death. Since he couldn't find out exactly who it was, he figured that he would simply eliminate as many as he could from that era. That is why you found such a heavy concentration of deaths within the ranks of retirees from Pharmacor.

Eventually the killing got out of hand, and it almost became a game to kill as many Pharmacor employees as possible. In his egotistical arrogance, he figured that no one was bright enough to catch onto the fact that he was the one behind the scenes pulling all of the strings to make everything happen. At the same time, the killing of the retirees had the added benefit of making the company more profitable, because they no longer had to pay the pensions. This had the perverse effect of adding millions to Jonas Trina's personal wealth due to the contract he had structured with the board upon his joining Pharmacor."

"Excuse me John, but how did the terrorists enter into the picture?" asked Ernesto.

"Good question. That came about because of contacts made previously with Afghan nationals years before. When Trina worked at Sutton Industries in the early nineteen-eighties, he was sent to Afghanistan by our government to get the bugs out of a weapons system that we were supplying to Afghan rebels to fight the attempted Russian takeover. Trina saved the day and became a hero to the Afghans. They never forgot the help Trina gave them in their fight for freedom. Now when he wanted to advance the rate at which he killed off his own employees, he figured that an alliance with terrorists would be a natural, as it turned out to be. Furthermore it provided him with an alibi. According to his notebook, when he was in Europe as his Social Center was burning to the ground in Cleveland, he was actually meeting with "Fist of Rage" operatives to join forces. In fact it was Jonas' willingness to torch his own Social Center that convinced "Fist of Rage" forces of his resolve. That actually was the integral part in their joining forces. He of course being in Europe at the time could not possibly have had anything to do with the fire at the Social Club."

"That bastard." spat out Jenny.

"Yeah, he was a real piece of work. However, thanks to our heroine Holly-Brit, we won't have to worry about the likes of Jonas Trina anymore," said John with an air of finality.

"Speaking of Holy-Brit, I was wondering, what made you believe that Trina was the one who was behind all of the killings?" asked Jenny.

"Well for one the timing of all of the deaths. It all began virtually with his arrival. Then I learned that he stood to make a great deal of money if Pharmacor became more profitable. The retiree's deaths were accomplishing that. By sabotaging some of Pharmacor's key competitors, the profitability was further enhanced. Also, call it intuition if you will, but just the man's general demeanor led me to think he might have had a hand in all of the bad things happening at Pharmacor. His arrogance and aloofness, and just the way he treated people like they were something to be walked on and spat upon. However, our buddy Jane supplied the real evidence. Show her if you will Jane."

With that, the group stopped walking as Jane rummaged through her purse for something. She pulled out a piece of paper that had a good deal of print on it.

"You'd think that I'd treat this paper with a bit more respect, wouldn't you Holland," said Jane as she un-crumpled and straightened out the piece of paper now on her lap. "Actually this is just a copy. Holland, the one you and I looked at in the hospital is tucked away in a safe sheltered place at home. I kind of think that it just might have some historical significance. Who knows, maybe someday it'll end up at the Smithsonian."

"Excuse me, but can I please be let in on the little secret?" asked Jenny rather demandingly. "Just exactly what do you have there?"

"It's something that we all were given Jenny, a copy of Jonas Trina's riverboat cruise invitation to the poor souls at our Cincinnati plant. Didn't you save yours?"

"I think that I threw that thing in the trash before I even left the meeting that day. Why is that so darned important?"

"Because within this piece of paper lies the crucial evidence which ultimately brought the mighty Jonas Trina to his knees. Do you remember how angry Jonas got when Nancy McKinney said that she'd made some changes to the invitation?"

"Yeah, so?"

"Read the invitation."

"Why? What could possibly be so important about the wording of a stupid invitation?"

"Jenny, could you please quit being so darned difficult, and just read the damned thing, "PLEASE!"

"Oh alright, if it's that important to you, let me see it."

With that, Jenny was handed the paper and she began to read the invitation aloud.

An Invitation to an Enchanted Evening

You are cordially invited to attend a gala event on Saturday September 21st. It will feature a riverboat cruise aboard the paddle wheeler Buckeye Belle, with all costs provided. The food, beverages, and musical accompaniment will kindly be donated by the Cleveland Pharmacor staff members. Surely you'll be blown away by the musical entertainment, and you are certainly guaranteed to enjoy the Middle Eastern themed cuisine. Feast upon delicacies such as warm pieces of baklava, or perhaps taboule, or stuffed grape leaves. Alcoholic drinks and softer beverages shall be in abundance, and with advance notice perhaps we will be able to furnish your personal favorite. The captain says this cruise is "to die for", and the scenery at this time of year is breathtaking. Other interests maybe in store for you as well. Gaming tables will be set up below, with shuffleboards on the deck. An assortment of video games will also be available. We think that with the Ohio moon overhead, far and away the most popular activity shall be dancing upon the river. We're sure that all who attend will have a great time Hope to see you there!!!!!!!!!!!!!!!!!!

Now Jane took Jenny's index finger and placed it on the invitation. Starting at the top left with the word "You", Jane moved Jenny's finger down the page in a diagonal line. The diagonal line ran from the word "You" at the top to the invitation to the word "river" on the next to last line. Jenny slowly pronounced the words as Jane moved her finger down the page.

"YOU...WILL...ALL...BE...BLOWN...TO...PIECES...AND WILL...DIE...IN...THE...OHIO...RIVER!"

As Jenny finished mouthing the final word, the reality hit her and her mouth hung open in shock at what she had just read aloud. A subdued "I understand now," was all she could eventually manage to say.

"As you can see, that left absolutely no doubt as to Jonas Trina's involvement in the murderous tragedy. His ego proved to be his Achilles heel. He thought that he was too clever for anyone to become wise to his tricks, but he took one chance too many and it cost him everything."

"Thank goodness he slipped up Jane. Otherwise he'd still be at large plotting how to eliminate more of us, and he'd probably succeed. Speaking of succeeding, I wonder who'll succeed Trina as the C.E.O. of Pharmacor," said Daniece?

"I don't know, and I don't care," said Ernesto. "Let's stick with something a lot more relevant like where are we going for lunch Miss Matthews. You've been so secretive about it all day. All I know is that I got an e-mail saying to join you guys for lunch, and you were treating."

"How would Szuter's Steakhouse strike you all?"

A stunned moment of silence came over the group as they slowly continued their trek.

"Are you serious?" asked Jane from her seated position

"Sure, why not?"

"For a group of six for lunch counting tax, tip, and a drink apiece would have to run you at least $275.00 is why," countered Jane.

"Good, then that'll leave us with $25.00 to take something back with us for the rest of the department."

"Tell me Miss Moneybags, how did you suddenly become such a woman of means? And remember before you answer that I see your paychecks," said Daniece.

"Well I was going to keep it a secret a little longer, but what the heck I guess that I'll tell you all now while we're walking together. It seems that I've made a new friend. Some guy in Washington named Lawrence Ambrose, although he insists on putting this word President in front of everything that he sends me. Anyway, I guess that something I did made an impression on him, because the other day a large envelope arrived at my place from the White House. When I opened it there was a smaller envelope inside with a $300 bank gift card in it. Instructions from the President said that I should use the money to treat some friends to lunch. He wrote that it had something to do with thanks for my help in the Trina affair. So there you have it. Oh I almost forgot. There was another note in the envelope. It was written on this really neat White House stationery. It said something about if myself, John, and some of our closest friends weren't too busy next Friday night, our presence was requested for a little dinner get together at the White house with the Prez, the First Lady, and..."

A loud shriek erupted simultaneously from three different sets of pipes as Daniece, Jenny, and Jane screamed their elation.

"Are you serious?" asked John in amazement

"See for yourself," said Holland as she pulled a copy of the letter from her purse for all to see. They all good-naturedly fought to get the first look at the precious document.

"Girl it really is true isn't it?" gushed Daniece.

"Are any of us invited?" asked Jenny somewhat hesitatingly.

"Well, I don't know. I have been the subject of an awful lot of jokes at the office, and of course there was the time when... Oh hell I can't keep this up... Of course you're all invited. I'm going to be allowed to have Rosa and my parents there as well."

"This is too good to be true," stammered Jane.

"Just out of curiosity, you wouldn't have any idea what they're serving would you?" asked Ernesto

"Hell Ernesto, it's the damn White House for Chrissakes. Even the peanut butter and jelly sandwiches would taste fabulous," chided John.

"Surprisingly, the menu is pretty much up to me," said Holland. I was thinking of maybe Chateaubriand or perhaps prime rib with a salad and an elegant vegetable like glazed carrots or petite peas with pearl onions. One thing I'd better make perfectly clear. Jenny, regarding your past culinary exhibitions, it's considered poor manners to fill your plate more than four times when dining at the White House." With that the group had a good laugh.

Daniece gave a quick sideways glance in Jane's direction. Jane responded with an almost imperceptible nod and look of approval as if they were involved in some type of secretive collusion. Ernesto happened to catch the non verbal communication between the two women and silently mouthed the word "Now" in Daniece's direction. With that, Daniece cleared her throat, and as all looked on, she began to speak;

"Holland, we were wondering if you would mind doing us all a small favor?"

"Well that all depends on if public nudity, felonious actions, or anything to do with large reptiles is involved," she responded gleefully.

"Actually it has more to do with your name."

"My name?"

"Yes, your name. We would like to discontinue calling you Holly-Brit, and only refer to you as Holland from now on."

"But I don't understand. Have I done or said anything to offend any or all of you? Is that why?

"Oh honey it's nothing like that," Jane chimed in.

"But you guys have all been fine with calling me Holly-Brit for years. Why not any more? What have I done wrong?" implored Holland.

Daniece answered; "Sweetheart, it has absolutely nothing to do with anything you've done wrong. On the contrary it has everything to do with what you've done right. Holland the nickname Holly-Brit, while very cute and sweet, brings to mind thoughts of a school-girl. Along with the cuteness and sweetness come the insecurities, a tendency towards irresponsibility, reliance on others for approval and support, plus remembrances of adolescent behavior in general. We as a group no longer feel that applies when we look at or talk to you. Whereas before we saw an insecure young lady who was hoping to somehow make her mark upon the world, now we see a supremely competent and confident woman standing before us. We see a person who is ready, willing, and able to take on the world on her own terms. The things you've accomplished in the past several months are nothing short of amazing, what with saving the city, saving countless lives, conversing with Presidents, etc. We stand in awe at the person you've become. The beautiful butterfly has truly emerged from her cocoon, spread her wings, and taken to glorious flight. Hooray for you Holland Matthews!! So you see Holland, you've simply come too far and done too much for us to somewhat denigrate you by referring to you any longer as Holly-Brit. The nickname simply no longer fits. Agreed everyone?"

The other members in the group nodded their approval and all looked to Holland for her response. Tears were flowing freely down her pink-hued cheeks as she sought to find the right words for the moment.

"Daniece, I believe that those may have been the nicest words anyone has ever spoken to me. Thank you. Thank you so very, very much! I admit that while these past months have certainly taken their toll, apparently I could have done worse in how the situations were ultimately handled. I owe a tremendous debt of gratitude to each and every one of you for your help and support in helping John and I cope with all that came our way. I love each and every one of you very much, and if you all agree that calling me Holly-Brit makes you in the least bit uncomfortable, then we should do away with it. From now on it is strictly Holland Matthews! Out with the old and in with the new!

With that done, the group once again resumed their trek towards their luncheon destination. The somewhat heavy previous conversation seemed to have briefly sapped their ability to converse because the next several seconds were covered with no talking whatsoever. Ernesto broke the silence when he said; "Hey guys, I don't think that we resolved exactly what to have at our upcoming White house dinner. I mean surely we have to have more than just one choice of entrees. Also I don't recall any discussion about rolls and butter. Furthermore, what types of expensive wines should we insist on?

"Also what about dessert?" Jane asked.

As the words were being spoken, the group happened to be adjacent to Lou's Bakery. The front door of the bakery opened, and a blast of wonderfully scented air engulfed them with the aroma. Daniece and Holland looked at each other and joyously shouted out together the dessert choice... "HAPPY CAKES!!"

EPILOGUE

Sixty four year old Devin Shrop sat down on the metal bench and began to unlace his work boots as he'd done thousands of times. This time it was more meaningful. For this would be the last time. He was retiring from his janitorial position at Thomas J. Helms Junior High in the Modesto California school system. This was a career that he had arduously continued with these past thirty four years. Though the job wasn't glamorous, or high paying as many California jobs were, it had done what Devin needed it to do. It had provided. He took off the boots and opened the thin metal door of his own personal locker. Taking out his worn black leather shoes, he slid his right foot in first and then his left foot next. It was funny how solemn even the smallest tasks now seemed at this austere moment.

One's retirement is a day that most aspire to, yet dread as it approaches, and many fear when it arrives. It signifies many things. It signifies closure as one's working days come to an end. It signifies a beginning as a new chapter of life begins. Alarm clocks lose much of their relevance. Days of the week somehow seem less significant. Retirement also signifies realization. One is struck by the realization of one's mortality. While this certainly isn't the end of the road in one's life, it is a very meaningful milestone. Assuredly one can look towards the future at such a moment as this and contemplate all the experiences yet to be pursued now that the time will be available. Conversely, many find it a time to look backward and think about the experiences that have brought us to this particular time and place in our lives. This is what Devin Shrop was reflecting upon as he busied himself clearing out personal effects from his locker on this, his final day.

He absent-mindedly brushed aside a cobweb from the inside corner of his locker as automatically as he would blink. Decades of cleaning up ingrained that sort of thing in a person. Devin took down the picture of his son and his family that he found on the top shelf. He wiped a thin film of dust from the photograph. The beaming twenty seven year old man with his beautiful young bride and baby girl pictured there exemplified everything life should be. Ah, the radiance of youth! Pleased with today, and yet filled with dreams of the future for an even better tomorrow. He was once like that young man grinning back at him from the picture. He said a silent prayer that his son's aspirations would be fulfilled, in direct contrast to his own which had been dashed upon the rocks of life. In truth, most of those rocks could have been avoided. But no sense in spending his entire last few career moments revisiting a maudlin past that was far too late to change.

Devin adjusted his thoughts as the locker emptied and the boxes now holding its contents filled. He reminisced on the hallways. How many miles had he covered on these tiled hallways? Hour upon hour spent behind the long handle of a wide cloth push broom sweeping up the refuse of youth. A smile came to his face as he recalled the laughter. It was funny how something that he often found obnoxious and irritating, like the raucous guffaws of pimply faced teens, was now fondly remembered. It was a sound he should have cherished throughout his time within these hallways, for it spoke of the joy, energy, and resilience of the human spirit. It was a sound that he would miss.

The tedium was remembered as well. The hundreds of chair bottoms from which he'd scraped dried chewing gum. The endless hours spent washing windows. And then there were the bathrooms. It was almost unspeakable what children could do to bathrooms. Not to mention the garbage! There were always the mountains of garbage to contend with. And yet even these would somehow be missed. Not because he missed the duty. Rather, it was because they represented something that he no longer could claim. A sense of belonging! That was what he would miss. No longer would he be part of this rich slice of pubescent life and all that it entailed. After today, he no longer belonged here. The hallowed halls of early academia, while grateful for his decades of service, were now going to move on without him. A palpable wave of despondency swept over Devin as this realization and the finality of the moment sunk in.

He reached into his pocket and extracted his newest possession. A gleaming gold pocket watch, presented to him a few days ago at the retirement dinner held in his honor by a small group of teachers and well wishers. Thirty-four years. This watch represented the sum toll of roughly half of a lifetime. He opened the watch and compared that time to the wire-covered clock on the wall. The gold watch seemed to be running a little fast. Devin turned back the minute hand two minutes, almost as if by so doing he too could somehow turn back the clock of his life. Alas, he knew better.

How had he come to this place in life? He thought back to the call his older brother had made to him so many years ago. Come on out to California, little brother. The land of opportunity he'd said. This call had had a resounding influence on the direction of his life. Certainly there was nothing in Northeast Ohio where Devin lived at that time which bound him. He had a boring job at some pharmaceutical plant, and he was looking for a change. California held the air of excitement, promise, and a chance to make a brand new start. Out with the old and in with the new.

Now in retrospect all he'd really accomplished was to trade one dreary boring existence for another. Sure he'd met a girl here. Got married. Had a kid. Hell, he'd even managed to stay married for seven years. But he could've done any of those relatively unremarkable things back in Ohio. He wondered for a second how things might have turned out had he never left the suburbs of Cleveland where he'd grown up. Probably about the same, he decided.

Speaking of Cleveland, what was the name of that old company he'd worked at so long ago before he'd gone west? Pharmex, Pharmacent, no wait... Pharmacor. That's right Pharmacor. He thought back briefly to one of his last days there, recalling with a grin the prank that he'd played by filling some of the asthma bottles with rubbing alcohol. He'd certainly gotten a chuckle out of that. He wondered if anything ever came of that. Probably not! He imagined that if anything bad would've happened because of that, he would've heard about it long ago. "Oh well, just like my life, that's water over the damn now," he thought as he closed the now empty locker door for the final time.

Devin Shrop put the boxes on his handcart and wheeled them out the front door to his car. The late afternoon sun was setting as he finished closing the trunk with the boxes now safely stowed away. As he reached in his pocket for his car keys, he inadvertently also pulled out his new gold watch. The sun's rays reflected brilliantly off the polished gold casing sending beams of light in many directions. The simple lightshow had a positive revitalizing effect on Devin as he put the key into the ignition and turned the switch.

"Snap out of it you old fool. You're just retiring! You've got plenty of living yet to do. Hell it ain't like retirement is some kind of death sentence someone passed on you."

The thirteen year old Buick coughed a couple of times and then sputtered to life. He pushed it into gear and slowly began to pull out of the school parking lot into the waning sunlight, renewed and filled with hope for a bright new tomorrow.

****

"Hey wait up you dorks," twelve year old Andrew Moncrief yelled to his two classmates as they raced along the Southern Ohio brook.

"If ya weren't such a slow poke, maybe you could keep up. Why don't ya have another cream stick doughboy?" Logan yelled back.

"To tell you the truth, I wouldn't mind stopping for a couple minutes," Dylan said to Logan.

"All right Flash, we'll stop and wait for you under this group of trees," Logan teasingly threw back in Andrew's direction.

The two lead boys settled down at the base of a tall elm tree. Dylan produced a squished candy bar from his back pocket. He broke off half and offered it to Logan as the boys waited for Andrew to catch up.

"What do I look like, yer dog? I don't want something to eat that's been touching your butt! Wait, I know! When Andrew gets here give it to him. I'm sure he'll eat it."

No sooner were the words out of his mouth when a dirty and tired looking Andrew appeared from around the tree. He plunked down beside the others and began eyeing the remaining half of the candy bar.

"Do you want it?" asked Dylan.

"Sure, why not?" said Andrew as he reached to take it from Dylan's outstretched hand.

"No reason that I can think of," snickered Logan.

The threesome sat on the moist leaf covered ground beneath the canopy of green foliage above, supplied by the many trees nearby. The late May sun was sending shafts of golden light through the branches to illumine whatever their rays touched upon on the forest floor. One particular beam was sending out a reflection unlike the other beams that mainly fell upon mud or wet leaves.

"Hey guys, it's almost the end of school. Do either of ya have anything lined up for the summer?" asked Andrew.

"Naw, not really. How about you Logan?" said Dylan

"Just doin' a little fishin', playin' baseball, and doin' whatever chores that I can't get out of. Hey, you guys see that light over there?" Logan asked

"Where?"

"I'll show ya," said Logan, and with that he picked up a stone and threw it fifteen feet away where it landed next to a shaft of light that was being reflected."

"Wonder what's making it do that?" Andrew questioned.

"It's probably shining off a beautiful diamond tiara dropped by some fairy princess running through the forest," laughed Dylan.

Well I'm gonna go see," said Andrew as he rose from his wet seat and brushed the leaves and mud off the back of his jeans. Walking the short distance to where the light was playing off the item's surface, Andrew bent down and picked up a metallic object. It was mostly covered with mud, however, enough of the shiny surface had remained clean to reflect the sunlight and reveal its presence to the boys.

"Well what is it?" demanded Logan.

"I'm not really sure," said Andrew as he scraped off the caked on mud with his thumbnail.

"Give it here, I'll bet I'll know," said Dylan.

Andrew flipped the shiny object to Dylan who caught it in one hand. He pushed a button on the object's side, and it opened up in his hand.

"Well ya big dummy! You know what you got here is a pocket watch. A gold plated pocket watch. My grandfather's got one just like it. I think he got it when he retired or something.

"Throw it here and lemme see it," cried Logan.

Dylan lofted the object in Logan's direction, but it overshot him and he had to retrieve the watch from a small pile of leaves it had fallen into. As he reached to pick up the watch, he noticed another object sticking out slightly from amongst the leaves. He plucked the other object up also and gave out a gleeful yell.

"Well ain't this just our lucky day! Lookee here. I found a wallet!

"See if it has any money in it," the other boys said in unison.

Opening the wallet, Logan found two weathered twenties and one solitary dollar bill. He also pulled out a driver's license and a couple of credit cards.

"According to what I've got in my hand here, I'd say that a certain David Clayton Spangler had himself a real bad day awhile back. He lost his wallet and all of his identification. My dad lost his wallet once and said it was a real bitch replacing all the stuff. Well guys we're now the proud possessors of forty one dollars and a watch. What do you say we go into town and treat ourselves to some ice cream!"

"That doesn't seem right Logan. We should try to get in touch with the owner and give him his wallet and I.D.'s back," said Andrew.

"I wonder who's watch that is?" asked Dylan.

"I'll check to see if there's anything inside that tells." With that Logan pressed the button on the watch and once again it popped open. "Listen to this, guys! It's got an inscription that says; To David Spangler. Thanks for your help. May you always fly high! Boy this Spangler dude really did have a bad day, losin' both of these."

"Gee guys; I wonder how these things got here? I mean we are pretty far off the beaten path you know," commented Andrew.

"Our boy Spangler was probably out here in the woods getting it on with someone if you ask me," kidded Logan.

"No seriously. Andrew's right. I wonder what the real story is behind these things and how they got here?" agreed Dylan.

The alabaster answer to that question could be found in the gleaming skeletal remains, permanently lodged, seventy three feet above their heads. In a stately Ohio elm.